I0714190

Parlatheas Press Titles:


## <u>The Cayn Trilogy:</u>

Son of Cayn
City of Cayn
Blood of Cayn


## <u>Chronicles of Damage Inc.:</u>

Phantoms of Ruthaer
Mask of the Vampire*


* Forthcoming

# City of Cayn

## The Cayn Trilogy
### Book Two

Jason McDonald
Alan Isom
Stormy McDonald

Parlatheas Press, LLC
Hollywood, SC

# DEDICATIONS

To my mom, for always being there for me.

– Jason

To my mother for always supporting my love of science fiction and fantasy even though you did not share it.

– Alan

To Shirley and Steve, who took the time to introduce their precocious young niece to the realms of Middle Earth, Narnia, and Pern.  Thank you.

– Stormy

# CHAPTER 1
# THE BYAL KRŬG

**October 25, 4235** K.E.

**11:08am**

Standing in a clearing surrounded by teamsters, five days from the nearest town, Jasper knew of only one place to find help: Trakya's *Byal Krŭg*, or White Circle. According to their historian, the White Circle was the oldest Mages' Guild on the continent of Parlatheas, having received its original charter more than three thousand years ago, during the height of the Korellan Empire. Despite a long and sordid history, including multiple wars and a fire which gutted the building and destroyed many of its original tomes, the White Circle remained one of the three largest repositories of learning in the civilized world, alongside the *Academia des Artes Magicae* in Gallowen, and Vologda's *Taynaya Biblioteka.*

He concentrated on his teleportation spell, driven by hope the White Circle could find a remedy for the Blood of Cayn.

The moment he spoke the last incantation, Jasper felt something *other* slither through his magic. He recoiled at the alien presence, but it was already too late. It altered his spell ever so slightly. With some arcane magic it might not have mattered, but accuracy was paramount with a teleport spell. A wave of nausea seized him, and, for an instant, he felt his feet materialize inside stone before the failsafe triggered. Wrenched from death, he found himself guided like a novice.

Helpless and more than a little embarrassed, Jasper arrived safely inside a dark, round chamber. Breathing a sigh of relief, he waited for his eyes to adjust to the low lighting. Set in the stone floor immediately surrounding him was a narrow band of burnished gold, intricately engraved with arcane runes of both protection and guidance.

Outside the circle stood two men dressed in dark robes. Each carried a tall, wooden staff of darkest oak. Their hoods were up, hiding their faces. Raising their staves in unison, they chanted and pointed with their free hands. Jasper felt the air around him constrict.  Tucking his chin, he inhaled sharply, filling his lungs, and poked out his stomach without being too obvious.  When they finished, Jasper relaxed, creating a small gap between him and the wall of air.  It wasn't much.  He still couldn't move, let alone cast an immediate counter spell, but it was something.

One of the mages patted him down and removed his belt and sporran.  The dark mage rifled his belongings and fished out the small sliver of soap.  Evidently satisfied, he dropped it back in the leather pouch and carried the pilfered items from the room while the other mage stood guard.

This was not the reception Jasper had anticipated.  The only thing he could figure was the guild knew about the soap and had set up some sort of detection spell.  Either they had discovered it was the cause of the sickness — or they had known all along.  The more he thought about it, the more concerned he became.

Beyond the guard, he noticed fresh scorch marks on the wall.

Jasper didn't have time to waste; he needed to find Marcus Marchenkov, second-in-command of the Eyes and Ears of the Kral.  Barely able to move his lips, he called upon his own magic and used it to probe the binding spell.  He searched for any weakness that might help him.

The two mages had cooperatively cast the spell. Although the binding was exceptionally strong, he found the wood of his own staff had interfered with their spell by absorbing some of its energies.  Thankfully, they hadn't thought to utilize the magic circle at his feet.

Sweat beaded on his forehead as he layered magic upon magic into the staff, using it as a conduit.  The staff, in turn, focused and amplified his power until the binding spell developed tiny cracks.  He would have to be quick.  Both casters would know the instant their spell failed.  He pushed more magic into his staff.

With a flash of light and a haze of ozone, the binding collapsed.

The guard reacted a half-second too slow.  Jasper swung his staff with all his might and struck the guard hard on the side of the head, knocking him to the floor.  He knelt beside the fallen mage and placed his staff across the man's throat. Using his bulk to maintain leverage, he applied pressure, little by little, with his knee until the mage stopped struggling.

Reaching down, he threw back the other mage's hood to reveal his face.  It was Ivo Indzhev, one of Jasper's old instructors from Tydway.  He had seen him a few times in the halls, but the two rarely traveled in the same social circles.

The mage glared at Jasper with cold, dead eyes.  Something alien had replaced the man's humanity, and it saw Jasper not as a person but as an object — a mere bug.  If positions had been reversed there was no doubt Ivo would have taken his life.  It sent an icy chill down the portly mage's spine.

Jasper grabbed the dark mage's hand.  The fingers and fingernails were pitch black, and the hand felt warm to the touch.  Worried furrows creasing his brow, Jasper pressed his hand flat against the other's forehead: a high-grade fever.  Shifting his weight slightly, Jasper pressed even harder with his staff and cut the mage's airflow.

After making sure the mage was unconscious, Jasper crossed the room and listened at the door.  Not hearing any traffic on the other side, he peeked out.  A massive, barrel-vaulted corridor trimmed with a dark wainscot along each side stretched into darkness.  Sticking his head out farther, he looked up and down the hallway.  Concern etched his features as he felt how quiet this once-busy thoroughfare had become.  He stepped cautiously out of the chamber and closed the door behind him.  With a quick weave of magic, he locked it.

At the far end of the hallway was the central stair that led down to the ground floor.  Trying to remember the shortest route out of the maze-like guild, he moved in that direction, the sound of his boots echoing eerily in the deserted hall.

A tingling sensation coursed through his hands, followed by another wave of nausea that caused his steps to falter.

'*Kcab emoc, Repsaj.*'

He leaned against the cool stone wall, clutching his stomach until the spasm subsided.  Taking a deep shuddering breath, he brought up a hand to swipe at his suddenly damp brow.  The tips of his fingers and his fingernails had turned grey. Images of Gregori's corpse swam before him.

The thudding echo of Ivo banging on the door jarred him from his thoughts. It wouldn't be long before someone heard him and raised the alarm. Putting aside his symptoms for the moment, Jasper fled, not caring how much noise he made. At the head of the stairs, he heard the echo of voices below, followed by the opening and closing of a door as someone released Ivo.

His thoughts racing, Jasper retraced his steps. Going out the front was no longer an option, and if he didn't come up with a real plan, he would be trapped.

At a side passage, inspiration struck. Tilting his staff so the charred tip angled back toward the central stairs, he summoned a thin sheet of ice. Once the floor was covered, he tossed out a bit of fleece and whispered, "Psévdo íchnos."

A solid-seeming image of himself raced across the ice and down the hallway toward Ivo and the arrival room. Jasper snuck down the narrower side passage. Maintaining his concentration on the image, he let it get close enough for the men to see it before he made the phantasm turn and flee to the central stairs.

Jasper rounded a corner and stopped. He glanced back toward the main corridor just in time to see two armed soldiers flash by with Ivo right behind them. All three were hot on the trail of his simulacrum. Back pressed to the wall, he listened to the curses of the men as they slipped on the ice and fell down the stairs, bringing a satisfied smile to his face. From the sound of it, they were broken but not dead.

He continued down the new hallway until he came to an intersection. An elaborate arch adorned each side passage. Jasper turned left and found himself at the entrance to the private chambers set aside for visiting mages.

A dark-robed mage patrolled the hall. He walked with an odd shuffle, as if he couldn't bend his knees properly and leaned against his staff with every other step. Luckily, the mage had his back to Jasper, allowing him to retreat and prepare.

Taking the chance he could talk his way through, Jasper strode confidently down the hall. As he approached the dark-robed mage, the pungent stench of decay and excrement assailed his nostrils. On either side, doors stood wide open.  He caught glimpses of groaning men and women on straw pallets, their bodies consumed by the contagion.

He wondered how the sickness spread so fast.  Then it dawned on him: a communal bath.  If the guild had bought a block of that soap, it would only have been a matter of time before everyone became sick.

"Stop!  This area is off limits," the dark-robed mage commanded when he saw Jasper.  "What are you doing here?"

"I'm on my way to the kitchen," Jasper answered.  He patted his stomach and gestured toward the door at the far end of the hall.

"The kitchen is closed," the other mage said automatically.  "Return to your quarters."  He cocked his head as though listening to another voice.

'*Damn it,*' Jasper thought.  '*What is going on here?*'

Not taking any more chances, he threw a fistful of iron filings at the other mage, intending to bind him with a similar spell to what the dark mages had used against him earlier.  The other mage countered it with a simple wave of his staff.

'*How did he do that?*'

The dark-robed mage flicked his left hand, sending three streaks of searing red energy down the hall.  Jasper concentrated, and the air in front of him shimmered.  The lights struck the barrier, causing it to buckle and ripple, but it held.  They ricocheted off the magic shield, blasting the corridor wall.

Jasper didn't understand what was happening, but he knew it wouldn't be long before others showed up.  He tightened his grip on his staff and struck the floor with its tip.  Magic flowed through the wood shaft and out.  A shuddering boom of thunder blasted the dark-robed mage off his feet and slammed him against the far wall.  Jasper ran past the dazed man without looking back.

At the end of the hall, he threw open a narrow wooden door.  With shouts and the sound of footsteps close on his heels, he dared not look back as he ducked inside the antechamber.  The landing led to a tight-radiused spiral stone stair intended for servants, not portly mages.  Sucking in his gut as best he could, he wound around and around, passing several doors, all marked with white, stylistic numerals.

The walls around him stretched and distorted as if alive — someone was trying to trap him, using the building itself. He raced on, fighting the vertigo blurring his vision, until he reached the bottom.  There, a utilitarian hallway stretched into the distance, each side lined with doors labeled with simple block letters.

Ducking into a soot-stained corridor, he felt the weight of the centuries embedded in the old and immovable walls here.  It never ceased to amaze him how old the guild was. By comparison, the Academia de Artes Magicae at Tydway, where he had originally learned his trade, was still in its infancy — not even two hundred years old.

Jasper came to a door with *КУХНЯ* written above and threw it open.  Silence and the smell of rot greeted him. Shutting the door behind him, he surveyed the kitchen.

Dust motes danced in the thin streams of light filtering through tiny windows set in the ancient block walls.  He had made it to one of the original perimeter rooms.

Pots and pans cluttered long rows of countertops and cabinets.  Along the far wall sat several wood-burning stoves, now cold and dark.  Cutlery and cooking utensils hung from racks built under tall, overhead cabinets.  From the looks of it, the staff were hustled out in the midst of their work, and no one had been down here for at least a week. Jasper worked his way around the counters toward the iron-bound door at the other end.

The door from the main dining hall burst open, and a pair of guards armed with short swords rushed him.  With a wave of Jasper's hand, sharp knives leapt out of their blocks and flew toward the men.

Although they tried, there were too many blades to fend off.  The men fell to the ground screaming as various sized knives and long-pronged forks buried themselves in their forearms, stomachs, and chests.

Jasper exited through the back door and found himself in a narrow alley.  He breathed a sigh of relief when he found the way clear. After closing the door behind him, he frowned in concentration as he wove magic through the lock and fused the bolt in place.

Abrupt banging and yelling from the other side rattled the door. The men had already thrown off the effects of his illusion. Jasper ran toward the street in front of the guild, the noise fading with each step. As he approached the main thoroughfare, a black wrought iron gate with sharp spikes barred his way. Jasper used his staff to push on the gate.

Locked.

Three stories above, a man exited the conical turret and leaned over the crenelated edge of the roof, peering down into the alleyway. With one eye on him and another on the gate, Jasper threaded his magic into the locking mechanism and rolled the tumblers. When the lock gave, he whispered, "Metaschimatízetai," and then boldly stepped out of the alley into the daylight. Dressed in the dark robes of a mage, he tugged at the edges of his illusory hood, making sure his face was completely concealed.

The area around the mages' guild was prosperous, lacking the accumulation of filth found elsewhere in the city, especially Lower Pazard'zhik. Along each side of the Bulevard na Kralete stood two- and three-story live-work affairs, housing the merchant class. Board and batten upper floors overhung walls of mortared stone and provided sheltered porches where people could avoid the traffic and harsh weather. In a few more weeks, their steeply pitched roofs would shed the weight of heavy snow into narrow alleys between buildings.

With a purpose in his stride, Jasper walked up the hill toward the Kral's estates. Using the porches for cover, he ducked inside a nearby store and cancelled his disguise spell.

He turned to leave, and found himself facing the sharp end of a crossbow aimed at his chest. Holding the crossbow was a buxom woman with shoulder-length, curly, dark-brown hair who stood a few inches shorter than the mage.

"Who are you and what are you doing in my shop?"

Glancing around, he noticed he was in a women's dress shop. There wasn't anyone else in the store except himself and the proprietor. Anger and fear warred for dominance in her expression, and she struggled to control the trembling in her hands.

"What's going on around here?" he asked, keeping half an eye toward the door.

"You answer my questions first."

"My name is Jasper Thredd.  I'm a mage from Tydway," he said truthfully.  "I'm here to help the Kral."

"You're not sick?"

"Do I look sick?"

"I heard all the mages were ill.  Some say the Plague has returned, and war is coming."

"I know.  I'm searching for the cure."

"In my dress shop?" she asked, still pointing the crossbow at him.

Shaking his head, Jasper said, "Actually, I was hiding."

"In my dress shop?" she repeated.

"I promise, I intended no harm.  I only needed to get off the street."

Looking out the window, he noticed several dark-robed mages questioning passersby.

"I don't have much time," Jasper pleaded.  "I really am trying to help the Kral, and I have friends who will die if I don't help them soon."

Her face softened, and the tip of her bolt dipped slightly.  Apparently reaching a decision, she nodded toward the window.

"You may need a better disguise," she said.

The dark-robed mages were approaching her door.

"Can you hide me?" Jasper asked quickly.

"Sure, there's a dressing room in the back."  She pointed with her crossbow toward a small work room.

Jasper shut the curtain behind him just as the two dark-robed mages walked inside.  Listening, he heard them ask the proprietor if she had seen a fat man enter her store.  Everything grew quiet.

His hands shook and he tried to steady them.  The expenditure of magic was taking its toll.  Finding his center, he called up what magic he had left.

The curtain slid open.  "They're gone," she said.

Jasper slowly peeked out from behind an elevated cutting board.  He let out a deep sigh of relief.  The proprietor still held her crossbow, but, thankfully, there was no sign of the dark mages.

Eying the wares in the back room, he thumbed through several dresses hanging on the racks and said, "You make your own dresses."  After a moment Jasper asked, "Do you have one my size?"

Several long minutes later, a rotund woman appeared at the door to the dress shop wearing a plain blue dress that just brushed the ground.  She wore a matching hat and gloves and carried a tall walking stick wrapped in strips of dyed leather.

"You'll need this."

Jasper looked around and saw the proprietor holding up a brightly colored scarf.  He stepped closer to let her tie it around his face.

"Thanks.  I forget I've let my beard grow out."

"Don't get yourself killed.  I would hate for you to ruin my dress."

Jasper's face was unreadable behind the scarf.  He took her hand and said, "Thank you.  I'll let the Kral know what you have done."

"Just come back and see me when this is all over."

Letting her hand go, Jasper stepped outside and made to head toward the Kral's estates again.  Before he took a step, he stopped and looked back at the proprietor.  "I never got your name."

"Violeta Galabova," she answered and pointed.  "It's on the sign."

"Oh, yeah," Jasper said, flummoxed.  "Thanks."

Walking in a dress proved more challenging than Jasper had anticipated.  The skirt billowed this way and that with any errant breeze, and he found himself afraid the unruly thing would blow up and reveal his pants underneath or get snagged on something and rip off.  At least he was wearing comfortable shoes.

Jasper strode past the dark-robed mages, giving them the same wide berth everyone else did.  He continued up the hill toward an imposing stone wall and gatehouse.  Behind him, the Bulevard na Kralete aimed straight toward the Majna i Vira and the stone buildings atop the edge of the Escarpment, the three-hundred-foot cliff that separated Upper from Lower Pazard'zhik and the Maritsa River.

Along the way, Jasper noticed several shops with doors marked with freshly painted crimson crosses, their windows dark and wares abandoned. The merchant traffic was steady, but most of the conversations he overheard dealt with this person or that person being sick. He hoped Chert was right and the Blood of Cayn wasn't contagious, but he had a sinking feeling in his gut.

The men at the mages' guild had taken his pouches, which also meant they had taken his identification. He wasn't sure how he was going to get past the guards at the gatehouse. As he approached the stone wall, he came up with and discarded more than a half-dozen ideas. On the other side resided the royalty of Trakya and their various estates, most related to the Kral in one way or the other. Most, but not all. High-ranking dignitaries were also allowed to lease property from the Crown and build their mansions.

It was on that side of the wall where the Krakov estate once stood — before the Kral discovered the Baron and Baroness were in league with the Dark One. Security increased at the gate after that incident, but only the royal family and the Kral's Eyes and Ears knew the real reason for it. It had stung the Kral deeply to learn the Dark One's cult was not just at his front door but inside his proverbial house. Jasper had never met the Kral, but he respected Marcus Marchenkov, who had hired him for this mission. Jasper just wished he could get a message to him.

In mid-stride, an epiphany struck. At the next intersection, Jasper turned left and walked parallel to the wall. He continued, passing block after block. It was well past noon by the time he left the merchant district and entered the section of town that catered to the military. Walking around in his blue dress, he felt conspicuous, but he didn't have the time to change or magic to waste.

Stopping in front of a thick door with a stylized chevron painted in bright red, Jasper thought, *I guess this is what's meant by girding up your loins.*

Taking a deep breath, he opened the door and walked inside. Dim light filtered through high windows, illuminating a rustic tavern full of soldiers, most of them female, eating a late lunch. All were of similar appearance, with shoulder-length hair and petite, athletic builds. Each wore a tight-fitting uniform consisting of sky-blue leather tunics and breeches with a different-colored chevron emblazoned on their right shoulders and, on their left, embroidered patches of various types: eagles, gryphons, dragons, and hippoæti. Next to them on tables or empty chairs sat blue, fur-lined leather flight helmets with a sable-colored Parlathean lion, the symbol of Trakya, stitched onto the front.

All conversation stopped when Jasper stepped inside. Even the bartender stopped polishing her glass.

Jasper scanned the bar and noticed various military awards and plaques hung on the wall. Quickly finding who he was looking for, he walked confidently through the crowd to the back of the common room, ignoring the open stares. He waited in silence.

In front of him were four fit-looking women dressed in the same type of uniform. They stood in a line, side by side, and as the one on the left counted, they drew and threw daggers in smooth, fluid motions, aiming at a row of small targets on the wall. Even to the casual observer, the contest wasn't just one of skill and accuracy, but also of patience. Each person had to hit their target dead center or run the risk of obstructing the target of their teammate next to them. These four soldiers competed against other squads, and watching them practice, Jasper understood how they had won three of their last four annual competitions.

After the round, the one on the left stepped up to the target board and calculated their score. She turned, about to congratulate her team, and stopped. Her mouth remained partly open; the words that had rested there forgotten.

He simply waited and watched the play of emotions unfold, unable to avoid the inevitable chain reaction he knew was coming. Surprise quickly turned to raw bewilderment, followed by denial and, finally, dawning recognition.

She burst out laughing. Her teammates turned and discovered a plump woman standing behind them dressed in a frilly blue dress, wearing a dainty scarf over her face. They didn't know what to do, causing their team leader to laugh harder.

Jasper yanked off his scarf and complained, "Yana, you could've done the decent thing and waited until I had my back turned before you laughed at me."

It took several minutes for Yana to collect herself, but she eventually managed and motioned for the bartender to bring her team a round of drinks.

"And bring one for my mom, will you?"

"Funny.  Very funny," Jasper said, finding himself thinking he should have kept the scarf on.

Once their drinks arrived, Jasper and Yana found a quiet table away from the front door.

"You look silly in a dress," she said, wiping a tear.

"I need your help."

"Sorry, I'm not that kind of girl."

"Would you stop?  I'm serious."

"I know, sorry.  Go ahead."

"I need to see your brother."

All merriment disappeared.  She turned up her glass and finished it in one swallow, slamming it back down on the table.  "You can't.  They have him at the chapel with the others.  They say he's dying," she said sadly.  "Our aunt's with him now."

Jasper reached over and placed his hand over hers. "Yana, that's why I'm here.  I'm trying to find the cure.  Have you heard if anyone has made any progress?"

"The mages' guild is supposed to have one ready any day now but, no offense, I think they're just sitting on their collective arse."

"I just came from there," Jasper whispered.  "They tried to hold me prisoner."

"What?  That's insane.  They wouldn't dare do that."

"They would if they didn't want me to tell the Kral what they're doing."

"What *are* they doing?"

"I have my theories, but no evidence — at least not yet — so let's pass on that question."

"You just said they tried to hold you prisoner.  Isn't that evidence enough?"

"It's my word against theirs, and I don't think that would hold up if I took it to the local constable."

"Why didn't you go straight to the Kral instead of coming to me?"

"The mages took my papers and my pouch when I arrived.  I wouldn't be able to get past the gate."

A knowing look came over Yana and she said excitedly, "Put your scarf back on, Mom.  You and I are going for a ride." She left the table to collect her team.  While she was away, Jasper reached for his drink, downed it, and asked the bartender for another.

# CHAPTER 2
# THE RISING STORM

### October 25, 4235 K.E.

**11:08am**

The caravan's ten Percherons cantered quickly down the road with their heads high. Grendel was amazed at their speed and endurance. Listening to Dragahn and Pyotr over the past few days, he had anticipated the team would slow down to conserve the horses' strength. Instead, the new drivers had them practically galloping. For their part, the Percherons seemed as fresh as the day they passed the Stena.

Skeletal tree limbs overhung the roadway, but the road ahead was open as though someone or something had cleared it in advance. Only brown grass and dirt remained.

By midday, dark clouds on the horizon chased after them, and Marko Madasgorski signaled for a break. Once the horses stopped, everyone jumped down from their seats to don their rain gear. The two Zhitomiran horsemen, wearing the red sleeve sinister crest of the Madasgorski family, worked their way through the Percherons, giving them water and checking their harnesses.

While they prepared for the coming storm, Grendel remained seated and took the opportunity to watch the orcs who joined them after Marko abandoned the teamsters. The humanoids seemed to work well together, but there was a definite hierarchy from their leader to the grunts. Each orc knew his place, and if anyone stepped out of line, the orc above him in rank quickly stepped in with brutal efficiency.

The tall, bald-headed man they called D'yakon Krovos, jumped down from the chuck wagon. He wore pitch-black robes and carried a two-handed claymore. His bearing and demeanor reminded Grendel more of an executioner than a priest, but he was what Xandor called a Sha'iry — a priest of the Dark One.

Krovos joined Marko, and the two turned their eyes skyward. Even though Grendel couldn't hear what they discussed, by their expressions he could tell they were trying to gauge the weather.

"Aren't you going to walk around a bit?" Sacha asked.

Grendel shrugged and climbed down from the wagon. He squatted a few times in place to limber up his legs and get the circulation flowing again. The orcs nearest him kept their hands on the hilts of their weapons. He stood and stretched, revealing his full height was head and shoulders over their leader.

Sacha flinched as Teodor passed her and unconsciously took a step back. He walked with a purpose and confidence that was out of character for the youth just a couple of days ago. Grendel expected some recognition but received none.

Not daring to say anything, the bodyguard followed Sacha as she followed Teodor to join her brother, Marko, and the D'yakon. Out of the corner of his eye, he caught the orcs passing around a paper-wrapped package filled with bloody meat. The warm, coppery scent lay heavy in the air.

"We can't outrun that storm, Marko," the dark priest said.

"D'yakon, we must stay on schedule." The knight's eyes kept darting west, back down the road.

"What are you worried about? It's not the storm, is it?"

"He's worried about the Kral's ranger," Gregori butted in.

They both turned and stared at the mage who'd stolen the youthful body of the teamster named Teodor.

"He's still alive. He and his companions escaped my lab."

"How can that be? You assured me your trap would work!" Marko snapped.

"Don't raise your voice at me," Gregori said. "I guaranteed nothing. I only said it had a high probability of success given the limited information you provided."

"Are you saying it's my fault your trap didn't work?" Marko demanded, his hand straying to the hilt of his sword.

"It was not the ranger who discovered my trap. It was a mage... and a powerful one, at that."

"Jasper," Marko cursed.

"So, you *knew* there was a mage amongst the teamsters," Gregori accused the knight. "Why didn't you tell me?"

"I suspected but wasn't sure, and if he was, I figured the dwolma would take care of any loose ends."

"Your loose end escaped the dwolma and found my lab. He knows about the blood and the soap. This loose end may cause us trouble yet," Gregori said, giving Marko a stern look before continuing. "I went ahead and took the liberty of informing Master Asenov in case this mage decides to return to Pazard'zhik."

D'yakon Krovos cupped his right elbow in his left hand and raised his fingers to pinch the bridge of his nose while he thought. After a moment, he asked, "What do we know about this mage and the ranger? Are they working alone?"

The two men stared at Marko, waiting on him to answer.

Sacha stepped in front of Marko and answered for him. "We know the ranger traveled with a dwarf. Based on what Mladen told us about the encounter at the bunker, I expect he has some proficiency with the art of healing."

"Anyone else?"

"Not that we are aware."

"D'yakon, what about Sabe and his men?" Gregori asked.

"My orcs were harassing them when I left this morning to come here. They'll chase them all the way to the gates of Chernigov."

"How many men does Sabe have left?"

"I'd say around two score."

Looking from the mage to the priest, Sacha said hotly, "You were supposed to take care of those men before we reached the Stena. The last thing we want is to come across an armed patrol of Rhodinan soldiers. What happened?"

Staring intently at the D'yakon, Sacha waited on an answer. The dark priest returned her gaze, his face turning red with anger.

Before the two could break into a full-scale argument, the largest of the orcs interrupted them and said, "The snow warriors have been hiding in the old bunkers. We caught up to them a few times and killed many, but we ran out of time. As the D'yakon says, we had to hurry back here to clear the roadway."

"They're a day or so ahead of us. By the will of Sutekh, their crucified corpses will guide our way," D'yakon Krovos added.

"Did we ever figure out what Sabe was doing in the Haunted Wood?" she asked, turning to the priest.

"They were foraging for old artifacts left behind when Trakya retreated from the White River," Gregori replied. "I wouldn't worry. Anything of importance has long been gone — probably buried in Bregu Kraagor's vaults beneath Chernigov."

A cold wind suddenly blew down the roadway. Marko glared at the approaching clouds and ordered, "Mount up. I want to be moving before that rain hits."

"What about the ranger and the dwarf?" D'yakon Krovos asked.

"We will kill them," the orc leader replied confidently.

Marko grabbed the pommel and lifted himself into his saddle. "Take seven of your best and finish them."

The orc captain struck his left breast with a closed fist in response and quickly set about organizing his warriors.

**1:06pm**

Xandor and Chert studied the Väkiljós elf in the cage. He had begun changing into the dwolma, and it wouldn't be long before the transformation completed. Probably within the hour, by the look of things.

"We have to kill him before he turns," Chert said grimly.

"I know," Xandor replied. He looked up at the position of the sun. The day was getting away from them. "I hate doing this."

Unsheathing his longsword and lighting the blade, Xandor saluted the elf while Chert administered last rites. The elf's skin began to undulate, as if the developing dwolma anticipated what was about to happen and tried to emerge faster. Xandor thrust his sword into the cage, igniting the black mucus. Tiny mouths appeared on the exposed portions of skin and screamed in pain.

All around the clearing, hands were clapped to ears to block out the noise. Xandor stood rigid, absorbing the horrific sound and adding it to the growing list of Marko Madasgorski's crimes. The mouths caught fire and slowly dissolved into a black liquid. Smoke from the burning body rose high into the sky and briefly obscured the light from the sun.

Chert stood with Xandor until the last of the black slime disappeared into the earth.

They both turned when Dragahn said, "You'll need to leave soon if you want to catch up to them."

The ranger sheathed his sword and stared at the caravan chief. Finally, he said, "We don't have much in the way of weaponry to spare." He took a couple of daggers from his belt and handed them to the teamster leader.

"Thank you. I'll make sure you get them back."

An awkward silence set in until Dragahn asked the question that was on everyone's mind, "Do you think Jasper will find the cure?"

"I've worked with Jasper for little over a year, now. While he doesn't know everything, he always seems to know where to look for the answer. He'll find the cure," Xandor replied.

"Thank you," said Dragahn. "We all appreciate what you've done for us. We deserve worse."

Xandor didn't respond. They both knew leaving them was most likely handing the teamsters a death sentence.

Pyotr stood next to Chert and took a swallow from Dragahn's hooch. He handed it down to the dwarf, who looked at it first before sniffing the top. He turned up the tin and took a swallow of the fiery liquid.

Handing it back to Pyotr, the dwarf slapped the horse doctor on the arm and said, "All is not lost. You still live."

Pyotr took another swallow, but his eyes strayed over to where Lucky lay resting. The youth was still pale with blood loss, but at least some color had returned. "What about Lucky?" he asked as they walked toward him.

Chert knelt beside the youth and laid a hand on his forehead. "He's made it through the worst of it. Probably be up and about later, but a day or two of rest would do him a world of good."

Dragahn and Andrei drifted closer, sensing the time had come to part ways with their erstwhile rescuers.

Looking around at the group, Chert said, "Have faith, my friends. Good will prevail. Please join me in a moment of prayer." The dwarf bowed his head. "Eternal Father, thank you for this day you have given us. We ask that you guide our steps o'er Gaia's lands and help us choose the path of greatest good. Please be with those gathered here today, our friends, and our families as we strive to fight evil and thwart those who would serve its cause.  And when our work is done, may you gather us to thy heart forever.  Zal es zeyn, Adonai."

"Xerxes, Sky, Ginger!  Let's go," Xandor yelled when the dwarf finished.

The three horses quickly trotted up to the ranger.

"Chert, you ready?"

With a curt nod, Chert climbed into Sky's saddle, a spot where he still wasn't completely comfortable.  He could only hope Xandor wouldn't set a punishing pace.  The ranger quickly mounted Xerxes and looked at the teamsters. "Gentlemen," he said with a nod.

Reins held loose in one hand, the ranger guided Xerxes across the clearing toward the roadway, followed closely by Chert on Sky, and the rouncey he'd dubbed Ginger.  They turned and looked back before they entered the woods and raised their arms in farewell.

# CHAPTER 3
# ARREST THIS MAN!

### October 25, 4235 K.E.

**2:27pm**

"If you weren't so heavy, this thing would fly like it's supposed to!" Yana yelled to Jasper over the screaming wind. She wore crystal lensed goggles that gave her the appearance of having bug eyes.

The two hung horizontally from a V-shaped hang-glider that flew through the air more than four hundred yards above Upper Pazard'zhik. The glider consisted of a light blue silk airfoil supported by interconnected struts and rod bracing. Yana held the sway bar tightly in her hands as she piloted the Trakyan flyer, trying to compensate for Jasper's weight. Still, the thing flew like a drunken goose, with one wingtip dipping lower than the other. It was not meant to support such an unbalanced load.

"Stop fighting! Are you trying to kill us?"

Around them the other squad members, each with her own single-person glider, literally flew circles around Yana and Jasper. They performed a synchronized dance of aerial acrobatics that caused people on the ground to look up and stare in awe.

"It's this blasted dress! The wind keeps riding up the skirt!"

"At least you're wearing pants!"

Swinging the sway bar this way and that, Yana piloted her flyer downward in a slow spiral toward the Kral's estate. She landed outside the chapel, where a group of men had gathered. Once she disengaged her harness, she helped Jasper out of his.

The two raced under the canopy of trees toward the gathering. One of the men, dressed in the robes of parliament, stepped forward and said, "Yana, this is highly irregular. Explain yourself immediately."

"Uncle Bate, this is my friend, Jasper Thredd, one of Marcus' agents. He needs to see my brother."

The nobleman eyed Jasper and his dress with some disdain but otherwise ignored him. "I'm afraid that's impossible. Marcus has lost consciousness and can't speak with anyone."

Jasper asked urgently, "Who has taken over the search for the cure? Maybe I can speak with them instead?"

A man dressed in burgundy robes, carrying a tall white-oak staff, stepped forward and said smoothly, "The White Circle holds that responsibility."

Another nobleman, with the silver double-headed eagle of the Eyes and Ears embroidered on his right shoulder, stepped forward and demanded, "Jasper Thredd, why did you attack members of the guild?"

Narrowing his eyes at the new speaker, Jasper kept quiet, all the while looking for a place to run.

Alarmed at the accusation, Yana turned and stared icy daggers at the portly mage.

"We have your papers and evidence of your treachery," the man stated. He glanced over Jasper's shoulder. "Arrest this man, Sergeant!"

Royal guards dressed in shiny steel armor marched toward the crowd, their swords drawn. The leader commanded, "By order of the Kral, Jasper Thredd, you are charged with espionage. Surrender your staff."

Yana looked frantically from her uncle to Jasper and back again. "What kind of trouble are you in?" she hissed under her breath.

Jasper simply shrugged and whispered back, "The usual."

She rolled her eyes and said, "You owe me."

With a shrill whistle, she grabbed Jasper by the bodice and pulled him back toward their flyer. Above them, two of her teammates threw small pellets into the crowd. As soon as they struck the ground, the pellets spewed smoke, and everyone began coughing.

Jasper shook his head and pointed toward the chapel.

"Damn it!" Yana yelled.

"I'll meet you."

"How?"

"Don't worry. Just keep hovering. Give me fifteen minutes."

Cursing all the way back to her flyer, Yana quickly strapped in and took off, climbing vertically.

Using the confusion for cover, Jasper ducked inside the chapel's infirmary in search of Marcus. All around him, the healer's prayers held a note of desperation. Hope could be found within these halls, but only in small doses.

Jasper didn't recognize Marcus when he first saw him. Sleeping on a narrow cot in one of the alcoves off the main hallway, he hardly resembled his normal self. He had a grey pallor about him and had lost a lot of weight in a short period of time, giving him the appearance of a skeleton draped in loose skin. An elderly lady sat next to the bed with her head down.

"Excuse me."

She looked up, surprised to see a strange man in a blue dress.

"My name is Jasper, and I work for your nephew. May I try to talk with him?"

The woman was about to shoo him away, but Marcus stirred and opened his eyes. In a dry voice he said, "My fever must be causing me to hallucinate. I'd swear you're wearing a dress."

"Marcus, there's no time to explain right now. We have a serious situation." Jasper quickly summed up the events as best he could. Marcus zoned in and out, but he seemed coherent enough to follow the conversation. "...and now your sister is a fugitive, and I need to get some help for the teamsters."

Marcus motioned weakly for Jasper to come closer. With help from his aunt, he sat up slightly and tried to pull a gold chain over his head. Jasper cautiously reached over and took the necklace. It held a heavy, gold ring engraved with Marcus' symbol of state. The movement caused Marcus to grow weaker, and he fell back into bed.

"Take it and use it. Get help."

Marcus' aunt looked at Jasper with desperate hope in her eyes and said, "We can't get him to eat. If you don't find the cure soon, he won't make it."

"Yes ma'am. I know." Jasper paused before asking, "Lady Marchenkova, can you do me a favor? It would help me help your nephew."

Outside the chapel, the smoke had cleared, and the grounds swarmed with royal guards.

"Find him. He's around here somewhere," the sergeant shouted.

Standing under a barren oak tree, the mage dressed in burgundy robes glared at Yana's uncle.

"Lord Marchenkov, why did your niece help this criminal?"

"I don't know, Master Asenov. This is completely unlike her."

"Until we discover the cure, we are all in danger. This man, this Jasper Thredd, must be captured and interrogated."

"I agree, but if he truly worked for my nephew, we should give him some latitude."

"I spoke with the Eyes and Ears. They have no record of this man working for Marcus. Lord Marchenkov, the man is lying."

Jasper continued his streak of great timing by entering the courtyard at that precise moment. He stared across the yard and made eye contact with the acting guild master.

"Sergeant!" Asenov yelled as he pointed.

Guards ran from either side, effectively trapping the man in the blue dress. Before they could lay a hand on him, Jasper shouted, "Ouranos!" and rose into the air, climbing higher and higher.

Asenov pointed his staff at the fleeing mage, focusing his magic.

With the sun behind her, Yana streaked toward Jasper in her flyer. The portly mage grabbed hold as she passed.

Lord Marchenkov followed Asenov with the intent of helping, but when he recognized his niece in the flyer, he shoved the burgundy-robed mage. The spell intended for the flyer burst into a dark cloud of garnet-colored smoke several yards away.

Turning on him, Asenov demanded furiously, "Why did you do that? You're letting him get away."

"That's my niece up there. You will not hurt her."

"Lord Marchenkov, I respectfully submit that your niece is now harboring a fugitive. Once word of this reaches the Kral, her career in the Wind Rider Legion is over," Asenov hissed venomously as he turned on his heel and stalked away.

The rest of the men assembled on the chapel lawn looked up and watched as Yana and Jasper flew over the wall and disappear past the escarpment.

"I really hate you, you know!" Yana shouted into his ear.

"I get that a lot!  Take me down over there!"

Above a small clearing on the other side of the Maritsa River, Jasper let go and floated down while Yana landed.  She unbuckled her harness and stepped away from the glider while Jasper took off the dress.  Underneath, he still had on his traveling clothes, so he folded up the dress as best he could and laid it on a boulder.

Yana waited until he finished before she strode up to him and punched him solidly in the jaw, knocking him to the ground.

"What the hell was that?" she yelled.

He had a good five inches on her in height and outweighed her by at least a hundred pounds, but her explosive nature made her seem bigger than she actually was.  She towered over the mage, her fist poised to strike again.  His lip busted, Jasper spat blood and rubbed where she had hit him.  He cautiously stood back up.

"I told you.  I'm trying to help your brother."

"If you're trying to help, why is everyone after you?"

"Not everyone, just the White Circle."

"Seemed like everyone to me.  I can't go home now.  None of my team can, thanks to you."

"Listen, I didn't mean for that to happen.  I needed to see Marcus, and, as it happened, your aunt." Jasper said the last part quickly and avoided eye contact.

"Oh, no!  You didn't!" Yana yelled as she suddenly closed on him and made to punch him again.

Jasper backpedaled, holding his arms up.

"My aunt!  You brought my aunt into this?  I hope I heard you wrong!"

"Stop shouting.  Somebody might hear you."

"I'm going to kill you!"

"Wait until I've told you everything.  *Then* you can kill me."

"You get one minute, fat boy.  Go."

Jasper took longer than a minute, but he described their mission, and the events that had occurred along the way.  He described the encounter with Marko and the Northmen as well as the final events when Aleksandra Madasgorski-Krakova revealed her true identity.  He then retold the elf's tale and spoke of how Xandor and Chert were going to stop the caravan before anyone else was exposed to the Blood of Cayn — the poison hidden inside the bars of soap.

"What else could I do?  I had to ask your aunt to relay these events to the Kral."

"Do you think the guild will find out about her?" Yana asked.

"I don't know, but she's my last hope."

"We have to stop that caravan," Yana mused.

"I know."

"How can I help?"

"It's a lot to ask, but could you fly out there?"

"How far away are they?"

Jasper calculated and answered, "I'd guess five hundred miles as the crow flies, maybe more if they sped up.  We were four days' ride from Chernigov when they tried to feed us to the dwolma."

"There's not enough time," Yana said, defeated.  "We'd need to grab our gear, prep, and get away from the city without anyone knowing.  I just don't see that happening.  And if we get caught in an aerial fight with the other squadrons, we all lose."

"What if I gave you a little boost?"

She eyed him warily and asked, "What do you mean, 'a little boost?'"

"Well, if your rig can take it, I can put a little lift in your sail, if you know what I mean."

"How much lift?"

"A small gust — say, forty knots, maybe fifty."

"For how long?"

"Four to five hours, max."

A sparkle lit Yana's eyes, "Could you help my whole team?"

"I think so.  But after that, you're on your own."

"Where will you be?"

"I need to get back to the teamsters before nightfall."

It was Yana's turn to calculate times and distances. She took a moment and said, "Around here, we've been averaging wind speeds of twenty to twenty-five knots. Trakyan flyers have a glide ratio of roughly twenty-to-one, which will help us between lifts. With a little luck with the wind, we should be able to catch up to the caravan within twenty-four hours after takeoff, plus or minus. But I still need to retrieve our gear from the armory."

"Here, take this. You may need it." Reaching into one of his pockets, Jasper pulled out Marcus' signet ring and handed it to Yana. She took it, and, when she recognized whose it was, tears filled her eyes.

Jasper put both his hands over hers and said, "I promise I will do what I can to find a cure. I was hoping the guild would help me, but they have bigger problems right now. If you can stop those wagons or even delay them a little, maybe it will give me time to come up with a plan before someone else dies. And remember, Chert and Xandor are chasing the caravan, and Grendel's still out there somewhere. He may still be with the wagons; I don't know."

She looked up, smiling, and said, "The caravan won't know what hit them."

Letting her hands go, he said, "Let's meet back here in two hours. That should give you enough time to enter the garrison and collect your squad while I prepare my spell. Use Marcus' ring if you run into trouble."

As Yana turned to leave, Jasper had a sudden thought and asked, "Do you know where Sehraine will be tonight?"

She stopped in her tracks and replied hesitantly, "Why?"

"I have to go back to Pazard'zhik and pick up a few things, and I could use her help."

Yana gave Jasper a hard stare and said, "You've already exiled me and my team, and you sent my aunt to meet the Kral. You will not drag Sehraine into this."

Giving her his best innocent look, he replied, "I need a disguise. I can't keep wandering around in a dress."

In the blink of an eye, Yana stood in front of Jasper, his collar in her tightly clenched fist. "You'd better not be lying to me, Mage." There was a look of hot violence in her eyes.

"I have to get back my things, and I'm going to need a disguise. That's all. Sehraine is the best, right?"

"That's it? Swear to me you won't take her with you."

"Why would I take her with me?"

She relaxed a little and said, "You need to watch what you say to her. She may look like an adult, Jasper, but she's still an adolescent. If you tell her you're going to break into the mages' guild, she'll want to go with you — if for no other reason than it'll sound fun. She lacks a sense of her own mortality."

Jasper gave Yana a quizzical look and noted she still hadn't released her grip on his collar. "I'm sure you'll see her before you go, so warn her, if you think it will help."

The wind rider stared into his eyes for several long moments before she finally said, "She'll be performing at the Naroden Teatar tonight."

"Wow. That's the perfect job for her," Jasper said, more to himself than to Yana.

"Promise me you won't involve her in this. It would kill me if something happened to her," Yana said. The dangerous look returned.

"I can't promise that," Jasper said seriously, amazed his courage held.

Yana looked as if she were going to say something else but decided against it. Instead, she ran to her flyer. Before sliding her crystal lensed goggles down over her eyes, she gave Jasper one last knowing look. With a stomp of her foot, the glider lifted vertically into the air. Jasper watched her fly away, unaware he was wringing his hands until she was gone.

# CHAPTER 4
# SIGNS AND PORTENTS

## October 25, 4235 K.E.

**2:31pm**

Kneeling near the trees at the edge of the roadway, Xandor pieced together what had happened to the caravan the previous evening. He cast a scornful glance at the scraped ground where someone had tried to hide their tracks, giving them more the appearance of a land-shark migration than a caravan.

Xandor studied the signs before him, tracing them with his eyes. Patches of crushed grass held the hard lines of several pairs of footprints on top of one another. The outline was just slightly smaller than a typical human, but they were heavy and pressed deep into the earth. Based upon their uniformity, Xandor guessed they were soldiers of some sort. Closing his eyes, he pictured the soldiers standing there. As he did, a faint, unclean scent caught his attention: orcs.

He opened his eyes and followed the tracks out onto the roadway, where they split up. A pair of orcs each walked to the front and rear wagons, while the others appeared to head toward each of the three horsemen. Their steps didn't meander. They knew exactly what to do. Xandor picked one of their trails and followed it until it stopped at a set of hoofprints: one of the caravan's rounceys. Next to the prints was a slight depression where someone had fallen from their saddle. Reading the signs, Xandor guessed the orc must have picked up the horseman.

Turning, Xandor backtracked a set of prints down the road to a spot where the ground was disturbed. He scanned the area, walking in a circle, and found four distinct areas where prints had deeply gouged the road. "Four men dropped from above," he mumbled to himself, noting the heavy branches overhanging the road. Beneath them, Xandor discovered tiny shards of glass pressed into the dirt. Picking one up, he examined it in the afternoon sun. The glass was thin and had a greasy residue. He suspected it was some sort of poison, but he couldn't be certain.

Frowning, Xandor oriented himself. He had to differentiate between the different layers of time. The lowest layer told of the caravan's arrival, the middle layers told of the ambush, and the upper layers told the story of what happened afterwards. The Percherons and wagons had stopped on the road. Not long afterward, the Frisian and the Shire met up with two other horses that had trotted out of the woods. Then a dozen orcs led the caravan toward the clearing where the teamsters had been caged.

Even though some of the other layers were hard to decipher, he could distinguish between the caravan tracks when they first left the road and when they returned. He estimated there was an eight-to-ten-hour difference, meaning they had left a couple hours before sunrise. It also meant they could easily be forty miles ahead.

Chert remained beside Xandor for a little while but grew bored and left to see what he could find. He continued down the road, with Sky following. They walked a quarter of a mile before the wind changed direction, and they caught the smell of death.

Pulling out his hammer, Chert cautiously followed the scent, Sky close on his heels. Ahead a huge wake of black-winged buzzards jostled one another for better access to their feast, unconcerned by the approach of the living. More birds wheeled and circled overhead. The dwarf yelled and waved his arms to drive them off. It took both him and Sky making noise before the buzzards moved enough to reveal the desiccated carcasses of four horses.

Ignoring the damage the buzzards had done, Chert examined the corpses, but couldn't find what had killed them or why they looked the way they did. Of course, he couldn't roll them over, but given their condition, he suspected there wouldn't be any telltale signs on that side, either.

"I don't know if you can understand me, but I need you to bring Xandor," Chert said to Sky. He felt a little foolish at first talking to the pony, but hanging around a ranger's horse must have done something, because Sky seemed to understand and quickly trotted back down the road.

Xandor followed Sky to where Chert waited; a score or more of buzzards perched impatiently in the trees. On the ground were the remains of four rounceys. However, instead of the wet mess he expected to see in the middle of a carrion feast, he found skeletal remains wrapped in grey flesh.

At the sight of them, Xandor stopped dead still, and all the color drained from his face. In his mind, the warrior returned to an unholy chapel dedicated to the Dark One, and the loss of a good friend.

"Xandor, what is it?" Chert asked gently. "What did this to these horses?"

Xandor reached inside his leather jerkin and pulled out his bronze Korsun cross. Rubbing it absently with his thumb, he stared at the carcasses.

"Evil," Xandor replied in the barest of whispers. Choosing his words carefully, he continued, "Do you recall what the elf said in the clearing?"

The dwarf nodded and stepped closer.

"Back before you and I met, Jasper and I worked with another team, and we crossed paths several times with the Sha'iry, followers of the Dark One. Most were charlatans using the cult for their own personal gain; however, there were a few who could weave truly evil curses. One of the Sha'iry we faced could steal a person's health. Steal your life force, if you will."

Gesturing toward the four horses, Xandor said, "These horses were killed by one of those Sha'iry, and their life force stolen to be used later, maybe to keep the other horses fresh. Who knows?"

"How can you be sure it was them?"

Xandor stared down the road. "I've seen this before."

The ranger turned back, his face completely devoid of emotion. "We were in the middle of raiding one of their temples when one of our team members became separated. We searched through all the rooms and corridors until we found him. When we did, he looked just like the corpse of one of those horses."

The horror of what had been done to his friend raged through Xandor's system like wildfire, leaving his senses raw. Every sound and scent bombarded him, magnified a hundredfold. He fought the vision in his mind's eye just as another part of his brain cataloged the sounds and smells around him until it found something that conflicted with the memory.  It latched onto the smell of raw earth and worked metal that defined Chert.  His grip on the cross at his neck tightened.

"It's not your fault," the dwarf said.

Xandor blinked owlishly.  Trying to conceal the emotions inside him, he swallowed hard and turned away.

Chert let the ranger go without pressing the matter and went back to examining the horses.

A minute passed, then two.  Finally, Xandor turned and said, "This thing has gotten bigger."

"What do you mean?"

"One of the times we ran across them, we captured a number of their books and scrolls.  One of them contained a story similar to the one the elf told.  The primary difference was, it cast the Dark One, Sutekh, as the hero.  According to their legends, Sutekh saved Havel from being consumed by his brother, Cayn, and was charged with defending Gaia against Chaos."


**5:05pm**

Dusk was falling when Jasper stood in front of three women in the small clearing outside of Pazard'zhik.

"What happened to your fourth wind rider?" Jasper asked.

"She didn't make it," Yana replied, flatly.  "They arrested her before she could make it back to her flyer."

Not wanting to push it any further, he held up three raptor feathers and tucked the fourth back into his jacket pocket.  He handed one to each of them and said, "When you're ready, yell the word 'Pnoés' as loud as you can, and hang on."

Moving behind them, he quickly studied their hang-gliders.  Unlike the previous trip, the wings of these sleek flyers bore a series of small, leather pouches that dangled down like Espian decorations.  Jasper was curious about what they carried but held his tongue.  The women seemed calmer now and understood the urgency of their mission, but when they first arrived, Yana had to intervene to keep the ladies from pummeling the mage.

"How fast did you say this wind of yours would travel?" Yana asked.

"Forty to fifty knots.  Why?"

"On the way here, we caught winds around twenty knots."

"Can your rig handle this trip?"

Yana shrugged and replied, "I guess we'll find out."

Each of the warriors turned to strap themselves into their glider.  As Yana cinched the last belt tight, she commented, "You know, we're probably going to lose our jobs over this flight."

"Why?"

"Are you joking?  We're taking an unsanctioned flight to attack a civilian caravan, not to mention aiding a wanted criminal — that's *you*, by the way."

Instead of the goggles she wore earlier, Yana settled a T-slit barbute with a smoky crystal visor onto her head and looked at her two team members to verify they were ready. Jasper noted the other two wind riders wore crystal goggles like Yana wore earlier and wondered absently if they were standard gear or not.

With a hard stomp, they lifted off the ground and into the air.  Higher and higher they went until they caught the westerly wind.  Other Trakyan flyers streaked down out of the clouds, chasing after them.  Yana's team flew eastward, pursued by the Kral's flyers.  For a moment, it seemed the other teams would force Yana and her squad-mates down. Suddenly, they picked up speed and disappeared into the darkening sky.  He swore he heard one of them yell out in excitement as they raced forward.

Twenty-four hours — maybe faster if the wind held. Would they catch the caravan in time?  The mage could only hope.

Some of the flyers broke away from the chase and headed for his clearing.  Using his staff, Jasper drew a circle on the ground around him and marked each of the cardinal directions with a rune.  With a surge of magic, he vanished.

# CHAPTER 5
# FALLEN HERO

## October 25, 4235 K.E.


**5:08pm**

Sheets of rain fell, and the grassy road quickly turned to mud. Four orcs wearing blood red mail jogged along each side of the road, splashing through the puddles. It was late afternoon, and dark clouds covered the hateful brightness of the falling sun. The orc captain kept them moving at a quick pace, but not one that would overly tire his warriors if they came across the ranger and his dwarf early.

After several hours, the orc captain gestured, and two of his orcs climbed into trees with branches spanning the road while the rest hid behind the thick trunks. The orcs readied their armor and double-checked their weapons as they waited.

They heard talking from down the road, and the orcs hiding in the trees signaled their captain when they spotted the ranger. He rode atop a black Andalusian, followed closely by a small pony carrying a dwarf, and a riderless rouncey.

"I take it chasing Sha'iry is more than just a job for you," Chert said.

"You could say that," Xandor replied absently, his eyes on the ground. He frowned as he tried to concentrate on the tracks, but the rain was washing them away. Fearful of losing the trail, he slowed in anticipation the caravan might veer off the road for one reason or another.

Timing their jump, the orcs in the trees waited until the ranger was directly underneath. They leapt down, one over the ranger, the other over the dwarf, and knocked the two riders from their saddles.

Fierce yells and growls erupted as the orcs rushed in from all sides, brandishing their cruel scimitars and cutlasses.

Sky and Xerxes both screamed and reared on their hind legs. They flailed with their forelegs, trying to defend their riders. The rouncey bucked and kicked at the orcs, instinctively aware the humanoids viewed her as food. Although it didn't stop the orc advance, it gave Chert and Xandor the time they needed to recover.

Xandor rolled to his feet, drew both longswords, ignited them, and attacked the orc who knocked him down. However, instead of just one orc, he faced three. He swung his swords side to side and the flames hissed in the rain; a cloud of steam surrounding him.

The orcs backed up as doubt wormed its way into their heads. Xandor read it in their bestial faces and yelled an Alashalian war cry.

Responding with a yell of his own, the orc captain flew through the rank of faltering orcs and struck at the ranger with a strong overhead blow from his curved scimitar. Bringing up both his longswords, Xandor deflected it and pushed it to the side.

The three orcs, emboldened by their captain, rushed forward, and joined the attack.

Even though the captain wasn't an expert swordsman, he was an excellent fighter. He faced the ranger head on and managed to bind Xandor's blades with his sword. Pressing forward, he brought up his knee to strike Xandor in the groin.

Xandor shifted his weight to avoid a direct hit; when he did, it left him open for a left hook. The blow struck the ranger in the side of the neck, and he staggered back.

The other orcs lunged forward, wicked sword points first. Xandor swept his left blade through the attack, blocking two of the orcs. Pivoting, he made a left to right stomach swipe with his right blade. The third orc stopped short. Even though the orc's sword slipped past Xandor's hastily constructed defense, it lacked any power and resulted in a shallow cut to the ranger's bicep.

Again, the captain rushed forward, pushing his way through the orcs, and raised his scimitar to attack. Xandor pivoted and swiped at the captain's head with the sword in his right hand. The captain ducked under it, evading the fiery edge. Xandor followed up with a thrust from his left sword, which the captain neatly parried to the side.

Letting his momentum carry him, the captain pushed the ranger back with his weapon.

Xandor twisted at the hip and attacked with his right. The diagonal swipe caught the captain on his shoulder and sliced through his hard chain armor. Screams of agony-fueled rage filled the road as the captain's flesh parted and his hair caught fire. Black blood sizzled in the flames.

Stepping past the captain, Xandor faced the other orcs who edged forward, trying to flank him. The first orc leapt and swung his cutlass recklessly at the ranger. Xandor pushed off with his right foot and lunged with his left blade, thrusting it into the chest of the advancing orc all the way to the quillions. The other two danced back, avoiding Xandor's swipe with his right blade.

Before the orc captain could fully recover, Xandor shifted rapidly to his left and closed again. He delivered a hard right cross, smashing the captain's nose with the crossguard of his right sword, causing him to drop his weapon and fall to his knees, stunned.

The second orc came at Xandor from behind.

Raindrops scattered as the ranger pivoted a hundred and eighty degrees, wrenching his sword from the chest of the first orc with a sickening crunch. Xandor bent his left wrist as he turned and dropped the tip of his sword. He brought the hilt across his chest, the point still down. The orc rushed forward with a two-handed thrust aimed toward the ranger's heart.

Xandor continued his motion and parried by briskly sliding his left-hand longsword along the flat of the orc's scimitar, back toward the guard. The movement knocked the second orc's blade aside and redirected it to strike his captain in the chest, piercing a lung but not killing him outright.

The orc's eyes went wide when he saw what happened, and he failed to see Xandor swing with his right longsword. The horizontal stroke cut cleanly through the mail shirt and opened the orc's stomach, spilling a steaming pile of entrails. The last orc stopped, turned, and fled into the woods.

Yelling as he dropped on Chert, the orc grabbed the dwarf by the helmet and shoved him off Sky, riding him all the way to the ground.

Surprised, the dwarf could only hang on and prevent the orc from bringing his blade to bear. When they hit the earth, Chert let go and rolled through the mud. The orc followed him and tried repeatedly to stab the moving target.

Sky stuck with her rider. She chased after the orc, scoring several bites in the process, and saving Chert's life.

Another orc charged out of the woods and attacked the wild pony. Rearing, she used her bulk as a shield, but she didn't have the training to use it and not get hurt.

The dwarf could only watch as the orc struck Sky with a saw-toothed falchion, slicing her leg, and opening a long wound along the side of her belly. She screamed and fell, her blood mingling with the rain and the mud. Seconds later, the orc squealed, pig-like, when he got too close and was struck by her flailing hooves.

On his last roll, Chert loosened the shield on his back and brought it around in front of him. He reversed direction, catching his attacker by surprise. Building momentum on the roll, Chert struck out with his shield and smashed it against the orc's knee, fracturing it. The orc went down with a groan, but two more quickly replaced him.

Jumping to his feet, Chert raised his shield just as two orc blades crashed down. He deftly pulled out his hammer and swung under his shield, crushing the rib cage of one of the attackers.

With rain and sweat streaming down his face, Xandor held his right-hand blade, now extinguished, against the neck of the captain and yelled in Rhodinan, "Drop your weapons, now!"

He looked around to find only one orc remained standing. Of the rest, three were dead, two injured, one unaccounted for, and their captain captured. The remaining orc gave his captain a parting glance before dropping his sword in the mud, and then he, too, fled into the woods.

Ripping off his helmet, Chert threw it down along with his shield and hammer and ran to Sky, who lay on the ground atop a dead orc.

"You stupid, stupid horse!" Chert cried.  He knelt beside Sky and tried to staunch the flow of blood with his hands.

The orc captain stared at the ranger with a sly smile that revealed pointed teeth.  He lunged forward with a battle cry. Xandor reacted instantly and sliced through the orc's neck, severing the jugular.  The captain fell face first into the mud with a splash.

Keeping his longswords ready, the ranger walked past the dead captain and surveyed the roadway.  He found one orc lying unconscious from a kick by Xerxes and another slowly escaping through the woods with a broken leg.  Letting them go, Xandor turned his attention to Chert.

He found the dwarf sitting in the mud, holding Sky's muzzle, and whispering Last Rites.  Through it all, Xandor couldn't tell if it was the rain or if the dwarf wept as he chanted.

# CHAPTER 6
# SEHRAINE

## October 25, 4235 K.E.


**5:12pm**

Jasper reappeared in Violeta's dressing room. The shop was closed, and there was no sign of the owner. He stepped out of the crude circle drawn on the floor behind the cutting board and laid the folded blue dress on the work counter where she could find it. Passing quietly through the shop, he exited the front door and, with the barest whisper of magic, locked it behind him.

The sun, hidden behind the mountains, illuminated the western sky in deep golds and reds. He caught faint glimpses of the Trakyan flyers circling in the distance as he dodged the early evening traffic and crossed the street. Looking back toward the mages' guild with its armed guards and turreted roof, it was obvious how crazy he was to even consider returning, but he needed his cookbook, spices, and the tiny sliver of soap. He needed his sporran. Without them, he might as well go home to Tydway.

It took Jasper the better part of an hour to reach the Naroden Teatar from Violeta's shop. He found it at the intersection of two broad avenues in the embassy district, where foreigners and dignitaries lived and worked under the watchful protection of the Kral.

The Naroden Teatar was a tall building with walls constructed from glossy, black obsidian. Behind massive Doric columns, the front entrance boasted a pair of ten-foot-wide doors sheathed in bronze and embossed with comedy and tragedy masks. Catering to the wealthy by providing them a place to go and be seen, the theater promoted the latest in entertainment. It was a popular social center for Upper Pazard'zhik, and with so many people ill, it seemed those who were healthy wanted a diversion more than ever.

Tonight's play was a portrayal of the battle of Tsarevets and the defeat of the demon-lich. Advertised as a military piece, the local drama troupe planned to use the latest pyrotechnics and props, including a new cable system, which enabled them to re-enact the portion of the battle with the Kral's Wind Riders.

Despite the warning from the Kral that everyone should stay home, the theater drew a record crowd. Already, people gathered in tight cliques outside, waiting for the theater to officially open. Before leaving the shadows of the sidewalk, Jasper looked down at his grimy shirt and pants and whispered, "Katharizo." Instantly, his clothes and hair looked as fresh, new, and well-groomed as the other wealthy patrons of the theater.

Jasper ducked into a side alley and aimed for the backdoor. As he approached, a hulk of a man wearing the formal tabard of the theater stepped away from the recessed entry.

"Good evening," Jasper said politely.

"Good evening, sir," the guard replied, eyeing the wooden staff warily, not quite sure if this was someone of importance or someone he should run off.

"I was hoping to visit with one of the members of the drama group tonight before their performance."

"Sorry, sir, they're prepping for the play and cannot be disturbed."

"I see." Jasper reached down and tapped into his magic. He layered it around his words and said, "It's extremely important that I get inside. I have an urgent message that cannot wait."

The guard struggled. He had his orders, but maybe he could make this one exception. It was an emergency after all.

Jasper continued, "I will only be a minute or two, and I promise to not disrupt the performance."

Looking up and down the alley to see if anyone was watching, the guard quickly stepped aside and gestured toward the door. "Since it's an emergency, go on in, but make sure you come back out this door. It would mean my job if the managers found out."

"Sure. No problem. I'll return shortly."

Jasper rushed inside, only to find himself staring down a long corridor flanked by doors. A steady stream of men and women moved down it, preparing for the night's performance. He had never been in the back-of-house before, and the thought of getting lost sent a ripple of panic through him.

'*Have to find the dressing rooms,*' he thought.

Following three men who seemed to know where they were going, he passed several rehearsal rooms and peered inside each one.  Not finding who he was looking for, he continued deeper into the theater.

He came to an intersection, and a strident voice cut through the cacophony.  Deciding to head that direction, he fell in with a line of people carrying props.  Someone, probably the director, shouted orders beyond a curtained arch. Jasper pushed past the heavy drape and found himself on stage.  He stopped and stared.  The view of the theater from where the actors stood was, in a word, intimidating.  Row after row of seating disappeared into darkness.  The seats were empty now, but he could easily imagine them filled with the aristocracy.

"There you are!" someone shouted.

Jasper hid his staff behind him and slowly turned.  A lean man with a mop of curly hair stomped toward him.  The man wore the latest fashion and literally vibrated with energy.  As he crossed the stage, Jasper watched at least five people approach him with urgent questions.

Before Jasper could explain why he was there, the director said, "Tell Ivan he will get his seat."

Dumbfounded, Jasper just stood there a moment.

"Well, run along and tell him.  The play starts in half an hour."

"Yes, sir," Jasper stammered.

As the director walked away, he said, "Oh, and make sure he brings *white* roses this time."

"Yes, sir," Jasper repeated.  He looked down at his clothes, wondering why the director thought he knew Ivan.

Beside him, a soft female voice whispered in elven, "The beard suits you."

"Nice to see you too," Jasper replied in kind as he turned toward the voice.

"You know this is the last place you should be hanging out.  The militsiya has orders to arrest you on sight."

Partially hidden by the curtains was a breathtakingly beautiful young woman with long silver-blonde hair.  She wore a deep green dress made from the finest silk that shimmered slightly when she moved, giving her an ethereal look.

"What about elven women who happen to be standing near me?"

"Don't know anything about that," she replied in a huskier tone and pure Trakyan accent. "Only humans work in *this* theatre."

Cutting to the chase, he whispered, "Sehraine, I need your help."

"With what?"

"I need a disguise to get into the White Circle."

Sehraine pulled Jasper behind the curtains and replied, "The building people around here refer to as *that spooky place with the crazy people*?"

"That's the one." He pulled an edge of the curtain aside to peer out into the main house. "I need to find a way in tonight."

It became so quiet Jasper dropped the curtain and looked to see if she was still there. Her blue eyes stared intently at the mage, and he could tell she was trying to judge if he was serious. Finally, she asked, "You're not talking after the play, are you?"

"No."

"Aren't you a member or something?"

"The last time I was there, they took away my membership robe, and I need it back."

"Must be a fancy robe for you to want my help."

"All I need is a disguise — that's it — and then I'll be on my way."

Sehraine frowned and said, "No one's ever broken into the guild before — at least, not that I've ever heard."

"Always a first time," Jasper said with a shrug.

"This better be damned important."

"It is."

Grabbing his arm, Sehraine hastily led Jasper farther backstage and down a hallway. She came to a door, laid a hand on Jasper's chest, and motioned for him to stay put. He remained by the door, silently waiting, hoping Sehraine would agree to help him.

People passed him in the hallway with stares that could only be interpreted as hostile. He was a stranger, and everyone here made sure he knew it.  Jasper could understand that.  He, too, was part of a team that didn't take kindly to strangers, especially at first.

The door opened, and a short, pudgy monk in leather sandals and hooded, brown habit stepped out, a beige rope knotted about his waist.  His hair was cut in a clerical tonsure, and a skullcap covered his bald pate.  He carried another brown robe in his hands, along with a long-beaded necklace with a wooden wheel-cross, sandals, and pocketed wrist bracer.

"Follow me," he said.

Jasper peeked through the door behind the monk, looking for Sehraine.

Whispering, the monk said, "Stupid, it's me.  You know, for such a smart man, sometimes you are really dumb."

Jasper's jaw dropped in astonishment.

"You want to get into the White Circle, don't you?" Sehraine asked, walking down the hallway and ducking into a side room used for storing stage sets and props.  A layer of dust covered most of the items.

Jasper hurried to catch up.

After he closed the door, Sehraine dropped the clothes she held in her hands on a crate and gestured for him to put them on.  The mage expected to struggle into the monk's habit, but found it fit over his clothes with room to spare.

"You'll have to take off your pants," she said.

"You've been waiting all night to say that, haven't you?" he replied.

"Monks don't wear pants."

"Are you wearing any?"

Ignoring him, she continued, "And you'll have to leave your rings, boots, and staff.  Anything you have that radiates magic."

Jasper stopped adjusting his clothes and asked, "My staff?"

"You asked me to help you, and I agreed.  I'm going to give up a role I've rehearsed for months for your little adventure, and you and I both know there's a real possibility that we'll be arrested or killed or both," Sehraine said as she stalked toward him.  She grabbed the neckline of his brown robe and jerked his head down until they were almost nose to nose.  "Not only that, but you've sent Yana on a midnight flight that could get her killed.  The least you can do is give up your damned staff!"

Jasper handed her his staff and a handful of rings, toed off his boots, then lifted the hem of the habit to pull off his pants.  Sehraine quickly averted her eyes and stared up at the ceiling.  She took his belongings and placed them inside a wooden miniature of a yellow-sailed pirate ship.

He slipped on the wrist bracer she provided and inserted his remaining spell components into its pockets.  "I'm sorry, Sehraine.  I wouldn't have asked Yana if it wasn't necessary.  As for you, you don't have to come — in all actuality, you shouldn't."

"And miss the opportunity to be the first person *ever* to break into the infamous stronghold of the mages?  You have got to be kidding!"

She held out her hand and helped him up.  When she did, she noticed his darkening fingers and nails.  "What's this?"  He told her the abbreviated version of what was happening, repeating most of what he had told Yana.  For some reason, he held back the portion about the old elf and his tale, and only described to her the elven story of creation and the Blood of Cayn.

During his story, she gestured for him to lean closer.  While he spoke, she combed her fingers through his dark brown hair with both her hands, wrapped a tight hairnet made of silken threads around his head, then made sure all his hair was tucked into it.  Next, she took a piece of strange-looking leather from the folds of her robe and placed it over his hair; it immediately conformed to the shape of his head.  After she applied a little cream from a small canister, Jasper found himself bald with a clerical tonsure just like Sehraine, complete with matching skullcap.

Jasper straightened and placed the necklace with the cross around his neck.  Sehraine stood in front of him silently assessing his appearance.  A pair of scissors appeared in her hand, seemingly from nowhere, and she trimmed his beard and mustache.  The scissors disappeared into the folds of her robe, and she pulled out a couple of paintbrushes, which she used to draw grey lines on his face.  He watched Sehraine work in a tall, oval mirror that stood several feet behind the petite actress.  Wrinkles formed where she touched him, and Jasper began to look older.  After a few more strokes, the hair on his face turned a yellowish-grey, and red splotches appeared on his skin.

She examined her work and, after some minor adjusting, turned her attention to his hands and feet.  Careful not to cover up his fingernails and greying skin on his fingers, she used another brush and removed some of her previous work.  Standing back, she gestured for Jasper to turn around.  Apparently satisfied, she replaced her brushes.

Looking at their attire he asked, "What made you decide on this outfit?"

"Simple.  We're going to break into the mages' guild, right?"

"Yes."

"They're the local masters of magic?"

"Uh huh."

"Wouldn't it make sense that they would be prepared for something magical, even expect it?  They've had centuries of practice."

"Yes."

"Seems like something ordinary might be our best ticket.  How many are we up against, and what do we have to do once we're in?"

"I don't know how many.  All I saw were a few mages and armed guards, but I didn't stick around for long.  Once we're in, we just need to find Asenov's office."

"Acting Guild Master Asenov?"

Jasper nodded.

"Oh, this just keeps getting better," she said and became lost in thought.  "You know, he has a box seat in the balcony," she recalled suddenly.

"Admit it.  You're enjoying this, aren't you?" Jasper asked as he dipped his finger into the pocketed bracer and traced a magical marker only he could see on the wall.  It would serve as a beacon if he needed it.

She answered, "I *love* impromptu performances."

# CHAPTER 7
# DOBRI AND YORDON

## October 25, 4235 K.E.

**7:00pm**

The lights in the theater dimmed, and the curtains opened. Smoke billowed from the stage as lightning crashed, painting the audience in jagged streaks of whites and blacks. In the orchestra pit, the conductor waited for his cue. When it came, music poured out, signifying the advance of the demon-lich's army.

Asenov, wearing emerald robes trimmed in white, held a pair of theater glasses to his eyes, watching the drama troupe perform. His white-oak staff lay next to him, propped within easy reach against his seat.

Loud voices behind him attracted his attention. Annoyed, he lowered the glasses and turned to see a theater doorman with a helpless expression on his face standing behind two rotund monks, their heads bowed. Their brown habits were dirty and stained, as if they had traveled a great distance. Not sure how they had managed to get this far, he became intrigued and motioned them forward.

The doorman said something quietly, and the smaller of the two monks nodded and stepped out onto the balcony.

"Master Asenov, we apologize for disturbing you. We bring you terrible news, but we also bring you hope," the monk said wearily. "We have traveled for several days to meet with you. We are from the province of Sliven, where the governor and his family have become very ill, stricken by the very symptoms that prevail here."

"Have you discovered anything about this plague?" he asked quietly, half an eye focused on the action on the stage.

"Maybe. Which is why we had to see you immediately. My brother and I have been tireless in our efforts to find the cause of this disease, and we feel we may have stumbled upon it."

"What have you discovered?" Asenov asked, his full attention now on the monk. After looking around to see who was watching, the monk stepped forward and whispered in Asenov's ear.

When he finished, the monk gestured toward his brother, who approached timidly. The first monk grabbed the other's hand and displayed the greying fingernails to the acting guild master as if he was presenting evidence.

"Have you or your brother discussed your suspicions with anyone else?"

"No, sir, not even the Kral."

"Good. Good. Let's go back to the guild and see for ourselves what you have discovered. Did you bring a piece with you?"

"No, sir. We were unsure if traveling with it would cause the disease to spread."

"No matter. Let's go and test your conclusion."

Master Asenov led the two monks past the doorman and down the stairs to the main lobby, where he motioned to the valet standing next to the door.

"Young man, hurry outside and tell my carriage I am ready to leave."

Leaning forward, the valet asked, "Was the play not to your liking, sir?"

"No, no. I just received some information that needs my immediate attention and must return to the guild. Please give the director my regards and tell him I would like to call upon him sometime next week at his convenience."

"Yes, sir," the valet replied, bowing.

While they waited, the arch-mage scrutinized the two monks. Jasper stood beside Sehraine with his eyes downcast, trying not to be nervous. They were saved a few minutes later when the valet returned.

"Master Asenov, your carriage awaits."

"Thank you," the arch-mage said graciously.

Outside was a black carriage pulled by a magnificent team of four Clydesdales with the characteristic brown coat and white fetlocks. There was no driver, just an empty seat.

"To the guild, if you please," Asenov said, walking quickly to the carriage.

Jasper looked around, trying to see who the arch-mage had spoken to. Sehraine had to pinch him to get him to stop. Fortunately, Asenov had his back to them and didn't see the motion. As they approached the carriage door, a pair of stairs unfolded in front of them, and the door opened of its own volition.

Moving to one side, Asenov motioned for the monks to enter. Once inside, Jasper was amazed at the lavish, midnight blue interior. Small silver stars embroidered in a diagonal pattern streaked the seatbacks. Sehraine gently pushed Jasper toward the seat facing the rear of the carriage and sat next to him.

Asenov took the seat opposite, and the door closed behind him. Jasper had a sinking feeling in his gut, and, when he looked at Sehraine, the worry in her eyes mirrored his — this was stupid. At least they had two things going for them: in the long history of the White Circle, no one had been crazy enough to steal anything from it, and no one would suspect a pair of monks riding with the guild master.

Out the window, it was obvious they were moving, but the carriage felt as if it floated over the street.

"I must apologize for the rush, but any news of this devilry, however small, might put us on the trail of a cure," Asenov said. "You never told me your names."

Sehraine said quickly, "My name is Brother Dobri, and this is Brother Yordan."

"Why does he not speak for himself?" Asenov asked.

"He has taken a vow of silence to show his dedication to the Eternal Father."

Jasper signed something, and Sehraine asked, "My brother wants to know if you have made any progress in finding the cure to this disease."

Asenov looked out the window and let out a defeated breath. "No. Our attempts at finding the cause, let alone the cure, have only ended with my administration becoming its latest victim. That is why your news of the cause is so important. Not only to me, but to all of Pazard'zhik."

Signing again, Jasper posed another question. Sehraine frowned slightly and asked hesitantly, "Has anyone died from the disease yet?"

"Fortunately, no, though several of our members who were the first to display symptoms appear to be nearing the end. Where did you say you were from again?"

"Sliven, sir."

"I'm not familiar with that province."

"It's on the other side of the mountain range west of here."

"When did you first discover the soap was the cause?"

"A week ago.  It was the only common factor that made sense.  Yordan boiled it down and found something, didn't you?" Sehraine asked, turning to Jasper.

Nodding, Jasper signed back.

"That's right," Sehraine agreed, facing Asenov again.  "We found something hidden inside, something alive.  We don't know what it is, which is why we came to you."

The carriage moved quickly through the streets until the guild loomed outside.  All the windows were dark, giving the building an ominous feel.  They passed the front entrance, a wide portico with marble steps flanked by fluted columns, and turned down a side road, stopping midway down the building.  A shimmering light appeared on the surface of the facade, and the Clydesdales turned to enter it.  Once past the masonry wall, the carriage descended a broad stone ramp lined with fire-lit sconces.

Jasper stared, wide-eyed.  Although they appeared to be entering the basement, he knew it was part of the extra-dimensional space created by the mages long ago, after a fire gutted most of the building.

At the bottom of the ramp, the carriage stopped, and the door opened.  Two dark-robed mages waited with their faces hidden deep within the recesses of their hoods.  They held tall, dark staves with fingers stained black as pitch.

Around them rose a vast double barrel-vaulted chamber supported by a grid of thick masonry columns that flared out at the top and the base.  Beside the nearest column, a spiral stair climbed to the ceiling and disappeared into the darkness.  A faint glow emanated from the shaft about which the stairs wound but did little to fend off the shadows.

Jasper and Sehraine locked eyes briefly and took a deep breath.  As she climbed out of the carriage with Jasper close behind, Asenov addressed the mages in a gracious voice. "Gentlemen, I would like to introduce to you Brothers Dobri and Yordan of Sliven.  They have found the cause of what has befallen the guild."

The mages' dark hoods turned toward the monks.

Asenov said apologetically, "Forgive us if we seem less than enthusiastic.  We've had many visitors come to us, only to have our hopes crushed.  I took the liberty of asking my staff to prepare a lab so that you can recreate your experiment, Brother Yordan."

Jasper signed something, and Sehraine replied, "Certainly.  We understand.  Is there a place where we can freshen ourselves before we start?"

"I will see to it personally.  Please follow these gentlemen up the stairs, and I will meet with you shortly."  With a quick gesture of his staff, the arch-mage disappeared.

As one, the two silent mages glided toward the stairs, trailing the scent of decay.  Jasper exchanged a worried glance with Sehraine.  Her earlier comment about the guild being spooky came back to him.  For all the noise their guides made, they could have been ghosts.

The first mage positioned himself on the fifth stair tread while the second mage stepped aside and gestured for the monks to precede him.  After the monks each took a tread, the second mage stepped onto the stair and tapped his staff on the step.  The spiral stair twisted with a grinding noise, and they wound around the central shaft and up into the guild proper.

Once above the basement, the vast masonry cylinder rotated around them, making it impossible to know if it was the stairs, the shaft, or both which moved.  Eventually the stairs, or the shaft, stopped its slow spin and a lone door slid into view.

The first mage motioned with his staff, and the door opened, revealing a long corridor beyond.  As he stepped out of the stairwell, the mage croaked, "This way, please; we have a room where you can rest while we finish preparing the lab."

"Thank you," Sehraine said.

Passing several unmarked doors on their right, the group came to a stop at a door flanked by wall sconces.  The lead mage opened it and gestured for them to enter.

Inside was a pleasant, well-lit room with a rectangular, wooden table and two plush chairs comfortably arranged beside it.  Atop the table were a pair of small towels folded neatly beside black bowls of steaming water and a plate of fruit.  Sehraine leaned over the table and picked through the fruit.  Jasper took a moment longer.  Everything seemed in order, but nothing felt right.  Nothing at all.  Behind them, the mage closed the door.  It locked with an audible click.

Sehraine was about to speak but Jasper placed a finger to his lips for silence.  Looking around, he studied the table, chairs, fruit, water, and towels.  There was nothing obvious to alarm him, but there were no obstructions, either.  The room was too large and the table too small, making it difficult for something or someone to hide.  *'Fool me once,'* Jasper thought.

Closing his eyes, he opened his mind, letting a little of his magic enhance his senses.  Opening them, he saw it.  An oversized, disembodied eye floated in the corner near the ceiling.  Pulling a bit of mirrored glass from his bracer, he constructed an illusionary image in front of the eye — an image of the room, exactly as it was, with the two of them freshening up.

Taking Sehraine by the elbow, he walked her to the corner where the magical eye floated and pointed up.  Next, he held out his hand to the room and made a sweeping gesture.  Seeing that she understood, he returned to the table.  With Sehraine close behind him, he used his enhanced senses to inspect the items on top of the table, but everything seemed normal.  Everything that was except the black bowls of water.  Instantly, he felt something tug at his mind.  Sehraine grabbed his arm.

Rainbow colored swirls bubbled to the water's surface.  Jasper grabbed the bowl nearest him and tossed it against the far wall, shattering it.

Before he could grab the other bowl, a streak of black oil oozed over the side.  Black on black it was hard to see, except that it cast no reflection.  Less than a teaspoonful, it stretched toward the monks.  With a slurp, it darted toward them.

"Sonnova..." Jasper cried out.  Using one of the chairs like a shield, he pushed in front of Sehraine.  It hit the seat with a sickening splat and dripped onto his foot.  Jasper shrieked when he felt the cold oil slither up his leg.

Nausea tore through his gut.  The presence of something else's psyche brushed against the edges of his mind.  Jasper pulled together his magic and erected a mental barrier, but the evil intelligence was already inside him.  It probed the mental cage he had set. It wanted his magic — it wanted to feed.

Sweat beading on his forehead, Jasper turned to find Sehraine staring blankly. Gripping her by the shoulders, he shook her hard. Her jaw clenched, and he could feel her tremble under his touch. Anger filled her eyes, replacing the blankness, and he saw her return, slowly at first, but then stronger with each breath.

'*Sehraine is going to be alright,*' Jasper thought as the alien intelligence inside him redoubled its efforts. Just like earlier that morning when he entered the guild, something *other* slid through him, disrupting his concentration and twisting his magic, as if inviting the new presence, and Jasper's own magical defenses cracked open. The alien personality flooded into his mind. Try as he might, he could not stop it.

The psychic intruder told him to give up, to relinquish his magic, and a single word became his world: *CAYN.*

Sehraine watched with horror as Jasper slowly lost himself. Not knowing what else to do, she placed her hands on each side of his head and stared into his eyes, trying to lend him the strength to resist. Jasper's mouth went slack, and she felt his muscles relax.

Standing on her tiptoes, she placed her forehead to his and whispered softly in elven, praying to Dioth Cyela, with words she had not used since she was a little girl. Memories wrapped around the prayer — memories of her father, of her turning away from the Elder Ways and, later, her people. Walking amongst the humans had brought her distraction, but deep down, she had never forgotten the old ways. With the memories came the knowledge that she would eventually have to face her people again.

Tossing away her pride, she begged Dioth Cyela to give her strength to Jasper. At first, she thought she imagined the warmth where her forehead touched his, but then soft golden light seeped through her eyelids, growing stronger with each passing moment.

Like a will-o'-wisp, the light danced to and fro, and no matter what Jasper did, it stayed just beyond his touch. He reached for it again and again, and each time the light gradually grew closer. The *something* inside him fought the light. It twisted and turned in his gut and tried to pull him back. Soft elven words drifted in the blackness and surrounded him. Though he couldn't understand the words, they quieted the alien presence inside him, giving him the chance to touch the light.

Suddenly, he felt Sehraine's flesh pressed against his and heard her whispering. A loud shriek echoed in his mind as the light grew, and, with a final surge of magic, severed the connection to the alien presence.

With a deep, shuddering breath, Jasper wrapped the tiny elf in a gentle hug even as he felt her tears. Smiling, he gently removed her hands from his face. She opened her eyes and stared into his, searching.

"It's me," he said quietly. "Thank you."

Backing away, she looked him over and gasped.

"What?" Jasper asked, alarmed by the expression on her face.

"The stains on your fingers. It's worse."

He looked at his hands. His fingers were now almost totally black, and his nausea returned with a vengeance. Once the wave passed, he asked, "How did you save me?"

"Don't worry about that. Let's just get out of here."

Grabbing her wrist, Jasper searched her face and asked, "Did you get any of that stuff on you?"

"What stuff?" Sehraine asked. "I didn't see anything. What was it?"

Jasper spun her around and searched her robes. "You look clean."

"What was it?"

"The Blood of Cayn," Jasper hissed before turning back toward the table. There was no sign of the oil, and the knowledge brought him no comfort. He knew the fight with the alien presence was not over, but at least it had given them a reprieve. He also knew the alien presence controlled the guild. He had felt it. Any mage who had been in contact with the black oil was now its slave. His thoughts went to the acting guild master. Why was he unaffected? Or was he? One thing he knew for certain, the alien presence had no interest in the theater. So Asenov had to have some resistance to it, even if he was doing its biding. Then there was Gregori Saso, the necromancer from the clearing who had let loose a dwolma. He recalled the handful of gems in the drawer and understood at least some portion of what he had seen in the ransacked laboratory. The black oil fed off a mage's power, making them sickly, until it ultimately consumed them — killing them.

What about Sehraine? Was she telling him the truth? He quieted the thoughts racing through his head and caught up with her at the door.

Studying the lock, Sehraine stood with the hem of her robe pulled high, revealing a shapely thigh. Poking out from underneath her robe was a collection of tiny picks and tools.

"That's more than a little disturbing," Jasper whispered with a tired smile.

"What?"

He waved a hand at her bare leg. "The monk's habit does not suit you."

She returned his smile and selected a pick and a rod. Dropping her robe, she knelt and inserted them both into the keyhole above the doorknob. His senses still magically attuned, Jasper watched her tools slip past the magical barrier inside the lock and manipulate the tumblers. He turned away and focused on his illusion in front of the wizard's eye. With a few manipulations, the illusion recreated the past few minutes, but instead of the two of them surviving, the illusion showed the two of them lost to the power of the black oil.

"Ah-ha," Sehraine whispered as she turned the lock, disengaging the bolt.

Crouched down, Jasper called up his magic while she replaced her picks. With a cautious hand, he cracked open the door and peered out. The two mages still guarded the hall.

"Don't look," he mouthed to Sehraine. Taking a scrap piece of paper from his bracer, he flicked his thumb, causing a tiny flame to appear at the tip of his thumbnail, and caught the paper on fire. Yelling, "Flás pátagos," he tossed it out the open door.

A blinding flash of light erupted in the hallway and white smoke poured around the door.

On the other side, the two dark-robed mages had their eyes clenched shut and a hand covering their mouth. Even so, violent coughing spasms shook them, and they let go their wooden staves as they fell unconscious.

Staying low to the floor, Jasper looked up and down the hallway to make sure no one was around. He gave Sehraine a quick nod, and the two dragged the mages inside and collected their staves.

Sehraine closed the door behind her and asked, "What's happened here?"

Kneeling beside the mages, Jasper searched their clothes and pockets, but found nothing. He pushed aside the edges of their hoods and shook his head sadly as he replied, "You heard me talk about the Blood of Cayn."

"Yes," she replied.

"Every mage here is under its control."

"What? You must be joking."

Jasper shook his head. "It consumes them."

"To what purpose?"

"I don't know."

Based on his limited exposure to the disease, it appeared the two mages had advanced symptoms. Dried blood crusted their nostrils, and their skin looked paper-thin. Open sores on their flesh oozed pus and blood, and when Jasper pulled back their hoods the rest of the way, clumps of skin and hair stuck and peeled away from their scalps with a sickening slurp.

"They were so young."

"They were both my students this past summer," said Jasper.

"Really?" She laid a hand on his shoulder. "I'm so sorry."

"They were at the top of their class."

"Are they still alive?"

"Maybe. I don't know. Their bodies need sustenance, but as for their spirits..." Jasper couldn't finish. He bowed his head and said a silent prayer. This would have been his fate if Sehraine hadn't intervened.

"Help me tie them up," Sehraine said removing the beige rope from about her waist. "Do you know where we are?"

"Yes. We're on the top floor of the guild. Asenov must have used his personal entrance to bring us here. I wasn't even aware of a stairway that led from the basement to here."

"Can you find his office?"

"Maybe. I've only been up here once, when I met Dimitri Velkov, the true Guild-Master. Asenov's office was next door."

"We need to get moving before these two are missed. Let's get out of these monk's habits and swap with the mages."

Nodding, Jasper undid the robe on the smaller of the two mages and handed it to Sehraine. The stench of sickness was awful, making her gag. While she changed disguises, Jasper moved to the next mage and removed his clothing. He had to stretch and pull the material, but he eventually managed to fit into the dark robe. He wasn't normally squeamish, but being inside the robe made his skin crawl. Jasper could only imagine how Sehraine felt.

After picking up one of the staves, Sehraine reopened the door and stepped into the corridor. Jasper picked up the other staff and followed her. He closed the door, pulled up his hood to hide his face, and headed away from the spiral stairs that led to the basement.

Asenov stared into a basin of water that glowed with an inner light, providing the only illumination in the chamber. A small smile crept over his face as he watched the image of the two monks on the surface of the scrying bowl. They stood holding their heads in their hands, trying to resist the power of the blood. As with everyone else, they eventually succumbed to the possession. The image flickered a little, causing Asenov to frown, but when it cleared, the monks lay on the floor, unmoving. His smile returned, and he waved his hand. The image changed, and the youthful face of Teodor filled the basin.

"Is everything taken care of?" Gregori/Teodor asked.

"Yes, the monks are no longer an issue."

"Good. Did you believe their story?"

"I don't know. I expect they were probably telling the truth."

"Have you found the location of the Tear of Havel?" Gregori asked.

"No, we are still searching the library, but there's no record of it in the archives after the elves sealed their village."

"Keep looking."

"We will.  How's the schedule?"

"We should reach Chernigov in three days."

"Good.  I don't believe Velkov will make it through the week."

"That's excellent news.  Let me know when he passes."

Asenov waved his hand across the water, and the image disappeared, along with the light, leaving the chamber a stygian crypt.

# CHAPTER 8
# THE GREY MEN

## October 25, 4235 K.E.

**7:43pm**

Two dark-robed mages walked down the hallway on a mission. Mages parted to let them by without a second glance. Jasper led Sehraine down corridor after corridor, left then right and left again until Sehraine had the impression Jasper was lost. The only thing that saved him was that they never passed the same door twice.

Eventually, the doors grew farther apart. Symbols appeared over some of them, but she couldn't decipher them; they looked more like random lines and circles than anything intelligible.

In the next corridor, the walls changed from grey stone to red brick, and Sehraine felt fresh air from outside pass down the hallway. They turned a corner, and Jasper stopped at a door marked with a small eye on a green field. The lurid eye followed them as they approached. Jasper and Sehraine searched the door, but there was neither knob nor handle or anything else to suggest a way past it.

After a moment, Jasper continued down the corridor, causing Sehraine to hurry to catch up. At the next door, he stopped. This one had a knob and a keyhole, but it was locked. Motioning for Sehraine, he stepped aside while she retrieved her picks and started to work. A few seconds later, she had the door open.

The room was an office of sorts, with a window overlooking the street. Using the light from the window, they navigated their way through the room. Abandoned for some time, a thin film of dust covered the desk, chairs, shelves, and little knick-knacks. Spotting a set of bookshelves filled with expensive-looking tomes and scroll cases, Sehraine studied the books with a critical eye. The coating of dust was disturbed on two shelves. She reached to pull out one of the books, expecting to find a secret door, when Jasper's voiced hissed through the gloom, "Don't touch anything unless I say."

Irritated, she replied, "Well, what's your plan then?  We have to touch something."

"How do you feel about dangerous schemes with little chance of success?"

"Oh, I don't know," she said sarcastically and then suddenly became serious.  "I didn't bring you here to get us both killed.  You better have a plan to get into that room."

"I do," Jasper said, but for some reason, his words didn't reassure her.

"You get me killed, and I swear I will haunt you."

Walking to the wall shared by Asenov's office, Jasper selected a spot in the corner.  He leaned his borrowed staff against the wall and began rearranging the chairs and end tables, nodding for Sehraine to help.  By the time they finished, it looked as if they had painted themselves into a corner with the furniture surrounding them.  He motioned for her to stand directly in front of him, less than a hand-span from the bare stone wall.

When she stepped into position, he wrapped an arm around her waist.  She made a face and whispered, "This is going to hurt, isn't it?"

"Don't know.  Never tried it before."

Taking up his stolen staff, Jasper faced the wall and hugged Sehraine close.  "Close your eyes," he instructed. Following suit, he called up his magic.  Jasper felt the power surge through him as it whirled about them.  He expanded the cyclone of magic, but something restricted its flow.  The furniture barred its way.  Jasper tried again, but everywhere the magic turned, something solid blocked it.  With no place for it to go, the magic backlashed and turned in upon itself, trying to rip Jasper apart.  Gripping his staff with one hand and Sehraine in the other, he gritted his teeth and held on, letting the magic course through them.

When it finally stopped, Jasper and Sehraine breathed a collective sigh of relief.  They opened their eyes to discover the office, walls, and furniture had vanished, replaced by mist that seemed alive.  Jasper stared, amazed at all the variations of the color grey.  He waved his staff through the mist, causing it to swirl and dance.

Still holding Sehraine, Jasper took a tentative step forward, and felt something ripple over his skin as they passed through an unseen barrier. Shapes appeared in the mist, but he couldn't tell if they were shadows from the furniture, wall, or the remnants of something else. The swirls intensified, and a biting cold wind ripped through his clothing, turning his fingers and portions of his face numb. Frost formed in Sehraine's eyelashes, and her breath blossomed in the air. Fighting the deadly cold, Jasper guided Sehraine another step. The shapes in the mist solidified, surrounding them.

"No matter what happens, don't let go of me," Jasper said, tightening his grip on her. He could see a half-circle of shadow figures reflected in her wide eyes, mirroring the men standing before him. Their skin and clothes were the color of dark storm clouds. They bore tall staves, which seemed solid enough, but the men themselves appeared hollow.

Jasper bowed his head in respect.

"You are forbidden to travel here," a voice said in the mist.

"I apologize for this intrusion, but I have need to travel the misty road."

"What is your purpose, young mage?"

"Masters, my name is Jasper Thredd, and I have reason to believe the charter of the White Circle is in jeopardy. Master Asenov has usurped leadership of the guild and means to harm the Kral."

The grey men seemed surprised at this news and, after some discussion, one of them asked, "Have you proof of this?"

"No, sir. My proof was taken from me by Master Asenov. It is my intention to enter his office and retrieve it."

Shocked murmurs echoed through the mist, and the grey men pressed closer. One stood aside from the others and said, "The mages of today are much bolder than they were in my time."

"Master Kolev, I deeply regret disturbing you, but I beg you to let us pass."

"Daughter of the Elves, what say you?"

Sehraine turned in Jasper's embrace until she faced the ghost. She shivered, but he couldn't tell if it was from the cold or fear.  "Sir, I am Jasper's friend, and he needed my help," she replied weakly.

"It means a lot to us, young lady, that you befriended this man.  Does he speak the truth?"

"Yes, sir."

Kolev stared at Jasper and said, "I have felt a wrongness in the guild of late and have tried to discuss these matters with Dimitri.  I can no longer see him.  Is he well?"

"He has fallen to the Blood of Cayn."

Harsh whispers spread amongst the grey men, and Kolev's misty form grew more solid.

"What do you know of the Blood of Cayn?"

"Not much, Master," Jasper answered.  "Elves of the Haunted Wood told me the story of the creation of the elves and the fall of Cayn.  During their tale, they told me the origins of the blood.  I am tasked with finding its cure."

"Asenov must have used the *Veritas autem Sutekh* to hide this from us."

Nods of agreement spread and suddenly, Jasper felt the presence of other mages.  The feeling pressed down on him and made it hard to breathe.

"I am unfamiliar with this reference," Jasper said.

"Find the book, and you will find your answers, but beware, young mage.  The *Veritas autem Sutekh* corrupts all who possess it, but it can also protect you from what is to come."

Grey clouds swirled violently about Jasper and Sehraine, and the two felt as if they were falling.  The real world slowly came into focus, and Jasper rushed to position himself and Sehraine so they would not appear inside a piece of furniture.

Asenov's office was a mirror of its neighbor.  It, too, had a desk and chairs, a couple of bookshelves, and a broad window overlooking the street three floors below; however, this one had the look and feel of recent use.  A small lamp illuminated scrolls scattered across the surface of the desk, waiting for their master to return.

Releasing Sehraine, Jasper went to work searching for his sporran.  It was an educated guess that his belongings were here.  Of course, Asenov could have destroyed them, but considering the guild had confiscated his things earlier that day, Jasper was hoping the guild master had kept them.

Behind Asenov's desk hung a small tapestry depicting an eye on a green field.  This one appeared to be sleeping, but it was hard to tell.  They worked around it, searching through the piles of items and various drawers with no luck.

Gesturing toward the tapestry, Jasper said quietly, "I bet there's something behind that."

"Could be.  Is it trapped?"

Jasper studied the layers of magic woven into the tapestry.  There was no telling what would happen if they touched it.  It could be a simple alarm or something much, much worse.  He stepped to one side, eyeing the heavy rod that held the woven cloth a few inches off the wall.  In the narrow space, he could just make out the edges of a darker shadow but couldn't be certain what it held.

"This Asenov, is he an arch-mage?" Sehraine asked while she searched the room, making sure not to touch anything.

"Yes," Jasper answered, still staring behind the tapestry.

"What's his specialty?"

"Divination and scrying."

"Have you ever met him prior to today?"

"Not really.  I only saw him once or twice in the hallways."

"Is he powerful?"

"Probably."

"Would he fry us if he knew we were here?"

"Yep," he replied, stepping back from the tapestry.

"You definitely know how to show a girl a good time."

"Just wait — it gets better."

She looked up from her search, an eyebrow arched.  "Is that eye watching us, too?"

"It's asleep.  I can only guess that, if we touch the tapestry, it will wake up."

"Can we move it without touching it?"

"I can generate a slight breeze behind it.  That should give you enough room to work, but..."

"But what?"

"I can only maintain it for a few minutes."

"You sent Yana and her team on a flight with a steady tail-wind; why can't you do that here?"

He turned back to her and answered, "For one thing, that was a single-purpose spell that needed no finesse.  Secondly, you're going to be on the other side of the tapestry where the breeze will originate; I doubt you want wind blowing in your face — or wherever."

"Good point."

"You ready?"

Sehraine rubbed her hands together and nodded.

Whispering words of magic, Jasper took a blank piece of parchment from Asenov's desk and folded it into a small fan, pinched together at one end. As he waved it back and forth, a faint breeze fluttered about the room, and the tapestry rippled slightly. Slowly, the breeze concentrated, and the tapestry began to rise. Still whispering and waving his fan up and down, Jasper caused it to rise even higher and move away from the wall.

As soon as she had enough room, Sehraine ducked behind the tapestry and saw the small metal vault built into the wall. She stared in wonder with lips parted and tears glistening in her eyes. It was a Thēsauros Reposito, built before the Korellan empire fell. An antique by all standards, they were legendary among both locksmiths and thieves. Refraining from touching it, she stared at the faceplate and whispered, "Aperio." She waited, but nothing happened for several long moments, making her wonder if she'd misspoken the command word.

Relief flooded her when the faceplate shimmered slightly, and a keyhole appeared in the middle. Pulling up the hem of her robe, she selected a small pick with a bent end and a blue rod with a V-shaped groove that ran along the length of the shaft.

Inserting the rod into the keyhole, she twisted it until it caught. Next, she inserted the small pick, placed it along the upper surface, and turned it counterclockwise for half a turn. Sehraine heard a barely audible click. Pushing the rod into the lock, she twisted it again until it caught, and, again, she turned the upper pick for half a turn until it clicked. Repeating the process twice more, the rod slowly disappeared into the locking mechanism. After the last tumbler, she let the rod lie at a slight angle in the lock, the v-notch facing up. From the folds of her robe, she produced a tiny glass vial with a silver-lined stopper. Using her teeth, she opened it. With exceptionally steady hands, she tipped the vial and let one drop of the liquid fall in the groove. Replacing the stopper and sealing the vial, she secreted it back into her robes and waited.

Behind her, the tapestry fluttered slightly but remained high enough not to touch her. The drop of liquid slid down the shaft of the rod and into the lock, where it disappeared. Smoke hissed from the keyhole, and she quickly turned the pick clockwise three times while simultaneously removing the rod. The faceplate opened without a sound, and inside, she found Jasper's belt with his sporran, a black, leather-bound tome, and a small white pouch with silver runes.

"What do you want?" she said with a smug smile. Not getting an answer, she shrugged and grabbed everything. Just as she made to pull back, the tapestry fluttered again. This time, however, the corner of the tapestry drooped, unsupported by the breeze. It gently touched Sehraine's shoulder.

The eye opened and screeched in alarm.

Snatching Sehraine by the arm, Jasper yanked her out from under the tapestry before it trapped her. Struggling to keep on her feet, she quickly dropped the book and the pouch inside the sporran and wrapped the belt around it tight.

Jasper reached for a chair as he ran toward the window and threw it, shattering the glass and sending the chair tumbling to the street below. Cold air rushed into the room, blowing the scrolls on the desk all about.

Dark-robed mages burst through the door to the office. When they saw the two thieves, they immediately started to chant and gesture toward them. In the middle of the room, Asenov's image began to coalesce.

Jasper's lips were moving but Sehraine couldn't tell if he was casting another spell or trying to tell her something. With a flick of his wrist, Jasper tossed something into the room and yelled "Jump!" Holding the sporran in the crook of her arm, she clutched Jasper's hand.

They jumped out the broken window as an explosion rocked Asenov's office. Fire engulfed the room, pressing against every surface as it sought to escape. It found the broken window and roared out over their heads. Burning chunks of debris flew out the window and rained down.

Chanting as he fell, Jasper held Sehraine close. Even so, they hit the ground hard enough to knock the wind out of them.  Finding nothing broken, they staggered to their feet and ran past the people gawking and pointing.  Before anyone could stop them, the two disappeared into the alley across the street.

Asenov stood at the window, unaffected by the flames, his face a mask of fury.  Behind him, the fire raged, fueled by the antique wood and abundant papers.  He turned and disappeared from view.  Almost instantly, the raging fire became nothing more than a plume of smoke.

Down below, dark-robed mages burst out the front door of the guild.  Some took to the streets and ran down the hill toward the Majna i Vira while another group followed Jasper and Sehraine's trail.

Midway down the alley, Jasper stopped briefly and touched the alley walls, whispering, "Toíchos omíchlis." Sehraine turned, urging him to hurry, but he only gestured for her to keep running.  He caught up with her at the far end, huffing and puffing.

The streets of Pazard'zhik were laid out like the spokes of a wagon wheel with all roads leading to the Kral's estates. This created semi-circular grids that made it easy for travel but difficult for fugitives.  The two turned and raced up the hill a short distance then turned down another alley, all the while working their way back to the theater.

Matching Jasper's pace, Sehraine commented, "You know the whole militsiya will be after us now."

"I know.  We need to get out of these clothes."

Pointing toward a city park with tall firs and birch trees, she said, "Let's find a place to change."

# CHAPTER 9
# FLIGHT OUT OF THE CITY

### October 25, 4235 K.E.

**8:18pm**

Six mages followed the sounds of Jasper and Sehraine's footsteps into the alley. The one in front, confident they would catch them, missed the line of powder on the pavement. As he passed over it, thick, billowing fog filled the alley and swallowed the first four mages whole, congealing like tree sap around them.

The remaining two mages, ignoring their trapped comrades, took to the air and flew over the foggy trap. One behind the other, they hovered over the intersection. Below, a group of people waved their hands to get the attention of a militsiya patrol marching down the street. They all pointed toward a narrow alley and the treed park beyond it. Splitting up, one mage flew directly toward the park while the second veered away and dropped to the ground beside the sergeant of the militsiya, who was trying to calm an older couple.

"Sergeant, several members of the White Circle have been killed." The mage's voice cut through the air like a knife and interrupted their conversation.

The sergeant apologized to the couple and asked his second in command to continue speaking with them. After taking a quick moment to make sure they were cared for, he approached the dark-robed mage and commanded, "Bring your people down and let us handle this. They're scaring everyone."

"Didn't you hear? You must set up a cordon at once or the killers will escape," the mage said, unaccustomed to being questioned.

Keeping calm, the sergeant replied, "I heard you, but if you start a panic, you can forget about catching them."

Gnashing his teeth, the mage tried to control his anger and said, "Sergeant, there are two of them. We have a chance to corner them if you act quickly." He pointed the way his companion had flown.

The sergeant looked where he indicated. With a gesture, he sent a squad of ten men running toward the alley entrance. He made another gesture and several of his men ran back up the hill toward their post.

"Your cordon will be set up shortly. Now, please, tell us what happened and describe these men you are after."

Flushed out of the park, Jasper felt like he and Sehraine were mice in a maze. He cast a quick glance over his shoulder. Closing in behind them, a dark-robed mage flew above the pavement.

"Damn it. Hold on," he gasped.

The look on Sehraine's face screamed, '*Are you crazy?*' but Jasper was already casting. She waited nervously beside him as the dark robed mage flew closer. Ice formed on the stone walls of the alley, and the temperature dropped at least twenty degrees. The mage slowed, unsure of what was happening.

Jasper gave a quick wave of his hand and tossed up a small bit of quartz. "Klouví págou." Instantly, the air solidified into thick bars of ice trapping the mage in an icy cage anchored by the alley walls like a crystalline spiderweb.

"That won't last long," Jasper said with a frown and resumed running.

Dressed in a fur-lined, sable and argent surcoat with a single gold chevron at his collar, a militsiya sergeant moved cautiously down the alley with his sword drawn. His men followed behind him, their footsteps punctuated by the crunch of ice. To either side, the slick walls glinted in the light cast by their lantern bearer. Above them, the dark robed mage hovered inside the cage and tried to work himself free, his breath visible in the frozen air.

"Don't let them get away!" the mage shouted.

Spurred to motion, the squad leader hurried under the cage. Even though there was plenty of clearance, the soldiers instinctively ducked under the icy magic as they continued after the fugitives.

At the next intersection, Jasper and Sehraine turned left. The theater wasn't much farther. They passed several recessed back-alley entrances. At each one, Jasper dipped his finger into his pocketed bracer, drew a little sign, and then continued past.  At the fourth door, he marked it like the others but, instead of continuing, he backtracked and stepped into the recess of the third door.

"This is stupid," Sehraine whispered.

Jasper didn't reply.  He simply looked at her and motioned toward the door.

She made a face at him as she retrieved her lockpicks.  In no time at all, the door opened, and the two stepped inside a dark foyer, closing and locking the door behind them.  A set of wooden stairs disappeared into the shadows of the second floor.  Beside it, a long hallway lined with doors on each side led to a showroom with several full height windows fronting the street.  Outside, members of the militsiya shined a light through the glass.

"There's probably a safe in here somewhere," Sehraine whispered excitedly.

"Stay focused."

Frowning, Sehraine disappeared inside her dark robes.  Jasper stood and watched with a mixture of fascination and awe as she wrestled inside them.  Not paying attention to what he was doing, he made to take off the mage's robe but stopped when it dawned on him that he wasn't wearing much of anything underneath.

With a slight grunt and a "ta-da," Sehraine's robe dropped to the floor, and she was back in her evening wear with all traces of the robe's previous owner's filth gone.  Unlike earlier that evening, she let her pointed ears poke through her silver-blonde hair, and her angular elven features were no longer softened by make-up.

Sehraine's eyebrows arched mischievously, and her almond-shaped eyes practically sparkled with excitement.  She frowned when she saw how far Jasper had gotten.  "What's wrong?  Why aren't you ready?"

Shrugging, Jasper looked down at his feet and felt his face glow a pinkish hue.

"Don't worry, its dark enough.  I won't be able to see you," she said with a straight face.

"I don't think so.  You have better night vision than most owls."

Sehraine stepped closer with a sly grin.  From behind her back, she produced a pair of silken pants and a shirt.

When he saw what she held, his face lit up, but then he realized they were several sizes too small.

"Ever been an elf?"

"No," he replied hesitantly.

"Well, clean up, and I'll help you, but you'll have to do something about your weight."

"My weight?  What's wrong with my weight?" he asked defensively.

"Just clean up, and we'll work out the rest."

With a single word, all traces of the dirt and grime coating Jasper disappeared, leaving the mage clean and fresh looking.  Her eyes grew wide at his appearance, and she said, "My, you do come in handy.  Now, can you alter your shape to look more like an elf?"

Taking a moment to prepare the spell, Jasper concentrated and said, "Gínomai xotikó."  The air shimmered, and his body began to morph.  The magic started with his feet and worked its way along his legs.  It traveled up his torso to his neck and head, and finally down his arms to his hands.  As it went, his body shrank and became slimmer.  When it finished, a perfect full-blooded elf stood in front of Sehraine.  A smug expression fixed itself on Jasper's now clean-shaven elven face.

"No, no, no," she said, shaking her head.  "This won't do."

"What?  I'm an elf, aren't I?"

"How does your magic know what an elf looks like?"

"I don't know — my imagination, I guess."

"Well, there's your problem."

Insulted by her remark, Jasper threw his hands up and argued, "It will do just fine; let's go."

"No, it won't," she replied, mocking his tone of voice. "The first guard we come to will know you're a fake.  Redo your face, but this time let me help you."

Taking her hands and placing them on his face, he whispered, "Prosōpo."

At first, she didn't understand, but as the magic glow reappeared, she began to sculpt his cheeks and brow.

They were gentle manipulations, and he felt her change the shape of his face into something less than perfect.  As she worked, his face remained that of an elf, but gained character and emotion instead of being a blank slate.

He watched her work and felt the stirrings of an attraction for her.  She caught him staring at her and said, "You know, if Yana sees you looking at me like that, she'll beat you up."

Jasper replied, "I think she's going to do that anyway."

"Why?"

"For dragging you into this mess."

"You needed my help."

"We all needed your help."

"Yes, but you were the one who asked."

Dropping her hands, she inspected her work with a critical eye and nodded approvingly.  "Now we're ready," she said.

At that moment, the backdoor jarred when someone outside tested the lock.


**8:30pm**

Asenov stood in the middle of his office, the empty vault in front of him.  His mind reeled, but through the confusion came clarity — with the *Veritas autem Sutekh's* whispers silenced, all that remained was the horror of what he had done.  He fell to his knees and buried his face in his hands.

A dark-robed mage entered his office, stirring a billowing cloud of soot with each step.  Others crowded behind him, wielding rune-marked silver daggers.  Each struck Asenov, driving their daggers deep into his body.

Asenov's emerald robes darkened as his blood seeped into the expensive fabric.  He tried to call upon his magic to escape his attackers, yet his voice would not obey him.  The skin around the edges of the wounds blackened and peeled back, exposing purple veins.  Succumbing to the pain of his flesh slowly dissolving, a weak gurgle escaped from his numb lips.  With his magic stripped and his life fading, Asenov silently cursed the dark-robed mages standing over him.

However, the black oblivion of death did not come for Asenov.  Instead, his office faded to mist, and a ring of grey men replaced his tormentors.  He struggled to meet the weight of their stares. One by one, their faces grew clear and, when recognition dawned, it brought no comfort.

Nikolai Kolev raised his staff, and a bright light engulfed the dying mage. "You are now one of us, doomed to an afterlife of repentance. Thus, have we maintained the terms of our charter," Nikolai said, addressing both Asenov and the mist.

A regal voice echoed back, "We accept your judgment."

**8:57pm**

The backdoor rattled a second time, and Sehraine and Jasper heard several muffled voices outside. With the robes of the mages now piles of ash on the floor, they raced up the stairs. They were in a multi-story office building that appeared to be dedicated to the business of mining. Maps of the mountains covered the walls, each with little circles drawn in wax.

"How are we going to get back outside?" Sehraine whispered.

"You'll see."

They entered one of the offices that had a clear view of the street. Below, the militsiya detained everyone, asking questions, and seeking answers. Jasper had expected they would establish a blockade around the guild and surrounding neighborhood, but he hadn't expected all this.

As he watched, soldiers pulled aside a couple and subjected them to the blue light from a bull's-eye lantern. Jasper had never seen the lantern before, but he had heard about it — so had everyone else. The militsiya used it to penetrate illusions and reveal the true appearance of a person.

Pointing to the street's far side, Jasper said, "Let's make our entrance over there."

"No good. How about there?" Sehraine asked.

"No, that's in the line of that lantern."

The door below crashed opened, and they heard voices echo up the stairs. Sehraine gripped Jasper's arm and pointed, the expression on her face saying, *trust me.* Taking a deep breath, Jasper poured forth his magic and a shimmering portal appeared on the exterior wall. The two stepped inside and vanished as the thud of booted feet in the stairwell heralded the eminent arrival of soldiers to search the second floor.

Embracing one another, Jasper and Sehraine stood within the recess of a doorway fronting the main street, concealed by shadows. They remained still, half expecting the closest soldiers to rush over and arrest them. A minute passed, and they remained unnoticed.

"Follow my lead," whispered Sehraine. Not giving Jasper time to reply, she slipped from his arms and handed him his sporran. The movement was enough to attract a guardsman's attention.

"You, there! What are you doing?"

Sehraine thought that was a stupid question but bit her tongue. They stepped out of the doorway still holding hands.

"Sorry officer, we were... distracted," she said, her voice husky with desire.

"Well, keep moving."

Jasper tried to nudge Sehraine toward the opposite side of the street, away from the lantern, but she tugged on his arm and led him directly toward the light. While walking, she surreptitiously adjusted the neckline of her dress.

"What are you doing?" he whispered urgently.

"Watch and learn."

Walking directly up to the soldiers holding the blue lantern, she schooled her expression into an appropriate mixture of concern and curiosity. "Gentlemen, what happened?"

The squad leader held up their blue lantern. Her face glowed in the light, leaving no doubt she was a true elf — a rarity in Trakya. Her natural beauty caused everyone to pause, guards as well as passersby. With everyone distracted, Jasper boldly continued past them without a second glance.

"Milady, we apologize for the rudeness of our presence, but something has happened at the mages' guild."

"What?" she asked in a hushed voice. Behind the guards, Jasper continued past several more buildings before stopping to wait for her.

"We're not supposed to say," the sergeant said.

Sehraine tipped her chin upward, so the lantern shone more fully on her widened eyes and leaned toward the guard. He, in turn, leaned closer and whispered conspiratorially, "Three mages have been murdered."

Bringing up her hand to cover her mouth, she emitted a tiny gasp at the news. "By whom?"

"A rogue mage."

"Really? Are we safe?"

The sergeant puffed out his chest and gestured to his men. "Have no concerns, Milady. We have the situation under control. However, we recommend you stay clear of this area for the evening."

"I will, Officer, thank you."

She awarded each of the militsiya with one of her best smiles and continued up the street, where she rejoined Jasper.

"That was fun," she whispered.

"Flirt."

"Damn right."

The two walked casually up the street and away from the guards without looking back. Along the way, Sehraine told Jasper what she had learned. When he didn't respond, she looked up at him and saw his brow furrowed.

In front of the White Circle, two dog-like creatures with snow-white pelts sniffed along the pavement. Larger than a bullmastiff, their piercing red eyes gleamed above muzzles filled with dagger-like canines that hung over their lower jaws. Clawed forefeet, shaped like human hands with opposable thumbs, gripped the stone pavers as they followed the scents gleaned from abandoned monks' habits — female elf and human mage. Whenever they came across a crowd, their forms melted, becoming invisible to all except the most observant.

After the cordon, Jasper and Sehraine stuck to the well-lit streets but turned this way and that, taking an indirect route to the theater, just to make sure no one followed them. It was that time of day when people were going home after an evening dinner or heading to a social event. The two tried to mingle with groups as often as they could and use the hustle and bustle to hide from watching eyes.

They rounded one final corner, and both let out a sigh of relief. Directly ahead stood the theater, its doors open and flanked by uniformed attendants ready to assist patrons into carriages lining the street. Lights from the massive building reflected off the underside of low-lying clouds, forming a kind of halo effect.

Sehraine made to cross the street, but Jasper pulled her to a stop.  He felt the weight of evil eyes watching them.  For a brief moment, he stood transfixed by two dog-like distortions in the air bounding toward them.  "Demon dogs," Jasper said with a curse.

With a sharp slap to his shoulder, Sehraine snapped him into motion, and the two raced toward the theater as people flooded out the front doors.  Jasper aimed toward the alley with the backdoor, hoping to lead the things pursuing them away from the crowd.

The demon dogs shed their cloaks of invisibility and appeared amidst the mass exodus.  Screams ripped the air.

Sehraine grabbed Jasper's hand and ducked into the crowd.  As they ran up the steps, Jasper cast a quick glance over his shoulder, only to see the creatures gaining ground.

Happy that his disguise made him slimmer, Jasper dodged between couples, trying to keep up with the lithe elf.  She made their flight appear graceful while he, on the other hand, managed to bump into almost every person he passed.  They ran through the main entrance, dodging the various groups congregated in the vestibule.

Pushing and shoving his way through, Jasper came face to face with the play's director, who held red roses in his arms and was thanking the crowd profusely for their attendance.  Turning at the last second to avoid him, Jasper plowed directly into a small, pale-skinned man beside the director, which sent all three crashing to the floor.  The small man's head smacked against the tile floor, knocking him out cold.

Jasper winced as he silently thanked him for breaking his fall.  Crawling over the unconscious body, the mage disappeared into the crowd.  He had lost Sehraine, but he knew where she would head.

Screams followed in the wake of the two dog-like creatures, marking their arrival at the doorway.  They reared up on their hind legs, rising above the crowd.  Their red eyes scanned the area carefully, seeking their prey.  Frustrated by the overwhelming blend of perfumes and colognes, the demons roared and flailed with their forelegs, clearing a path. Like a herd of frightened animals, the pools of people in the vestibule fled in a stampede toward the exits.

Swimming against the tide, Jasper aimed for the main auditorium and the stage. He burst through the last of the crowd and through the doors, only to find himself surrounded by stygian darkness. As his eyes adjusted, he saw the dim glow of a ghost lamp centered on the stage. The heavy curtains hung closed behind it.

Jasper raced down the main aisle and didn't look back when light from the vestibule flared behind him, or when he heard the sickening crunch and clatter of something or someone landing on the seats to his right.

A primeval roar echoed, and adrenaline coursed through Jasper's body. Taking advantage of his sudden energy surge, he leapt onto the stage with the demon dogs close behind and landed in a spinning turn. Raising his hands with the palms outward, he yelled, "Vlíma!" A stream of red flame erupted from his palms and struck one of the snow-white creatures in the chest just as it leapt over the orchestra pit, flipping it backward into the front row of seats. Its fur blackened where the flame singed it, and Jasper caught the acrid smell of burnt hair. Unfortunately, it seemed to feed off the pain like a berserker. Growling, it bounded toward the stage, followed closely by its mate.

Not looking back, Jasper ran for the middle seam of the drawn curtain. Stage handlers on the other side, unaware of their danger, were still dismantling the evening's props and preparing them for storage.

Yelling as loud as he could, Jasper tried to get the men to run, but it wasn't until one of the creatures ripped its way through the curtain that the stagehands dropped their tools and fled for the exits. The two demon dogs, distracted by the men, sniffed the air, searching.

Jasper felt the pull of the magical rune he had traced on the storage room wall, hoping Sehraine would be there waiting for him. Letting it guide him through the maze-like back of house, he found the passageway he and Sehraine had taken just a few hours earlier.

Howling, the demon dogs chased after Jasper single file down the narrow corridor. He skidded to a halt and turned back in one motion.  "Istós!"  The dust in the air sprang to life, coalescing into thick, sticky fibers that filled the hallway. Layer upon layer wrapped itself around the creatures, entangling their arms and legs.

The dressing room door on his left slammed opened, and Sehraine scurried out, her hair mussed, and her face flushed from the run, carrying an oversized leather knapsack bulging at the seams.

"Sorry," she said.  "Just grabbing a few of my things. Glad you could make it."

"Me too," Jasper replied as they turned and ran down the hall toward the storage room.

"Can you get us both out of here?" she asked as they rushed inside the old prop room and locked the door.

"Maybe.  Let me have your bag."

She handed it to him, and he unceremoniously dumped clothes, shoes, and sundry other items which sparkled or glinted onto the floor along with his sporran.  Her mouth went wide with disbelief.  "What are you doing?"

Instead of answering, he placed the empty bag on the floor and waved his hands over it, his eyes closed in concentration.  When finished, he folded back the edges to keep it open and turned to the pile beside it.

To Sehraine, it looked as though he had stopped breathing.  Her eyes followed his to the black, leather tome she had pulled out of Asenov's vault.  Had she done something wrong?  She was about to ask, but he came back to life and quickly motioned for her to hand him the black tome.  She did, and he immediately dropped it into the bag, letting go as if it stung his hand.

"How much do you weigh?" he asked.

"How much do you weigh?" she countered, her hands going to her hips.

Jasper retrieved his staff and the other items they had stowed away, taking the time to slide his rings on his fingers before he dropped his clothes into the bag.  As he worked, he answered, "I weigh around two-hundred and fifty pounds."

"No, you don't — look at you."

Outside, they heard a triumphant roar and the distant click-clack of clawed feet.

Shaking his head, Jasper said hurriedly, "Magic knows how much space you take up, no matter what shape you take.  It's a constant that cannot easily be altered, magically or otherwise."

"You're talking a magical reality, not physical."

"Yes and no," he said absently, stuffing his boots into the leather bag.

"All right," she said with some reluctance.  "I weigh around ninety pounds."

"With or without the dress?"

"Without," she said, giving him a strange look.  "What difference does it make?"

"A lot," he said as he tossed her the sack.  "Put some boots and traveling clothes in there and get out of that dress."

"I take back what I said earlier about you getting beat up. Yana's going to kill you."  Despite her comment, she shimmied out of the gown, revealing a lightweight chemise that hinted at her shape beneath.  Just on the other side of the door, they heard dog-like sniffing.

Her back turned to Jasper, Sehraine collected the rest of her clothes from the floor and stuffed them into the leather bag, noticing that it neither bulged nor grew full.  Picking up her boots, she looked inside, astonishment lighting her face.

Jasper grabbed his sporran, opened it, and dug out the sliver of soap.  He quickly replaced it and noticed a small, white pouch stitched with silver runes.  He pulled it out briefly, his eyebrows raised in surprise.  Not having time to investigate, he dropped it back inside.

The wooden planks of the door shivered, and the hinges groaned as one of the creatures struck it a solid blow.  Jasper took up his staff and motioned for Sehraine to stand next to him.  Using the charred tip, he drew a circle on the floor around them and began to chant.

Another blow shook the door, and the topmost hinge broke, causing the door to cant crazily. The demon dogs snarled viciously through the new-formed gap, saliva dripping down the face of the door.

Drawing the last of his magic, Jasper closed his eyes and focused on his spell; everything else was a distraction. In his mind's eye, he saw only the magic flowing around them and heard the words that told his magic what to do.  At the edge of his vision, he saw a shadow forming.  He fought to keep his concentration, but the shadow crawled across the floor.  It wasn't a demon dog; it was *something* else.

'*Repsaj, evig flesruoy ot em.  Uoy era eno fo su.*'

The shadow reared up, and Jasper raised his free hand to defend himself.  That was when he noticed his blackened fingers: there was no flesh, only bones.  Where the skin ended, tiny maggots devoured his flesh and with it, the last of his magic.

None of that mattered.  He had to finish the spell.  He had to save Sehraine, no matter the cost.

Centering his focus, he traced over the circle he had drawn on the floor and poured his magic into it.  The shadow wrapped itself around the protective circle, methodically searching for a weakness in Jasper's defenses.

Horrified, Sehraine watched the door splinter and form long cracks.  She glanced up at Jasper.  He had his eyes closed and his lips moved, but no sound came out.  She prayed his spell would work even as part of her mind tried unsuccessfully to not think about what would happen if it failed.

There was another loud crack from the door.  She stifled a cry when a white fist broke through the door near the knob and groped for the lock.

Within the circle of Jasper's arm, she quivered with fear.  It took all of her trust in Jasper to hold her ground.  Doubt wormed its way into her thoughts.  Sehraine looked at the door, up at Jasper, and back at the door.  She wanted to run.

The demon dog found the lock and released it, allowing the door to fall inward with a clatter.  They entered, one behind the other.  Random spatters of fresh blood streaked their white pelts, some still dripping.  Their dog-like muzzles broke into malicious grins, and their clawed hands flexed in anticipation.

They both leapt.

Sehraine screamed and gripped Jasper tighter, burying her face into his side.  The circle on the ground blazed with a bright, white light.  Closing her eyes, she tensed in anticipation of the pain and death she knew would come.

# CHAPTER 10
# FROM DOGS TO WOLVES

## October 25, 4235 K.E.

**9:04pm**

After the standoff that morning, Grendel and Sacha's day had been, relatively speaking, pleasant. The rain followed them down the road and eventually caught them after lunch. As soon as it started to fall, Sacha removed her scarf, closed her eyes, and turned her face up to the sky while driving, letting the rain settle on her cheeks and lashes like glittering gems. Normally, Grendel paid little heed to the weather beyond the necessity of warmth in the depths of winter. It had never really occurred to him that he might find pleasure in something as simple as rain.

Sitting like that, swaying gently in time with the wagon's movements, Sacha seemed as innocent as she was beautiful... and by the beard of the Eternal Father, she was beautiful. She basked under the touch of the light rain on her face for only a few minutes, but it stirred a longing in Grendel, one he dared not acknowledge. Instead, he fixed his gaze down the road ahead, careful that neither she nor anyone else saw him watching.

By the time the caravan stopped for the evening, the rain fell in earnest. The remaining orcs quickly led the Percherons off the road and onto an area of high ground among the trees. Unfortunately, the skeletal boughs were barren and afforded little protection. While the two Zhitomiran soldiers worked with the horses, the orcs unloaded the tents from the chuck wagon and set up camp in a small clearing nearby.

Shortly after the evening meal, Gregori arrived at Sacha's tent with Marko and the dark cleric close behind. Grendel couldn't see their faces, but he could hear enough of their whispering to know something was awry. They entered the tent without preamble and closed the flap behind them.

The voices inside grew in volume as they argued. What Grendel heard didn't make much sense, but it was clear someone important had died.  He thought he heard Jasper's name but couldn't be certain.

Grendel stepped a little closer, trying to make out what they were saying.  Kourash slipped around the corner and said, "You can't hide behind her forever.  She will tire of you like she does everyone else, and when she does, I'll be waiting."

Turning slowly, Grendel kept the outward appearance of being relaxed; inside, however, his muscles were ready, even eager, for action.  Off in the distance, lightning flashed, glowing on Kourash's pallid skin and ruby-colored eyes.  Grendel's hands itched to grab his battle-axe, but he kept them loose by his side.

The two were of comparable heights, and Grendel looked the Seldaehne straight in the eyes.  "You want a piece of me? Why wait?" he asked in a low growl that matched the rolling thunder.  The glare on his face was a carryover from his days in the arena.

Never having fought a Seldaehne before, Grendel had difficulty reading Kourash, but this wasn't his first dance. The two kept in each other's faces, not wanting to be the first to back down, but also not wanting to be the one to throw the first punch.

"What's going on out here?" Marko yelled over the din of the rain.  The tent flap snapped open, and the knight stood at the entrance with his helmet in his hand.

Sacha's voice responded from inside the tent.  "Brother, call off your dog before he gets hurt."

Marko forced out a laugh and said, "Sister, I think it's your dog that would get hurt."

"Enough, both of you!  I tire of your constant games," D'yakon Krovos commanded as he exited Sacha's tent.

Grendel remained facing Kourash, not backing down.  A light hand on his shoulder released the tension building inside him.

"Let it go," Sacha whispered.

Kourash's malicious grin revealed a mouthful of sharp, pointed teeth.  "Yes, cur, go sit at your mistress' feet, lest she have you neutered."

"Kourash!  You can kill him another time," Marko said. Strapping on his helmet, the knight stepped into the rain.

Sacha stayed beside Grendel, both her hands wrapped around his wrist while Kourash followed Marko into the darkness. Their hoods already up, Gregori and D'yakon Krovos disappeared into the storm, still deep in discussion.

Later that night, the pounding of the rain became deafening. Grendel stood rooted in the mud, water running down his face. His leathers had kept him dry for a while, but after so much rain for so long, everything was cold and saturated. Behind him, the tent flap shifted, and light chased his shadow across the camp. He turned to see Sacha standing at the entrance with one hand on her hip, silhouetted by the light within. Gone was the image of innocence from that afternoon, replaced by someone far more wanton.

"Why won't you come in out of the rain?"

"I can do my job better out here," he replied.

"Your job is what and where I tell you it is! Come in here. Now!" Her voice was sharp with frustration.

"No," Grendel growled. His days in the arena made him all too familiar with the game she was trying to play. She acted like some of the trainers. They needed to feel like they had total control over their fighters. Sex was an obvious reward, but sometimes the trainers played mind games, making their slaves think it was something more, but in the end that's what they were: slaves. He had no intention of falling into that trap.

She swept her hand toward the other tents. "Even the Seldaehne has gone to his bed. Who do you think you're protecting me from out here? Come in. Get dry... and warm."

The wind shifted and rain blew into her tent, pelting her and quickly saturating her hair and clothes so that they clung to her skin.

"I am not your slave, woman!" Grendel yelled with more emotion than he intended.

The rain forgotten, Sacha stared at her bodyguard, confused. He took a step toward her and said, "You are paying me to keep you alive. You want an ammissarius to warm your bed? Go find someone else."

Her eyes widened in shock that quickly gave way to anger. "No one says 'no' to me!" she spat.

"I just did," Grendel replied. He stepped forward, looming over her. His eyes glowed with violet light between the flashes of lightning. "What happened to your previous bodyguard?"

Sacha opened her mouth to answer then snapped it closed.

He bent down, so he didn't have to shout to be heard. "I asked you a question. What happened to him?"

The noise of the rain grew distant. She met his gaze unflinching and defiant. "He's dead," she answered. "Is that what you want to hear? Or maybe you want to hear me confess that I killed him while he slept?"

He knew he shouldn't be, but Grendel felt disappointed by her answer. "Why? Did he fail to satisfy you?" Grendel asked.

Her eyes narrowed, and she balled up her fist. "How dare you! How dare you stand there and question me like that!"

"I guessed right, did I not?"

With a rage-filled yell, she aimed a punch at Grendel's jaw. His hand enveloped her fist and stopped it mid-swing. Her other hand swung toward his face, but Grendel caught that one as well. Twisting her arms behind her back, he held her tight while she struggled.

"Bastard, I'll have your head for this! I'll —"

Transferring both her wrists into his right hand, he seized her hair in his left fist and pulled her head back. Lightning flashed and thunder shook the ground, but the two remained fixed in their odd embrace.

"I am done with the games," he growled. "Sometimes, I think you know more about me than I do. The rest of the time, you are so blind.

"Know this: I am not your slave to be commanded. When you figure that out, let me know." Letting her go, he took a few steps back and resumed his position outside her tent. His deep voice carried over the rain. "You better wake up, woman, or we are both going to end up dead."


**11:13pm**

'*Am I dead*?' The thought came unbidden.

Miraculously still standing, Sehraine opened one eye, then the other. Her brain only registered one thing at a time.

She looked down and frowned when she noticed the pale circle of silvery light that surrounded her and Jasper — a light, she guessed, left over from Jasper's spell. Then she felt the cold rain running down her back beneath her chemise. She shifted her weight and felt the mud seep between her bare toes.

Slowly, her eyes adjusted to the dim lighting, and she could make out her surroundings — a clearing with four surprised faces staring back at her. When she recognized the trees at the edge of the clearing, she involuntarily shivered, though not from the cold. Stories abounded about the Haunted Wood. At first glance, she thought the faces belonged to the images of ghosts, but as her vision improved, she realized they were just men.

Their grim features, combined with their steely eyes, reminded her of the time she had witnessed a man sentenced to the executioner's block by the Kral. These men had that same hard look. They knew they were going to die.

Jasper's staff fell to the ground with a splash. Sehraine turned just in time to catch him as he collapsed. Caught by surprise, she barely managed to keep from falling down herself. Jasper's face pressed against hers, and she fought the urge to let him fall into the mud. Pushing against his dead weight, her knees began to buckle, and she took a step back, trying to brace herself.

"Don't just stand there gawking! Help me," she pleaded through clenched teeth.

One of the men, a youth by the looks of him, helped pull Jasper's unconscious body off her. He stooped down, and with Jasper's arm draped around his neck, hoisted the limp elven body up and off Sehraine.

"Thanks," she huffed.

A bright smile lit his face, and his eyes lingered on her chest. The small circle of light glowing around her threw off just enough illumination for the boy to see, and it didn't take her long to realize what the rain had done to her chemise.

"Great! Just great! Jasper, I'm going to kill you for this," she muttered to herself.

"Hi! I'm Lucky," he said good-naturedly.

"Of course you are," she replied. "Can you tell me where I am?"

A middle-aged man stepped forward and interrupted before the boy could respond. "Did Jasper send you?"

Exposed and surrounded, she studied the man addressing her. He had the appearance of a ruffian, but he also had the commanding presence of a leader. "Yes," she answered warily.

"Are you it?" the man demanded, looking around as if he expected others to be hiding in the trees.

Reaching into the bag, she retrieved a heavy cloak, put it on, and stepped out of the circle. When she did, the glowing light winked out, throwing everyone into darkness.

"Damn it, Jasper! Why don't you tell me these things?" she cried out, her frustration building.

With the pale light gone, Sehraine's eyes had to readjust, and her elven vision presented the clearing in varying shades of black, white, and grey. Four men stood around her, completely blind. The youth holding Jasper stood frozen. He stared out, his eyes wide with fright.

Sehraine saw that they only carried two daggers amongst the lot of them. Beyond them were several steel cages: some filled with bodies and others that were empty. In the trees, black birds perched on the branches, no doubt waiting for the people to die.

'*What was Jasper thinking, bringing us out here?*' she thought.

"Elf, can you see?" the leader asked.

"Yes," she replied.

"Will you help us?"

Before she had a chance to answer, a deep-throated howl echoed through the forest. Sehraine suppressed another shiver. That single howl would be their only warning, meant to drive them into panicked flight. The hunters already had them surrounded.

"What's your name?" she asked.

"Dragahn."

She stared at each of the men — these were the caravan men Jasper had told her about. She recognized Pyotr by the flask in his hand, which meant the fourth man was Andrei. Her shoulders drooped as the weight of responsibility struck her. These men were counting on her.

"My name is Sehraine.  The elf you helped off me is Jasper, still in disguise."

The four men bombarded her with questions.  She raised her hand but put it back down when she realized the men couldn't see it.

It took a few minutes before Dragahn calmed his men. "What happened?" he asked after everyone quieted.

"The guild was a trap.  We barely escaped Pazard'zhik with our lives."

"What happened to Jasper?"

"I don't know.  I'm hoping he just needs some rest."

"I'm afraid you may have escaped one death only to face another.  The light from the circle that brought you scared off a pack of wargs, but they'll be back."

"Why don't you make a fire?" she asked and then immediately regretted the stupid question.

"We tried, but the wood's all wet," Lucky answered anyway.

Shadows shifted under the trees at the edge of the clearing.  She stepped closer to the men and said, "I have my daggers and can see in this darkness.  We'll make it to dawn."

# CHAPTER 11
# CONVERSATIONS AFTER MIDNIGHT

### October 26, 4235 K.E.


**12:09am**

Grendel stood outside Sacha's tent. Not for the first time since taking this mission, he felt alone. The rain had finally stopped, leaving the intermittent patter of water dripping from the tree branches. Staring into the woods, Grendel missed his dwarven friend.

Before this, Chert and he had always traveled together, sharing many adventures. The dwarf had a way of keeping him centered, something he hadn't been aware he needed until now. He recalled the events of the past few days and couldn't help but feel abandoned. If Jasper had only stopped the caravan sooner, none of this would have happened. He didn't even know if the mage still lived. Sacha said he was alive when she left him, but if that were the case, why hadn't he shown up yet?

A light touch on his shoulder broke him from his thoughts. He whipped around and found Sacha standing next to him.

"What are you thinking?" she asked.

"Do you ever sleep?"

"Do you?"

He turned and stared into the darkness. "I was thinking of my friends."

She eyed him curiously. "I don't have any friends," she said softly. Grendel wasn't certain, but he thought he caught a hint of regret in her voice. She stood close, and her sleeve brushed the side of his hand.

He glanced at her from the corner of his eye, suspicious of her change in mood. "It takes two to make friends."

"Where I'm from, we don't make friends, only enemies."

"Sounds like the arena."

"Similar."

The two stood quietly.  A few late season frogs called out to one another, and an owl hooted in a nearby tree.  In the distance, Grendel heard the faint echoes of howling wolves.

"Trust and friendship are foreign concepts to me," Sacha said.  "Neither have any place in the courts of Zhitomir.  Both are weaknesses that get you killed." She glanced up at him. "I imagine the arena was the same."

"Pretty much," he replied.  A chill breeze whispered through the camp.  "Why are you doing this?" Grendel asked.

"Doing what?"

Gesturing toward the wagons and the nearby tents, he gave her a questioning look.  "This caravan.  I do not understand why it is important enough for you to kill.  Is it what you want, or what *they* want?"

Sacha stared at the other tents.  Grendel watched the play of emotions over her face in the darkness.  "Fear and hate are a dangerous mix," he said.

She gave her bodyguard a startled look and backed away, her emotions now focused on him.  "If I wanted your opinion, I would have asked for it," she hissed.  "Remember, it was you who came to me looking for this job, and at no time do I recall asking you to be my conscience."

Grendel's jaw clenched.  Sacha's mood swings tried his patience, but he wasn't ready to give up on her — at least, not yet.  "I am not trying to be your conscience," he growled. "Just your bodyguard."

She eyed him narrowly, full of suspicion.  "Why should I believe you?"

"Because I am telling the truth."

"Do you always tell the truth?"

"Most of the time."

Her face softened again, and she said, "It's hard for me to speak the truth unless there's something to gain from it."

"Do you not eventually lose yourself in the lies?"

"Have you ever lost yourself to the lust of battle?"

Not sure where she was going with the question, Grendel stood quietly before answering, "Yes."

"Same thing."

"No, it is not."

"It is if every day is a battle."

**12:12am**

Rain continued to fall, and a pack of dusky wargs surrounded the small group in the clearing. Larger than a common wolf and more intelligent, their heads stayed low as they sniffed the ground, silent, hungry shadows prowling the darkness around the teamsters.

Dragahn and Lucky manhandled Jasper up on top of one of the cages, face-down to keep the rain from drowning him.

Sehraine stood among the men, holding a thin-bladed dagger in each hand. As the wargs closed, she looked this way and that, yelling out their locations. At first, they retreated from her shouts, but as they gained confidence, the pack drew closer and closer.

One lunged toward Lucky, and Sehraine yelled again. When the men converged, the warg ducked back only to have another strike from behind. Dragahn sliced with his dagger and scored a shallow cut in the beast's pelt.

"Stay in a circle! Stay in a circle!"

From the opposite direction, another warg charged Andrei. Feet apart, the young teamster held a heavy branch in front of him with both hands. The creature crashed through his swing, splintering the brittle wood, and knocking him to the ground. Screaming, Andrei raised his arms to shield his face. Saliva and blood mixed as the warg bit the man's forearm and dragged Andrei away.

With a shout, Sehraine ran forward and stabbed the warg in the haunch. It yelped in pain and let Andrei go, even as several of his pack mates bounded toward the teamsters.

Holding his injured arm, Andrei staggered to his feet. Smelling hot blood, the pack closed. They snapped at Sehraine, herding her back and separating her from the injured teamster.

Dragahn cried out as one leapt on him. He had just enough time to steady his dagger before the weight of the warg bore him to the ground, its slick, white teeth glinting in the darkness. Pushing up, he plunged his dagger into its chest. Warm blood ran down his hands and traced along his arms.

Shaking its head, the beast tore at Dragahn's shoulder, but the chief didn't let go. The dagger dug deeper and deeper between the mighty warg's ribs, finally piercing its heart.

With a violent shudder, the lifeless form of the warg became a dead weight, trapping Dragahn underneath.

Spinning, Sehraine lashed out at the retreating pack with her daggers, but they moved like wraiths in the night and, more times than not, she hit empty air. The wargs focused on Andrei, snapping and biting at the man's flailing limbs. The young man's screams mingled with the vicious snarls of the hunters.

Silently begging for forgiveness, Sehraine averted her eyes from the carnage as she backed away to rejoin the remaining teamsters. She found Dragahn buried beneath a warg. Pyotr and Lucky stood back-to-back, rooted in place. She had to get them beyond the pack's reach.

Andrei's screams suddenly ended.

Time had run out.


**12:16am**

"My position here is tested every day by the ones who travel with us," Sacha explained. "If I show any signs of weakness, any at all, my brother will exploit it. He already sees you as a way to get to me. Be careful around him and Kourash."

Grendel glanced toward Marko's tent.

"So, I weave lies and keep my brother at bay. In the end, I'll probably have to kill him before I return home to our family."

The way she said it, cold and calculating, reminded Grendel of the political maneuvering among the arena owners. He had heard stories from the other gladiators. Stories of how many of the matches were no more than thinly disguised executions. So much had gone on behind the scenes. Manipulation and treachery constantly plagued fighters, but it was the world in which Sacha lived and breathed, even thrived.

"We should leave." Grendel surprised himself when he said it.

Tears formed in Sacha's eyes. "I can't."

"Why not? Let us leave, right now. They cannot stop us."

Sacha didn't answer. He saw her thinking about it, which only encouraged him. She looked at Grendel, her expression unreadable, but before she could open her mouth to speak, the air around them turned frigid.  The coldness of the grave seeped up from the ground beneath their feet, accompanied by the miasma of death.  Sacha fled inside her tent without saying a word, the smell of fear following her.

The tent flap closed, and Grendel was again left in the darkness, but he wasn't alone.  A pair of yellow eyes the color of brimstone peered out from the woods.

## 12:22am

*'It's always darkest before the dawn.'*  Who coined that phrase?  Or was it a proverb?  If Sehraine could have found the person who first uttered those words, she would have punched him in the throat.

The wargs dragged Andrei's body to the edge of the wood, but she knew they wouldn't leave — not with easy prey still at hand.  The only good news was the rain had slacked off to a drizzle.

"Inside the cages!" she yelled.

"No way!" she heard Pyotr shout.

"Get in there now before they attack again!"

"Not without Dragahn!"

"I'll get him.  You worry about yourself and Jasper!"

Pyotr took a deep breath and ran.  Growling, a warg charged the doctor.  Pyotr grabbed Jasper off the top of the cage and dragged him inside.  The metal door clanged shut just as the creature snapped its teeth into his coat sleeve, tearing it loose.

Two more wargs joined the first and began sniffing around the cages.  One sneezed and shook its head.  The other whined.  Whatever it was they smelled around the cages held them at bay.

Sehraine crouched beside the dead warg atop Dragahn and struggled to roll it over. It was no use.  She wasn't strong enough.  As she straightened, trying to figure out how to help, Lucky came to her aid.  With a grunt and a shove, the two rolled the carcass off the chief.

"You don't have a dagger!" Sehraine said, alarmed.

Lucky wrenched Dragahn's blade from the warg's chest. "Now I do."

Sehraine knelt and felt Dragahn's breath.  There was so much blood.  She could only hope most of it was from the warg.  Shadows shifted behind the young man, drawing her eyes to the three wargs that edged closer.

Calculating positions and distances, she said, "Get ready."

"What are you going to do?" Lucky asked.

"Give you and Dragahn a chance.  Don't waste it."  She leapt to her feet, emitting a frightened cry as she hurdled the warg carcass, and ran in the opposite direction from the cages, counting on the predators' instinct to give chase.  Behind her, Sehraine heard a single, excited yip before the rhythmic drum of padded feet filled her ears.

In her peripheral vision, wargs streaked from the trees to join the chase.  She reached up and unclasped her cloak, letting the heavy fabric fall way.  Bare feet digging into the soggy ground, she sprinted for the tree line.

Paws splashed in a puddle, behind and to her right.  She darted across the warg's path, hoping it would overshoot her position.  As it passed, the creature slapped her heel with its paw.  The force knocked her foot into the back of her opposite knee, sending Sehraine flying toward the base of a tree.

Rather than sprawling in the mud, she let her momentum roll her back to her feet and spun in a crouch, dagger leading.  The tip of the blade slashed across the warg's sensitive nose.  It yelped and leapt away, colliding with one of its pack-mates.

Sehraine sprang into the air just as another charged.  She grabbed a branch and swung her legs up, wrapping them around it.

A warg flung itself into the air and snapped its teeth, catching the trailing edge of her chemise.  For a horrible moment, she struggled to keep her hold on the branch and bear the weight of the warg, then the fabric ripped, and the creature fell.  It gave the tattered garment a frenzied shake before dropping it and turning its attention back to her.

Lightning struck the clearing.

Sehraine clenched her eyes shut and clutched the branch tighter as the world around her shook in the thunderclap that followed.  She and the wargs both cried out in terror.

The thunder's echo died away, leaving the world silent and still.  Sehraine opened her eyes and saw Jasper, no longer disguised as an elf, slumped over, clutching his staff.

Dropping to the ground, she raced toward him and caught him before the last of his strength escaped him.

He gave her a faint smile and said, "Always wanted to see you naked."

# CHAPTER 12
# WIND RIDERS

## October 26, 4235 K.E.

**2:30am**

Tired and hungry, Yana and her squad flew high through the air. Riding the winds that pushed the rain clouds ahead of them, they hung between the sea of darkness below and the blanket of stars above. She fought the numbness in her limbs by shifting her weight. The chill wind tugged at her boot, and she shifted back. It made her thankful for the thick fur lining in her helmet and gloves, and the layers of clothing she had on under her uniform.

She wished she could actually *see* the road. They could only hope to maintain a heading that would leave the main road within sight come the dawn. Bored by the seemingly unending expanse of dead trees, Yana turned her attention to the stars, trying to gauge how much time had passed since they'd crossed the Stena, but navigating by the stars wasn't part of Wind Rider training. If... No, *when* she returned to Pazard'zhik, she'd be certain to recommend it to their commander. Assuming she wasn't condemned to the mines for her part in Jasper's escape from the city.

Yana pushed aside the worry and glanced to either side to check on her teammates. They seemed to be holding up to the grueling journey. Her jaw clenched in grim determination, she flew on through the night.

**5:58am**

After burying Sky in a shallow grave topped by a mound of stones, Chert and Xandor resumed their chase. Mladen's rouncey was too skittish for the dwarf to ride, so they rode double, using the spare horse as a pack animal. Riding through the night, lost in their thoughts, they only stopped for short breaks. All four were tired and wet, but Xandor was determined to catch the caravan.

It was long after midnight when the rain stopped. Shortly after the clouds cleared and the stars became visible, the temperature dropped, creating thin layers of ice over the many puddles of mud. Xerxes tried to avoid them, but occasionally he crunched through the thin layer and snorted at the sudden cold around his fetlock.

When dawn came, it painted the sky in brilliant hues of red and orange. "Wake me if something happens," Chert grumbled, and dropped into a fitful doze.

Xandor chafed at the slow pace forced by the condition of the road. His eyes roved constantly, scanning the tracks to gauge their progress, and searching the trees for signs of danger. He feared they were losing ground, despite traveling through the night.

As the day progressed, the temperature rose, melting away the rime of ice. He found the place where the wagons stopped for the night and took the time to study the remains of the camp. All total, there were signs of roughly a half-dozen orcs and ten people, but only four tents. Outside one of those lay the tracks of huge hobnail boots, a nail pattern Xandor had only ever seen in one set of footprints. "Chert. Grendel's alive."

Chert said a quick prayer of thanks, and they returned to the road in better spirits. The ranger had a good feeling they would catch the caravan before sundown.

**8:11am**

Signaling for a halt, Marko stopped the caravan at the edge of the Haunted Wood. Ahead of him, the road continued through a bizarre landscape of sporadic groves of short, stumpy trees and irregular pools of greyish white mudpots formed by springs hot enough to kill a man.

Marko dismounted and stood near a pool, watching it bubble and steam. Along the far edge, several red and pink spots oozed to the surface. In the distance, something coughed and a mudpot spit mud at least five feet into the air.

With the toe of his boot, Marko tested an area at the side of the road. The thin crust broke under the slightest of pressure. He raised his voice so everyone could hear. "Stick to the center. I don't want to have to pull a wagon out of this mess." He climbed back into the saddle and led his Frisian down the center of the road.

D'yakon Krovos and his driver guided the chuck wagon, letting it fall in behind the knight, with an orc loping along on either side.  Behind them, Sacha and Grendel eased their wagon forward, flanked by another pair of orcs.  Next in line came Gregori and Ognian with their orcs, while Kourash and two Zhitomiran horsemen guarded the rear.

Sacha and Grendel rode together quietly, the night before not forgotten, only set aside.  Of the two, Sacha seemed the more distant.  With a worried expression, she constantly looked back at the Haunted Wood as if searching for something.  When Grendel asked her about it, she subtly shook her head but otherwise didn't answer.


**1:11pm**

Wide, fast-moving shadows passed over Xandor, roughly following the path of the road.  Looking up, he saw three Trakyan flyers and immediately nudged Xerxes to stop.  He pulled out his spyglass and aimed it at the lead flyer.  When he zoomed in, he recognized Yana by her helmet.

"Jasper, what have you done?" he said aloud, waking Chert.

"What?"

"Take a look," he said, handing the spyglass to the dwarf.

"That's Yana!"

"I know."

"What's she doing here?"

"What do you think?"

"Jasper?"

"That's my guess."

"They're going to hit the caravan, aren't they?" Chert asked.

"Did you see those pouches under the wings?"

"Looked like they had something in them."

"Hang on!"

Lowering his head, Xerxes leapt forward and galloped down the road, drawing the rouncey along with him.  Xandor leaned close to the stallion's neck, and the staccato beat of hooves echoed off the trees.  Ahead, they saw the edge of the Haunted Wood and the field of mudpots beyond.

Galloping as fast as they could, they watched the three gliders dive at the caravan.

**1:16pm**

Fiery explosions rocked the caravan and threw chunks of mud and earth into the air. The panicked screams of horses, men, and orcs followed. Caught out in the open, they had nowhere to run.

Scanning the skies, Marko knelt beside his Frisian and squinted through the thick plumes of smoke obscuring the roadway.

D'yakon Krovos yelled "Scutum!" and the blasts skimmed up and over the chuck wagon in a roaring wave. The Percherons screamed and reared in panic, jostling wagon and cleric. Krovos snarled a curse at the horses, rooting them in place. Their eyes rolled wildly, but their muscles wouldn't obey. Jumping down, Krovos scanned the skies for the flyers and prayed to Sutekh for another spell.

Staying crouched, Marko picked his way through the roiling smoke, silently cursing the Kral and those who served him. Orc parts lay strewn across the road. Using the bed of the chuck wagon for cover, Marko assessed the damage. Thanks to Krovos, the chuck wagon had escaped relatively unscathed, but Sacha's wagon had completely disappeared, replaced by potholes filled with mud. The third wagon was all but destroyed, and there were no signs of his horsemen.

Marko broke into a run that brought him to the burning remains of the third wagon. Rage overtook him. He yanked out his sword and struck a screaming Percheron repeatedly. In front of him, Teodor's shattered body lay at odd angles.

"Quick. We can still salvage this if we hurry," D'yakon Krovos said calmly, appearing out of the smoke.

"What are you talking about? Everything is destroyed!"

"No, it's not. Look," D'yakon Krovos pointed. Sure enough, through the smoke, Marko saw Kourash and one of the horsemen unloading crates from the bed of the burning wagon. "We need to get those loaded on the chuck wagon before the wind riders return."

Marko wiped his sword and sheathed it, then ran to help Kourash and the warrior. Of the sixteen crates, Kourash stood next to the only four that remained intact. The others lay in pieces with greasy stains marking what was left of the bars of soap. Burning fragments of wax paper floated in the air.

"You," Marko said, pointing at the Zhitomiran warrior. "See if you can salvage any more bars."

"I'll need your help," the warrior replied.

The tone in the other's voice struck a nerve, and Marko placed his hand on the hilt of his sword.  "How dare you address me that way, soldier."

"I'll address you any way I damn well please," the warrior replied with a dark smirk.

Cold seeped down Marko's spine.

"Gregori?"

"Of course.  Now shut that mouth of yours and help me salvage what we can."


The wind riders swooped around and came back for a second run.  They aimed for the smoke, seeking survivors. Spotting the chuck wagon, they dove toward it, their incendiaries ready.

A billowing cloud of blue-black flames appeared directly in front of them.

Yana snatched at her sway bar and tried to veer away, but the cloud spread, making it unavoidable.  She and the flyer next to her dropped all their incendiaries before entering the wall.  Flames engulfed them, catching their sails, struts, and uniforms on fire while the incendiaries wasted their fury on the mudpots along the north side of the road.  The third squad member wasn't so lucky.  Too close to the wall of flame, her incendiaries exploded, consuming her and her flyer before she even had a chance to scream.

Concussion from the blast tossed Yana and her wingman haphazardly through the air like toy kites.  Flames devoured the fabric and frames of their gliders, and gravity quickly took over.

Incongruously, the image of a stooping falcon rose in Yana's mind as she tried to pull up to slow her descent. Trailing smoke, her flyer streaked across the sky toward the Haunted Wood.


With a satisfied grunt, D'yakon Krovos turned and walked to the rear of the caravan to help Gregori.

# CHAPTER 13
# SACHA AND GRENDEL

### October 26, 4235 K.E.

**1:20pm**

When the first blast erupted between the second and third wagons, Sacha's four Percherons screamed and jostled against each other, searching for a way to escape the noise. Several more explosions shook the ground around them, and the frightened horses bolted into the field of mudpots.

Shouting at them to stop, Sacha tugged and pulled on the reins, all to no effect.

"Jump!" Grendel yelled, white knuckling the seat.

Her chin set in determination, Sacha wrapped the reins around her wrists and hauled back on them with all her might.

With a sudden lurch and a splash of mud, the Percherons plunged headfirst into a bubbling mudpot. Their screams cut off as hot sludge filled their noses and mouths, choking them. The suction of the mud and the struggles of the draft horses became too much for the yoke to bear, and it snapped with a sharp crack.

Sacha, still gripping the reins, flew forward into the mud near the struggling animals. She landed with an audible splat and quickly went under.

A spider web of fractures in the thin crust spread from the deep grooves cut by the wheels, and the wagon tilted. Hot mud, now free of its shell, oozed between the loosened boards of the bed, and it slowly began to sink.

Grendel saw no sign of Sacha, only the struggling of the Percherons as they fought to remain afloat. Leaving his battle-axe in the bed of the wagon behind him, he inched down the length of the broken yoke and fished out the horses' reins. He pulled, hoping she still held on, but there was none of the telltale tension.

Drawing in a deep breath, he dove into the mud and followed the reins down. The milky sludge felt oddly warm as it oozed around him. Grendel pushed deeper, and the mud grew searing hot, burning his skin. Just as quickly, it cooled. Reins in one hand, he groped blindly with the other as he swam farther into the mud. His lungs screamed for air, but he refused to give up. He had to find Sacha.

Something brushed his hand. Stretching with his fingertips, he found Sacha's wrist and pulled her toward him. With a mighty heave, he fought the weight of the mud and clambered up the horse's reins while holding Sacha's limp form as gently as he could. Grendel found a Percheron's leg and climbed up until he broke the surface.

Grendel spit mud from his mouth and gulped a lungful of sulfurous air to ease the burning in his chest. Turning his full attention to Sacha, he brushed the warm mud away from her face as best he could and felt a ragged pulse at her neck. Relief flooded him. Miraculously, she had managed not to drown, but he couldn't tell if she was injured. Her head lolled to one side, so he hugged her closer, letting her cheek rest in the crook of his neck. She twitched and softly moaned as if trapped in an unpleasant dream.

Half-buried in the mud, the dead Percherons became fleshy islands of white and grey. The wagon lay canted, one side submerged deeper than the other. Wooden planks stuck out of the mud like the broken hull of an old derelict. Nearby, crates floated on the surface, but they, too, slowly sank. All around them, fat bubbles plopped as they surfaced.

Before their Percherons disappeared altogether, Grendel grabbed the yoke of the wagon and, with a mighty effort, hauled himself and Sacha within reach of the driver's seat. Refusing to release them, the mud swallowed the wagon's toe board and inched toward the driver's seat.

Chest deep in hot sludge, Grendel pulled himself and Sacha along the wagon's side toward the edge of the mudpot.

Suddenly, the air turned icy cold, and a shadow covered them, despite the cloudless sky and bright sun overhead. Grendel glanced up and saw a tall, darkly handsome man with yellow eyes standing on the brink of the pit. He was dressed as a rakish nobleman, with his wide brimmed hat and heavy jacket, but something about the deep maroon clothing didn't look right. Grendel was no expert in fashion, but even he could tell the clothes were outdated and meant more for the courtroom than outdoors in the mud.

"Thank you, Grendel. I'll take over now," the man said.

Still working his way along the side of the wagon bed, Grendel eyed the man suspiciously.

"She is mine, after all," the man continued nonchalantly.

"You know my name, but I do not know yours," Grendel said.

The horrible semblance of a smile twisted his features. "You may call me Razrushitel."

"I will not give her up," Grendel said stubbornly.

"Really?" the man responded with a hint of mirth in his eyes.  "Do you want to save her?"

Unsure of what the man meant, Grendel answered, "Yes. I want to save her."

"Even after all she has done to you?"

Perplexed by the question, Grendel didn't respond.  He struggled past the rear of the wagon and stretched for the bank.  His fingertips barely brushed against the crusty shore, causing it to crumble.  The wagon sank deeper into the mud, taking Grendel and Sacha with it.

"You are alone in this quest, son of Cayn."

Razrushitel walked near where Grendel's fingers had broken the crust.  Using the toe of his shiny black boot, he gently stepped down and broke up the adjacent portions along the edge.

"No one can save you now.  Not your friends.  Not anyone."

Pointing toward the road and the smoldering wagon, Razrushitel said, "That attack.  Did you know that it was Jasper who ordered it?  You were supposed to die today."

Disbelief coursed through Grendel.  In the distance, the chuck wagon fled down the road.

"What are you going to do now? You can't save her. Your friends have turned against you.  Give her to me.  It's the best thing for her."

"No," Grendel growled.

"She's lied to you, and she's used you, Grendel. Regardless of what she told you, she left those teamsters to die.  That was her plan all along.  And poor young Yosif, he bled out soon after you left him," the man said, kneeling just above the edge.  "Do you still want to save her?"

Sacha stirred in Grendel's arms.  She murmured and cried out, as if trapped in a nightmare.

"She has unleashed evil in the city of Pazard'zhik and caused hundreds to die, including Marcus. You're the Kral's man — you must know she can't be saved. The Kral wants her dead."

The wagon lurched when Grendel climbed into the bed. Grabbing one of the crates, he threw it at the man. Razrushitel easily dodged aside, letting the crate shatter behind him, spilling its contents.

"You're lying," Grendel growled.

"That's just it. I don't have to lie. The truth is so much more entertaining."

A sudden realization dawned on Grendel, and he said, "You are Sacha's demon."

Razrushitel's smile disappeared, and his face lost all emotion. The demon's yellow eyes bored into the half-orc as he said, "She told you about me? Did she show you the scars?"

Grendel returned the demon's gaze and felt himself drawn in. He saw Sacha reflected in Razrushitel's eyes. Images flashed in his mind. He saw the grotesque form of the demon standing naked in a room surrounded by people wearing purple and black robes of velvet. They chanted and prayed to Sutekh to accept their offering. Out of the crowd, a young Sacha approached the demon, clad all in black. The silken robe slipped from her shoulders with a soft whisper. Wrapping her in his arms, the demon took her in the pool of dark silk while the humans watched. It wasn't exactly as she had described it. Grendel tried to look away but found himself caught.

"Did she tell you she liked it?" the demon purred. "That she wanted it and screamed for more? She's in love with power and gave me her soul that night to get it. She is mine by right."

Finally wrenching his eyes free from the demon's gaze, Grendel lay Sacha atop one of the crates and hefted his battle-axe. "You want her, come and get her."

"You're sinking," Razrushitel smirked. The wagon lurched and mud breached the sides of the bed.

With a growl, Grendel threw his battle-axe at Razrushitel. Slinging Sacha over his shoulder, he planted his foot on the wagon's gunwale and jumped the remaining distance to the edge of the mudpot.  "I saved her without your help, demon."

"No.  No, you haven't.  You still have a long way to go," the demon said, his smile returning.  "Remember what I've told you."

The shadow departed, and Razrushitel was gone.

Placing Sacha on the ground, Grendel knelt beside her and gently brushed more mud away from her face.  He needed to talk to her.  He had questions only she could answer.

Sacha's eyes snapped open, and she slapped his hand away.  "You bastard!" she snarled.  "You lied to me!"

Grendel jerked back, raising his hands in a gesture of surrender.

"You work for the Kral!" she spat as she rolled to her feet.  She took a menacing step toward him and jabbed a finger against his chest.  "This whole time, you've been spying on me!  You... you *mudak*!"

She waved her arms wildly, and a rapid torrent of Rhodinan poured from her mouth, faster than Grendel could follow.  Seeing her words had little effect, she spun on her heel and stalked away, even more enraged.  After a few steps, she reached down and, with a yell, threw a lump of hardened mud at him.  He deflected it with his hand, causing it to explode into a cloud of white dust.

Grendel's ire broke the surface.  "I do not know what you just said, woman, but you had better control that temper!"

They stared at each other across the field of mud.

Grendel yelled, "You and your brother killed those teamsters and that boy, so do not yell at me about lying!"

"I did not lie about that," she snapped, switching back to Trakyan.  "I told you they were alive when we left them.  They even had food and water.  I saw Gregori prepare it personally.  Besides, what difference does it make?  You've killed before," she said as if that explained everything.  She turned her back on him, moving deeper into the field of mudpots.

"Even though you did not kill them outright, you still left them to die.  I never killed like that!" he shouted.  He hefted his axe and strode after her.

"Dead is dead," she said flippantly and took a few more steps before he heard her mutter, "I cannot believe you're a damned spy."

His jaw clenched as he bit down on his irritation. "Woman! Look at me!" he said with a growl, grabbing her shoulder a little harder than he meant and spinning her around. "I was sent to spy on Dragahn and the caravan, not you," he said through clenched teeth. "Everyone thought they were smuggling something." His grip dug in a little harder, and he saw Sacha wince under the pressure. Bringing his anger under control, he let go and said, "Those men did not deserve to die."

"And everyone you've killed deserved it? What about your fights in the arena... or was that a lie, too?" she asked, her voice dripping venom.

"The arena was real, but there I did not have a choice!"

"Same with me, except my arena doesn't have the neat and tidy boundaries yours did," she spat. "One wrong move, one uncertain step, and I'll end up just as dead. Kill or be killed, Grendel. It's the world we live in. Face it; there's not much difference between you and me."

Grendel stopped, letting her words sink in as she backed away, first one step, then another, and eased out of his reach. Rubbing her shoulder, the look on her face was a mix of pain and hatred.

"Sacha, what the hell did you do to Pazard'zhik?" Grendel asked.

"Why do you want to know?" she asked. "Are you communicating directly with the Kral, or are we being followed?"

The look on Grendel's face gave him away.

"The ranger and the dwarf! They're with you? Besserdechnaya dvornyaga!" Sacha screamed, her anger flaring again. Still cursing, Sacha wound her way around a broad mudpot, continuing her course away from the road.

"You cannot keep going that way. It is too dangerous."

"Well, I can't go back to the road, can I? That ranger's probably sitting there waiting for me, and you'd lead me right to him."

"I will stop you," Grendel growled threateningly.

Sacha turned around, hands on her hips. Globs of mud dripped around her. "Then stop me, but you might as well kill me yourself if you plan to take me to the Kral."

"What. Did. You. Do?!" Grendel roared.

"I got revenge on the Kral."

"Why do you hate him so much?"

The sad tone in his voice caught her by surprise. She tilted her head slightly, causing her hair to fall and hide her face as her shoulders slumped in defeat. "He killed my husband."

Silence reigned between Sacha and Grendel while they stared at each other. The only sound for several long minutes was the occasional plop of mud when a bubble broke the surface.

"I heard about that," Grendel finally sighed.

"What else did you hear?"

"I heard the Baron was killed while trying to sacrifice innocent people."

She laughed bitterly when he said *innocent* and turned her head, staring eastward. She watched the chuck wagon move toward the edge of the horizon. A few minutes more, and it would disappear altogether.

"The Kral took everything from me that day," Sacha said, still staring at the road. "My title, my station, my home. Everything was burning down around me, and I fled with my demon. I had to go into hiding after that night... pretend I died in the fire with so many others. With the demon's help, I contacted my husband's few remaining associates.

"Gregori knew what to do; he always does. He laid out this elaborate plan, but I only halfway listened. All I wanted was revenge on the Kral and the people of Pazard'zhik. Gregori told me my husband had a caravan that had already driven twice to Chernigov, with a third planned before winter closed the passes. He said it would be easy to use the soap to exact my revenge, and I could leave on the last train out. So, I agreed and took Sachin's place, delivering orders of soap while they handled the rest."

"People have died because of what you did."

She met his accusatory glare unflinching. "Don't you see? My family sent my brother, Marko, to bring me home.

In their eyes, I am a failure.  If he succeeds, he will take my place as the favored sibling."

"Was it the death of your husband or the fact you were disgraced?"

"What?"

"You have been so focused on taking revenge that you failed to see what was really happening," Grendel said. "Marko, Gregori, and D'yakon Krovos were already working together.  Could you not tell?"

Sacha looked back toward the chuck wagon traveling down the roadway.  Her eyes narrowed.

"You never stood a chance," Grendel said and took a tentative step toward her.  "Please.  Let me help you."

"Why?" she asked.

His eyes never wavered as he held her gaze.  "Because I may be the only one left who can."

# CHAPTER 14
# THE MUDPOTS

### October 26, 4235 K.E.

**1:42pm**

When asked later what it felt like, Yana could never recall exactly. It seemed to her that it should have hurt more, especially when she flew directly into one of the trees in the Haunted Wood.

With their flyers trailing smoke, she and her remaining squad member hurtled past the caravan and over the field of mud. Yana pushed on the sway bar, but it didn't respond. She was only dimly aware of the road passing a hundred yards or so to their south.

Then she hit the tree.

Smaller branches snapped off and showered the ground below, but the larger branches tore through the remains of her silk airfoil like the razor-sharp claws of a Volhynian cave bear. Her harness held her fast to the frame, and all she could do was bring her arms up to protect her head and prepare for impact when she struck the bole. The last thing she remembered was the smell of burnt hair and leather.

"Yana's coming around."

The gravelly voice seemed far away. Pain lanced through her forearm — it felt broken — and, just as quickly, was gone, replaced by a sharp prickly sensation. Portions of her skin, especially her neck, felt hard and crusty. She could only imagine what she looked like.

When she opened her eyes, the world was a blur. The first thing to come into focus was a row of tombstone-sized teeth. As her vision cleared, she could make out Chert leaning over her and staring down with a relieved smile. Grateful she was among friends, she relaxed and stared up at the blue sky through the forest canopy.

Kneeling on her other side, Xandor laid a hand on her shoulder. "You had us worried."

"Rumiana?  Maria?" she croaked.  Xandor shook his head and helped her sit up.  Chert held out a canteen, and she gratefully drank it dry.

"What happened?" she asked.

Xandor made a wry face and answered, "From where we sat, it looked like you were blown up."

"Feels like it," Yana said, staring down at her uniform and grimacing.  The scorched leather was black from ash and soot, obscuring its normal blue, and every seam had stretched.  Some exposed blackened wools, but others revealed her singed, red skin.  There was a bloody gash along her right forearm.  All in all, she felt lucky to be alive.

She caught them watching her.  "What is it?"

"Your hair.  It's a bit short," Xandor replied.

"It was short before."

"Not this short."

Yana reached up and touched her head.  Sure enough, the brittle ends of her hair ended just above her earlobes, where the fire snuck inside her helmet.  "It could be worse, I guess," she said.  "What happened to my weapons and gear?"

"Over there, with what's left of the flyers," Xandor replied, hitching a thumb over his shoulder.  "Once we were sure you'd survive, I figured you'd want to go through everything and see what you could salvage."

"Yana, what happened to Grendel?" Chert asked her gravely.

She looked down at her hands.  "I'm sorry, Chert.  I don't know.  I thought I saw him on the second wagon, but when our incendiaries went off, the horses and wagons got all jumbled.  I gave my ladies explicit instructions not to hit Grendel, but you can never tell with an operation like this."

Xandor asked, "What are you doing here, anyway?  You're a long way past your usual flight range."

"You didn't know we were coming?"

"No.  How could we?"

"Jasper sent us," she said, still trying to clear her head.

"Jasper... Not the Kral?"

"No.  The Kral thinks we deserted."

Xandor and Chert exchanged looks.

"What happened?" Xandor asked.  "Tell us everything."

"Not much to tell.  I met Jasper yesterday, and he told me about the soap.  He said we had to stop that caravan;

using our flyers was the only thing we could think of that would be fast enough to catch them before they reached Chernigov."

"Where is Jasper?"

"I don't know.  The last I saw, he was still in Pazard'zhik."

"Why didn't the Kral send soldiers to help you?"

"We never got a chance to talk with the Kral.  I do know Jasper talked to Marcus."  Yana slowly reached inside the leather breastplate of her uniform and showed them the gold chain with her brother's signet ring.

"How is Marcus?"

"Not good.  Jasper said he was in and out of consciousness when he saw him, but our stay was cut short when the Kral's Ochi i Ushi chased us away."

"Did Jasper find help at the White Circle?"

"I don't think so.  He said they tried to capture him."

Xandor swore and started pacing.  Occasionally, he stared toward the column of smoke and the smoldering wagon.

"Can someone tell me what's going on?" Yana asked.

"We're not really sure," Chert answered quietly.  He told her what they had learned at the clearing, repeating a lot of what Jasper had said previously.

Returning to their side, Xandor commented, "They've set a few ambushes for us along the way, but the attacks have only served to delay us, not stop us.  I'm afraid that may be part of their plan.  If they get to Chernigov first, we'll lose them."

"Xandor, would you make a small fire and heat some water?" Chert asked.  "Our prayers are helping her right now, but Yana isn't fit for travel.  Before we go after them, I want to make sure she's ready."

"I'm fine," Yana said.  As she made to rise, the world suddenly pitched to one side, and she had to steady herself.

Placing a gentle but firm hand on her shoulder, Xandor pushed her back down.  "You're not fine.  We'll stay here long enough for you to get your feet under you."  He glanced at the dwarf, who had walked to the rouncey and opened one of the saddlebags.  "Chert, you know what this means?"

"Aye.  No help means no cure."

"That's what I was thinking, too," Xandor said, collecting kindling for the fire.  "What do we do now?"

Chert retrieved a jar of ointment and a tin cup from his bag and said, "First priority is to get Yana up and moving." Stooping by the side of the road, he scooped up a handful of dirt and dropped it into the tin cup.  "While I do that, you go check out what's left of the caravan and see if there are any survivors.  I know you've been itching to go out there."

Xandor nodded, and the dwarf took the ranger's place at the fire.

When the water finally started to steam, Chert poured some into the cup, and let it steep a few minutes before helping Yana sit up.  "Here, drink this.  It will take the sting out of the burn, and this" he said, motioning toward the ointment, "will prevent scarring."

"What's in it?" she asked, giving the muddy water a tentative sniff.

"Do you really want to know?"

"If you want me to drink it, I better know what's in it."

"Hornblende, mica, sulphur, and a little kaolinite for the pain.  Tastes better with honey, but I'm out."

"You must be joking.  You really want me to drink this?"

"Aye."

Closing her eyes, she tilted the cup and gulped it down, grit and all.  She made a face and nearly gagged.  A spot of warmth spread from the back of her throat, and she felt it move through her body.  She gave the dwarf a wide smile when the sharp prickly sensation turned to a dull ache, and she found she could move without being dizzy.

Setting the cup aside, Chert helped Yana out of her armor.  With a prayer on his lips, he dipped his fingers into the ointment and spread it over the angry, red skin of her neck and hairline.  "Look up."  He covered her throat and the skin below her chin.

Turning to her shoulder, he said, "Now, let's get the rest of you."  Once complete, he surveyed his work to make sure he hadn't missed anywhere.  Satisfied, he nodded to himself and recapped the jar.

"Join me for a quick prayer."

"Sure," she replied and bowed her head.

Chert knelt in front of her and took her hands in his.  As his words implored the Eternal Father to grant a boon of healing, blue light emanated from his hands into hers and spread to her limbs.  It gave Yana the sensation of slipping into a perfect bath after a difficult mission.  Tension eased from her muscles, and the deep ache that accompanied serious bruising and fractures diminished.  When he finished, she felt almost normal.

"Thank you," she said simply as he sat back.

"Don't thank me, thank the Eternal Father," he responded.  "And he says you are welcome."  He grinned at her.  "Go walk around and tell me if you feel any pain."

While Chert put away his pot and cup, Yana stood, touched her toes, and stretched out the kinks.  As she straightened, she noticed a pile of stones near the edge of the road and tears came to her eyes.

"She was dead when we found her."

"Her name was Rumiana," Yana said.  After a moment of silence, she continued, "Thank you for burying her.  She deserved better.  Did you find Maria?"

"No.  I don't hold much hope that she'll ever be found."

The wind rider followed Xandor and Xerxes with her eyes as they made their way toward the hazy battlefield.  "Maybe they'll find her."  She scrubbed her hands over her face and turned back to the dwarf.  "Maria had been with me almost two years.  But Rumiana had only served with us for six months. So much potential and a love of life. I led her, them, here.  To this."

"You may have led them here, but I am sure they both knew full well and accepted the risks.  You fought dangerous foes.  And by the looks of it, your run was at least a partial success."

She nodded at his words but kept focused on the pile of stones while he spoke.  A moment later, she removed a small spinel pendant and, walking over to the cairn, hung it on a branch overhead.

"I'm sorry," she whispered.

Moving to the remnants of the two gliders, Yana shook her head.  She dug through the scraps of silk and broken struts, and it didn't take long to realize both were beyond repair.

With nothing else worth saving, she gathered her sica, the curved Trakyan shortsword that was standard issue to all members of the Wind Rider Legion, a matching dagger, and her father's bone-handled karakulak hunting knife, which rivaled the sica in length. After securing them to her belt, she scooped up her soot-covered barbute.

"You know, that thing saved your life," said Chert.

She crooked an eyebrow at him. He walked up, and she passed him the helmet, letting him study it.

The dwarf hadn't seen one before, but he had heard of them. He rotated the steel helm until the smoky crystal visor, inset into its T-slit opening for the eyes and mouth, faced him. "Its pre-Korellan — a Le'Urian helmet, if I'm not mistaken. Where did you get it?"

"To the victor go the spoils," Yana replied.

Giving it back, he commented, "I know one thing. I couldn't have healed you if the flames had cooked your head."


**2:03pm**

Keeping to the road, Xandor rode Xerxes out of the Haunted Wood and into the field of mudpots. The two moved at a fast clip, but not fast enough to cause a lot of noise. Thoughts of Grendel kept distracting him from the terrain.

Near the remains of the caravan, Xerxes slowed and cautiously avoided several smoking craters. The stench from the bodies — human, orc, and horse — clung to the road like a heavy pall. Xandor looked about, amazed that only one wagon remained. What appeared to be Ognian's charred remains sprawled across the driver's footboard.

Xandor jumped down from the saddle and inspected the wagon bed. Other than a single charred and broken crate, a few grey puddles, and the odd scrap of waxed paper, the soap was gone.

There was no sign of Grendel's body among the wreckage. Shielding his eyes with his hand, he quickly scanned the field of mudpots but didn't see anything resembling the tall half-orc.

Ignoring the bodies for the time being, Xandor tried to piece together the sequence of events. The attack and subsequent panic obliterated most of the tracks, but he was able to retrace the path of the caravan to the site of the first explosion. Based upon what he saw, the incendiaries landed directly atop the third wagon and spread forward. The corpses of the four Percherons attested to the severity of the aerial bombardment.  Their bodies lay in barely recognizable lumps of charred hair and meat.  Only the left lead horse appeared to have survived the initial strike, but the head and neck looked to have been the subject of a frenzied sword attack.

Xandor stepped around the orc body parts strewn across the cratered road.  Several of them had taken a direct hit from an incendiary.  Near the crumbling shoulder of the road, dark red and black swirls lapped the edge of a new, bubbling pool, making odd patterns on the surface.  Edging carefully around the oozing sludge, the ranger searched the vacant position of the second wagon.  A haphazard path of churned-up dust and dried mud led into the field of mudpots on the road's south side.  Seeing the deep craters, Xandor could understand the horses' panic, but the incendiaries had missed their target.  He visually followed the wagon's zigzagging trail to its abrupt end where it literally disappeared — with no sign of the wagon or its riders.

Turning back to the road, the ranger knelt beside the broken pieces of the abandoned chuck box.  Xandor suspected Marko's men had tossed it aside to make room for the salvaged soap.  Around the chuck box, the road held a puzzle all its own.  On the right-hand side, charred orc parts lay scattered about, while the left was scoured to bare dirt and ash in a rough semi-circular pattern.  However, nothing marred the middle of the road except wagon tracks and footprints.  Stranger still, there were only a few hoof prints showing agitated movement.  The lead Percherons had stood still during the whole attack!

Brow furrowed in thought, he picked his way back toward Xerxes.  Among the equine corpses, he found the scorched body of a boy who couldn't have been more than fifteen summers.  Still steaming, his heavy canvas pants, thick wool shirt, and sheepskin vest had fused with his skin.

"What in the world were you doing here, kid?" Xandor murmured.  Shaking his head, he continued on behind the lone wagon, where Xerxes guarded two more bodies.  They were dressed like warriors, but the heat from the blast warped and melted metal, charred leather, and rendered their bodies unidentifiable.

All in all, there weren't as many bodies as Xandor expected. He counted four Percherons, still strapped to their wagon, two rounceys, and four men in all. However, with all the carnage, it was impossible to tell how many orcs had died.

Xerxes stomped the ground nervously. The ranger patted his neck to calm him and said, "It's all right, boy. There's nothing here to harm us." As the sound of Xandor's soothing voice carried across the field, the crackling of movement answered it.

Not seeing anything, Xandor reached into his saddlebag and pulled out his spyglass. Panning across the field, he spotted two people walking at the edge of the southern horizon. Even though it was impossible to tell who they were at such a distance, he had a strong feeling Grendel was the taller of the two. However, they weren't what he had heard.

Adjusting his focus, he searched closer to the road. He still didn't see anything. Frustrated, he lowered his spyglass. After a minute, he saw movement at the end of the second wagon's trail. Its color just about matched the greyish white of the mud: a Percheron.

Xandor brought up his spyglass to confirm it. Sure enough, a draft horse still lived. He said to Xerxes, "You're not going to like this." The Andalusian eyed the ground between them and the Percheron. The look in his eyes said it all.

"It's not a crazy idea."

A snort escaped the horse.

"Look, we have to try."

Xandor retrieved his rope and tied off one end to Xerxes' saddle. "Hold this end for me."

He tied the other end around his waist and placed the remainder over his shoulder.

"You ready?"

Xerxes shook his head.

"Well, I'm going. Remember, if something happens to me, you'll have to handle Chert and Yana by yourself."

The horse cast a quick look back toward the edge of the woods. He glanced at the field of mud and back to the woods once more. Making up his mind, he cautiously stepped onto the thin crust.

"He's not that bad," Xandor said as he took another step.

He didn't need to look at Xerxes to get an answer. The horse responded with a rude noise that sounded remarkably like flatulence.

"Where did you learn to do that?"

Silence.

Xandor stopped and caught Xerxes staring at him.

Offended, Xandor protested, "That wasn't me."

A derisive snort echoed across the field.

"All right, but it wasn't just me. I heard some serious noise coming from your side of camp the other night."

Taking another cautious step, Xerxes quietly worked his way forward. He kept at least three feet on the ground at all times, causing him to gradually fall behind the ranger.

Xandor let the rope on his shoulder fall, loop by loop, as he followed the erratic trail of panicked horses and bouncing wagon. Here and there, hot mud oozed from a tracery of cracks where one horse or another hit the edge of a pool with a single hoof. As he went, he studied the terrain, working out how to tell solid ground from crusted over mudpots. The safest places seemed to be near the small, stubby trees scattered over the field like dark islands in a sulphureous lake.

It wasn't long before Xandor neared the end of the second wagon's trail. Twenty feet away, the draft horse floated in the bubbling mudpot, covered nearly to its withers. His broken traces swam around him like a pair of snakes, and the short length of chain attaching them to either side of the horse's halter jangled every time he moved. Wounded and tired, the Percheron attempted to climb up onto the crusty bank, but it gave way under his weight, causing him to sink deeper. Between Xandor and the horse, myriad cracks marred the surface of the ground, giving a clear indication how many times the horse had tried to escape.

The ranger weighed his options. There weren't many. Behind him, Xerxes stood near a stunted shrub. Xandor made sure the knot at his waist was still secure before easing out onto the broken ground. With each step, a loud, crunching sound met him and his feet sank below the surface. Stooping, the ranger crawled on all fours, distributing his weight. More cracks spread with each touch, and he laid down fully and crawled on his belly. He had done this once before when crossing a frozen river and could only hope it applied to dried mud as well.

The ground felt hot under his hands, but not from the sunlight. It came from underneath. Not needing any further motivation, he crept forward, keeping a steady count in his head to pace himself. All the while, he listened for signs the ground was about to give way but didn't hear any. Ahead of him, the Percheron waited, watching the ranger's progress.

Inch by inch, Xandor eased forward until he could reach across a short expanse of bubbling mud and press his hand against the Percheron's neck. The horse became excited, and Xandor had to wait for him to calm before trying his next trick. With an ominous crunch, the hardened mud beneath him shifted, forcing him to hold his breath until it stopped. He feared it wouldn't take much for it to collapse completely.

The ranger talked quietly, soothing the horse, and the ground stopped moving. With the Percheron relaxed, Xandor untied the rope from his waist. He wound the free end around the horse's harness and cinched it tight.

"Now comes the hard part," Xandor said aloud. "Xerxes, you ready?"

Xerxes responded with a soft whinny.

"Go ahead. Back up slowly, but make sure you stay near the trees."

The rope lifted as Xerxes stepped backward. A few more seconds, and it became taut, suspended in the air with mud dripping from it. The Percheron's throat touched the crusty edge of the mud. Eyes rolling, the horse panicked and began to kick.

"It's alright, boy," Xandor soothed. "We're going to take this nice and slow, but we have to crack this shell to get you back to shore." He pushed down on the false edge, breaking bits free as he wormed his way back.

Time seemed to stand still as they progressed by inches. At this rate, he feared the sun would set before they escaped back to the road. It came as a surprise when the toe of his boot touched the slight rise of shore.

"Hold," he called to Xerxes.

Rolling to one side, Xandor intended to get clear, but the Percheron became agitated and started to climb out of the pool again. The weakened ground instantly gave way, and Xandor fell into the bubbling mud. His first thought was that it wasn't as hot as he expected. The mud felt warm as it oozed inside his leather armor. Suddenly, it started to burn his skin.

With a shout, he grabbed the Percheron's harness and frantically hauled himself onto the horse. The added weight caused the Percheron to sink farther.

Xerxes steadily backed and pulled the draft horse through the pool.

Grimacing, Xandor hugged the horse around the neck. The Percheron's eyes rolled wildly when mud covered his nose. Praying the rope would hold, Xandor reached over and wiped the mud away from the horse's face.

Mud wrung from the rope as it creaked under the tension. Xerxes kept walking backward, his muscles bunched, but the rope only stretched. They were five feet from the edge, and Xandor thought he could jump for it. Apparently reading his mind, the Percheron gave the ranger a pleading look.

"Alright boy, we're in this together."

His words helped calm the Percheron. Together, they floated toward the bank and finally bumped it. Xandor tightened his arms around the horse's neck and yelled, "Now!"

Kicking with his back hooves and using the rope for leverage, the Percheron brought both its forelegs out of the mud as Xerxes hauled back on the rope for all he was worth.

Xandor and the Percheron exploded from the surface while the Andalusian continued backward, making sure they were clear. Reaching stable ground, the ranger let go of the horse and hastily peeled off his armor and boots. He took a spare shirt from his saddlebags and rubbed the horse's coat, wiping off the hot mud, revealing bright red skin under the white hair. As he did, he checked the horse for injuries. Other than favoring his right rear leg and being partially cooked, the Percheron seemed healthy.

"Let's not do that again," Xandor said with a gentle pat on the horse's shoulder.

The Percheron eyed him curiously, his muscles still shaking from the exertion.

"Alright, let's get out of here."

Back on the road, Xandor took one more look around the ruined remains of the caravan before he mounted Xerxes and directed him toward the Haunted Wood.  As he rode back to their makeshift camp, the ranger pulled his thin journal from a saddlebag and began writing a short note.  When finished, he glanced south where he last saw Grendel, but the horizon was empty.

# CHAPTER 15
# VERITAS AUTEM SUTEKH

## October 26, 4235 K.E.

**2:09pm**

Meditating in the middle of the clearing with his eyes closed, Jasper sat with the black tome in his lap and one of his cookbooks beside him. Busy thoughts kept intruding on his attempts to find his center.

Last night, the Blood of Cayn had whispered to him in his sleep. It wanted him to abandon these people and go back to the guild. He tried to block it, but the incessant muttering would not stop — it was driving him insane. Then came a moment of clarity. It told him he'd made a grave error. What it told him was serious enough that he had stayed up the remainder of the night wrapped in his cloak. Even now, it sent chills down his spine. He was scared, and when he found the two adults dead in their cages early this morning, it brought everything into focus for him. It was the Plague War all over again.

Jasper had sat next to Sehraine, watching her sleep. The whispering in his mind taunted him. It kept repeating, '*uoy yrrac ym doolb edisni dna won os seod eniarhes.*'

He could tell it had been more than a little disturbing for her to wake up with him staring at her. He remembered her asking what was wrong and when he didn't answer right away, it only made things worse. It tore him up when he told her that she might be infected with the Blood of Cayn. He had said it so quietly; she had asked him to repeat himself. At first, she denied it, telling him she felt fine, that he was being paranoid. Then her denial turned to anger as she stood over him with clenched fists. "How can you be sure?" she had asked heatedly. "You're not an expert. All you are is a troublemaker."

"You're right," he replied. "You're not showing any symptoms, but I need to know: did any of that black oil touch your skin when we were at the guild?"

A look of horror overcame Sehraine, and she buried her face in her hands. "I told you I didn't see anything, but everything happened so quickly."

Rising, Jasper wrapped Sehraine in a hug and held her. She pushed him away and wiped the tears from her eyes with the back of her hand. "If it did touch me, what do I look for? What's going to happen to me?"

He started by describing the elves that had been in the clearing. How they had changed. The look of horror on her face only grew as he went on, and he couldn't bring himself to tell her the worst of it. It didn't matter; she understood. After that, she hadn't said much, even going so far as to stand at the edge of the clearing. She blamed him, of course, but what else could he have done?

He looked down at his blackened hands, holding the book in his lap. As much as he disliked the idea of opening it, he needed answers. He cleared his mind of distractions like he was casting a spell, but instead of directing his magic outward, he focused it and wrapped it around the key elements of his psyche. His encounter at the guild made him realize just how vulnerable he was to that kind of attack.

Sorting through his memories, he chose those he felt best defined who he was. It was all subjective, but the course the necromancer, Gregori, had taught a lifetime ago stressed the importance of Self and being in the Now. Those lessons came back to him, and he followed what Gregori said to the letter.

Jasper didn't claim to have an eidetic memory; however, when it came to magic and arcane lore, he had a knack for retaining complex formulas. His teachers had been adamant that to be a good wizard, a student had to be good at memorizing spells and maintaining the level of concentration necessary to bend the forces of nature to his will. Jasper had learned exercises to enhance his memory, but most of the time it just came naturally. He went through what he had been taught one last time.

Feeling he was as ready as he was going to be, he opened his eyes. He slowly opened the tome and was immediately disappointed. Leafing through the first few pages, he found the writing indecipherable.

Kolev had, with very specific language, warned him about possessing this book. So, as Jasper turned the pages, he kept his mind neutral. By treating the book as if it belonged to someone else, he tried to distance himself from the writings. Some magical texts could only be read by their owner — he hoped this wouldn't be the case with the information he sought.

Midway through the book, his blackened fingers stuck to the pages, leaving fingerprints. Great. Keeping his focus, he scanned the pages for anything useful. As he moved through the book, he noticed the handwriting changed styles, but the content remained gibberish.

Turning page after page, he expected to get closer to the end of the book but was still only midway through it. Thinking he would try skipping to the end, he attempted to close the book. Nothing happened — his hands wouldn't respond. He tried turning to the next page, and his hands and fingers acted normally. Weird. Changing tactics, he reversed course and flipped through the pages backward. Odd diagrams and sketches appeared on the pages where writing had been just moments before.

In the margin, someone had scribbled an incantation. Before he could stop himself, he whispered the arcane phrase, infusing it with his magic. As he spoke the last word, a tremendous force grabbed hold of him and pulled, sucking him towards the book. Panic seized his heart when he realized it was not just towards but *into* the book. Jasper resisted. He felt his back bowing under the weight, and his face drew closer and closer to one of the diagrams. The more he resisted, the faster his thoughts whirled. His mind spun, disorienting him, and causing his nausea to grow. The taste of bile collected at the back of his mouth.

When the world stopped spinning, he found himself standing among the ruins of ancient homes. From the way the structures flowed into and out of the tall trees, he knew it must have once been an elven village. It was the same abandoned village he had seen when he touched the magical cabin in the clearing but now in vivid detail. All the trees and plants were bleached of their color, warped and twisted like an old man's fingers. He felt a great sadness about the place, but also a great fear. Something was out there.

Jasper looked up, expecting to see the sky; instead, he saw the inside surface of a magical dome of green light that covered the entirety of the village.

He cursed silently. How could he have been so stupid? If the book had taken in an arch-mage, what chance did he have? Why was he taking this huge risk? Was it pride?

"A sin," said a voice. A dark form appeared out of nowhere. It wore a hooded robe to conceal its nature, but Jasper saw bright silver eyes peering from the cowl.

"Where am I?" Jasper asked.

"Nowhere," it responded.

"I don't recognize this place. What are you showing me?"

"Do you know who I am?"

"You are the *Veritas autem Sutekh* — the truth of the Dark One."

The bright silver eyes shone with amusement. "You are not an arch-mage."

"No. I'm a simple mage looking for answers to a riddle."

"Speak your riddle, simple mage."

"I seek the cure to the Blood of Cayn."

Somehow, the light in the village dimmed, and the air turned foul.

"There is no cure."

"There has to be a cure; there must be."

"In the pages of the tome you possess, you will find a formula. One of Unity. One with roots founded in the origins of elves and all the other races. The Blood of Cayn is a part of that; it cannot be undone."

"*Veritas autem Sutekh,* as you say, there may not be a cure, but there must be a balance."

"Then you have the answer to your riddle."

Looking around, Jasper saw the image of an old trader's wagon. Laying on the tailgate were the remains of a broken barrel. Its wooden bands were split, and the top lay on the ground. Black oil from the barrel covered the warped tailgate and constantly dripped into a pool beneath it; however, every time one drop fell, another drop fell upwards, maintaining a constant volume between the two levels. Footprints traversed the pool and left a trail of black slime leading toward the edge of the village.

"Where am I?" Jasper asked again. "And don't tell me nowhere."

"You are at the beginning, of sorts."

"This looks more like the end."

"It may be, but it also represents one of the origins of the Blood of Cayn."

"Is this what caused the Plague War?"

"Yes."

A part of Jasper wanted to study the substance and understand it. Instead, he asked, "Can it be destroyed?"

"No."

Damn. Jasper tried to think of another way to ask the question but drew a blank. Using a brainstorming technique he had learned in school, he replayed the past few days. He went over in his mind the story related by the elves and suddenly recalled something they had mentioned.

"Where do I find the Tear of Havel?" Jasper asked.

The evil presence grew, and Jasper resisted the urge to turn and flee. The scene before him changed. He stood in an old, dilapidated chapel. Masonry walls, black from soot, surrounded him, but what caught his eye was an odd-shaped opening where a window once resided. The jagged edges resembled a sawtooth pattern — the same pattern from the window now in Tsarevets.

The sun shone down from above. A bluish-purple crystal, resting on the altar, sparkled in the light. Taking a step forward for a better look, he estimated the crystal to be about ten inches long. It had a wide, rounded edge along one end and tapered to a sharp point, like a teardrop. While he stood at the altar, the *Veritas autem Sutekh's* power seemed somehow diminished. It gave him hope.

"Why did Asenov want the Blood of Cayn?"

"He didn't."

"Then who did?"

"Who can say?"

"You must answer me," Jasper pleaded.

"You do not yet possess the *Veritas autem Sutekh*. If you require such knowledge, then you must claim me as your own."

Wrestling with himself, Jasper thought of all the things he could do with this knowledge. He could cure Sehraine and himself. He could... "No. Keep your secrets. I've seen what you have done."

"Just remember: the knowledge is at your fingertips," the *Veritas autem Sutekh* whispered.

With that, Jasper lifted his blackened hand and found himself back in the clearing.  He hadn't moved.  The black tome still occupied his lap, but now it was closed.  The remaining teamsters stood around him, watching.  It hadn't felt that long, but when he looked up, the evening's first stars dotted the sky.  A small campfire flickered next to him, providing warmth for their makeshift camp.  He heard the ragged breathing of the children in the cages.

"Are you alright?" Sehraine asked, sitting beside him.

"What?" Jasper responded, still deep in thought.  "Yes.  Yes, just thinking."  Part of him felt relieved she was talking to him again.  Yosif and Dragahn stood behind her, casting frightened glances toward both the mage and the surrounding trees.

"What did you find out?"

"I'm not really sure," Jasper murmured.  "Have you ever heard of an elven village hidden by a green light?"

"No.  Can you describe the village?"

As Jasper described the homes and general layout of the streets, tears formed in Sehraine's eyes.  Jasper kept talking, his focus on the images in his mind rather than his companion, making him blind to the rising horror and pain he caused.  When he described the wagon with its broken barrel and the pool of black blood, she covered her face with her hands and slowly crumpled to the ground.  She lay curled in a fetal position, shaking.

"Jasper, stop," Dragahn said softly.

Shocked by her reaction, Jasper gently lifted Sehraine back into a sitting position and pulled her close so she could cry on his shoulder.  "Sehraine, what's wrong?"

"M...m...my father," she sobbed.

"Oh, god, Sehraine, I'm sorry.  I didn't know," he whispered, holding her tight.

When her tears finally slowed, and she pulled away from Jasper, Pyotr stepped forward and produced a handkerchief.  Taking it, she gave the horse doctor a sad smile and used it to dry her face.

"It's your home?" Jasper asked.

"Enough, Jasper.  Leave it alone," Dragahn said.

"I must know," Jasper said.

"You're right," Sehraine said. "It was my home... once." She closed her eyes and took a shuddering breath to bolster her courage. "My father drove that wagon."

"Sehraine, I'm so sorry," Jasper said.

"Don't be. I haven't spoken of it for years, not even to Yana. I need to tell someone," she said. "Before the great plague, my father ran a trade route between our village and Pazard'zhik."

"You traded wine, didn't you?"

A surprised look came over her face, and she asked, "How did you know?"

"Not important," Jasper answered quickly, avoiding her gaze. Then he asked, "What happened?"

"I was stupid," she murmured. "My mother died when I was born. Once a year, my father and uncle took wine and crafts to Pazard'zhik to trade. Most of my childhood was spent with my grandparents, hoping my father would hurry home. He always brought back such interesting *things*. When I was old enough, he let me travel with them. Normally, when we went to Pazard'zhik, we stayed a few days, took in the sights, and, sometimes, my father would take me to the Naroden Teatar. The Elders frowned upon us spending so much time with humans, but they granted my father some leniency because of the goods he brought back to the village.

"During our last trip, the theater was all I could think about. I told him I didn't want to trade wine forever and one day would move away from the village and become an actress. Looking back now, I can see I hurt his feelings. When I asked my father if we could go to the theater, he refused, saying we needed to get back before the pass closed for winter. We argued, of course, and I think that only made him more determined. On the last day, we hardly spoke to one another. He told me to watch the wagon while he traded our last barrel of wine. Something snapped, and I yelled at him — I told him he had wasted his life trading, and I didn't want to end up like him. Afterward, I ran away. To this day, I don't know why. I just ran and ran. I don't even know if my father and uncle looked for me. All I know is that I didn't want to go home. Then the Plague War started, and I was trapped behind the Stena."

"But that was over thirty years ago!" Yosef exclaimed. "How old *are* you?"

"Hush, Lucky," Pyotr admonished.  "It's rude to ask a lady her age, no matter how young she looks."

Jasper ignored the byplay between the teamsters. "Have you ever been back?" he asked.

"No."

"Why?"

She started crying again.  "I don't know.  I guess I was scared of what I might find."

Jasper turned and knelt in front of her.  He placed both hands on her shoulders and felt her shudder.  "Sehraine, I have reason to believe that we will need to go to your village, and if I'm right, no one, especially you, will like what we find."

She stared at him, wide-eyed.  "Don't ask me to do this," she said in a tiny, scared voice.

"I won't ask you, but there are things I feel you should know.  Things you must see."

"What are you not telling me?"

Jasper's expression turned grave when he answered, "I would rather not say.  Not until I know for sure."

On the verge of more tears, she eyed him fearfully.

Taking a deep breath, he asked, "Have you heard of anything called the Tear of Havel?"

"Yes.  It was an artifact the Elders of my village kept at the lodge."

"What was it?"

"A dagger made of crystal."

"A dagger?  That's not what I saw."

"If you knew what it was, why did you ask me?"

"Testing a theory."

"Do you think what you saw may be a lie?"

Jasper answered slowly, collecting his thoughts.  "Not a lie in the truest sense, but not necessarily the truth, either.  At least, not as we see it.  Is this dagger still at your village?"

"I don't know."

"The *Veritas autem Sutekh* showed me a place.  I'm pretty sure it was moved before the war to a monastery outside of Chernigov."

Dragahn made a noise, and the other teamsters grumbled at the name.  "That's bad news, then," the teamster chief said.  "The place is crawling with orcs."

"Orcs!" Sehraine exclaimed.

Jasper huffed out an exasperated sigh. "Nevertheless, that is where we must go," he said and turned to look at Sehraine. "I can't ask you to go. If you want, I'm sure Dragahn will let you stay here with him."

Drying her eyes, Sehraine looked around and exclaimed, "You can't just abandon these men and the children!"

Jasper raised his blackened hands and said, "I don't have a choice."

"He's right," Dragahn said, stepping closer. "I wish you could have brought help with you, but it doesn't change the fact that a cure *must* be found. Tomorrow morning, we'll start back to the Stena after we make some litters to carry the children."

"Jasper Thredd of Tydway," a hollow voice said from the edge of the firelight.

The words startled everyone, causing them to glance around. Grey men dressed in grey robes surrounded them. They brought with them no light. In fact, they seemed to darken the campsite, stealing the warmth from the small campfire.

Rising, Jasper approached one of the figures. He bowed deeply and said, "Master Kolev, I did not expect to see you outside the White Circle."

"We were sent to tell you the Kral received your message. He is aware of your progress."

"Good. Do you or he know of a cure?"

"No, and with the White Circle in the state it's in, there is little hope they will find it. We tried questioning the mages who took over the guild, but all we found was madness."

Jasper thought for a moment and said, "Master Kolev, I think the Tear of Havel somehow holds the key to the cure."

"Did the *Veritas autem Sutekh* tell you that?" Kolev snapped.

"Yes and no. It did not give me any straight answers."

The ghostly arch-mage drew close to Jasper and warned, "You, too, are bound by the same charter we are. The Kral will consider your oath broken if you fail. Be aware of the choices you make." The arch-mage glanced at Sehraine before saying, "They affect us all — not just you."

Taking a step back, Master Kolev surveyed the crowd around him and announced, "The Kral sent us to bring all of you back.  He wishes to speak with you."

Fear crept into everyone's eyes.

Gripping his staff tighter, Jasper said, "You can't take us to the Kral now.  Sehraine and I must find the Tear of Havel.  It's our only hope."

Sehraine nudged Jasper and asked in a low whisper, "Can you even find this Tear of Havel?"

"Yes.  It's either that or give up now, and I'm not ready for that."

"Me either," she said with quiet determination.

Kolev stared at the two people, weighing them.  "You have done us a great service by alerting us to the evil in our own guild.  I will grant your request and delay your audience with the Kral."

"What about the *Veritas autem Sutekh*?" Jasper asked.

"Keep it, but remember my warning."

Jasper shuddered at the thought of serving the Kral in perpetuity.

Kolev looked around impatiently at the teamsters and said, "We must go.  The Kral awaits."

Sehraine stood and handed the handkerchief back to Pyotr.  He waved his hand and said, "I won't be needing it."

"Thank you," Sehraine said.  "All of you."

Pyotr slapped Jasper on the shoulder and said, "You owe us a meal."

Jasper replied, "You're on.  Make sure you burn everything you don't take with you."

Pyotr nodded with a grim smile and said, "Don't mother us; we got it."

Next in line was Yosif.  Jasper gave the youth a bear hug.  "Take care of these men, will ya?"

A muffled voice answered, "You got it."

Letting Yosif go, Jasper gripped Dragahn's hand and shook it firmly.  "Good luck."

"You, too."

The teamsters, along with the hollow men, watched the two prepare for their journey.  Jasper packed his books into his sporran, including the black tome.  When they were ready, he and Sehraine stood apart from the others, and Jasper drew a circle in the dirt with his staff.

"Where are we going?" asked Sehraine.

"To find Xandor, Chert, and Grendel."

"Where do you think they are?"

Holding the mental image of his spice container firmly in his head, he pointed and said, "That way."

# CHAPTER 16
# RATS

October 26, 4235 K.E.

**4:41pm**

At the far edge of the field of mudpots, Grendel and Sacha walked through the remains of a ghost town. By the looks of it, the people had abandoned it some time ago, maybe even before the Kral ordered his people behind the Stena. A single street stretched before them, dotted here and there with weeds. On their left, a three-story brick building loomed, its windows hidden behind weathered and warped shutters. Farther down on the right, two shorter brick buildings huddled under grey-green creeping vines. Along the rest of the street, where wooden buildings once stood, old masonry foundations lay partially buried beneath dirt and debris.

Grendel stared northward, hoping to catch a glimpse of the road. Behind him, tree-covered foothills dotted the southern horizon. Returning his attention to their immediate surroundings, he scanned the area for signs of trouble. Pieces of wooden boards and planks littered the ground, left over from homes and shops that had fallen over from rot and neglect. At a quick guess, it appeared that at least ten to fifteen structures had stood here at one time.

The two had successfully traversed the field of mudpots, but the constant tension had taken its toll. With no food or water, the desperate need to find a hospitable settlement weighed on the bodyguard. "There should be a well nearby," Grendel said. "Let us find it and then rest."

In front of Grendel, Sacha said quietly, "We're being watched."

He glanced up at the nearest brick building, thinking he saw movement. "I feel it too."

Beside an old foundation wall, the remains of a humanoid rib cage jutted out from under some brush. "These are fresh," Sacha said as she picked up a loose rib bone. "I think it's an orc."

Grendel stopped as the hairs on the back of his neck stood up. Even though he took deep, regular breaths, adrenaline coursed through him. Whoever was out there wouldn't watch them forever.

"Take a look at this," she said, handing him the rib. "Feel these scratches."

Grendel rubbed his fingertips where she indicated. Deep grooves scored the bone.

"What did that?" she asked. "Vermin?"

"Maybe. They seem too large for a field mouse."

"I've seen some big rats."

"Have you seen rats big enough to leave marks like these?" he asked as he tossed the bone back among its mates.

"It may not be safe to stay here," she said, her eyes darting from one shadow to another.

A scuttling sound echoed off one of the masonry buildings, and loose mortar trickled from the windowsill. Grendel unslung his battle-axe and walked cautiously toward the building.

Picking up a thick thighbone, Sacha followed him. Silence settled around them, and the fading sun cast bleak shadows across the faces of the abandoned buildings.

Out of the corner of his eye, Grendel caught a flash of brindle-colored fur. A huge, squealing rat leapt from one of the dark windows. Slipping past his axe, it hit the half-orc's chest like a missile, taking them both to the ground. Nasty yellow-brown teeth snapped at his neck, and thick saliva spattered his tunic. Grendel dropped his axe and frantically grabbed at the rat, trying to stop it from reaching anything vital.

With a shout, Sacha swung her makeshift club and struck the side of the rat's head. The thighbone snapped with a loud crack.

The squealing rat turned its beady eyes toward Sacha, who stood rooted in place. It stared at her with eyes that shone with human intelligence.

Grabbing a handful of fur, Grendel flung the rat at the masonry wall as hard as he could. The impact crushed the bricks. He grabbed his battle-axe and rolled to his feet in a single motion, placing himself between Sacha and the stunned rat.

Snarling, the rat shook itself.  Its muscles bunched and loosened as it shifted its weight.

Grendel tightened his grip on his axe.

The rat jumped.  Grendel took a step back and smacked the rat with the haft of his axe, sending it to the ground. Changing his grip, he brought one of the axe blades down, cleaving the rat's body in two.

Transfixed, he and Sacha watched the rat's legs twitch on the blood-soaked ground.  With a cracking of bone and sinew, the rat's body changed.  Grendel took another step back and placed a hand protectively on Sacha's arm.  The rat's body reverted into that of a small, naked man.

From the windows and doorways on either side of the street, pairs of beady eyes stared down at them maliciously. Sacha gasped and pointed with the broken bone still clenched in her fist.  "Look," she whispered.  He jerked his eyes away from the body on the ground and saw the creatures glaring back at them.

"There are so many of them," she said urgently.

"Let us make a run for it," Grendel suggested.

"Where?"

"Depends."

"On what?"

"Will you trust me?"

He felt her tense, heard her breathing.  Grendel didn't take his eyes off the buildings; he didn't have to.  He felt her worry and suspicion.

"What do you have in mind?" she asked.

"We need to go back to the road."

"Why?  Won't they follow us?"

"Yes, but they are rats, confident in their numbers.  We need to even the odds."

"How do you expect to do that?"

"Wait for my friends and hope they have not already passed us by."

"No!" she exclaimed, backing away.

He threw a quick glance over his shoulder.  Sacha glared at him, the broken bone raised as if to keep him at bay.

"Sacha, we need food, water, and allies.  We will not find any of those things out here."

"How do I know you won't turn me over to the ranger?"

"You do not.  That is why it is called trust."

The silence was palpable.

The eyes peering out from the buildings slunk back into the darkness followed closely by scrabbling sounds throughout the ghost town.

"Sacha, you have to make up your mind, or we are both going to die."

"It's not that easy."

"Nothing ever is."

"What's that supposed to mean?" she asked with an edge to her voice. She crossed her arms and pressed her lips together tightly.

"It means we are out in the middle of nowhere, surrounded by the gods know what, and you are more worried about a single ranger than making it out of here alive."

"You can't force me to see the Kral."

"Yes, I understand, but right now, I have more pressing matters on my mind."

Giant rats crawled over the nearby foundations. Instead of charging, they changed shape into a hybrid form of both rat and man. They stood on legs like men but retained much of their rodent-like appearance.

"We have to run."

"Damn it."

"Can I take that as a 'yes'?"

"*Yes*, you big lummox. We'll do it your way."

Side by side, the two ran for all they were worth. Behind them, a relentless tide of rat-men and huge rodents flowed around the mudpots. Grendel had never experienced being on someone's menu and decided rather quickly he could have happily done without it.


**5:25pm**

The road came up faster than expected. Grendel stopped and turned. The sun had dropped below the horizon, painting the western sky in swathes of blood and dark purple bruises. From the east, the black cloak of night raced toward them, and the landscape swam in the half-light before true darkness fell. Everywhere he looked, vermin clung to rocks and limbs. Sacha stood next to him, quivering with fear. Grendel tried to imagine what it must be like for her, the coming night slowly devouring her ability to see the danger lurking all around them. It took true bravery for her to stand rather than continue running.

Swinging his axe to loosen his shoulders, he watched the mass of vermin boiling beyond the edge of the road while the rat-men hung back. '*Cowards*,' he decided. Placing Sacha in the center of the road, he said, "Stay here. Do not move."

She opened her mouth to protest, but he turned his back on her and drew a circle around them with one of the blade-tips of his battle-axe. Facing the rats, Grendel lifted his axe in front of his heart onehanded and dipped his head. "Alea iacta est." *The die is cast.*

Grendel began his dance. At least, that was the closest word she could come up with to describe it. His battle-axe became an extension of his body and swept about him in wide, fantastic arcs. Each time his axe dropped, loud squeals and coughs followed.

His body flowed as he moved around her, staying within the circle he had drawn. She became mesmerized by his grace and precision, but she didn't dare move. Not from fear of rats, but because Grendel's axe moved faster and faster, a whistling blur in the darkness. It passed so close she felt the rush of air in its wake.

The wave of rats kept coming. Grendel's swings became more desperate as the rodents constantly tested him, causing him to waste energy. Behind the ranks of fodder, the rat-men waited patiently, and Grendel silently cursed the terrain. There was nowhere for them to go.

Sweep after sweep, he tried making each dead rat an example, hoping the rest might turn and run, but they knew it was just a matter of time before his strength failed. Sweat dripped from his forehead, and he felt his timing start to slip. He swung his battle-axe in long sweeping arcs, but most of the rats either scampered out of its way or flattened themselves and let the blade ride over them.

While their tactics were partially successful, the mounting pile of bloodied bodies along the edge of the circle attested to those rats who were either too slow or too clumsy to avoid the axe. Grendel used the small barrier to his advantage, but he couldn't be everywhere.

When the next wave attacked, two hybrids slunk into the circle.  Sacha shrieked when one grabbed her arm and stabbed wildly with her dagger.  The hybrid stiffened under the magic, and Sacha's next blow plunged into the creature's heart.  The other hybrid shoved her into Grendel's back, almost catching her on the swiftly moving axe blades.

Grendel stumbled forward and planted his axe into the surface of the road.  "Duck!" he growled.

Sacha bent just as Grendel's axe swept over her, separating the hybrid's head from his shoulders.  With Grendel's rhythm disrupted, the rats raced into the circle.  The two stood back-to-back, their weapons out, and kicked, stomped, chopped, and stabbed at the fleet forms.

Over the sound of the battle, they heard a high-pitched voice from beyond the rats.  "Kill yourself now, humans!  Save us the trouble!" it laughed mockingly.

Grendel kept quiet.  He brought his axe back around and was rewarded with several squeals.  Focused on the rats as he was, he didn't feel the ground vibrate.

However, the rats did.  They all turned toward the staccato sounds of horses galloping toward them.

"Hee-ya!"

Xerxes raced through the swarm of vermin, trampling them.  Igniting his longswords, Xandor jumped and landed outside Grendel's circle, sweeping his swords back and forth.  Chert rushed in with his hammer and shield ready.

Squealing rats fled across the field toward the abandoned town.  At the edge of the firelight, the hybrids stared malevolently at the ranger, but they, too, quickly turned tail and ran.

"Glad you could join us," Grendel said, feeling as if a great weight had been lifted from his shoulders.

"Wouldn't miss it," Chert replied, smiling.

"Where'd they go?" a female voice asked from beyond the edge of Xandor's light.

"Yana?  Is that you?" Grendel asked, his eyes wide with surprise.

"Heard you were having a rat party and couldn't resist."

"I think they're gone," Xandor said, stepping over the border of rats into the circle, Yana right behind him.

"I've never seen or heard of rats that big," she said. "Have you?"

Probing the dead rats on the ground, the ranger said, "Never seen any myself, but I've heard rumors."

"There were shape-shifters among them," Grendel said.

Sure enough, they found two humans buried among the dead rats. Chert reached into his pouch and produced a piece of quartz, about the size of a man's thumb, which cast a pale light. He examined the bodies, closed their eyes, and murmured a prayer over their still forms.

Burning blade held high, Xandor crossed back to the edge of the road, searching for the glint of eyes, but found none.

Grendel remained near Sacha while he watched his friends work. He hadn't realized just how high strung he had become. For the first time since leaving Pazard'zhik, he could breathe easy.

"Are you injured?" Chert asked as he walked up to the two of them.

Adrenaline still pounding in his veins, Grendel had to look to be sure, but he appeared unscathed. The dwarf and the half-orc turned to Sacha. She had a long scratch across her shoulder where the hybrid had pushed her.

Chert's expression turned grim when he saw it. "I need to tend that."

"I've had worse."

"Maybe. Now let me see it."

"Keep your hands off me, dwarf!" Sacha said, backing up.

"Look, human, you have a choice. Either I tend to it, and it heals nice and easy, or you run the risk of infection. Have it your way, but with these being shape-shifters..." Chert glanced at the position of the stars before he continued, "I would guess you have two days before you turn."

Horror spread over her face, and she stepped closer to Grendel, as if the dwarf had threatened to attack her. Grendel thought he saw a hint of disapproval in Chert's expression.

Xandor remained outside the circle of light and sheathed his swords. He made no secret of listening to everything being said.

"Can you help me?" Sacha finally asked.

"Maybe.  It depends if their saliva got in the wound.  A scratch, I can heal, but a bite wound..."

"Fine.  Just do it."

While Chert tended to Sacha's scratches, Xandor motioned Grendel aside.  "That's Baroness Krakova," he whispered harshly.  "What is she doing here?"

The half-orc looked down at the ranger, not sure what to say.  He had gone over this moment in his head several times, but still had not come up with a good answer.  Grendel looked away when Yana joined them.

Xandor stared at the half-orc, waiting for him to speak.  Beside them, Yana shifted impatiently.  "What's going on, Grendel?"

"She needed my help," Grendel said simply.  His eyes followed Sacha's every move.

"What?" Xandor asked incredulously.  "Have you lost your mind?  She's the enemy."

"I know how this looks but give her a chance."

"Xandor, he doesn't know," Yana said quietly.

"Know what?"

Leaning closer to Xandor, she lowered her voice, "He doesn't know you're the one who killed her husband."

Grendel's face turned ashen.  Recalling all her protests, he began to suspect Sacha's motives.  Had she tricked him so she could have a shot at the ranger?  He looked from Sacha to Xandor and back again.

"The question is, does *she* know," Xandor said.

"Let's find out," Yana replied.

# CHAPTER 17
# SECRETS REVEALED

### October 26, 4235 K.E.

**5:43pm**

"Chert!" Xandor called.

"Done," came the dwarf's swift reply.

Sensing she was in danger, Sacha surged to her feet, but the dwarf's spell was cast.  She managed a single step before something wrapped around her legs.  A second struggling step, and she looked down to find herself encased up to her waist in rapidly solidifying mud.

"Dwarf!  I swear by Sutekh if you don't let me go, you'll regret it!" she screeched.

Chert's face turned beet red, and his beard bristled. "There will be no swearing here, young lady, especially to the Dark One."

"I'll swear any way—"

"Any more curses or oaths to the Dark One," Chert interrupted, "and we'll see how you enjoy life as a marble statue.  Got it?"

Sacha's eyes darted from the dwarf to Grendel, but the half-orc stared at her, his expression guarded.  Xandor walked toward her, unsheathed his sword, and placed the tip against her throat.

"No more games, Baroness."

She stared up the length of the ranger's longsword into his heterochromatic eyes.  One the color of spring leaves, the other the frozen grey of a winter sky, neither held a hint of mercy.  His professional detachment comforted her — this was something with which she was familiar.  "You want no more games?  Fine.  Kill me now, ranger, like you killed my husband, and let's get this over with."

A cold wind swept across the group.  Grendel stepped forward, and Sacha saw him search the darkness for her demon, ignoring the wind rider's restraining hand on his wrist.

With a bitter smile, Sacha met Xandor's narrow-eyed stare, resigned to face her death unflinching, but he dropped the tip of his sword.

"You knew all along?" Grendel asked, jerking his hand from Yana's grip and taking a few steps closer toward Sacha.

"No, not the whole time.  Let's just say a friend told me."

"That demon is not your friend," Grendel growled.

Yana gasped and Chert made a sign against evil.  Even Xandor took a step back.

"What demon?" Chert demanded.

"She has a demon protecting her."

Sacha eyed Grendel suspiciously and asked, "When we were at the mudpot, you talked with him, didn't you?"

"Yes.  He told me some of what you have done, but I also know he lied — or at least spoke in half-truths."

Sacha could hear the pain and betrayal in his voice.  She took in the expressions the others wore, particularly the dwarf, and wondered if that was what sympathy and compassion looked like.  *'How does it feel to have friends like these*?' she wondered.  *'To know there are people who won't use your every weakness against you*?'

"Even here, at the end, you used me," Grendel added.

Her eyes downcast, she whispered, "It's the only way I know how to survive."

"Release her," Grendel said firmly.  "You have my word she will not harm anyone here."

Chert searched the face of his longtime friend and finally nodded.  He closed his eyes, and Sacha lurched forward, no longer bound.

Grendel caught her and pulled her against his chest, stroking her hair.  The others fidgeted and looked away from his open display of affection, keeping a watchful eye out for the demon.

Turning to Yana, Grendel said, "I have to ask.  There were some things the demon told me, and I need to know the truth."

"Sure.  Anything."

"Is Marcus dead?" he asked carefully.

"No," Yana answered quickly, but then, in a softer voice, she added, "He's tough; he'll pull through."

Pausing, Grendel looked Yana in the eyes and asked the hardest question of all. "Did Jasper send you to kill me?"

Yana blinked in surprise. He saw her shake her head, even as she considered her answer. Finally, she said, "No. He asked me to stop the caravan, not kill you. He warned me that you would be on the second wagon, and to be careful. You have to believe me. He did everything he could to prepare me and my squad. Even though I lost two of my girls on this, I don't blame him."

"I'm glad to hear you say that," a weak voice said out of the darkness.

"Of course, if he were standing here, I would still punch him in the eye," she quickly amended.

The light from the crystal Chert held aloft intensified, driving away the darkness for a score of yards in every direction. Caught in the sudden glare, Jasper raised his arm from Sehraine's shoulder and pulled his hood lower over his eyes.

"How long have you been there?" Xandor asked.

"Just arrived, actually," Sehraine replied.

The world spun a bit too fast for the mage, and he swayed on his feet. Only Sehraine's support and his white knuckled grip on his staff kept him upright. "I need to sit," he murmured to the elf. Together, they staggered over to the side of the road, where she helped him down, then arched her back in a joint-popping stretch.

"What's wrong? Are you hurt?" Xandor asked, alarmed.

Yana rushed over and wrapped the young elf in a hug, then held her at arm's length and looked her up and down for injuries.

"Tired," Jasper replied. "Tired and sick."

"Not that I'm unhappy to see you, Sehraine, but *why* did you come?" Yana asked.

"I didn't have much choice," Sehraine replied with a shrug.

Wrinkling her nose, Yana glared at the mage. "Jasper, you smell like death."

"Thanks."

"You were a part of this, too?" Sacha demanded.

"Yes, Baroness. I'm afraid so." Jasper turned his gaze to Xandor, his expression filled with sadness laced with fear.

"I've contracted the plague that's running rampant through Pazard'zhik.  Every spell I cast makes it worse."

Xandor glanced at Sehraine and then back to Jasper and asked, "What happened?"

Jasper recounted all that had happened to him, including his encounter with the Blood of Cayn and escaping from the mages' guild the second time.  With Sehraine filling in portions, it wasn't long before everyone was caught up.

"How can you be infected and not me or Sehraine?" Yana asked.  "We've all just come from Pazard'zhik."

"It's the soap...  It *chooses* its victims," Jasper answered.  "It acts as if it's alive."

"Alive?" Xandor asked.  "How is that even possible?"

"It's Gregori.  Something he learned from the helrúnan in Chernigov," Sacha declared.  She stepped away from Grendel, her eyes probing, noting what she could see of Jasper's face and hands.  "He wanted to infect everyone in that camp, including you and the teamsters, and study you."

"You bitch!" Yana yelled.  "It was your soap!"  The wind rider charged forward with hot tears in her eyes, her hands aiming for Sacha's throat, and her blades forgotten.

Sacha's hand flew to the dagger at her waist.  Grendel grabbed her wrist with one hand and blocked Yana with the other.  The wind rider tried to slip past, but the half-orc kept himself between the two women.

Sehraine darted behind Yana and caught her in a hug that pinned her arms to her sides.  "As much as she might deserve it, killing her will not save Marcus." Her words hit everyone like a splash of ice-cold water.  Sacha glared at Yana and Sehraine for a moment, then dropped her gaze.

"She left us to die — to be eaten by the dwolma," Jasper said.  His blackened fingers tightened their grip on his staff as he added, "In case anyone forgot, I was jammed between the hors d'oeuvres and the slimy green salad."

"Jasper, who else is sick?" Xandor asked.

Still staring at Sacha, he replied, "Other than the entire White Circle?  At least a third of Upper Pazard'zhik, maybe more, and let's not forget whoever ended up with the other two loads of soap Dragahn's team hauled this summer."

"What about Sehraine?" Yana demanded, glaring at the mage.

Jasper quickly glanced at the elf and saw her give the barest shake of her head.  "I haven't seen any of the symptoms," he said.

"That's not an answer," Xandor said darkly.

"I know, but it's all I have at the moment," the mage replied.  He huddled in his jacket, shivering and miserable.

"Don't talk about me as if I'm not here," Sehraine said, stepping away from Yana, who continued to stare murderously at Sacha, all the while clenching and unclenching her fists.

"Sorry," Xandor and Jasper replied.

"Let's take a closer look at this plague," Chert said.  He had the mage remove his jacket and tunic.  Grey striations started at Jasper's hands and climbed his arms to his torso.  A scattering of ulcers and boils broke the skin.  Muttering to himself, the dwarf walked around the mage, investigating his hairline, eyes, and back.  He even had Jasper pull up a pants leg and take off a boot.

After he finished, Chert let out a big sigh.  "They're faint, but those dark veins run all over your body," he said.  "Do you want me to try to heal it?  Just to warn you though, it didn't work on any of those poor souls in that clearing."

"It's worth a try."

Chert handed his light stone to Xandor.  With both hands, he gripped Jasper's arm tightly and stared intently into the mage's eyes.

"You ready?"

"No."

Chert closed his eyes, and calm spread over his demeanor.  The dwarf whispered a prayer in his native tongue, and a blue glow leapt from his stubby hands into Jasper's arm.

Jasper's blood turned to lava in his veins.  His face contorted in pain, and his lips drew back in a silent scream.  Something dark and ugly swept through him, sending horrific spasms through every muscle, until he felt as though his bones would shatter from the abuse.  Jasper became a distant spectator in his own body.  The alien presence squatted inside his head like a fat toad, daring the cleric to remove it.

Sweat beaded on the dwarf's forehead and his brow creased in concentration.

Jasper gnashed his teeth and fought a losing battle against the thing in his head, drawing on his magic. As he gathered his power, a palpable pressure built up within the circle of light, and everyone took an involuntary step backward. Everyone, that is, except Chert.

Shimmering golden-brown eyes bored into the inky blackness staring out from Jasper's normally jovial face. Chert slapped a palm to Jasper's forehead, his chanted prayer increasing in volume. A second, brighter burst of blue slammed into the mage. Dark veins on Jasper's body stood out like stark lines on a map, illuminated by a dark indigo glow that contrasted with the bright light Xandor held aloft. At first, it looked as if the healing might work. The dark veins receded, and blackness in Jasper's hands faded to grey.

With a loud 'pop' the deep blue glow winked out, taking the light from the crystal with it. Darkness claimed the road, and everyone stood quietly, listening to Jasper's labored breathing.

"Xandor, are you hurt?" Chert asked.

"No, but your quartz cracked up the center. Can you use it again?"

"Not for light," the dwarf replied, and produced a second piece of quartz. Another prayer restored the light.

Everyone looked at Jasper. His body heaved and shuddered as he slowly regained control. He opened his eyes and gasped. "That... hurt."

"Sorry about that," Chert said, "but the lines have receded somewhat."

Jasper said, "I can't feel a difference." He kept silent about the presence he felt and the voices.

Chert shrugged and said, "That's the best I'll be able to do for you until we find a real cure."

Xandor handed the dead pieces of quartz to Chert and crouched in front of Jasper. He studied the mage intently. "You going to make it?"

Knowing what the ranger meant, Jasper struggled to recover. It was important for him to be able to carry his own weight and contribute. He used his staff to lever himself to his feet and gave the ranger a curt nod.

The two walked slowly to Grendel and Sacha, standing quietly at the light's edge.

"Baroness, we need information," Xandor said.  "We have to know where those crates have been sent."

Grendel placed a gentle hand under her chin, drawing her face up until she met his gaze.  "Sacha, this is far bigger than your desire for revenge on the Kral.  I do not believe you set out to destroy the world.  Gregori, though... I can easily believe it of him.  Did he tell you anything that could help us?"

Chewing on her bottom lip, Sacha didn't respond.  Her eyes darted around the group like a cornered animal.

"When this originally started, was it sanctioned by your family?" Grendel pressed.

"What do you mean?"

"I am trying to understand how you and your brother became tangled up in all this.  You mentioned Gregori was the one who concocted this elaborate plan.  Does he work for your family, or did he work for your husband?"

She stiffened under his touch but answered, "I don't know.  Gregori came to Pazard'zhik from Erinskaya, so I assumed he worked for my family, but he had always been a part of Gavriil's inner circle."

"What reason would your late husband have to start a plague?" Xandor asked, picking up on Grendel's train of thought.

"My husband never mentioned anything about a plague to me before you killed him, so I don't know."

Ignoring her jab, Xandor continued, "Lady, this plan of Gregori's is utter madness.  From what little I knew about your husband, he had too much to lose to approve anything like this.  His business, if you want to call it that, required a stable government, which is something Gregori's plan undermines.  Do you think Gregori could have done this behind your husband's back?"

"Maybe."

"What were you and your husband doing that night?" Xandor asked.  "The house burned down to the foundations.  We dug but didn't find a bloody thing and, from what Marcus said, the people we saved couldn't tell us either.  Were you going to use the Blood of Cayn that night?"

Sacha's eyes darted to Grendel and then back to Xandor.  "Yes.  No.  Not like you think.  Yes, we were going to use it to kill the Kral and his family.  Trakya would have fallen, and

Zhitomir would have placed Gavriil on the throne with me at his side.  Our sacrifice to Sutekh would have given us his blessing and clenched our success.  Instead, it only brought our ruin.

"But the Blood of Cayn wasn't supposed to be contagious.  Each crate had a specific destination — a specific purpose."

Listening, Jasper stroked his beard and asked cautiously, "Where was Gregori when your husband died?  Was he at the estate?"

"No, he was away.  Why?"

"It's just curious that Marcus received specific information about your house and sent us in to investigate.  Is it possible Gregori provided that information?"

Sacha's brow furrowed as she thought it over.

Certain he was on the right track, Jasper concluded, "I'd bet good money Gregori had your husband killed, and he used the Kral to do it."

"I suppose it's possible, but why would he do that?" she asked.  "We were so close to success."

"You tell us," Xandor replied.  "Did they have a falling out?  Maybe Gregori had something personal against the Baron."

"Not that I'm aware of, but if Gavriil tried to stop Gregori..." Sachin offered.

"What about Marko or D'yakon Krovos?" Grendel asked.  "Could they have been involved in this from the start?"

"Until yesterday, I thought Marko had come to escort me home.  As for the D'yakon, he has always had delusions of being the next Maa'kheru Bolezni and leading a horde of humanoids to the very gates of Tydway."

"Is that normal for your family to send a relative to 'collect' you?"

"Sometimes," Sacha hedged.  "It depends."

"On what?" Jasper asked.

"On who it is, and their status in the family."

"So, do you know who sent your brother?" Xandor asked.

Her eyes narrowed, and her jaw jutted forward.  "Our parents, of course."

Xandor paced, deep in thought.

Silence reigned amongst the small group until Grendel asked, "What happens if Marko becomes the favored sibling?"

"He moves one step closer to the throne, and when our parents die, he gets their office."

"What happens to you?"

Rather than answer, she stepped away and turned her back on the group, facing the dark eastern road.

"Sacha, *what happens*?"

"I lose all my protections, and I'm given as a sacrifice to Sutekh," she answered quietly.

Grendel pulled her back against his chest in a hug and said, "If you want to prevent him from succeeding, you have to help us stop them."

Xandor stopped pacing and asked, "Where are those crates headed?"

"Marko's taking them to Bregu Kraagor at Chernigov. From there, they're to travel downriver."

"Boat or wagon?"

"Bregu Kraagor handled the logistics.  His orcs unloaded the wagons and took them to the city.  I don't know what happens to them after that."

"What about the previous shipments?  Are they still there?"

With a droop of her shoulders, Sacha answered, "No."

"You know the Blood of Cayn is in the soap," Jasper said. "You now know it's alive.  Where did Gregori get it?"

"Gregori never said where he found it, only that he'd received it as a gift from Ka'Sehkuur, Sutekh's brother."

Jasper, Xandor, and Chert stared at each other.

"People are dying.  My *brother* is dying because of you and your cult, you worthless bitch," Yana snapped at the Baroness.

Sacha pushed Grendel away, and took a step toward Yana, but before she could open her mouth to respond, Chert cleared his throat.  Facing Xandor and Yana, he said, "I believe the events Jasper described would have happened with or without her.  Regardless of her intentions, she is not the one to blame for what is happening."

"She bloody well isn't innocent, either," Xandor said heatedly.  "We know she worships the Dark One and helped that necromancer put his plan in motion."

Chert turned around and said to Sacha, "Baroness, what *are* your intentions?"

Sacha drew herself up.  Spine stiff, and face determined, she looked down on the dwarf.  "I intend to kill my brother."

# CHAPTER 18
# REINFORCEMENTS

**October 26, 4235 K.E.**


**5:56pm**

"Milord, permission to enter."

"Granted," responded a deep voice from within the grey pavilion.

"Orders from the Tower, Sir," squire Patrick Anders reported as he stepped through the tent flap. Lord Geoffrey Fergusson, sixth Baronet of Yorkshire, bent over a table, studying a map with several small markers positioned on it. In his mouth, he absently chewed the butt of an unlit cigar. The Knight Commander neither looked up nor acknowledged the squire's words.

In the bright light of the oil lamp suspended from the tent's ridge pole, the Knight Commander's broad-shouldered frame cast one end of the map in deep shadow. The squire had the irreverent thought that, in his striped surcoat, Lord Fergusson looked like a black and silver storm cloud looming over the paper landscape.

Sharp eyes lashed out at the squire, as if the man heard the boy's thoughts. Anders gulped and started to take a step back before he remembered the message he carried. He hurried forward and snapped to attention two long strides from the knight. He saluted, then presented the sealed leather pouch. Lord Fergusson adjusted one of the markers slightly farther north and nodded to himself before he pushed away from the table, returned the squire's salute, and accepted the missive.

While standing at attention, the squire watched his commander out of the corner of his eye and waited for his next order. Fergusson's long grey hair, braided back out of his face with strips of leather and bound at the end with a bit of black silk, contrasted with his darkly tanned face, which looked more like dried leather than actual skin. His most prominent facial feature, however, was his nose. It stuck out like a hawk's beak, slightly hooked at the end. Beyond Lord Fergusson, a narrow cot, a foldable writing table, and a large footlocker were tucked in the far corner of the tent. Anders briefly wondered if that footlocker held everything his commander cared to own, and who looked after the man's estate while he was out in the field.

Lord Fergusson's sharp inhale cut through the squire's wandering thoughts, and he saw the commander's eyes return to the top of the heavy parchment, re-reading the orders from the beginning.

The Knight Commander held a unique position in the Iron Tower. He had been with the order most of his life, and for the last twenty years he had served as one of the primary trainers of new recruits after they survived basic training.

Rumors surrounded the mysterious nobleman and ran rampant among the soldiers. Without a doubt, Lord Fergusson should have been one of the Tower commandants, but he had never moved up the ranks. No one knew for sure if it was because he had upset someone of a higher station and lost his political clout, or if he had requested the position.

Whatever the case, the Tower let him remain as a trainer rather than promoting or retiring him. That very exception added to his reputation among the military families. His long-term position, coupled with the fact that he was very good at turning green troops into well-disciplined soldiers, led many new recruits, or, as in Squire Anders' case, their parents, to request assignment to Fergusson's unit.

Five years ago, he and a small training company from the Iron Tower had relocated to Rhodina to consult with the Korol' of Michurinsk and participate in cold-weather training. For some, it was a less-than-choice assignment. The winters were harsh, and everyone in camp knew they were only a hard day's ride from the White River, where the humanoid tribes raided. For those who were unfazed by the frigid temperatures and loved to fight, though, there wasn't a better assignment.

Lord Fergusson walked back to his map and moved one of the markers west, next to the White River. "Assemble my officers."

A broad smile stretched across the boy's face. "Yes, Sir!" he replied, snapping a smart salute.

Before the squire could exit the tent, the Knight Commander said, "Young man."

Turning around, he replied, "Sir?"

"Be careful what you wish for."

"Yes, Sir," the squire replied.

Outside the pavilion, the night air was crisp with the smells of late autumn.  It wouldn't be long until the first snowfall.  He breathed in deeply, grinning despite Lord Fergusson's warning.

A small city of grey pavilions surrounded him, all with silver-and-black pennons snapping proudly in the evening breeze.  Oil lanterns hung from tree branches, keeping the oncoming night at bay.  Beyond the tents, voices rang out, followed by the clanging of steel as some of the warriors sparred.  It was the calm before the storm.  The squire walked across the grassy field toward a small knot of knights, overseeing the men train.

Anders held aside the tent flap to admit Lord Fergusson's second in command, Leftenant Brian Gallagher, followed immediately by their Rhodinan liaison, Poruchik Sokol Morozov.  Behind them came five knights in matching silver-and-black surcoats emblazoned with a silver tower.  These were Lord Fergusson's alterns, the junior officers charged with day-to-day training and oversight.  Unlike their commander and his second, they each wore their hair cut short, and appeared to be several decades younger.

They assembled in inspection formation and came to attention.  The Leftenant cleared his throat.  "Sir, the officers are assembled as ordered."

The Knight Commander continued leaning over his table, staring at the map.  Curious as to what held their leader's attention, the younger officers allowed their gazes to drift to the map, observing strange red flags along the river, and the new position of their company marker.  Without turning around, Lord Fergusson said, "Ladies and Gentlemen, our assignment is Chernigov."

"Chernigov?" Poruchik Sokol blurted.  "There have been no communiques from Kamenka-Tambov regarding the khumanoidi."

"Nevertheless, we aim for Chernigov," Fergusson replied. "What can you tell me about the area on this side of the river?"

"Korol' Melikhov's youngest brother, Knyaz Dorinkov, has command of the Semyonovsky Regiment, encamped in what's left of Glazok, Sir." Poruchik Sokol approached the table and pointed to a small dot slightly southeast of the orcnéan city. "Here, Milord, about six miles from the river."

"Are we going to take Chernigov from the humanoids, Sir?" one of the alterns asked.

"No," Lord Fergusson said. "We are to travel west and await further orders."

"What does that mean?"

"It means we travel west," Lord Fergusson said. "Poruchik Sokol, I want you to ride ahead with a message to Knyaz Dorinkov. Let him know we're coming. I'll have a courier pouch ready for you within the half-hour." He looked up and met the gazes of each of his officers. "Assemble your troops for inspection. We leave tonight."

"What kind of mission is this?" another young knight asked.

"One of a kind. Now go."

Dismissed, the knights disappeared outside; however, when the Leftenant reached the door, he stopped and turned around. "Sir, may I ask what's really going on?"

The Knight Commander walked to his writing table and picked up a small, leather-bound journal.

The Leftenant's eyes widened in surprise. "Geoffrey, if that fell into the wrong hands..."

"I know."

Lord Fergusson handed the journal to his Leftenant and waited expectantly. The Leftenant flipped through the pages and stopped on the last page with writing. It only had one word at the top. '*Chernigov*?'

"This is recent. Where is he?"

"I'm not sure. Intelligence suggests no more than two days' ride west of the orc city."

"What are we supposed to do?" the Leftenant asked.

"First off, I'm going to answer him."

"Sir, you can't do that. It's against protocol."

"To hell with protocol, Brian, that's one of *our* men out there."

Looking at the cover, the Leftenant said, "There's no name on the journal, Sir.  How can you be sure?"

"I know this ranger.  You do, too.  He was sent to us three years ago for his first mission."

"What's he doing on the other side of the river?"

"Special assignment."

"You could blow his cover," Brian stated as he returned the journal.

"He's asking us for our help.  I don't think he cares if we blow his cover."

"Sir, the High Council will not take kindly to you interfering with one of their agents."

Reaching into his pouch, the commander produced the message given to him earlier by the squire and handed it to his Leftenant.  "Read this."

As the younger knight scanned the document, his mouth involuntarily opened.  By the end, he was speechless.

"Exactly."  The commander resumed his study of the map.  Pointing to several small, red flags marking port towns along the White River, the commander asked, "See this and this?  These are the latest locations where this disease has appeared.  It's no longer contained inside the boundaries of Trakya, and if Xandor's right, there's a wagonload of the source contaminant out there and another waiting to leave Chernigov.  If we don't destroy it here and now, there'll be no stopping it, and we will have another Plague War on our hands."

Finding his voice, the Leftenant asked, "Has the Highlord spoken with the Kral?"

"I don't know.  Our orders are to help that ranger any way we can and find a cure, which means we have to get him to us, or us to him.  Either way, someone has to go through Chernigov."


**7:04pm**

The pleasant smell of supper drifted across the road. Jasper sat next to the fire, watching the stew gently bubble. He offered to cook the rats, but everyone had turned him down flat.  Instead, Yana and Xandor offered to 'go find something.'

Before they left, Jasper approached Xandor and asked for his spices back. "Being sick and all, you probably shouldn't be near the food," Xandor said, handing him the small container.

"What if I just watch?"

"Since when have you ever *just watched*?"

While they were away, Jasper had Sehraine pull together a few of their rations and start a vegetable soup. Chert stood off a distance with his tools, grumbling, still trying to fix the giant-inflicted damage to his shield. Grendel sat with Sacha. She had formed an uneasy truce with the group, but the half-orc continued to stay by her side. Jasper wasn't sure if it was for her protection or theirs.

By the time Xandor and Yana returned with field-dressed rabbits, the fire was ready and waiting. Jasper tried to give the ranger pointers while Xandor prepared the meal, and made noises every time an ingredient was added. It all stopped when the ranger turned to him and asked, "Who's doing this?"

When he finished with the meat, the ranger stepped back and said, "Jasper, tend the pot while I check on the horses."

Grendel waited for Xandor to leave before he approached Jasper. He stared into the flames and said, "I misjudged you, mage."

Jasper looked up at the tall man and asked, "Is that a good thing, or bad?"

"I do not know. At least now I know you did not try to kill me."

Jasper stood and said, "I'm sorry that I did something to make you even consider it a possibility."

"We have not been together long, and when you did not help me fight Marko's men... I thought the worst."

"I told you then it was premature, and nothing has happened to change my mind," Jasper said seriously.

"I know, but good decision or not, you gambled with my life, again."

Jasper's thoughtful expression reflected the light of the fire. "Next time, you warn me before you try something like that, and I promise to be prepared. Agreed?"

"Agreed."

Three rabbits weren't a lot of food for a group like theirs, but in the soup, it turned into a hearty meal.  After finishing, Xandor sat back and pulled out his journal.  He was surprised to find a note under where he had written 'Chernigov?'  In a bold hand it read, "Help is coming."  Before his eyes, someone sketched a rough map of the city, along with its proximity to the White River.  Next, a dark line appeared across the river indicating a bridge with one end anchored at the edge of the city and the other at a keep.  Under the city, the script continued and said, "15,000 orcs."

"Wow!  That's a lot of orcs!" Jasper exclaimed, staring over his shoulder.  "Where's the monastery?"

Everyone looked up from what they were doing.

Xandor almost closed the journal but stopped himself.  Yana walked over, curious.  She arched an eyebrow at the bold script but otherwise kept quiet.

"I don't see it," Jasper continued.

"Do you mind?"

Ignoring the ranger's personal boundaries, Jasper sat next to him.  Xandor took out his stylus and wrote in the journal, "Monastery?"

It took a few minutes before a response appeared on the page.  What they read didn't give them hope.  It simply said, "No information."

Jasper studied the heart of the fire and said, "It must be there."

"What's there?" Xandor asked, noting the hint of desperation in Jasper's voice.

"The Tear of Havel."

"The elven ghost said it was lost.  Did you find out more about it?"

"A little.  I'm hoping it's the cure."

"What does it look like?"

"A dagger, I think.  My information is somewhat sketchy."

Patting the mage on the back, Xandor said, "We'll look for it after we catch that wagon."

"We'll need more horses if we're going to catch them," Yana said, startling them.

Jasper glanced at the three horses: Xerxes, the Percheron recently rescued from the mudpot, and Mladen's rouncey.  He counted the people: Xandor, Grendel, Chert, Sacha, Sehraine, Yana, and himself made seven.

"How many do you think we need?" Jasper asked.

"At least two — three would be better — but where are you going to find them?"

"Where's my box?"

Yana stared at the mage, as though expecting him to conjure horses out of thin air.

Xandor began to smile and shook his head as he answered, "In my saddlebags, but the last time I looked, you didn't have any horses in there."

"Find me some worms, would you?"

Everyone's eyes followed Jasper as he rummaged for his box. Lifting the lid, he reached inside and slid the panels separating the interior compartments like a puzzle box, each manipulation revealing a new storage space, until he came to a small one containing several thin wands. Taking out a black one with finely inscribed red runes, he stuck it in his belt and closed the box.

Casting about, Xandor spotted a cluster of shrubs with an accumulation of dead leaves underneath. The ranger walked over and nudged the leaves with the toe of his boot, finding them still wet from the rain the day before. He knelt and dipped his hands into the moist debris, digging until he found two fat earthworms.

Alarmed, Yana said loudly, "What are you *doing*?!"

Setting the worms on the ground, Jasper plucked the wand from his belt. He touched the first worm and a bright light illuminated it, causing everyone to look away and shield their eyes. The mage turned to the other worm, and everyone had the impression it tried to squirm away as if it knew what was coming. It wiggled and bounced but wasn't quick enough. Jasper touched it with the wand and again the bright light flared. Smiling, the mage walked toward the saddlebags to put away his wand. Behind him stood two dun-colored horses, their eyes shining moistly, not comprehending what had just happened.

"That is so unnatural!" Yana shuddered.


**7:43pm**

Fergusson's troops assembled on the parade grounds. Each of the five knights stood before their troop of soldiers, flanked by a subaltern with a black-and-silver pennon bearing the company's emblem affixed to the tip of a lance. Planted into the ground before the assembly was a black standard bearing the symbol of their order: the Iron Tower. It fluttered gently in the evening breeze.

The Knight Commander strode onto the field, followed by his Leftenant.  Light from smoky torches mounted on tall poles around the field glinted off their armor.

The Leftenant quickly took his position next to the standard, and called out, "Attention!"

Everyone snapped to.

"We have been ordered to stand in harm's way," Lord Fergusson announced.  "Over the next few days, each and every one of you will earn that tower on your uniform.  Make your families proud."

The Knight Commander walked down each of the ranks, recognizing a few from previous campaigns, but most were fresh recruits from across the mountains.  They were sending him younger and younger soldiers these days.  Either that or he was getting old.

When he finished inspecting the troops, he walked back in front of them, nodded to his second-in-command, and said, "Leftenant."

Leftenant Brian Gallagher stepped forward.  "Light packs!  Forced march!" he called out.  "All other gear to the quartermaster for transport!"  Silence greeted the announcements, but excitement filled the air.  "Departure assembly in thirty minutes!  Dismissed!"

# CHAPTER 19
# CHERNIGOV

## October 28, 4235 K.E.

**6:14am**

For a night and most of a day, Xandor and his companions rode hard, stopping only for brief rests, but they didn't gain on Marko and his final wagon. The temperature dropped as they traveled east, and it seemed that winter had finally routed summer's hold. By mid-afternoon, the landscape changed to one of rolling, scrub-covered hills dotted with the rotten stumps of a once-majestic forest that had stretched as far as the eye could see. Hints of smoke rode the sharp wintery air, though no one could see its source. Tracks from the wagon rode over an ever-increasing number of orc-prints, and Xandor had them abandon the road, explaining there was too great a chance of running into a patrol.

For the remainder of that day, the group traveled on foot, all hopes of catching the chuck wagon gone. The ranger found areas less frequented by the humanoids, but it also meant slower going over rougher terrain. Weeds and brambles tugged at their clothing and exposed skin, as if the land itself tried to warn them away from their destination.

Twice, Xandor called for a halt by raising his fist just above his shoulder. Everyone, including the horses, dropped to the ground, not daring to breathe as they listened to the muttering and cursing of a passing patrol. Xandor's ability to slip past them bordered on the preternatural, earning him a new level of respect from his companions.

As evening approached, the smoke became thicker and covered the sky. Breathing became more difficult, and soon, everyone fought against the constant desire to cough.

Grendel seemed less affected by the foul air, but that brought little comfort, since it meant the orcs were probably unaffected as well. Following Sacha's example, everyone wrapped kerchiefs around their faces, shielding their mouths and noses from the smoky assault.  All except Yana, who wore her T-slitted barbute.

A little after midnight, they found a small grove of saplings suitable for making camp.  A thin trickle of a stream meandered through decayed leaves, but everyone was happy to have fresh, cold water.

During the night, the temperature plummeted, and everything froze, including their tiny stream.  When they woke, they were surrounded by glistening spider webs of frost.  Xandor brought the group together and explained that he wanted to do a little reconnaissance before proceeding farther, and he quickly disappeared into the underbrush.

The ranger belly-crawled up onto a ridge southwest of the city, trusting his cloak to hide him from the sharp-eyed watchtower guards.  A pall of smoke constantly vomited from the city obscured the rising sun.  Thick and unaffected by the air currents, it kept the entire valley in a state of semi-darkness.  He found a suitable spot to hide and stared through his spyglass at the nightmare below him called Chernigov and the bridge that overshadowed it.

Chernigov started out as a Trakyan border village with a moderate-sized inn, trading post, and ferry.  Later, a dock was added after several boats sought refuge during the harsh winters.  The soil nearby proved fertile, and soon farmers and herders arrived, eager to try their hands.  Gradually, people of all sorts moved to the area and began practicing their trades.  Relations with the Rhodinans helped bolster the town's commerce, and eventually the Kral and Korol' Melikhov III, ruler of Michurinsk at the time, met at the inn and signed a diplomatic treaty.

As a show of mutual cooperation, the two countries came together and built a stone bridge over the White River, permanently connecting the two lands.  Spanning almost a mile and soaring high enough to allow tall-masted ships to pass underneath, it was an incredible feat of engineering and magic.  Massive stone columns lined each side and, some said, were founded on bands of adamantine forged by dwarven blacksmiths.  Stone reliefs carved into the columns, representing the Korol' and the Kral, served as the guardians of the river.

Even with the mages and masons working day in and day out, it took five years to build. When it was finished, the locals nicknamed it the Rainbow Bridge, because, when the rays of the sun hit it just right, the stones glittered with all the colors of the spectrum.

Afterward, people moved to the region in droves. The Kral sent a governor to oversee the land, and the tax collectors followed. The river dock expanded into a long wharf that stretched a quarter mile along the shore, and commerce prospered.

By the time the Plague War struck, the town's population had grown to over six thousand people on the Trakyan side of the bridge and nearly two thousand people on the Rhodinan side.

The Plague War changed all that.

The Kral ordered the citizens to evacuate, abandoning the town to the marauding humanoids, who found the town made to order, complete with its stone buildings and underground sewers. It also had one singular piece of strategic importance: the bridge.

Orcnéan helrúnan, or witch doctors, crawled out of their dark holes and directed the destruction of the market at the city's center, replacing it with a huge pit. For an entire moon cycle, they prayed to their vile god and made blood sacrifices, tossing human bodies into the pit. Under the darkness of the new moon, fire erupted from the rancid pit, consuming the pile of bodies, and filling the air with ash and smoke. So long as the fire burned, the helrúnan proclaimed, the sun would not shine its face upon Chernigov. The once-famous bridge ceased to sparkle, covered by layers of filth and grime.

With the sun concealed behind the screen of smoke and ash, the new inhabitants went to work on the town's defenses and upgraded them — orc style. The defensive wall, originally a simple, ten-foot-high wooden palisade meant to keep wild animals out at night, was rebuilt with blocks salvaged from abandoned buildings or quarried from underneath the town. The new wall stood more than ten feet wide and fifteen feet high, with an additional four feet of battlements above. Regularly spaced buttresses braced it from the inside, acting as ramps for the more nimble orcs.

On top, long spears impaled partially decomposed humans as a warning to all trespassers.

Xandor tried to ignore the bodies. There was nothing he could do for them except pray the Eternal Father had granted their spirits peace. He forced himself to focus on the mission — he had to find a way in and destroy that wagon of plague-ridden soap. Despite its defensive wall, he knew the scattering of rundown and decrepit buildings reflected only a portion of the actual city. Xandor counted a dozen different flags planted atop what looked like half-buried structures of earth and brick. Each one had a well-guarded entrance that, more likely than not, led to an underground warren.

Lord Fergusson and the Iron Tower estimated the number of orcs to be around fifteen thousand, but the ranger had the sinking feeling their numbers were wrong. He opened his journal and read the latest entry from the Tower.

*'Intelligence reports tribes of ogres and dreyri among the orcs. A few savage men have earned a place among them, but the majority of humans within those walls are slaves or food. City is controlled by an orc named Kraagor, who gave himself the title Bregu, or king. Chernigov controls traffic up and down the river. It also controls the bridge and the keep on the Michurinsk end.'*

Xandor adjusted his focus on the gate tower overlooking the road to Trakya and the flag — a hand-drawn moon on a field of dark burgundy — flying above it. Inside the moon, a bloody orc skull with curving horns leered. He zoomed in on the orc archers patrolling the top of the wall. The ranger followed their path with his spyglass and saw something that made him stop and look twice.

Partially hidden behind the crenellations were several war machines that, at first, resembled common catapults, but they weren't. Instead of using manpower or counterweights to hurl their deadly missiles, these used metal leaf-springs. Much like an archer's bow, they were thicker in the middle while the ends, which rose high into the air, tapered to sharp points, allowing them to bend easily. Layer upon layer of metal bands were built up to create the spring, each shorter than the previous. Thick ropes, tied to the ends, wound around a solid wooden drum, which was attached to a long throwing arm fitted with a sling. Even from a distance, the timber frame, drum, and tethers that anchored it appeared heavy.

He couldn't see it, but Xandor suspected there was an oversized hand crank used to bend the spring and position the throwing arm.  He had no idea the range or accuracy but could see that the orcs had equipped each with a large enough windlass to move heavy boulders or any other projectiles they wanted.

Boulders and sharp rocks strewed the surrounding field.  Some appeared to be part of the foundations of former buildings that once stood outside the old city wall, while others were strategically placed to prevent any kind of organized charge of infantry or cavalry.  Xandor lowered his spyglass and sketched the city, the positions of the war machines, and penned a short description, grimacing unconsciously as he contemplated the tactical challenges of assaulting the prepared defenses.

Shouting caught his attention, and he quickly brought the spyglass back up.  Four hundred yards south of the city stood the ruined walls of a small estate, surrounded by several dozen orc warriors.  It was the only building still standing outside the city gates.

Knots of humanoids worked their way around the ancient walls, occasionally firing arrows up and over into the courtyard.  They kept circling, using the debris on the field as cover.

From his vantage point on the ridge, Xandor had a hard time understanding their odd behavior.  They didn't seem to care if they actually hit anyone; nor were they in any hurry to attack whoever was inside.

The range of the spyglass was limited, and he couldn't quite focus on the far side of the estate; however, he thought he could just make out the armored soldiers running to and fro.  A blurry wall rose up from the opposite side topped with a stone Korsun cross.

Adjusting his focus on the western wall, the one closest to him, he followed a soldier as he ran atop what appeared to be either a flat roof or catwalk — or both.

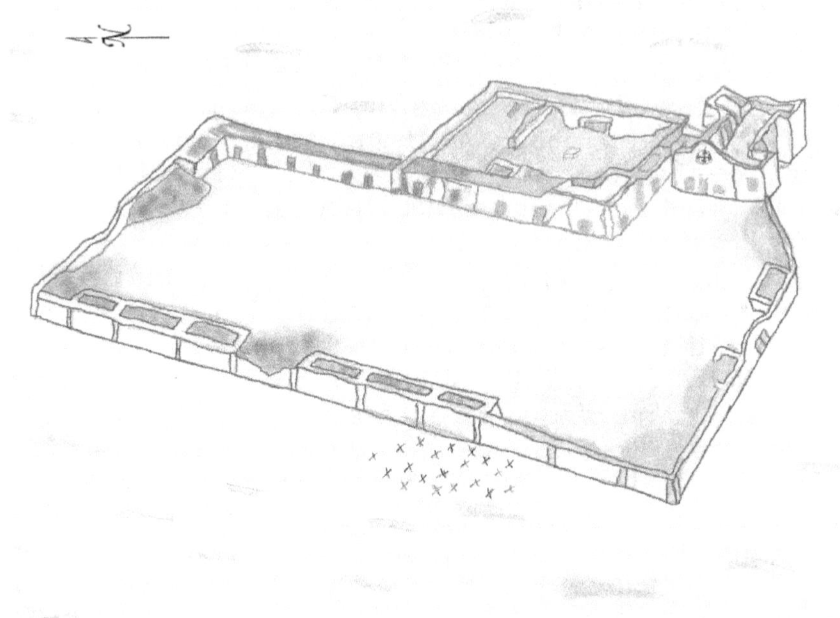

Xandor was too far away to gauge exactly how tall or thick the wall was separating the soldiers from the circling orcs.  He guessed it must have been around eight to twelve feet tall, but chunks of it were missing in a few locations where the orcs had partially battered it down.  Through one of these gaps, Xandor could see earthen embankments inside the courtyard that shored the corners of the wall as well as braced other weakened areas.

Panning to the far east side, Xandor spotted two buildings through the haze, including what he presumed was the chapel.  Built integrally with the wall, they jutted out from the monastery, giving the estate an irregular shape. Most of the roofs had collapsed, and mounds of dirt and debris filled the interiors.

A few yards outside the western wall of the monastery, dark forms became partially visible as the smoke drifted and flowed, drawing the ranger's attention away from the chapel. He looked closer and waited for the smoke to clear further. When it did, he saw the tips of several X-shaped crosses.  It was hard to tell from his angle, but there appeared to be a man crucified on each one.  He silently swore when he saw one of them move.

As the sun rose higher, the semi-darkness in the valley became a semi-brightness, marginally improving visibility.

Someone waved a flag back and forth from atop one of the shorter buildings.  It was a signal of sorts because soon after it went up, he heard shouts, and the fighting along the wall intensified.

He felt the urge to run and help, but instead kept his position and continued watching.  The flag looked familiar, but he couldn't quite make out the heraldic mark.  The azure standard fluttered, giving him teasing glimpses of a pointed, gold shape.

Holding the flag, a knight in plate armor shouted commands and rallied his men.  He didn't wear a helmet, so Xandor focused on the blurred image of the knight's face and waited for him to move close enough to focus.  When he did, Xandor's mouth fell open in disbelief.

'*August*?' he thought.  He lowered the spyglass, rubbed his eyes, and tried again.

The knight was on the move, making it harder to catch a good glimpse of him.  When he stopped briefly near the northwestern corner, there was no mistaking the way he carried himself.  It was August Sabe, a gallant warrior and friend, but what was he doing here?  He was supposed to be on the other side of the world.

Perplexed, Xandor slowly worked his way down the ridge and hurried back to camp.


**6:46am**

Lord Fergusson's breath steamed as he watched his men run through the assault rehearsal again.  They had traveled through the night and previous day to set up camp on the outskirts of Glazok.  It was close enough to the White River to be ready when Xandor gave the signal, but far enough away not to attract attention.

When they had arrived, he and Brian met with Knyaz Dorinkov and his second, Poruchik Vassily Tirinko.  The regiment from Michurinsk appeared competent.  Comprised of four companies, it included a troop which specialized in demolition.  Maybe, with the help of the Knyaz and his men, they would be able to pull off a miracle.

Divided into squads, soldiers in silver and black ran across the field, attacking mock fortifications with confidence. The men knew their jobs. Of course, that didn't keep him from worrying — not that they would see it in his face or mannerisms — that was not how the game was played. He maintained the appearance of certainty and assurance, and his troops pretended they were as confident of victory as him. His lips twitched at the familiar thought — it was something that went through his mind before every battle.

He watched his new recruits go through the motions of the assault. For some of them, this would be the first time they laid eyes on a humanoid, let alone fought one. This was no typical first assignment. Most new recruits were blooded against raiders or bandits, not in siege actions. He wondered how many of those same recruits would be cursing his name by the time all was said and done. Assuming they survived, of course.

His brow furrowed. Lord Fergusson found himself in a position no commander liked. He was moving to attack a fortified position with no serious reconnaissance, no solid preparation. The entire assault was unfolding almost of its own volition — they were making it up as they went, and he hated it. No sane commander assaulted an entrenched enemy without lots of thought, planning, preparation, and rehearsal.

Were it not for the Rhodinan probes over the last few years and the scouts he had out, they would have nothing; as it was, all those reports yielded little more than the exterior dimensions of the Keep at the foot of the bridge. It was something to start with, and they were making the most of it with rough timber layouts of the walls, running rehearsal after rehearsal in the short time they had.

He thought again about how he hated to rush an assault. They were certain to lose more men than they could afford, but if they did not take the Keep and push across the bridge to assist Xandor — or at the very least, provide him the distraction he needed — they might lose their only hope for a cure to the plague threatening friend and foe alike. So, they were going to throw themselves at the walls and the orcs, and they were going to overwhelm them.

They had to.

**7:30am**

"You're never going to believe who I just saw," Xandor said when he entered camp.

Everyone jumped, startled by his unexpected appearance. All except Yana, who casually walked in behind him and said, "You didn't have to make so much noise."

He turned to her and said, "I didn't want you to mistake me for an orc patrol."

"Little chance of that. A herd of buffalo, maybe."

Letting it go with a quick grin at her teasing tone, Xandor quickly recounted what he had seen while everyone packed. He finished by saying, "I swear it looked like August leading those men."

Jasper glanced up and said, "August? Here? That's impossible."

"I know. I swear it looked like him, and it was his family crest flying on the flag."

Not convinced, Jasper said, "Well, whoever it is, it sounds like they may need our help."

"I don't want to sound mercenary," Yana said, "but our job is to destroy those crates. We've already sacrificed too much to get distracted now."

"Yana, I couldn't see anything except stone walls and battlements," Xandor answered and held up his hand when he saw she was about to interrupt. "I'm not saying anything about giving up on the crates, but there's a possibility, however remote, that a friend of ours is down there and needs help; we have no choice."

A flood of emotion began to well in Yana's eyes and she said, "There's family we've left behind who need our immediate help. Marcus needs our help."

Jasper laid a calming hand on her shoulder and said, "Yana, we're not here only to destroy those crates. We have to find a cure, too. If what Xandor described is what I think it is, then we have to go there anyway. That's *the* monastery."

Everyone looked at the mage.

"The Tear of Havel is in there somewhere," Jasper said.

Xandor flipped open his journal and started writing hurriedly, describing everything he had seen. "We'll have to cross a field crawling with orcs to get there," Xandor said thoughtfully while he wrote. "I don't see how we can sneak across, and once we alert Chernigov to our presence, we can forget about catching Marko."

When Xandor finished, words appeared in the margin. *'Company in place, less than a half day's march to the city, east of the river.'*  "That helps," Xandor said and read the message aloud.

"Who are you?" Yana demanded, standing in front of him.  Her face was neutral, but the tone of her voice held more than a hint of anger.

The ranger looked up from his journal and put away his stylus.  "Yana, I'm a ranger.  That's all."

"Gluposti!  You're a spy!  Who are you talking to?"

Xandor sighed and weighed what he should say next. Sehraine and Grendel, surprised at the outburst, stood next to Yana and waited for Xandor's response.

Chert stepped between them and said, "Give him a chance to speak."

Xandor's lips pressed together, and his brow creased. "We're from Tydway."

"I know that!" Yana snapped.  "Tell me something I don't know."

"Have you heard of the Iron Tower?" Jasper asked.

Xandor threw Jasper a warning glance.

"Xandor, this isn't the time for you to keep secrets. People's lives are at stake."

Reluctant to divulge anything that would further compromise his position, the ranger kept quiet.  The tension became thicker.

Finally, Xandor looked Yana in the eyes and said, "I didn't want you to find out this way, but I — no, *we* — need help.  I once served the Iron Tower as a forward scout.  My first assignment was in Michurinsk with a group of knights. After my tour of duty, they gave me the opportunity to take what the Tower likes to call a special assignment.  In my case, it took me, most recently, to Pazard'zhik."

Yana grew angrier with each word and gripped the hilts of her weapons.  "You used my brother.  You used me!  Is the Highlord planning a war with the Kral?"

Quickly shaking his head, Xandor answered, "Of course not!  My assignment was to track down Sha'iry and relay any information on the Dark One's cults.  It worked out that your brother and I had similar objectives.

"Yana, Marcus knows I'm part of the Iron Tower.  I think it was one of the reasons he chose me for this mission.  He had to use someone outside his agency, someone with the wherewithal to take it to the end."

Xandor's explanation seemed to take some of the wind from Yana's sails, especially with the mention of her brother. She wanted to find fault in what the ranger said, some way to vent her anger.  She turned her eyes to Jasper, and he gave her a small smile.  "I suppose you work for the Iron Tower as well?"

"No, I'm just a cook," Jasper replied, still smiling.

"Just a cook," Yana scoffed.

"Listen," Jasper said in all seriousness, "Xandor and I have known each other for a while now.  He and I came to Pazard'zhik together, but for different reasons.  I was looking for a friend of mine who was supposed to be in the city. Turned out he wasn't, but I stuck around to study at the White Circle.  When Marcus approached Xandor about this job, he thought I would make the perfect grubmaster, which I did."

"Uh-huh," she said.

Xandor placed a tentative hand on Yana's shoulder. "Please believe me.  My assignment had nothing to do with the Kral.  In fact, it helped him."

Yana stared into Xandor's mismatched eyes and found no guile or hint of deceit.  Those same qualities had led her to trust him the first time they met.  She shook her head. "You may have an army to support us, but no amount of men east of the river will help us get across the field to the monastery."

"No, but it may provide us enough of a distraction to get into the city to destroy those crates," Xandor replied.  As an afterthought, he added, "Maybe even a way out."

"We go in there, we won't be able to take the horses," Jasper said.

Everyone looked to the mage.  All except Xandor, who kept his eyes on Xerxes, and said, "What can we do with them?"

Jasper turned to Sehraine, "Your village was north of here, wasn't it?"

"Yes, but we're on the wrong side of the river."

"How far?"

"From here?  I'd guess two days, maybe three."

"Even so, are you familiar with the lay of the land?"

"A little bit.  Why?"

"Can Xerxes swim?" Jasper asked Xandor.

"Sure."

"Can you explain to him what he needs to do and have the other horses follow him?"

"You want them to travel by themselves?" Xandor asked.

Jasper coughed and said, "It wouldn't be the first time he's done it."

"That was different.  It wasn't through a humanoid-infested war zone, and Xerxes wasn't the only battle-trained horse in the group."

"What else can we do?" Jasper asked.  "Have one of us go with them?"

They stared at each other.

"I'll do it," Sehraine said.

Everyone turned to her.  Yana's eyebrows drew down as she glared at the elf, the look on her face clearly indicating that she should have been consulted first.

Sehraine faced her friend.  "Yana, the land hasn't changed that much since I went to live in Pazard'zhik.  I can get the horses across the river.  It won't be easy, but I think I know a way."

"Fine.  We both go." Yana put her hands on her hips, daring anyone to argue.

"If you go, can you find the soldiers on the other side of the river?" Jasper asked.

"Sure.  As long as they don't mistake us for orcs."

"That's unlikely."

"Stranger things have happened," Sehraine said, "and happened to us."

"How will we find you?" Jasper asked.

"If we find Xandor's friends across the river, it shouldn't be a problem.  However, if you get to them and we aren't there, find us the same way you found Xandor."

Jasper and Xandor glanced at each other.  Then Jasper said, "This might work better.  If it goes badly, I would prefer for the ladies to not be there to watch... or worse."

"Yeah, we might make fun of you," Yana added with a glint in her eye.

Smiling, Jasper said, "That, too."

He reached into his pouch and pulled out a small container of spices. He stared at it for a moment, shook his head, and slipped it back inside. Instead, he removed his hematite and onyx signet ring and handed it to Sehraine, briefly touching her hand. "Be careful you don't lose this."

"I don't know you nearly well enough to accept your ring," she joked. She held it up and noticed the globe and dagger insignia inscribed on it.

"I'll have to fix that one day soon," Jasper said. "But seriously, that's one of a set of six, and there'll be no end of trouble if it gets lost."

"Six signet rings?"

"Jasper's in a secret society," Xandor supplied.

Jasper made a face. "It's neither a secret nor a society. We're more of a fraternity with strict membership criteria."

Yana stared curiously at the two of them but let it pass. "What about Sacha?"

"I go where Marko goes," she said with finality. "Don't worry. I can take care of myself."

"That's what we're afraid of," Jasper said.

"She goes with us," Grendel said. His tone gave no room for argument.

Xandor looked at the big man and asked, "Do you trust her?"

Everyone turned to Grendel. Under their combined gazes, he grimaced and shifted from one foot to the other uncomfortably. Finally, he shrugged.

"Look, if you don't trust her," Xandor said, "she can't come. From what I saw, we stand little chance of success, and if she alerts them to our presence at her first opportunity, we're finished. If that happens, there's no chance of stopping the crates or finding a cure."

Sacha watched Grendel, her face impassive.

Grendel stared back at her. "I do not trust her, but I also believe she has little to gain by handing us over to the orcs."

Xandor turned to Sacha. "You place us in a difficult position."

"If you hadn't blown up the caravan, we wouldn't be in this position," she responded.

"No, you'd probably be dead by now — or well on your way home."

Sacha looked as if she were going to say something but thought better of it.

"I don't trust her to go with Yana and Sehraine," Chert said, "and if we leave her, she will follow us."

"Not if we tie her up," Xandor said.

"With the temperature dropping, that would surely kill her."

"I am not baggage," Sacha said hotly. "I know I haven't given any of you reason to trust me, but you must believe me when I say that I will do everything I can to help you, provided you give me Marko."

Xandor studied Sacha for a moment. "It seems we have little choice. However, if you step out of line, I'll end you," he promised.

Sacha visibly relaxed, ignoring the threat.

"Don't get too comfortable, Baroness. You haven't seen where we're going," Xandor said quietly, erasing the smug look from her face.

With that decided, Xandor urged everyone to break camp. Jasper quickly went through his box and selected a few items that might prove useful, while everyone else cleaned up. It took a few minutes, but when they were done, the small grove of trees looked completely undisturbed, all traces of their campsite erased.

"Good luck," Sehraine and Yana said to the men.

"You, too."

Xandor stood next to Xerxes, rubbing his muzzle. "Take care of them, boy. Help them find the Iron Tower."

His horse nudged him gently and nickered softly.

# CHAPTER 20
# ILLUSION AND MISDIRECTION

### October 28, 4235 K.E.

**9:24am**

After seeing Yana and Sehraine on their way with the horses, the rest of the group followed the ranger to the ridge, where they could see for themselves what lay ahead. The siege at the monastery was still ongoing, but now Xandor spotted a pair of Repha'im, stocky giants not quite as tall as an Anak'im, lobbing boulders into the courtyard. It seemed to him their attacks were lackadaisical; something distracted them. The humanoids seemed to be holding back. They clearly had enough numbers to storm the walls.

Handing his spyglass to Jasper, he asked, "Can you get us to those crucified men?"

Jasper surveyed the field through the glass and asked, "Do you care how I do it?"

Looking askance at the mage, Xandor replied, "Not really. Just don't blow us up."

"Got it," Jasper said as he handed Xandor back his spyglass and ducked down the ridge. All the while, they heard him muttering, "Don't blow up friends. Don't blow up friends."

A worried expression crept over Sacha, and she tapped Grendel's wrist to get his attention. "What's he going to do?" she whispered.

Shrugging, he replied, "I have no idea."


**9:32am**

From the western rim of the valley, the shrill call of a clarion horn rang out. All activity stopped as though the orcs were frozen, then every eye sought the source of the sound. A single beam of sunlight cut through the smoke to shine down on two knights in heavy plate armor sitting atop warhorses protected by ornate black-and-silver barding. Each knight, wearing visored helmets sporting fancy white plumes, gripped the shaft of a long lance. At their tips, black-and-silver pennons snapped in the breeze.

Planted in the ground beside them was a tall sable standard bearing the argent symbol of the Iron Tower. The knights and horses did not move, not even the swish of a tail. They simply stood, awaiting the response to their challenge. Behind them, similarly dressed knights on horseback and foot soldiers wearing chain and leather armor materialized out of a low hanging haze, forming long ranks behind their commanders.

The impact on the humanoids was instantaneous. Vulgar shouts and curses erupted from behind the city walls, and the orcs and Repha'im attacking the monastery moved to meet these new arrivals. The southern gate of the city opened, and hundreds of screaming orc marauders flooded onto the field.

When the knights saw the orcs rushing toward them, they shouted in unison and struck their swords against their shields, the challenge accepted. The sound echoed throughout the valley and hit the city like a physical blow.

Lowering the tip of his lance, the commander shouted, "Charge!" Braying notes from bugles echoed the order. As one, the Iron Tower raced across the field. The ground vibrated with the thundering of hooves, and the light from the sun followed them into the valley.

The front rank of orcs from the monastery plowed into the knights, but the men and horses vanished within a thick cloud of smoke. Before the orcs could react, the marauders from the city charged in from their right, throwing themselves at the knights. The marauders attacked with a ferocity that bordered on madness, and the clang of steel on steel rang out.

All eyes on the wall turned toward the fighting along the western edge of the valley, and several catapults moved into position. The crack of whips filled the air. Grunts and screams followed in their wake.

"Jasper, this is not what I meant!" Xandor said between clenched teeth as they ran forward, surrounded by black-and-silver foot soldiers.

Behind him, Jasper gestured with a pale silver wand and replied plaintively, "I haven't blown anyone up!"

# CHAPTER 21
# CROSSING THE VALLEY

### October 28, 4235 K.E.


**9:42am**

Morning had come, but the sun had yet to shine on the Iron Tower's tree-shrouded encampment. Left to the mercy of the winds, clouds of heavy smoke drifted across the water, limiting vision on both sides of the river to just a few miles.

Rhodinan scouts were constantly on the move, watching for signs of movement from the enemy and reporting to base. One of them raced his horse through the trees toward camp. When he arrived, he found a hundred Iron Tower soldiers holding their own against four hundred warriors from Michurinsk in a mock battle with wooden swords.

Dismounting, the scout rushed past the city of tents and found Lord Fergusson watching his men while conversing with his Leftenant. After a brief conversation, Lord Fergusson called to his squire to bring his horse. He gestured to his Leftenant, giving him command of the exercise, then tugged on the reins and followed the scout into the murky forest.

As soon as they were gone, the Leftenant signaled, and the assault drill began again.


Lord Fergusson and the scout galloped along the forested trail to a bluff overlooking the southern side of Chernigov. When they drew to a halt, the shouts and sounds of fighting carried across the water to them. An improvised blind amid a cluster of trees provided a safe vantage point from which to see the ensuing battle beyond.

Knights of the Iron Tower were battling orcs.

The scout followed the action through a long-range spyglass and said, "Sir, I don't recognize their colors. What garrison are they from?"

Lord Fergusson stared through his own spyglass and replied, "I don't recognize them, either."

"If you don't mind me asking, Sir, were you the only ones sent here?"

"As far as I know."

"Who could they be?"

The Knight Commander chewed his cigar and watched the fight intently.  He moved his spyglass this way and that, keeping up with the ebb and flow of the battle.  Slowly, a smile crept over his face.  The scout looked to where the spyglass pointed.  At first, nothing happened, then knights suddenly charged through the smoke, outflanking the marauders.

"Sir?  How did you know they'd do that?"

"Someone's been studying our history."

"Sir?"

"The fight across the river isn't real.  It's pulled straight from the Battle of Sacile.  See how those knights flanked the orcs, and look there: foot soldiers are charging that cluster of orcs just north of that small building.  This battle occurred twenty years before I was born, son.  Look at their heavy armor."

"You mean those orcs aren't real, either?"

"Some of them are."  The commander pointed to a small knot of orcs standing in a defensive circle, caught away from the safety of the city wall and surrounded by charging knights.  They kept swinging their scimitars, but their blades passed completely through their foes.  For their part, the knights continued forward, not even acknowledging the attack.  In their wake, a cluster of infantry plowed through the orcs.  They marched across the field, building up speed as they went, and charged into the smoky ranks of advancing humanoids.  They fell on each other, hacking and slashing each other to pieces.

**9:55am**

"Keep moving!" Xandor yelled.  "We're almost there!"

The small band raced across the field behind the fighting.  Occasionally, they came across bewildered orcs flailing at the illusory opponents.  A flick of Xandor's blades or a swipe of Grendel's battle-axe made quick work of these obstacles, clearing the way once more.

Closer and closer, they approached the walls of the monastery, and Xandor had to reassess his appraisal:

Jasper's plan wasn't just insane, it was going to get them killed.

The farther east they traveled, the worse the fighting became. More orcs poured out of the city, and flaming missiles flew from the catapults toward the knights. Amongst them sailed clay balls. When they struck, intense, fiery blasts cratered the ground and threw huge chunks of earth into the air.

The ranger spared a glance at Jasper. Sandwiched between Sacha and Grendel, the mage gripped his wand tightly, eyes focused somewhere other than his immediate surroundings. The effort to keep the spell going must have been immense. Despite the freezing temperatures, sweat poured off Jasper's face as he ran, and a thin trickle of blood seeped into his mustache.

"Sir, a band of Iron Tower foot soldiers is nearing the wall!" a warrior shouted from the estate south of Chernigov. Dressed in a grey cloak that helped him blend with the smoke, he watched the battle from atop one of the buildings that braced the western wall.

Their leader, dressed in the same grey-colored cloak, shouted, "To the walls, men of Michurinsk! Let us show the Iron Tower that we, too, are a force to be reckoned with."

Two dozen archers lined the walls of the monastery, taking careful aim with their longbows.

"Fire!"

In unison, the archers fired point-blank into a roving band of orcs. Their arrows flew unerringly through the smoke, striking the monstrous sons of Cayn, real and illusion alike.

Only a paltry few actually felt the arrows. Some shrugged them off with a vicious snarl, while others fell. Most of their arrows flew through the phantom squads of orcs, hitting the ground and skittering off in random directions. For the archers on the wall, the results were far from satisfactory.

"What devilry is this?" their grey-cloaked leader cried from the rooftop. "Hold your shot! Hold your shot!"

Another fire-filled ball of clay slammed into the ground, spewing a fountain of hot dirt into the air. *'They're getting closer,'* Xandor thought.

Of the members of their tiny band, only Chert seemed unaffected by the trembling and shaking of the battlefield under his feet. Dirt, rocks, and burning grass rained down for a dozen yards in every direction around the blast point, creating swirls and eddies in the billows of smoke. Foot soldiers still surrounded them, but their images wavered and lost some of their solidity.

"Jasper, for the record, I hate this plan," Xandor announced.

"Almost there," Jasper gasped. His response was weaker than the previous one, and Xandor cast a worried glance over his shoulder. The mage looked pale and tired — more so than just from running. They needed to get inside those walls.

Some of the smoke cleared, and the top of an X-shaped cross loomed over them. Nailed through his wrists, a soldier in grey-green leather hung limp. His eyes stared down, unseeing. Dried blood from a deep gash along his scalp covered the side of his head. Someone or something had ripped open his stomach. At the base of the cross, entrails lay frozen in a lumpy pile. An errant breeze shifted the stifling haze to reveal a small forest of crosses, each bearing its own gruesome burden.

Leaving the others to catch their breath, Chert hurried amongst the crosses, checking for survivors. A faint groan guided him through the ghastly maze. The soldier hung limp, but his chest expanded and contracted as he breathed. Turning to call for help, Chert found Grendel a few steps behind him.

"Looks like the nails passed between his arm bones," the taller man said. "If I pry them out, it will hurt him worse."

Chert walked behind the cross, staring up at the heavy timbers. "An thou prayest for the ability to do good works, the strength of the Eternal Father shall flow through thee," he murmured. He pressed his hands against the cross and closed his eyes. Seconds ticked by while he stood silently praying. The air around the cross grew heavy. Crackling energy surrounded the stocky priest, moving up his arms to his hands before sinking into the cross. The glow traveled up the wood grain. With a loud groan, the heavy timbers split open around the nails, and Grendel caught the wounded soldier as he fell.

With sparks dancing in his beard and hands aglow, Chert allowed his faith to guide them to the next survivor. As they brought down the third soldier, Xandor's voice cut through the suddenly still air. "RUN!"

Chert looked around, alarmed.

The phantom knights and soldiers surrounding them had disappeared, exposing the tiny team to the real orc army. Hobbling toward the wall of the monastery, Xandor supported an unconscious Jasper on one side while Sacha supported the other. The wand in Jasper's hand turned ash grey and disintegrated.

A furious tidal wave of orcs surged over the field, intent on crushing the humans trapped between the wall of the monastery and the crosses.

"Fire!" a deep voice shouted from behind the monastery wall.

The front rank of orcs collapsed as a storm of arrows plunged into them. Trampling their comrades, the wave of orcs continued forward, cursing.

"Fire!"

A second volley of arrows struck the orcs, causing the line to falter.

Chert yelled at Grendel, who carried three of the crucified warriors, one draped over one shoulder and two on the other. Together, they caught up with Xandor, Jasper, and Sacha as they reached the monastery.

Leaving Sacha supporting Jasper alone, Xandor put his back to the wall and faced the orcs charging toward him. He gripped both his weapons and prepared to fight, but a lethargy seeped into his bones. Thoughts of the friends he had lost along the way clouded his vision. His hands dropped by his sides, the strength to fight ebbing away. Shrugging off the feeling of black depression, he looked around through teary eyes and noticed that it affected the others too.

He remembered the ogres' half-hearted attacks earlier, and it dawned on him: it was the monastery — the place was cursed.

"Fire!"

A cloud of arrows shot out over the wall and struck the orcs again.  Their charge slowed to a cautious trot.  A guttural shout and sharp whipcrack preceded a shuffling in the ranks, and orcs carrying oversized wooden shields moved forward.  They stood shoulder to shoulder and formed a solid wall of thick wood.

"Fire!"

Arrows flew at the wall of orc shields.  Although some passed behind the shield wall, most thudded harmlessly in the wood.

A loud whistling sound caused everyone to look toward the city.  Several enormous clay balls streaked across the sky, rolling and spinning along a trajectory ending in the forest of crosses.

Xandor fought the effects of the curse and yelled for Chert. The dwarf shook himself and began to chant. Despite not understanding the dwarven words, the ranger felt strengthened, and the sadness seeped away. Still chanting, the dwarf forced his hands into the wall and pushed.  A small, dark opening appeared. He kept working at it, making it larger and larger. When it was big enough to allow Grendel to pass, Xandor ordered, "Inside!"

The first of the clay balls flew overhead, crashed among the crosses, and exploded.  Naphtha spewed from the orb, igniting the wood and the bodies nailed to them.  The concussion from the blast shook the wall's foundations and a section of masonry near the top cracked off and shattered beside Xandor.

Not needing any further encouragement, Sacha ducked inside the dark cleft after Grendel.  Xandor quickly followed, dragging Jasper behind him.

Clay balls fell closer and closer.  With Chert outside pushing and Grendel inside pulling, they ferried the three injured men inside.

Several more projectiles arced through the sky.  Chert glanced up to see one heading their way.  "Move it, Grendel!" Chert shouted.  "This one's going to be close!"

The clay ball cast an ever-growing shadow over the opening.

With a superhuman effort, Grendel dragged the last warrior inside and reached back through the wall to snatch Chert in by his chain shirt.

The whistling shriek of the incoming incendiary pierced their ears.  Xandor cast a quick glance around the room. Grendel crouched over Sacha in one corner, his back to the incoming danger, despite the fact he could offer her no real protection from the naphtha and ensuing blaze in the tight space.  Jasper and the rescued soldiers lay slumped together in the opposite corner.  The ranger placed himself between the unconscious men and their impending doom, bracing himself to stand against the blast.

A loud *whumpf* struck outside, and a wave of heat blasted through the small chamber.  The wall snapped shut, cutting off the tongue of flame that darted inside to lick at Chert.  The whole room shook under the force of the blast, filling the air with dirt and debris.  Thin shafts of light trickled down from the ruptured ceiling, but the wall held. Chert pulled his hands out of the masonry and gave thanks to the Eternal Father.

Xandor brushed the dust from his short-cropped hair, then took stock of their situation.  Grendel offered Sacha a hand up while Chert administered what help he could to the four unconscious men.

Standing in the courtyard outside the open doorway, several soldiers dressed in chain armor partially concealed behind grey cloaks rested their hands on the worn hilts of their longswords.  Grim faces gave evidence to the type of life they led.

Xandor did not see much hope in their eyes.  One of them stepped into the room and held up his hand, indicating they were to stay where they were and keep quiet.

Outside, the marching of feet and beating of war drums replaced the noises from the bombardment.  It sounded like every orc in the city was just on the other side of the wall.

Suddenly, the pounding outside stopped, and everything quieted.

"Vityaz, this crude attempt to rescue these men will be your undoing!  What a waste of your precious resources," a harsh orc voice laughed.

A deep voice replied from above them, "Bregu Kraagor, as always, it's such a pleasure to see you again.  Have you come out from behind your walls to surrender to me?"

Raucous laughter echoed, and Bregu Kraagor responded, "Surrender?  Were you hit in the head when last we met?  You have no food and nowhere to go, while I, on the other hand, have both in abundance."

"The last time we met, I believe it was you who suffered a blow to the head, Kraagor.  You seem to have forgotten you were the one who fled the field of battle with your tail between your legs.  I have excellent bards who would be happy to remind you.  How many of your warriors did you lose that day?"

The silence was palpable.

Another voice — Marko's — shouted, "Vityaz, we are not here for you or your men.  This dispute between you and Bregu Kraagor can be temporarily put aside; however, we demand you hand over those who sponsored this unwarranted attack against a sovereign city at once."

"Who are you to address me?"

They could hear the jangle of gear as the orcs shifted their line.

"I am Marko Madasgorski, royal knight and cousin to the throne of Zhitomir."

Grendel laid a calming hand on Sacha's trembling shoulder.

"Knight, you have me at a disadvantage.  I was not aware Zhitomir took an interest in the affairs of orcs."

"You and I both know that Chernigov holds a special strategic significance."

After a moment's pause, the voice above them asked, "What terms do you suggest?"

Grumbling started on both sides of the wall but was quickly hushed.

"Terms, Vityaz?  They are simple.  You're free to go provided you hand over the men you are currently harboring."

"What assurances can you give us that as soon as we leave these protective walls, you and your men will not waylay us?  I do not mean to impugn your honor, Sir Marko, but Bregu Kraagor and I have known each other some time now, and our relationship is founded on a mutual understanding of one another."

"I appreciate your candor; however, I can give you no assurances."

After another moment's pause, the voice overhead replied, "Give me some time to discuss these matters with my men."

"You have the makings of a fine leader," Marko said.  "I give you twenty minutes to make your decision."

"Agreed."

Boots scraped lightly on the ground outside the doorway, and Xandor tensed when the guards stepped aside.  While it was true he heard someone with August's voice and manner of speech, he was at a loss as to how the youth could be here leading these men.  The ranger looked down at Jasper lying on the ground.  Chert wiped the blood from the mage's face, but Jasper had yet to show any signs of waking.

A shadow crossed in front of the doorway and a tall, broad-shouldered teenager dressed in plate armor stepped inside the room.  He looked older than Xandor remembered, and his face seemed grimmer than usual, but there was no doubt this was August Sabe.  All thoughts of the siege and the parley outside were pushed aside by the multitude of questions forming in Xandor's head.  With a smile, he said, "August!  Am I glad to see you!"

The ranger couldn't recall exactly what happened after that.  Everything went black and when he could see again, he found himself lying flat on the floor.  Chert and Grendel stood over him, their weapons drawn.

The young leader stood at the door with his hand on the hilt of his weapon, his face red with anger.  Behind him in the courtyard, men had unsheathed their longswords and held them threateningly.

His beard bristling, Chert said in a low voice, "Boy, take your hand off your weapon and tell your men to back away."

The men behind the knight pressed forward.

Xandor raised his hand in a sign of peace and slowly got to his feet.  He stepped cautiously in front of Chert and Grendel and gestured for them to lower their weapons.

"How dare you accuse me of being that honorless traitor to the Sabe family name!" the young knight exclaimed. "I am Vityaz Dobrynya Sabe!"

Rubbing his jaw, Xandor realized his mistake and said, "Lord, I mean, Vityaz Dobrynya, I apologize for my error. Please, let me explain."

Dobrynya recovered his composure and surveyed the room. His eyes roved the shadows, but they kept coming back to the hulking form standing behind Xandor. "You travel with one of the enemy, yet you risked your life to rescue three of my men. Why?"

Choosing his words carefully, Xandor answered, "Vityaz Dobrynya, I again apologize for mistaking you for August, but when I was up on the ridge, I saw you and your banner and thought a friend was in danger."

The words seemed to surprise Dobrynya, and he stared hard at the ranger. "The one who was my brother is not worthy of such an effort, warrior."

"Perhaps he wasn't at one time, but people can change."

A soft groan sounded from the corner, and Jasper opened his eyes. "What happened? Did we make it?" he asked weakly. He sat up and looked around.

Xandor tried to subtly catch the mage's attention before he saw Dobrynya, but it was too late. "August?" Jasper said a little firmer.

Red crept back into the knight's face, and his eyes bored into the seated figure.

Chert shifted slightly and placed himself in front of the mage.

"Did I miss something?" Jasper stood slowly and leaned heavily on his staff.

Barely moving his lips, Chert replied, "That's not who you think it is."

"It's not?!" Jasper exclaimed, his voice slurring. "Well then, who are you?"

Xandor turned and gave the mage a hard look. A surprised Jasper closed his mouth, but his eyes remained full of questions.

"Vityaz Dobrynya, please forgive my friend. My name is Xandor, a ranger in service to the Iron Tower. My dwarven friend is Chert Joalheiro."

Xandor continued with the introductions, gesturing to the hulking figure behind him.  "And this is Grendel.  You are right, he is half-orc.  Nevertheless, he has proven himself loyal and honorable many times over.  Behind him is Lady Aleksandra Madasgorski, and our rude mage is Jasper Thredd from Tydway.  Obviously, he is acquainted with your brother as well, and helped us reach your walls."

The youth's eyes lingered on Lady Madasgorski.  "Little good it has done you.  You are now trapped here like the rest of us, with the entirety of Chernigov outside, waiting for me to make the decision to turn you over to them or not."

Sacha stepped forward.  "You cannot trust Marko."

Dobrynya eyed her suspiciously and said matter-of-factly, "Lady, I am well aware of your family's reputation.  The saying goes: the only reason a Madasgorski purposely reveals himself is he feels he has the upper hand."  The youth glanced at Xandor and gave him a questioning look.  "You travel with strange company, ranger."

Smiling, Xandor replied, "I know we may look an odd company, but each one here has proven their worth.  Give us a chance to show you."

Jasper suddenly coughed and said quietly, "Let me catch my breath."

Everyone watched the mage close his eyes and chant a few words in an odd tongue.  Gripping his staff tightly with both hands, he jerked it back like a fishing rod that had just caught a fish.  His staff quivered, and his arms struggled with some unseen burden.

Alarmed, Dobrynya laid his hand on the hilt of his sword.

Xandor whispered, "Vityaz Dobrynya, give us that chance."

A pain-filled shriek echoed beyond the walls, and a disembodied eyeball hovered over Dobrynya's shoulder.  The youth ducked and drew his longsword in one smooth motion.  Before he could swing, Jasper's chanting changed.  Waves of heat rolled off the eyeball, and it glowed red as it started to melt.  It fled out of the room and over the wall.  Everyone stood, horrified, staring at the trail of ichor it left behind.  After it disappeared, Xandor and Dobrynya overheard Jasper say to himself, "Fool me once..."

"What was that?" Dobrynya asked, still alarmed.

"An old acquaintance."

His face ashen with fright, Dobrynya demanded, "Why are you here?"

Jasper said, "We need something the elves placed in the monastery before the orcs took over.  We need the Tear of Havel."

Dobrynya's eyes widened in surprise and said, "It's no longer here."

"Are you sure?  It would have been hidden in the chapel."

"You can search for yourself, but I'm afraid the chapel is no longer accessible.  The roof collapsed months ago, and we have been slowly filling it in with dirt.  Most everything is buried."

"What!" Jasper's face fell.

Xandor stepped beside his friend and laid a reassuring hand on his shoulder.  "We'll find it."

Dobrynya asked, "Why is it so important to you?"

Jasper glanced up at the vityaz and answered, "It may hold the key to the cure Trakya and, I fear, the world, desperately needs."

Dobrynya studied them both carefully before saying, "All is not lost, mage.  I know where it is." Before anyone could question him, he turned to Xandor and asked, "What was your plan?  I mean, now that you're here, how did you expect to get out?"

Giving Jasper a sharp look, the ranger answered, "My intention was to create a distraction — a *distraction*, Jasper — not bring out the whole bloody city."

"It was all I could think of on short notice," replied Jasper.  "Besides, we needed something big, and you know it."

Dobrynya's brow furrowed in confusion.  In a flash, it cleared, and he asked, "Who do you have on the outside?"

Jasper gave the ranger an almost imperceptible nod of encouragement, and Xandor faced the youth.  "There's a company of Iron Tower soldiers on the east bank of the river awaiting our signal.  We also have two other friends outside the valley.  They are currently making their way past the city to cross the river and help coordinate."

"Real soldiers, not the illusion I saw earlier?"

"They're real," Xandor said confidently.

Hope filled Dobrynya, and he said, "That's the best news I've heard all day.  Mage, are you fit enough to cast some more magic?"

"What do you have in mind?"

With a sly smile, the vityaz answered, "Maybe the question you should really be asking is, where did we get all that dirt to fill the chapel?"

# CHAPTER 22
# THE MONASTERY

### October 28, 4235 K.E.

**10:25am**

An icy breeze rippled past the gold and azure cloth bearing the Sabe family crest — a seven-pointed star. The smoke cleared a little, and Vityaz Dobrynya Sabe, dressed in plate armor covered by an azure surcoat, surveyed the horde outside the walls as he propped his kite-shaped shield against the parapet. At his feet, a bit of twine interlaced with tiny black beads ran sporadically along the perimeter of the monastery — something Jasper had pulled from a white pouch.

What remained of his men, fifty in all, guarded the wall. The curse of the monastery constantly reminded him of those they had lost. Deep inside, a reservoir of defiance welled, banishing their faces and his excuses.

Beyond the monastery, row upon row of orc soldiers and other slavering beasts, all armed with clubs, rusted swords, or long spears, waited. Intermingled with the group were heavy-set Repha'im, who stood twice as tall as those around them. Savage, unintelligent brutes, they were only good for causing massive amounts of damage.

Dobrynya searched the horde, but there was no sign of Bregu Kraagor and his entourage.

The sea of orcs kept their distance from the monastery walls, as if some physical barrier prevented them from getting any closer. The orcs were superstitious of the monastery and its curse, and over the past year, Dobrynya and his men had done everything they could to reinforce that superstition. All that effort was over now. Bregu Kraagor had allowed Dobrynya and his band of resistance fighters to play their little games, but Sir Marko Madasgorski would not. Of that, there was no doubt.

Taking off his helmet to wipe the sweat from his bald pate, Dobrynya's second-in-command watched the young lord struggle silently.  After a moment, Ilya Ergorov said, "Sir, the men are in position."

"Help the dwarf move the wounded and then report back to me," Dobrynya commanded, still staring at the horde.

Bowing, Ilya said, "Yes, Sir."  He started to leave the wall, but before he had taken his second step, the young vityaz turned to him and said grimly, "Ilya, remind the men that the sons of Cayn have a cleric of the Dark One.  Leave no bodies for him to use against us, especially our own."

"Yes, Sir."

Chert and Sacha, carrying Xandor and Grendel's cloaks and other equipment, led a small group of soldiers across the courtyard.  Borne by their comrades, the three men rescued from crucifixion lay unconscious in litters.

Halfway to the chapel, Chert pulled Sacha aside and said gravely, "Lady, I don't know what you are playing at, but you have my best friend convinced you're here to help us.  And now, Xandor has convinced the vityaz that you are one of us."  Chert waited to let his words sink in before continuing, "If you hurt my friend or prove Xandor wrong, I'll bury you."

Somehow, the visual he conveyed seemed more sinister after watching what he had done to the wall.  Sacha paled but otherwise kept her composure.  "Dwarf, threats are not necessary.  We all share a common goal.  I will not disappoint you or your friends."

Jasper waited at the chapel door while a soldier holding a short length of twine ran up to him.  The mage took it and counted the tiny black grains woven into it.

"We covered as much as we could," the soldier said.

"It will have to do," Jasper replied absently.  Each grain was spherical in shape, with a surface made from twenty hexagons and twelve pentagons.  Trapped inside was the barest trace of dark matter, a substance Jasper had learned about while studying with the White Circle.  Taking out the small white pouch stitched with silver symbols, Jasper loosened the cord, uncinched the top, and dropped the last of the twine inside.  Dismissing the soldier, he passed under the central arch and entered the chapel.

Dobrynya was right.  Everything was buried.  Nothing remained except for a hollowed-out building, open to the sky.  Soil and rotten timbers still frozen from the rain a few nights ago covered the entire floor and most of the walls.  An uneven mound of dirt and debris along the perimeter of the chapel sloped up from the main entrance to a height of roughly six feet.

Using his staff to help him, the mage climbed the mound and found what he was looking for: an opening near the top of the wall where a stained-glass window had resided.  It was the right size and shape, and, in his gut, he felt certain this was the right place.  It matched the glass window at Tsarevets perfectly.

Vityaz Dobrynya had said he knew where the Tear was.  Jasper hoped it was somewhere they could actually reach.

At the top of the earthen mound, Jasper felt a change in the atmosphere.  The feeling of sadness was strongest here; however, it didn't feel like any curse he had been exposed to or taught about.  This was different.  It was more like the emotion had soaked deep into every stone and was reflected back on anyone who came near.  '*Did the Tear of Havel cause this*?' he wondered.

He knew he had used too much magic to get here, but for some reason, he felt renewed instead of drained.  Even the voices inside his head had stopped.  Was it this place?  Shouting outside jarred him from his thoughts.

Turning to leave, he wasn't aware his hand had been gripping the *Veritas autem Sutekh.*

"Vityaz Dobrynya!  Have you made your decision?"
Standing on one of the short buildings buttressing the western wall, the vityaz glanced around one last time to make sure his men were ready.  Ilya and the ranger led the soldiers near the north wall while the half-orc, Grendel, stood with the men at the main gate to the south.

Three of his men dashed across the courtyard to get into position along the eastern edge of the monastery, where an amalgam of broken buildings and mounds of dirt braced a long stretch of grey wall.  Farther north, Chernigov lay partially shrouded by the perpetual clouds of smoke and ash that hid it from the sun.

Dobrynya stared back at Marko, who waited with the orc soldiers. Wearing his plate armor and helmet, the Zhitomiran knight was an imposing figure atop his stallion. He held his horse's reins with one hand and in the other carried a sharp-edged shield emblazoned with the red sleeve sinister on an ermine field. Behind him, the hulking, colorless Seldaehne sat on his Shire horse. Bregu Kraagor was conspicuously absent, which meant one thing: this was going to be a fight.

Taking a deep breath, the vityaz yelled back, "Sir Marko, we have! We elect to stay!"

"Fool! Can you not see the folly of that decision? We will overrun these walls. Your men will be tortured and killed in front of you while you are ransomed back to your father. You will go home in disgrace! And for what? A few men who are not even loyal to you!"

Walking his horse parallel to the wall, Marko continued, "Men of Michurinsk! Do not let your impetuous leader act stupidly! Save yourselves! All you have to do is give us what we want, and you are free to go!"

As one, the men behind the wall raised their bows high and yelled defiantly, taunting the knight of Zhitomir.

"We have made our decision!" Dobrynya shouted after the noise subsided. "Go back to Bregu Kraagor and tell him that he will have to spill blood in order to root us out!"

The horde of orcs on the field yelled and struck swords to shields, causing the walls of the monastery to shake. Weaker portions of stucco cracked and fell, revealing the salmon-colored brick behind. A constant trickle of sand from the mortar joints rained down the front face.

Noticing the effect the noise was having, Marko yelled, "We will march around your puny walls and bring them crashing down around you!"

One of the archers lowered his bow and began to sing a well-known battle hymn. His lone voice rang out clearly, echoing off the walls of the courtyard. At first, only those closest added their voices to his, but soon, the music spread as each warrior joined. The battle hymn took life as various vocal ranges blended together in defiance.

The acrid smoke over the monastery lifted slightly, giving everyone a breath of fresh air. Even the walls of the monastery seemed to settle down.  The cacophony caused by the sons of Cayn faltered as the singing coming from the Rhodinan soldiers grew stronger and filled the valley.

Marko made a disgusted face and raised his hand.  When he dropped it, ogres within the horde of humanoids hoisted ladders made of red iron.  Orcs along the front rank raised their tall wooden shields, forming a solid line.  Marko lowered the visor on his helm, unsheathed his sword, and pointed toward the wall with the tip of his blade.  "Attack!"

Humanoids on all four sides of the monastery surged forward, emboldened by their numbers.

Yelling from the northern defenses sliced through the singing and grabbed Dobrynya's attention.  He turned quickly and watched several dark objects fly over the combatants on the field.

"Incoming!" he warned as he unsheathed his sword and lifted his shield.  Facing one side and then the other, he ordered, "Archers, fire at will!"

Small groups of bowmen, standing on earthen embankments or the roofs of short buildings, took aim with their longbows from behind the parapet and fired into the mass of humanoids.  Arrows streaked unerringly, hungry to find their targets.  More than forty of the sons of Cayn fell, only to be replaced by a hundred more.

Orc officers yelled, and whips cracked.  Holding dark, Turkestani-style recurve bows with siyahs made of human bone, a line of orc archers advanced.  Barbed arrows flew over the horde, through the smoke, and into the courtyard.

Those not fast enough to find cover staggered and fell with black-fletched shafts riddling their bodies.  Men raced across the courtyard, dodging arrows, and dragged the bodies into the chapel.

The archers on the wall nocked their arrows while squatting behind the parapets, stood as one, and fired again.  They rained arrows on the orcs, devastating their ranks.  Heedless of their losses, the orcs continued their charge toward the foot of the wall.

After glancing toward the north, the vityaz shouted to his left and his right, "Hold!"

Everyone instinctively ducked when the deadly clay projectiles exploded against the northern defenses, splashing flaming naphtha over the top of the wall. Screaming soldiers dropped to the courtyard below.

For just a moment, smoke obscured the northern half of the monastery. When it cleared, the now soot-covered wall seemed intact. Those men who were able climbed back into position.

Arrows leapt from behind the walls of the monastery, striking the orcs again and again; however, it wasn't enough to slow the onrushing wave.

The front rank of orcs, concealed behind their shields, reached the bottom of the walls and stopped. Holding their shields higher, the orcs shifted as the ogres stepped around them. They planted one end of their heavy ladders into the ground and leaned them against the wall.

Seeing the tip of a ladder appear in front of him, Dobrynya ran forward, using his shield to protect him from the still-flying arrows. He kicked the ladder hard to the left, and it scraped against the side of the wall as it fell.

Others weren't as lucky, and orcs streamed onto the walls.

Steel on steel rang out as swords clashed. The Rhodinans along the wall fought defensively and slowly backed toward the edge of the buildings or down the earthen embankments.

The ladder reappeared in front of Dobrynya and clacked against the bricks. Before he could get to it, an ogre wearing hardened leather armor surged toward him, his brownish-green face painted in nightmarish shades of red. He bared his pointed teeth in a savage growl. Holding a crude axe, he rushed toward the young lord with a powerful, overhand cut.

Dobrynya brought up his shield to deflect the axe blade. Instead of letting the axe fall squarely on the face, he canted it slightly, causing the axe to slide and draw sparks. Expecting more resistance, the ogre lost his balance. He tried to recover, but it was too late.

The youth sidestepped the ogre, whipped around, and struck the creature on the back of the neck with the sharp edge of his broadsword. The thick vertebrae snapped, and black blood welled up, covering the wound.

Letting the creature fall, the vityaz backed toward the inner edge of the roof as several orcs approached him. He waited until they stepped near the string of beads and yelled, "Now!"

A loud horn sounded, and the Rhodinans leapt from the wall as a ring of searing black fire erupted along the top of the roofs and earthen mounds.

Caught by surprise, the invaders transformed into living torches. Howling, the pain-maddened beasts fled the searing heat; some falling backward into the sea of their comrades while others surged past the Rhodinans and threw themselves into the courtyard, where they fell to their knees. Portions of their skin melted under the heat of the dark flame and sloughed off the bone onto the ground, forming puddles of brown and black ooze.

Tearing his eyes away from the melting orcs, Dobrynya looked up at the whistling noises coming from overhead. Glowing boulders arced toward them through the smoky air. "To the chapel!" he ordered.

Dragging the wounded behind them, soldiers sprinted across the courtyard, aiming for the dark entrance to the chapel. Others dispatched the remaining humanoids mercilessly, making sure the way was clear.

The northeastern corner of the monastery exploded, and red clouds of brick dust obscured the courtyard.

Vague forms staggered along the fringe of the plume. The first was Ilya, still holding his sword. Blood ran from a gash over his right eye, and he blinked owlishly. Behind him, the dust cleared, revealing the boulders had pulverized a V-shaped section in the wall. For a brief moment, everything stopped, and the world held its breath. Then, a roaring torrent of sons of Cayn poured through the stair-stepped opening.

Carrying his double-bitted battle-axe in front of him with both hands, Grendel raced across the courtyard toward the opening and threw himself at the crowd of orcs. With his long dreadlocks flying behind him as if possessed, the mighty thews of his broad shoulders heaved and the blade of his battle-axe cleaved the first orc in half. He caught the next one with a sharp kick to the side of the knee and struck it with the haft of his axe, sending it to the ground.

Red with dust, Xandor emerged from one of the short buildings. Ilya joined him, and they rallied the men near the shattered wall, giving others time to pull out anyone who was injured or dead and head to the chapel.

More glowing boulders streaked across the sky, enchanted by dark magic. This time, they struck the short buildings that formed part of the eastern wall, and the bombardment shook the very foundations of the monastery. Various sized chunks of brick flew into the air and rained down on humans and orcs alike. Another red cloud of dust billowed out, obscuring the courtyard.

His ears still ringing, Dobrynya barely heard the clangor of fighting within the cloud. Shouting, "To me! To me!" he worked his way blindly across the courtyard toward the chapel entrance. Men carrying the injured ran to the sound of his voice.

The dust settled, and Dobrynya grimaced. The northern defenses were all but destroyed. A jagged line of pale red brick stuck up from the ground like an open wound, and the interior masonry walls had collapsed like a row of dominoes.

Gesturing for his men to hurry inside the chapel, the vityaz watched as, through the confusion, Xandor and Grendel fought their way to each other, leaving a trail of humanoids behind them. Their swords flashing in the dim light, Ilya and the Rhodinans formed ranks behind them and helped stem the flood of orcs and ogres.

Both his longswords coursing with golden fire, Xandor lunged and ran the nearest orc through with his left-hand blade while slicing a second orc across the throat with his right-hand weapon. The simple efficiency of the warrior's motions, combined with the fluid ease of long practice, turned the scene into a kind of horrific dance that swayed back and forth in the cacophony-filled yard.

Next to the ranger, Grendel growled and bared his canines, causing the orcs to mistake him for a friend rather than a foe. He swung his axe with both hands, lopping off orcnéan heads, several at a time. Grendel and Xandor fought well together, and, in short order, a pile of orc bodies lay in front of them.

A loud boom echoed, and the barred gate on the south wall buckled.

"Hurry! Everyone inside!"

Grendel grabbed a squealing orc by the neck and flung him away.  More orcs crawled over the rubble like ants.  "We have got to get out of here before they surround us!"  The half-orc's deep bass voice rumbled over the sounds of battle.

Sweat streaming down his face, Xandor nodded as he swept the edges of both his blades across the abdomen of an orc, spilling its entrails.  The two continued their display of swordsmanship and axe wielding while slowly retreating toward the chapel entrance.

Giant shapes appeared beyond the gap in the wall, and more boulders flew toward the soldiers.  Orcs and men scattered.  The boulders flew past Grendel and Xandor and dug deep furrows in the courtyard floor.

Again, a loud boom echoed as something heavy struck the gate.  This time, the heavy timber barring it split with an ominous crack.  Feeble movement in the shadow of the wall caught the young lord's eye.

"Mage!"  Dobrynya  yelled  as  he  brandished  his broadsword and ran to the aid of the trapped man.


**11:00am**

Jasper emerged from the chapel to see the young lord rushing toward the gate by himself, probably unaware he displayed the same caliber of reckless bravery as his brother.

With a thundering boom, the courtyard turned into a conflagration of burning bodies as naphtha-filled projectiles struck.  Confusion reigned as the foul-smelling smoke completely obscured the northern and western portions of the monastery.

Rhodinan warriors stopped, dropped, and rolled, but the liquid adhered to their armor and clothing.  When that failed, they stripped off their outer layer of garments and flung them, still aflame, at the orcs.

Grendel ripped off the remains of his leather jerkin and tossed it down, revealing a crisscross of faded scars on the front and back of his torso.  Miraculously untouched by the heat and flame, Xandor remained at Grendel's side, his swords burning even brighter than before.

Inadvertently, the last barrage from Chernigov helped the Rhodinans more than it hurt.  The orcs, rather than the humans, took the brunt of the damage, leaving their numbers significantly reduced.  Seizing the opening, the

Rhodinan rear guard pressed forward with their attack. It was a brutal, unglamorous affair, fighting over smoldering corpses, but the rally was enough to allow their comrades to pull out the last of the wounded and the dead.

Judging by the haphazard sounds of fighting, Jasper didn't expect many survivors. He scurried across the yard after Dobrynya, shouting in the direction where he had last seen his friends, "Xandor! Grendel! Hurry up! We don't have all day!"

He caught sight of the young leader hefting aside a chunk of debris pinning one of his soldiers. The freed man struggled to stand, but it was obvious his leg was broken. The vityaz ducked under the soldier's arm and hoisted him to his feet. They managed to get clear of the main gate moments before it crashed open with a shrieking of iron and splintering of wood. Outside, two Repha'im held a massive battering ram fashioned from a stripped tree trunk. The orcs behind them charged.

Standing shoulder to shoulder with Dobrynya, Jasper couldn't shake the idea it was August there with him. "Go on," he said. "Get that man out of here. I can handle this."

Not waiting for the vityaz's reply, he stepped forward, pointed the blackened end of his staff at the giants and the horde of orcs poised on the other side of the gate and yelled, "Vrontés kai boulóni astrapís!"

White lightning arced from the tip of Jasper's staff, split into two forks, and struck each of the giants with a deafening peal of thunder, knocking them off their feet. Grins turned to screams as the orcs standing at the entrance dropped their weapons and grabbed their ears, black blood streaming between their clawed fingertips.

From the corner of his eye, Jasper saw Dobrynya staring at him in astonishment. "What are you still doing here?" he asked. Beyond the fallen giants, the crack of whips drew his attention to see the horde moving again. "Damn! I thought that would be more of a deterrent," the mage huffed.

"Come, Feliks, it is past time for us to advance toward the chapel," Dobrynya said to the man leaning heavily on his shoulder.

"Let us go together, moy komandir," the injured soldier urged.

In the courtyard, Xandor and Grendel helped Ilya hold the ground in front of the chapel against the growing tide of humanoids, while the last few stragglers made their way inside. More scimitar-wielding orcs poured through the breached walls.

"Go," Jasper said. "I'll be right behind you." With a curt nod, Dobrynya and the injured soldier took off in a hobbling run.

Jasper took a deep, steadying breath, not allowing himself to doubt his strength. He lifted his staff, turned at a measured pace, and a wall of red and orange flames erupted around the courtyard, separating most of the orcs from the humans. Panicked orcs stumbled over one another as the ones closest to the fire tried to flee while the ones in the rear were driven forward by their officers.

Jasper leaned heavily on his staff, too out of breath to run. He heard the vityaz shout, "Move it, mage!" Jaw set in grim determination, he shuffled back toward the chapel.

The battle became more frantic as the Rhodinan ranks closed. Shouts and grunts accompanied the sounds of licking flames. Orc and human blood ran freely, and the earth beneath their feet turned muddy from the gore.

A geyser of flame exploded among the orcs, stemming the tide enough to allow the last soldiers to escape into the chapel. The few remaining orcs caught between Grendel, Xandor, and the fire threw down their weapons in surrender. The two ignored them and raced through the doorway.

Ilya appeared at Jasper's side and helped him cover the last few yards.

"Everyone's clear," Dobrynya said when they arrived at his side.

Jasper nodded. "Time for my last trick, then." He closed his eyes and waved his staff before entering the chapel, triggering the string of beads he had left behind. An explosion of black fire briefly engulfed the courtyard. Heat rippled, and corpses melted.

Skirting the edge of the debris mound, Jasper, Dobrynya, and Ilya followed a well-worn path into a side chamber. Chert greeted them with a nod and hurried the trio down a narrow set of stairs to a musty crypt.

Carved stone columns veneered in limestone flanked alcoves along either side of the chamber. A pile of bones rested at the bottom of each where someone had brushed them aside to make room for Dobrynya's fallen men. All of them, that was, except for the last one.

With a bandage wrapped around his forehead, a warrior held a torch above a dark tunnel dug into the back of the empty alcove.

Ilya caught Jasper staring at the ornate carvings, some of which were elven. He took the torch and sent the wounded soldier after the others. "Sir, we can't stay," Ilya said politely. The mage tore his eyes away from the column and entered the alcove.

At the bottom of the stairs, Chert knelt and prayed to the Eternal Father. He placed his hands on the ground, and the walls of the chapel shook. The already weakened masonry fractured along the mortar joints.

The last of his men to leave, Vityaz Dobrynya watched, wide-eyed, as the door to the crypt shattered and a slab of red brick fell across the stair opening with a deafening boom. When Chert stood, dirt still poured down the steps.

**11:38am**

Marko Madasgorski and Kourash walked the courtyard, surveying the devastation. Behind the two men, an orc captain waited silently, trying not to attract the attention of the knight or his henchman.

The Zhitomiran knight was livid. Orc bodies lay scattered, their burnt corpses adding to the stench, but not a single Rhodinan warrior was to be found.

Marko stared at what remained of the ruined chapel. "Captain!" the word shot out like a curse.

"Yes, muh lort?"

"They went underground! Find them! Find that exit!"

The orc captain, relieved to have something to do, scurried off, growling orders.

Marko turned to Kourash and said, "They're here. I know it."

# CHAPTER 23
# TIGHT SPACES

### October 28, 4235 K.E.


**11:40am**

The scent of raw earth combined with smoke from several burning torches slathered in pine pitch made an odd concoction for the olfactory senses. Chert reveled in it. He buried his hands in the tunnel walls and slowly shaped the rock and dirt, closing off the entrance. It was a precaution they had to take, but it also left them with no way to retreat. As soon as he sealed the adit, the air ceased flowing and grew stale. If anyone suspected they were claustrophobic but didn't know for sure, they were about to find out.

Every ten feet, a timber post and lintel system shored the tunnel ceiling. Carrying his helmet under his arm, Chert ducked under them with a smile. It wasn't often he found a place where he felt tall.

Crawling in the tunnel like they were, the company traveled only a few dozen yards before they stopped to rest. Eyes burning, everyone laid down where they were and tried to keep their heads below the acrid smoke. Chert went up the line, checking each man and healing those he could. He counted nineteen that could walk, and eight that either had broken legs or were unconscious. Despite being alive, there was a distinct lack of hope in the air.

Near the midpoint of the line, Grendel lay flat with his forehead resting on his arms, chest heaving. His frame was too large to travel down the tunnel like everyone else, forcing him to bellycrawl. Chert could see raw spots were already forming on his friend's shoulders and elbows where they'd rubbed against the walls.

Dirt trickled down from the ceiling onto Grendel's back, and he flinched. Chert prayed the Eternal Father would help everyone remain calm — especially Grendel. There would be no escape if anyone panicked and caused the tunnel to collapse.

There was one thing Chert could do for them. He dug around in his belt pouch, found four pieces of quartz, and prayed for light. Instantly, a warm glow illuminated the adit. Everyone breathed a sigh of relief when he passed the crystals up the line, and the soldiers put out their torches.

Their respite over, they traveled farther into the tunnel and felt the weight of the earth above them grow heavier and heavier.


## 12:00pm

During their next break, Dobrynya moved awkwardly up the line, squeezing past his soldiers, and found Xandor writing in his journal.

"I wanted to thank you," the young lord said.

"We're not out of this yet," Xandor said without looking up.

"I know, but without your help and that of your team, we would not have gotten this far. We would not have had hope."

Putting down the glowing stylus and closing the journal, Xandor glanced at the young knight. "You're a good man, Vityaz Dobrynya."

"Just Dobrynya, if you don't mind."

"Xandor gave him a quick nod and a smile.

Looking away, the teenager stared down the adit into the darkness. The youth's face grew distant, and Xandor knew he was thinking of the men he had lost. As the ranger continued to watch Dobrynya, a thought occurred to him. He broke the silence by asking, "How long have you been working on this tunnel?"

"Over a year."

"Wow. And Bregu Kraagor just let you pile up dirt in the monastery?"

"I don't know if he knew about it. For some reason, the orcs left the monastery alone, especially the chapel. Maybe they were afraid to do anything because it was holy ground. It wasn't until a few nights ago that they even knew we were there."

"What did you originally have in mind when you built this tunnel?"

Not answering, Dobrynya turned to his second-in-command and asked, "Do you have the map?"

Taking a scrap piece of paper from his pouch, Ilya unfolded it and handed it to Dobrynya. Glancing at it briefly, the young lord passed it to Xandor. The map showed Chernigov before the orc occupation. Several calculations were scribbled in the margins, along with various slope lines. Someone had drawn a red circle around the outline of a building located just south of the town's center. Faded, black dashed lines led from the building to the waterfront.

"My grandfather took this map from a smuggler before the war. I never really thought it would come in handy until now."

"What's that?" Xandor asked, pointing to the building circled in red.

"That building is the inn where the Kral and the Korol' signed the treaty that inspired the Rainbow Bridge. According to our records, there's a basement underneath it. We built this tunnel to access that basement and get inside Chernigov."

"Why?"

"To set the stage for a direct attack on Bregu Kraagor. We think removing him would fracture the power structure of the orcs and cause a civil war. They might even disperse enough that we could drive them completely out. Of course, that won't happen now. At least not this way."

Xandor turned back to the map, "What about those dashed lines?"

"That's our way out. A smuggler's run."

"Is it still there?"

"Maybe. That's a chance we have to take."

The ranger studied the map. "I recommend we separate when we get to the inn," he said pensively. "You'll have a better chance of escaping if we create a diversion."

"No. We go in together; we come out together."

Appreciating the youth's sense of loyalty, Xandor turned to face him. "Not this time, Dobrynya. We have unfinished business with Marko."

Taking back the map, Dobrynya said, "If we make it out of here, the least I can do is invite you to Pomest'ye Sabe to meet my father and help your friend find what he's looking for."

"Is that where the Tear of Havel is located? At your father's estate?"

Weighing the man in front of him, Dobrynya hesitated before answering, "Yes."

Clapping the younger man on the shoulder, Xandor said, "Thank you.  We'll be there."

Dobrynya had just given the map back to Ilya when they heard Grendel gasp, "Chert!"

Alarmed, everyone looked down the line.

Grendel lay on his belly and stared up the tunnel.  His eyes were wild and those near him backed away as best they could in the tight confines, expecting him to snap at any moment.  Some of the warriors had their hands on the hilts of their daggers.  They had seen him in action and knew there would be no stopping him if he lost it down here — at least, not without a fight.

Without hesitation,0 the dwarf walked down the line, pushing the soldiers aside.  Curses followed in his wake when he accidentally stepped on a hand or tripped over someone's leg.  Ignoring the outbursts, he found Grendel turning this way and that, sweat pouring down his face and his eyes filled with fear.

Laying a hand on his friend's shoulder, Chert bent down and prayed.  His words were calm and seemed to have an immediate effect.  Grendel's wild look disappeared, replaced with one of despair.  "I can't make it."  Grendel's breath came in gasps.

"Yes, you can."

"It's too tight.  The ground is closing in on me."

"Grendel, look at me," Chert commanded.  His friend slowly leaned his head to one side and peered at him from one eye.  The dwarf's voice was gentle but still carried a note of authority.  "I'm able to stand upright.  You are not wider than I am tall, and this tunnel is mostly square."

"I'm suffocating," Grendel gasped.

Chert crouched.  "Grendel, you'll be able to breathe better if you roll on your side.  We'll let the men behind us pass and give you some room.  Come on, let me help you."  The dwarf sent word up to Dobrynya and said, "Get the men moving.  We'll be along shortly."

Dobrynya gave the orders to continue deeper into the adit.  Immediately, everyone began crawling away.  All save Sacha and Xandor.

The ranger made sure Chert had Grendel under control before he pulled his journal back out.  He quickly sketched the map Dobrynya had shown him, including a rough line indicating the smuggler's run and where it exited at the river.  Closing the journal, the ranger gave Chert a questioning look.  The dwarf nodded once and then jerked his chin at the soldiers.  Xandor returned the nod, then hastened to catch up to the Rhodinans.

**12:07pm**

Lord Fergusson opened the journal and wrote, "How do you plan to get out?"

Nothing immediately appeared.

"I guess he's not just waiting on me, then," he muttered.

"Excuse me, Milord?" asked Patrick Anders.

"Nothing, young man.  Just thinking about our friend across the river.  Help me with my armor."

He flipped the cover closed and picked up his breastplate.  While Patrick finished adjusting the last of the straps, Fergusson checked the journal again.  A rough sketch of the city appeared on the page, and a dashed line connected the box labeled *inn* to the western shore of the river.  Underneath was written, "Dobrynya will use old tunnel to escape.  Need to create a diversion.  Start attack at dawn.  Need boat to cross river."

Fergusson closed his eyes and let out a long sigh.

It had begun.

**12:08pm**

With Xandor and the soldiers moving farther down the tunnel, the light faded, and everything grew quiet. Darkness reigned.  All Sacha could hear was Grendel taking long, deep breaths.  The faint golden glow of Chert's eyes and the intermittent violet flash of Grendel's was the only hint of light to guide her closer to them.

"I can help," she offered.

Chert stared at her with open suspicion, but his glare was lost upon her in the gloom.

"I have a necklace that can alter his size."

"You will not use your witchcraft on my friend," Chert said.

"Listen, I really can help," Sacha said, pulling out a thin gold chain and unfastening the clasp.

Chert eyed the necklace warily like it was alive but didn't stop her when she reached for Grendel.  As she whispered a few words, the thin gold chain stretched, fitting tightly to his thick neck.  Still holding the chain, she continued whispering, and slowly, Grendel shrank.

"Tell me if you want me to shrink you farther," Sacha said.

Grendel took a deep, steadying breath.  He could sit in the small confines, and the maneuverability seemed to calm him.  Holding his heavy battle-axe across his lap, he clenched and unclenched his fists, then stretched his arms and shoulders.

"How do you feel?" Chert asked.

"Better."

Sacha leaned back and said, "When you want to go back to your true size, just take off the necklace."

Taking out another piece of quartz, Chert prayed for light.  The semi-precious stone gave off a warm glow. Handing it to Sacha, he said softly, "Here.  We need to catch up to the others."

"You're welcome," she replied smugly.

Grendel cleared his throat, drawing their attention back to him.

Not meeting either of their eyes, Grendel pointed hesitantly to his tusks and asked, "Can you do something about these, too?"

"Sure.  Why?" Sacha asked.

Grendel just shrugged.

Touching the chain around his neck again, Sacha whispered softly.  Slowly, Grendel's canines receded into his mouth, making him appear more human.  He ran his tongue over his teeth.  Satisfied, he grabbed Sacha before she could release the gold chain and gave her an ardent kiss.

Letting her go, Grendel rose to a crouch.  In a matter of moments, he slipped past Sacha and crawled deeper into the adit, leaving her to stare after him in stunned silence.

# CHAPTER 24
# SEHRAINE'S TALE

### October 28, 4235 K.E.


**12:14pm**

"Milord!"
The shouted exclamation of his oh-so-youthful squire startled Lord Fergusson out of his musings. Turning around, he noted the excitement in his aide's face as the youngster burst through the door hangings and skidded to a halt, all signs of discipline abandoned.

"Milord, a pair of Trakyans are here!"

Sitting at his desk, Fergusson quietly muttered, "Finally," and fought to keep his expression neutral as he stared at his squire. The young man practically bounced in place. After a few seconds of the Knight Commander staring at him, Patrick Anders calmed himself and straightened his leather vestments. "Sorry, Sir. Won't happen again."

"Very good, Anders. Show them in immediately."

A moment later, Anders returned with the two women Xandor had described in his earlier message. Still, the bantam size of the two ladies surprised him. Fergusson stood and took a closer look at them. He noted their dirty faces and the dark stains on their clothes, the thick knit hats covering their heads and ears that seemed at odds with the rest of their gear, and the steely determination in both their eyes. He also noted the fresh blood seeping through bandages on one of the ladies as well as the slashed — and charred — condition of her armor.

"Laytenant Yana Marchenkova, Black Dragon Squadron, Trakyan Wind Riders," the one in charred armor said with a smart salute. "This is my cousin, Lady Sehraine Marchenkova. Xandor sent us to contact you and assist in the extraction of our party and possibly a contingent of Rhodinan soldiers fighting under the Sabe crest."

Lord Fergusson returned the salute automatically, his eyes narrowing as he recognized Yana as one of the Kral's elite corps of flyers — the recruits who joined that cadre were carefully selected. It also stirred a new thought regarding something the Rhodinans had brought to the fight.

"Welcome to our camp, Laytenant. I've been expecting you. But first things first. Anders, escort the Laytenant to the healers' tent. While they are tending to her, send a runner to Knyaz Dorinkov and ask him to send his antiques over; he will know what I mean."

"If you feel up to it, Lady Sehraine, I would like to hear about your experience on the western side of the river. When the healers are finished with you, Laytenant Marchenkova, please rejoin us and fill in any blanks."

"Of course, Milord," Yana replied. She turned and gestured to the squire to lead the way, then snorted in mingled amusement and exasperation as the boy practically ran from the tent.

Fergusson cast a long-suffering look after the squire and turned back to Sehraine. He found her staring at the floor. Following her gaze, he saw the fresh bloodstain on his rug, left by the wounded soldier. Silence settled over the tent. He gave the lady several moments with her thoughts before he softly asked, "Milady, what happened?"

Sehraine continued to stare at the bloodstain, letting the silence stretch. Just when the commander began to wonder if she had heard him speak, she sighed. "Xandor was up before dawn this morning, spying on Chernigov and getting a feel for the lay of the land. When he returned, he relayed that he had spotted someone he knew under siege in an estate south of the city. Whoever it was, he and Jasper were pretty fired up to rescue him.

"Yana and I separated from Xandor, Jasper, and the others, maybe a half-hour after sunrise, and took the horses north of the city. We thought it would be the best way to go since most of the activity would be focused to the south, and we were right. Mostly. Yana and I still had to dodge a few patrols.

"With me pointing the way, Yana led us for what seemed hours without any of the orcs catching sight of us. Then our luck ran out." She focused her sapphire eyes on Lord Fergusson.

He could see doubt and fear in those eyes, neither of which had been there a few minutes before when the

Laytenant stood by her side. Remembering his manners, he pulled the chair from his writing desk and offered it to Sehraine.

With a smile of thanks, she settled onto the wooden seat cross-legged, her feet tucked under her knees. "Yana was a few yards in the lead, on foot, and Xerxes was leading the horses. I'm not much of a rider, so I was glad I only needed to hold on and keep my seat." Her brow furrowed as she thought back to the morning. "I don't know what happened exactly, even now. One moment, we were riding along; the next was madness. It started with a rustle of leaves and breaking sticks, then Xerxes bolted toward Yana as a mob of dreyri appeared. It seemed like they burst from the very floor of the forest, spraying leaves and detritus through the air. A horrible banshee wail echoed through the trees, mingling with guttural shouts from the creatures.

"Within the blink of an eye, I saw Yana slice one from chin to belt while Xerxes kicked another hard enough to slam it into a tree. Another screech split the air, and Yana stabbed a dreyri through the neck. Beside her, Xerxes stomped his wounded opponent and killed him.

"Three dead just like that," she said, snapping her fingers, "in less time than it takes to tell." She paused again, looking down at the ground. "Then they charged," she continued, and her face clouded. "Yana and Xerxes, that is. Yana went left, Xerxes right. They fought viciously and killed two more without seeming to take even a scratch. All around, the horses were going crazy. I barely managed to jump off mine before he bolted. Maybe that was when the dreyri noticed me. I managed to get a decent-sized tree between us. You have to understand. I'm not a fighter, Commander, and have very few weapons skills to speak of. Looking back on it, I think the dreyri saw me as an easy target. I dodged him for a moment or two, but it was only a matter of time before he caught me.

"I can still smell his rank breath," she said with a shudder, lost in the past. "I don't know if he intended to bite me, or worse. I had no intention of finding out. He didn't realize I took his dagger until he fell on it."

"Fell on it?"

The young lady nodded, not looking at the man before her.  "I collapsed backward and pulled him off balance so that he fell on it... and me."

Lord Fergusson darted a glance at the doorway of his tent as Brian, his second-in-command, slipped in quietly.  He gestured for him to wait, then said, "Resourceful."

"But stupid," Sehraine replied bitterly, apparently oblivious to her expanded audience.  "I couldn't get out from under him.  Lucky for me, the remaining dreyri turned and fled into the woods rather than face Yana and Xerxes.  I don't think they were expecting that kind of resistance from a couple of girls.  Yana charged into the woods after them, shouting at us to keep going."

Sehraine looked at Fergusson with tears in her eyes.  He handed her a handkerchief from his pocket and prompted her to continue.

"She's my best friend, but at that point I didn't even recognize her.  My friend was gone, replaced by a... a creature... whose eyes blazed with rage and bloodlust.  I can't say for certain which scared me more, the dreyri or her.  Still, I didn't want to leave; I hoped she would return.

"Xerxes had to drag the dead dreyri off me before he rounded up the horses that had fled into the woods.  It didn't seem to take long, so maybe they didn't go far.  Then he tried to get us moving again, but I refused.  Minutes went by, and the forest slowly returned to normal, with neither sight nor sound of Yana.  Finally, I realized he was right.  We couldn't risk staying any longer.  It killed me to leave.  I was certain I would never see her again.  We traveled perhaps a half hour and found Yana waiting for us, bleeding from a dozen small wounds, but otherwise looking like nothing had happened.  She even apologized for the ambush!  Said something about the dreyri being downwind and looked embarrassed about it."

"Downwind?  Do you know if she has any training as a tracker?"

With an apologetic look, Sehraine shrugged.  "Some, but I don't think her skills hold a candle to Xandor's on the ground.  The saying in Pazard'zhik is a recruit has to be born half-hawk to make it in the Wind Rider Legion."  Sehraine's brow furrowed at the memory.

"Interesting.  Please, continue," the commander said.

"We were close to the river.  It took a little time, but we eventually happened across a boat big enough to carry all of us.  Once we reached the eastern bank, it was practically a walk in the park to find our way here."

Lord Fergusson pursed his lips as he mulled over the last bit of her tale.  He knew from Xandor's journal that she was an elf, and he understood why she had traveled in disguise this far north.  It was hard to believe that, even after more than thirty years, the common Rhodinan still blamed the elves for the Plague and the war that followed.

In the Confederation of Nations, people did not persecute the elves.  He had even met several at political functions over the years.  From what he knew, the lady before him was atypical and was obviously less comfortable in woodland settings than most of her folk.  Urban elves were not unheard of, but they were definitely in the minority.

"Milady, I have known people like Laytenant Marchenkova.  They are not like the rest of us.  They all have a core of... rage.  Did something happen to her when she was young?"

Sehraine gave the barest hint of a nod.

"Typically, it's centered on some harrowing experience and is a major part of what compels them to lead the lives they do.  When that rage breaks loose, death follows as surely as thunder follows lightning.

"Still, most of the Kral's soldiers I have met are good, honorable men and women.  The friend you know is certainly there, but inside, chained against a time of need, is the rage she holds."  He elected to let her figure out on her own that her other friend, Xandor, held the same wolf chained inside him, too.

Sehraine smiled tiredly.  "Thank you, Lord Fergusson.  Even though I've known her nearly ten years, I've never seen that side of Yana before.  I've heard the stories from her fellow wind riders, but I thought they were exaggerating.  Now, I think not.  However, we aren't here for you to help me understand my friend's emotional issues.  What can I tell you that's of actual value?"

"Much of what you said is useful.  Based on your account, I know that most of Bregu Kraagor's attention is focused south of Chernigov, with only a few patrols sent out to the other sides for basic security. That should give us some room to maneuver. However, what I need most is a firsthand account of what we face."

He picked up the cigar from his desk and chewed it while he absorbed what Sehraine had told him. After a few silent moments, he continued, "You said the patrol you encountered consisted of dreyri, yet the denizens of Chernigov are predominantly orc. I wonder what kind of relationship Kraagor has established with other tribes. The fact he has attained some kind of lordship over them is no mean feat. What can you tell me of their arms and armor?"

Sehraine began answering questions as quickly as she could, with Fergusson asking new ones as soon as she finished speaking. A few minutes later, Patrick Anders returned with Yana, and she filled in the holes with information more military in nature.

Finally, Lord Fergusson got around to asking the question which had been nagging him. "I have one question left. Xandor only mentioned you two ladies, but Lady Sehraine has repeatedly mentioned Xerxes. Who and where is he?"

"He's getting a rub down, Milord," Sehraine said. At his astonished look, she explained, "He's a horse, Sir."

"You... took tactical advice from — and followed — *a horse*?" he sputtered, staring at Sehraine as though she had grown a third eye.

"He's a very smart horse," she answered defensively.

Yana's throaty laugh filled the tent at his dumbfounded expression, then she said, "He's Xandor's horse, Sir," as if saying so explained everything.

Seeing that her words only brought about a vague understanding, Yana added, "Xerxes is very smart — smarter than a lot of people I know. I'd be willing to say he's the smartest battle horse I've met to date. Of course, I think Xandor has done a lot of extra training with him. Sehraine did well to follow his lead and leave the ambush site."

"Perhaps," Lord Fergusson said with a chuckle, "we need Xandor to train our steeds as well."

# CHAPTER 25
# YANA AND THE IRON TOWER

### October 28, 4235 K.E.

**12:35pm**

Lord Fergusson gestured for them to follow him to his map, and said, "Now, let me bring you up to speed on our situation here. We have one company of soldiers from the Iron Tower, roughly a hundred men and women. Well over half are green troops, but thirty-two are veterans with several campaigns under their belts. Of the hundred, seventy are dragoons, with a score of those being archers. Adding to our numbers, Knyaz Dorinkov and his troops have an established base nearby in the remains of an old village."

Yana asked several questions about capabilities of the troops and readiness. Occasionally, Sehraine would inject a question, but the discussion was obviously more in line with Yana's field of expertise. As the conversation continued, the elven actress fell silent, seemingly lost in thought as she stared at Fergusson's map.

Finally, Lord Fergusson said, "I've asked everything I can think of regarding both Pazard'zhik and Chernigov and brought you up to speed on where we are, unless anyone can think of anything we've left out."

"Just our objective, Milord," Yana responded. "We need to help Xandor, Jasper, Chert, and Grendel escape Chernigov, which, as far as I can tell, is infested with several thousand orcs allied with other humanoid tribes of unknown number and location. Making this even more difficult, Xandor expects us to extract an unknown number of Rhodinan soldiers, most of whom are probably walking wounded, from an as-yet-to-be-determined point, following a signal that could come at any time. I'd say it makes planning somewhat tricky — if not impossible." She quirked an eyebrow at Lord Fergusson. "Does that about sum it up, Milord?"

"Yes, Laytenant, that sums things up nicely. With three exceptions. First, I have already received the signal; second,

I know where the twenty-seven Rhodinans will be; as for the third, I'm going to need your help."

At her quizzical look, he continued, "We have no reconnaissance of what is on or behind the walls, beyond what we can see from the treeline."

He smiled grimly at her wince of sympathy. "Finding that out will set our as-yet-undetermined point of attack. Barring anything else, the front gate is the obvious weak point."

"Milord, I am happy to help in any way I can but slipping over those walls to skulk about is a tall order."

"Perhaps. Perhaps not."

Fergusson turned to the soldier standing silently in the corner. "Leftenant, allow me to introduce to you Laytenant Marchenkova." With a gesture to the seated lady, he continued, "And this is the Lady Sehraine. Ladies, Leftenant Brian Gallagher. He has been with me for years and usually knows what I'm thinking before I do. Still, I have to ask, Brian, how did you come by Knyaz Dorinkov's antiques?"

Brian grinned. "I was conferring with Vassily when your runner arrived. Naturally, I volunteered to deliver them."

"Your unnatural curiosity, I am certain, had nothing to do with your volunteering," Fergusson noted with a chuckle.

With mock severity, Brian replied, "As a good and loyal servant to Milord, I simply endeavored to be as efficient as possible." He dropped his tone and grinned as he shifted his attention to the ladies. "And my curiosity is entirely natural."

"Indeed. Show us what you have," Fergusson ordered.

Brian stepped to the covered entryway, retrieved an oversized bundle from the guards there, and laid it down in the middle of the tent.

"Laytenant Marchenkova, will you give me a hand, please?"

Yana crossed from her position and knelt to help him unwrap the bulky — but surprisingly light — object. As they unrolled it from the last layer of protective cloth, a sharp intake of breath gave away Yana's surprise. "Now, Milord, I believe I see what you have in mind with your reconnaissance request." She did not look up as she spoke, already beginning to check the pieces and parts of the Trakyan flyer for soundness. "Where did you get this? It's older than I am."

"It was left in Chernigov when you Trakyans pulled out. Knyaz Dorinkov's father acquired it in the short time Michurinsk held the city."

Lord Fergusson looked over Yana's shoulder at the various struts and bolt of silk and asked, "Can it fly?"

"I can't be certain until I finish examining it and get it assembled, but all the pieces look to be here.  The ones I have handled thus far seem to be sound."  She grinned wolfishly.  "We haven't flown this far east of the Stena in years.  Well, at least up until a few days ago, anyway.  The orcs won't know what's happening until I'm on top of them."

"We're counting on that.  Especially since what I have in mind is not just a reconnaissance."

Yana's gaze sharpened as she caught his tone as well as his words.  "What do you have in mind, Sir?"

"Leftenant Gallagher, show her what's in the cases."

Brian stepped aside and opened two small, ornate boxes. Yana gave him an intense look as he carefully pulled out small black orbs, each an inch in diameter.  On the sides were faded runes, some more legible than others, worn smooth by time.

"Is that what I think it is?" she asked delightedly.

"If you are thinking they look like explosives, then yes," Brian replied.

"Dragon Pellets" she corrected.  At his quizzical look she elucidated, "We call these orbs 'Dragon Pellets.'  It goes well with the primary maneuver we use them for, 'Dragon Stooping.'"  At their blank looks, she continued, "We dive from a high altitude, like a falcon.  A falcon's attack dive is called stooping, but our attack ends in fire, and dragons, as you know, are known to breathe fire.  Hence 'Dragon Stooping.'"

Catching the faintest hint of inflection, Brian queried, "Officially?  What about unofficially?"

Yana grinned impishly as she answered, "Dragon Pooping."  Her laughter peeled as he snorted in amusement.

"Why pooping?"

As the others continued to chuckle, she explained, "Think about it — when we attack, we stoop, good so far, but when we actually strike, we are dropping pellets behind us. So the main reason we refer to it as 'pooping' is because it's more like a bird dumping extra weight as it takes off."

"And the second reason," prompted Sehraine who had heard all this before.

"And the second," Yana continued with a nod to her friend, "is that the popular rumor is that those pellets are predominantly made of dragon dung." She grinned at her audience's shocked expressions. "Hey, that's magic for you — the ickier the better. Speaking of which, we need to examine them to make sure the glyphs are all intact. They are packed to minimize rubbing, but these are old and have had lots of time to rub against one another when moved. If the glyphs are damaged the pellet is useless. How many are there?"

"Unfortunately, this, plus three more boxes, is all we have," Brian replied. "We had planned on using slings or small engines to hurl them, but I think the Knight Commander has come up with a bit different — and more direct — use for them."

"Indeed, I have. What do you imagine that use to be, Leftenant?"

"To have the good Lay-tenant," he carefully worked through the unfamiliar pronunciation, "remove as many war engines from the walls as she can. What I have not decided is whether you view the engines on the Keep at the foot of the bridge as more valuable targets, or those on the city wall itself."

Lord Fergusson smiled at his Leftenant, then turned to Yana. "Thus, does my good Leftenant display the mind-reading skill I mentioned earlier; however, I think we have enough ordnance to make good on both targets, if we use them judiciously. Assuming, of course, that antique can get off the ground.

"I would like you, Leftenant Marchenkova," he said, slipping back into the Glaxon parlance as his thoughts focused on the new wrinkles he was adding to his plan, "to overfly the Keep. I want you to look for war engines by type, soldiers by estimate. Let me know the layout inside, and any weaknesses. Then go across the river and do the same for the eastern wall of Chernigov. Pay particular attention to the engines that can range the bridge. Also, when you fly over the river, identify any boats suitable to evacuate Vityaz Dobrynya and his people."

"Lastly," his gaze refocused on Yana as he continued, "strafe the eastern wall of the city and destroy as many of the war engines as you can, focusing particular attention on those that can range troops on the bridge. Questions?"

"Two, Sir. First, when do I go? Second, what is to keep the orcs from moving other engines into place?"

"You go as soon as you can get that flyer assembled and checked. I'd like you to make at least a couple of runs before it gets too dark for you to see. As for what will keep them from replacing, or repairing, the engines tomorrow morning, that will be you, Leftenant."

"I have a better idea, Sir," she replied. At his perplexed expression, she grinned and pulled her helmet from her pack. The smoky crystal filling the 'T' shaped slit reflected the overhead light. "My helmet is enchanted for night action. I can hit them after sundown and be pretty much invisible in the city's cloud cover."

Fergusson nodded his approval. "Even better. Hit them several times between now and tomorrow morning, at random times. That should keep them busy all night and have the added bonus of allowing you to destroy even more of the engines as they replace them."

"Milord, if I might make a suggestion?" Sehraine asked.

"Yes?" Lord Fergusson had become so focused he'd almost forgotten she was there. He turned to find her at the map, a new red marker showing the location north of Chernigov where they'd stumbled on the dreyri patrol.

"Consider hitting the northern wall of Chernigov, instead."

"To what end?"

"I was just thinking that the orcs are bound to miss that patrol Yana and I ran into and send another to look for them. If Yana hits the northern wall, and maybe if you have a few men make a little noise north of the city..."

"Ha!" he exclaimed. "An excellent idea, Milady! We can pull them even further off balance by making them think we plan on attacking from that quadrant, which would be logical, considering all of their attention has been south of the city recently. Your dreyri encounter will give further credence to that idea."

Turning back to the map, he quieted for a moment, thinking, and then said, "Laytenant Marchenkova, hit the northern wall first, and hit it hard.  On subsequent runs, hit multiple walls here, here, and here, but I want you to always hit the north wall again.

"I'm hoping they find the remains of the patrol you took out sometime this afternoon.  I'll ask Knyaz Dorinkov to spread a few of his men in that area to help make sure they do."

Lord Fergusson stared at the map like it was chess board.  He mused, "Kraagor might or might not waste resources sending more patrols out, but he will most likely pull engines from other areas to replace those you destroy; areas like the east wall, where he knows they have other layers of defense."

Focusing on Yana, he said, "The other runs are to make them waste resources, keep them off balance, and hopefully reallocate more engines.  However, the last run is your real objective.  You must destroy the engines in position to threaten troops on the bridge."

Yana's pensive look prompted Leftenant Gallagher to ask, "Laytenant, you have a concern?"

"Just some quick mental math coming up a bit short.  Do we have enough bombs to make four runs tonight and hit the Keep wall tomorrow?"

"Probably not.  But remember, your first three runs are meant to be distractions.  Save your ammunition for the last run, which will be the most critical," the Knight Commander replied.  "Let's play it by ear as far as the number of runs go.  Hopefully, the age of the bombs won't make any difference."

Yana looked at the small objects warily.  "How old are they?"

Lord Fergusson threw a questioning glance at his Leftenant.

Brian shrugged.  "At least as old as the flyer."

"That's good to hear," she said sarcastically.

Lord Fergusson stared at the young wind rider and said, "Laytenant, I could not order you to take this mission even if you were under my command, but understand you are our only hope in seeing what's beyond those walls and maybe saving your friends."

She visibly relaxed the tension that had built up in her shoulders.  "That glider is older than I am by a fair margin.

The design of modern gliders is a bit different, though the basic concepts are the same.  Ours are magicked for lift so that we can take off from any position.  The age of this one has me a tad concerned about what kind of lift I can get.  If the magic has died, or has diminished too much, we could have some problems."

He looked at her for a long moment.  Finally, he said, "Only one way to find out."

She nodded in reply.

"Anything else on your mind?"  When she shook her head, he continued, "Then you have your orders."

Yana nodded her understanding and willingness.  "Well then, let's get to it and blow up some stuff!"

Suiting actions to words, she collected the parts of the flyer, and Brian helped her roll them back into one of the blankets.  She picked up a smaller, loose piece of cloth, unfolded it, and froze.  Holding it up, she revealed a red pennon with a black dragon.  Grinning, she said, "This is my squadron!"

"Then you should keep it," the Knight Commander replied.

She rolled it and tucked it into a pouch, then she and Brian lifted the flyer and carried it out of the tent.

"Anders," Lord Fergusson called to his squire, who tore his eyes from the blanket.

"Milord?"

"I need you to run some errands."

After Patrick took off to attend to his assigned errands, Lord Fergusson sat at his desk and pulled out a battered journal.

He wrote, '*Lady Sehraine arrived unscathed.  Leftenant Marchenkova arrived wounded, but in good order.  Will reconnoiter the city for us.  You forgot to mention she is a member of the Kral's Wind Rider Legion.*'  He thought a bit about what else to say.  '*Working on getting the orcs stirred up,*' he continued.  '*Some confusion on their part may help you.*'  He paused a moment, deep in thought, and then wrote, '*Still working on Sabe's extraction.  Tunnel ends at waterfront.  Look for Black Dragon standard.*'

His next pause lasted longer as he sat staring at the book but not seeing it. Plans and contingency plans raced through his mind.  With a loud sigh, he turned to his map table.

"Anders, take notes.  First..."  He dictated thoughts for fifteen or twenty minutes, ordered messages delivered based on those thoughts as required, and then returned to his journal.

"Excuse me, Milord?"  The soft, feminine voice at his shoulder startled him.  Lord Fergusson looked around to find Sehraine holding a sheaf of papers.  There was no sign of Anders.

"Is there someone who can direct me where to go with these?"

The Knight Commander blinked.

Seeing his confusion, she said, "Anders hasn't returned from his errands, so I took the notes.  I hope you don't mind."

"Thank you, young lady!  You didn't have to do that, but I greatly appreciate it."

He took the sheaf of papers and continued, "I'll have Anders take care of them when he gets back.  In the meantime, is there anything you need?  Food?  A place to rest?"

"I'm fine, Milord, really.  With your permission, though, I would like to get familiar with the camp layout and check on Xerxes and the horses."

"Of course!"  He walked with her to the door of the tent. Just outside, a pair of boys sat playing a game of marbles.

"James, find my squire and tell him I have some more errands for him."  One of the boys hopped to his feet and took off through the camp, leaving his marbles where they lay.

Fergusson turned to the other boy.  "Zack, this is the Lady Sehraine.  I want you to be her guide.  Take her to the quartermaster first and tell him she needs a change of clothes for herself and her companion, her choice of weapons, and a place for them to rest.  After that, you're under her command while she's a guest in our camp."

"Yes, Milord!" the boy exclaimed, leaping up from the ground.

The boy led her away, chattering as they went.  Lord Fergusson shook his head.  "Zack!" he called after them. When the boy looked around, he shouted, "Don't talk the lady's ears off!"

**1:05pm**

Sehraine followed Zack, listening to the boy's seemingly random chatter about the camp and everyone in it. He was a treasure trove of information regarding names and places, as well as surprising tidbits of unusual information about the camp followers. It seemed that, when they weren't on errands for the knights, the runners were involved in a type of game where bits of information were the game pieces — the more secret and difficult to obtain, the higher the point value — and each child vied for the title of king.

She wondered if Lord Fergusson was aware of the game. Making a mental note to speak to him later, she followed the boy into the quartermaster's tent.

"Sir," Zack said, giving his best salute to a middle-aged man with short-cropped ginger hair. "Lord Fergusson asked me to bring this lady over for supplies. I have a note."

The quartermaster read the request from Lord Fergusson, his brow knit. "I don't have extra supplies and arms for everyone who wanders into camp," he muttered. "We barely have rations for the men we brought."

"Sir, I don't want to be any trouble," Sehraine said. "The Laytenant and I have been sleeping outdoors for the past few days. Another night won't hurt us."

Looking at her for the first time, the man's eyes widened in surprise. "Sorry, ma'am. I didn't mean to sound rude. We traveled rather light and fast, so our supplies are limited. I'm sure we can find tents for the two of you, even if we have to get them from a Rhodinan sutler."

"One tent will do, if you have one to spare. The main thing I'm interested in is a change of clothes for each of us."

"The note also says to give you weapons."

"Yes, your commander was rather insistent about that. I already have a brace of daggers. Perhaps you could spare me the use of a short bow and a quiver full of arrows?"

# CHAPTER 26
# ENTERING THE CITY

## October 28, 4235 K.E.


**1:15pm**

Brian Gallagher and Lord Fergusson watched Yana go over the ancient hang-glider with a practiced eye, looking for rot and damage. Finally nodding her satisfaction, she donned her harness. Pulling each strap tight, she hooked herself to the glider.

"You come up with anything new you need me to look for while I am up there?"

"No. Stick to the plan. Focus on numbers of engines and orcs, and the layout of defenses behind each set of walls. Basic strength estimate stuff — and any weak points in their defenses, of course." Lord Fergusson smiled down at her. "If I have not said it already, good luck and be careful."

She smiled back. "Thanks; I always am."

A snort of amusement sounded behind her, and she turned to find Sehraine, newly arrived, with a young boy standing beside her.

"You find something amusing?" she inquired with a fake glower.

"No, nothing. Except you are only careful when you aren't impatient, and you never like to wait."

"Hmpf. Baseless libel, I assure you, Milord."

Lord Fergusson grinned at the ladies' banter; however, his smile vanished as Yana donned her helmet and the crystal visor hid her eyes.

Around the clearing, work came to a standstill as everyone watched expectantly when she aimed the flyer for the sky and kicked off. It rose about a foot or so before it dropped back to the ground. Amused expressions spread among the onlookers.

She repeated the exercise. Twice.

"Need help?" Brian offered.

"Isn't it supposed to go higher?" Zack asked.

Yana wanted to glare at them and give them a piece of her mind, but she tried to remain focused on getting the flyer off the ground.  Finally, on the fourth try, she gained some altitude and cleared the shorter trees.  Ten feet, twelve feet, fifteen feet, almost to the inch, before the lift stopped and she glided back to the ground.  On her next try, she made it five feet when suddenly the lift reversed and slammed her into the dirt.  Everyone heard something snap.

Lord Fergusson asked, "Should we clear the area before someone gets hurt?"

Yana lay there stunned for a moment before slowly climbing back to her feet.  She unhooked her harness and doffed her helm with a false calm.  Sehraine hid her smile behind her hand, but her eyes sparkled with amusement.

The scene that followed had several of the soldiers within earshot alternately blanching or laughing aloud.  They didn't understand most of the words she used, being in Trakyan, but the intent was clear.  After yelling sufficiently at the old flyer, she took several deep breaths.

"Do you feel better?"

The Trakyan spun around to glare at the speaker and found Lord Fergusson staring at her quizzically.  Sehraine started laughing, unable to contain it any longer.  Realizing how ridiculous she looked, Yana relaxed and laughed with her.  "Actually, yes I do.  Now if I can just get this blasted thing to stay airborne."

She hooked her harness back to the hang-glider, resettled her helmet, said a quick prayer, and kicked off again.  The glider slowly rose into the air, wobbling a few times as it went.  Once it caught the wind, the flyer soared higher and higher until it vanished into the sky.

"Yelling at it seems to have helped," Brian noted.


Yana circled the Iron Tower encampment, slowly ascending until she was above the trees, getting a feel for how the antique flyer handled.  The lift was somewhat erratic, but once airborne, the basics of glider technique were no different from what she had been trained on early in her career, except the control cords were in slightly different locations.

Satisfied, she took it higher.

About five minutes into her test flight, the lift unexpectedly reversed again. The sudden drop took her breath away, and she struggled to control the craft. At first, she thought it was just a downdraft, but when she could not break out of it, she realized that she was experiencing an aberration in the magic of the glider.

Screaming in a mix of fear and frustration, she plummeted toward the forest. The magic released its hold a mere handful of feet above the canopy and the glider swept past, clipping the tops of the tallest trees, and dragging its pilot through the upper boughs.

Yana tried to get some lift out of the craft before they snagged on a branch and truly crashed. Nothing happened. Grasping limbs slapped at her, and the craft slowed a bit more with each impact. With a shudder, the flyer suddenly responded to her commands and lifted above the trees.

The wind rider spent a few minutes circling. It seemed the more time she spent in flight, the fewer hiccups she experienced with the glider's magic. Once she was satisfied with her ability to maneuver, Yana returned to the practice field and landed. With Brian's help, she loaded the antique bombs into the pouches in the wing and made her first run.


**1:17pm**

Marko Madasgorski scowled at the useless orcs bumbling around the valley in every direction, searching for tunnel exits. When a runner from the city told him the king requested his presence, he flew into a rage, killing the messenger.

He could tell something had happened when he and Kourash entered the city gates, something other than the debacle at the monastery. When Marko asked a guard at the gate where he could find the Bregu, the guard shied away and pointed toward a cobblestone street that led to a steep set of stairs along the east wall.

From the rampart, the knight looked out across the valley and noticed the orcs were moving back into the city. Fists clenched and a snarl on his face, Marko strode down the wall. He found Bregu Kraagor in the shadow of one of his larger war machines, studying the eastern sky through a spyglass.

The King of Chernigov was a stocky-built orc with stark white hair.  He wore a wine-colored doublet trimmed in gold — stolen, no doubt, from a ship captain who wandered too far north.  The repulsive creature was an insult to the title he claimed, and the Zhitomiran struggled to conceal his sneer.

Lowering the spyglass, Bregu Kraagor turned at the knight's approach and stared at him with beady, black eyes that reflected his cruel personality.  His tusks were brownish yellow from age, and ritualistic scars lined both his cheeks.  His right earlobe was missing, bitten off by a former challenger to his throne.  Handing the knight his spyglass, he pointed and said, "Look there and tell me what you see."

Marko snatched the instrument from the king's hand and glanced across the river.  Not seeing anything, he was about to give it back when Bregu Kraagor nudged the end of the spyglass, adjusting where he was looking.  He spotted a black speck on the horizon, hovering just above the treetops.  Whatever it was, it was too small to be a dragon and too big to be a bird.  Almost as if it had noticed their interest, it dipped back into the trees, and he lost sight of it.

"What was that?" Marko asked.

"You tell me, young knight."

"How am I supposed to know?"

On the other side of Bregu Kraagor, Gregori and D'yakon Krovos walked toward them.  Gregori wore a black patch over one eye.  Marko winced when he saw the deep, angry gouges that peeked from underneath it.  He had been there when Gregori's eye had burned inside its socket.  The mage had cut it out using the tip of a dagger.  It was a memory he would not soon forget.

"Bregu Kraagor, we cannot use the river until we know for sure what's happening on the other side.  Did you send scouts?" Marko asked.

"Do you think me stupid?  Of course I sent scouts."

"What did they find out?"

Bregu Kraagor stared back across the river and answered, "They haven't returned."

"What's Melikhov up to?" Marko said pensively.  "Surely he wouldn't dare attack this city.  He knows Zhitomir has sent emissaries to meet with you and reopen the river.  An act of aggression now might be viewed as a prelude to war."

"Are you so sure the threat of Zhitomir will keep them at bay?" Bregu Kraagor asked.

"Of course, I'm sure!  How dare you second-guess me?" Marko said.

"Does Empress Malraisa even know about the crates?"

Marko tried not to, but he couldn't help throwing a quick glance at Gregori.

The cunning king said matter-of-factly, "I thought not."

"What's that supposed to mean?"

"I've heard rumors about your cargo.  Sickness and death on the White River, traveling south.  Rumors saying the plague has returned, and war will soon follow.  They know we are coming."

"It was inevitable," D'yakon Krovos said with a gleam in his eye.  "The way had to be opened like it was in Maa'kheru Bolezni's time!  Like him, I will take this plague through the Alashalian mountains, lead our army, and defeat the Highlord and Highlady!"

"Who says you're going to lead this army?" Marko countered.

The dark cleric was furious.  "Of course, I shall lead the army!  It's my destiny."

With a flash of steel, Kourash slammed the flat of his heavy blade against D'yakon Krovos' head, knocking him unconscious.

Marko deftly stepped aside, avoiding the cleric as he fell on the hard stone.  "Bregu Kraagor, please have someone take that to our wagon."

"Of course, Sir Marko," the orc king said smoothly.  As an afterthought, he added, "Young Lord, might I also suggest that your crates be moved underground until we find out what Melikhov's doing?"

Gregori glanced across the river and turned back to Marko, giving him a slight nod.

Marko scrutinized the orc king, trying to gauge his intentions.  Reluctantly, he said, "All right, but if this is a trick..."

The king smiled benignly, but with his tusks and scars, it came off more as a grimace.  "Sir, you are paying me too well for me to pull any petty tricks.  If it makes you feel better, please oversee my orcs and make sure they store the crates in an acceptable location."

"Enough.  I'm losing my patience," Marko said.

Meeting his personal guard at the base of the wall, Bregu Kraagor led the small group down into the city and to the building housing the chuck wagon.  The surviving Percherons eyed the group warily from the small corral.  Behind them, a group of orcs unceremoniously dumped D'yakon Krovos onto the wagon bed.

Sometime after Sir Marko and Bregu Kraagor had left with the crates, the D'yakon stirred and Gregori shuffled to his side.  "You shouldn't have given Asenov the *Veritas autem Sutekh.*"

Confused, D'yakon Krovos tried to rise.  He lay in the bed of the chuck wagon and smelled horse.  Dim light filtered through gaps in the thatch roof.  He had trouble concentrating and his vision blurred.  "I don't know what you're talking about."

"Don't lie.  You had the Northmen give it to him, and now Jasper has it.  What?  Did you think you and that idiot, Asenov, were going to lead the humanoid horde into battle?"

Krovos stiffened.  "It was the will of Sutekh."

Gregori's eyes narrowed.  "No, you weren't planning to lead us.  You were planning to stop us.  Well, it's too late.  Ka'Sehkuur has woken.  Even now, his blood speaks to us."

Krovos jerked up, ignoring the nausea in his gut, and tried to flee.  Strong reptilian hands gripped his head and forced his mouth open.  Gregori shoved a piece of soap inside.  It turned to black oil and oozed down his throat and up into his nose.  Krovos bucked and thrashed, but Kourash held him tight.

Gregori knelt, his hands against the side of the wagon, and bowed his head.  "Ka'Sehkuur, we beseech you.  Accept our offering.

"The world will burn, and the ignorant will stoke the flames.  Let madness rule."

From the darkest corner of the room, feral eyes gazed out, and Razrushitel stepped forth.

**1:18pm**

Back against the side of the tunnel, Xandor pulled out his stylus and shook it to activate the light.  Opening the journal, he read the message from Lord Fergusson:  '*Lady Sehraine arrived unscathed.  Leftenant Marchenkova arrived wounded but in good order.  Will reconnoiter the city for us.  You forgot to mention she is a wind rider.  Working on getting the orcs stirred up.  Some confusion on their part may help you.  Still working on Sabe's extraction.  Tunnel ends at waterfront.  Look for Black Dragon standard.*'

Xandor grinned at the first part and turned to Jasper.  "Sehraine arrived 'unscathed,' to quote my source.  Yana arrived in good order as well but managed to get herself wounded along the way."

"In other words, Yana is Yana and attracts trouble almost as quickly as you," Jasper said finishing the thought for him with a little embellishment, pleased to hear the two women were safe.

"Neither of us attracts trouble like some others we know."

Jasper laughed.  "No one attracts trouble like those three!  Hector, Dave, and Aislinn are walking, talking, trouble-magnets.  I hope things are going better for them and August than for us."  His expression turned pensive.  "I wonder if they've caught up to Robert yet."

"Don't spend too much time wondering until after we get out of our own trouble."

The mage shrugged.  "Can't help but worry about them.  Part of me thinks I should be there."

"And the other?" Xandor asked.

"The other part knows I'm exactly where I need to be right now."

"That's good to hear," Xandor replied.  "Now let's go stop Marko and this plague."

Break over, they got back on their hands and knees and continued their crawl.


**1:25pm**

The tunnel ran approximately four to five hundred yards at a slight decline.  Leading the way, Ilya looked behind him at the trail of crawling soldiers that disappeared into the darkness.  Constant sounds of shifting and sliding echoed around the second-in-command as everyone progressed a few feet at a time.

Beads of sweat dripped off his face as he put one hand in front of the other, leaving random dots and scuffmarks on the earthen floor.  Developing a rhythm, he felt he was making good time, but it was hard to tell.

Light from his piece of quartz ate the darkness in small nibbles, revealing more tunnel.  Its presence settled the battle-hardened soldier and helped fight the monotony.  Beyond its limits, flakes of pyrite and calcite embedded in the wall winked back at him like tiny stars.  Ilya thought it odd that they seemed enormous when the light struck them, but when he got close, they were barely a speck.

When a dark shaft appeared in the floor directly in front of him, he almost didn't recognize it for what it was.  He glanced up, and on the other side of the hole were partially exposed stone blocks.  They had arrived at the foundation of the city walls.

The shaft dropped about five feet and hugged the bottom of the wall before continuing into a lower tunnel.  Seeing the thick wall suspended in the dirt and running the width of the tunnel was eerie, but it also gave Ilya a sense of accomplishment.  They had almost made it.

Dropping into the hole, he turned and helped the next man in line transition a wounded soldier down the short drop.  Once clear, he dragged the litter deeper into the lower tunnel and kept moving to give the soldiers room to follow.


**1:35pm**

Under the city, the group moved even more slowly than before.  The vibration from the movement above them caused the fugitives to go more cautiously, all too aware of the threat of a tunnel collapse.  At the front of the line, Ilya finally held up a closed fist, signaling the end of the tunnel.  Everyone stopped.  Light from his glowing piece of quartz revealed a solid wall of earth where the tunnel ended.

Streaked with dirt and sweat, Dobrynya, Xandor, and Chert slowly worked their way past the soldiers to the front of the line where Ilya waited.

"What's on the other side of that wall?" Chert asked quietly, studying the contours of dirt.

"If we did our math right, we should be halfway between the city wall and the old inn," Ilya whispered.

Xandor asked, "Do we need to go up?"

"No.  The basement should be directly in front of us."

"Chert, can you tell anything?"

The dwarf studied the wall some more and said, "No.  Not without digging."

Dobrynya and Xandor sat back while Chert dropped his helmet and shield.

"Is his shirt coming off too?" Ilya quipped.

"Do you need any tools?" Dobrynya asked when a soldier handed him a small shovel.

Smiling at the young vityaz, Chert said, "Watch my dirt."

The dwarf sank his hands into the clayey soil and literally pushed a section of it aside.  A slight tremor resonated down the adit, and the soldiers eyed the sides warily.  The soil began to compact near Chert and soon became hard as rock.  Pushing forward a step at a time, the dwarf worked the earth, molding it.

Dobrynya turned to Xandor and whispered, "What I would give to have a whole company of dwarves.  We'd drop the walls of this city around Bregu Kraagor and send him running back north where he came from."

"I don't think you could keep them focused long enough. All they do is talk about dirt."

"I heard that," Chert grunted as he pushed aside another section of earth.

"And rocks."

Dobrynya and Ilya chuckled at the mock glare the dwarf bestowed upon his friend.

After fifteen minutes of slowly moving forward, the dwarf stopped.  He leaned over with his hands on his knees, trying to catch his breath.

The soldiers were speechless.  Not a pinch of dirt had fallen.  The dwarf had simply moved it aside, using it to solidify the tunnel as he went.  In front of him, they saw irregularly shaped blocks of stone fitted tightly together by mortar — the basement wall.

Xandor crawled next to Chert and whispered, "Douse the lights."

With a wave of the tired dwarf's hand, the glow-stones extinguished.   Barely perceptible traces of light shone through the cracks in the mortar.  The soldiers couldn't see it, but Chert could.  He stood and walked cautiously toward the wall.   Behind him, he heard Xandor and Dobrynya shuffling, anxious to be out of the tunnel.

Chert couldn't hear anything beyond the wall.  He slowly forced his hands inside the stone, his palms facing out. Sweat dripped off his nose as he compressed the mortar joints and created a small opening.

A pinhole of light lanced into the adit, reflecting off dust motes floating down from the ceiling.  After peeking through, Chert backed away and motioned for Xandor and Dobrynya to have a look.  Inside, rotten pieces of tables, chairs, desks, bed frames, and other items, formerly used at the inn, laid about as if someone had simply tossed them into the room.

Heavy timbers, split and checked with age, spanned the ceiling and supported a dark tongue-and-groove wood floor. Warped boards, broken through in places, allowed weak streamers of light to trickle through.  On the opposite wall, a set of rickety wooden stairs led through a framed opening in the ceiling to a small alcove where a battered oaken door hung precariously from its hinges.

"It looks unoccupied," Dobrynya whispered.

The two men crawled out of the way, leaving Chert enough room to work.

"Weapons out," Dobrynya ordered.   "Pass it down." Instantly, the anxious shuffling stopped, replaced by the sounds of steel on leather.

Muscles bulging, Chert pressed his hands back into the wall and shaped the stone, widening the opening.  As he did, fresh air flowed through, and the sound of deeply drawn breaths filled the tunnel.  When the opening was large enough for a person to pass through, the vityaz crawled out. Xandor and Ilya immediately followed.  Behind them, the soldiers pressed forward, eager to escape the tunnel, but Dobrynya signaled for them to stop with a closed fist.

While Xandor crept up the stairs, Dobrynya and Ilya rearranged the furniture as quickly but silently as possible, making a space where a few men could stand.  When finished, Dobrynya held up four fingers, and Chert let four soldiers into the basement.  Once through, their commander had them search for the smuggler's run.

Xandor heard orcs shouting, and he peered through the crack between the door and the jamb.  Much of the hallway beyond the door lay hidden, but he could tell the inn had not fared well under the orc occupation.  Stained charcoal grey from the constant smoke and ash inundating the city, patches of tongue and groove paneling clung to bowed timber walls like scabs.

The thud of heavy boots preceded an orc in mismatched leather armor walking down the hallway.  Xandor motioned down the stairs, made a V with his fingers, pointed to his eyes, and held up a finger.  Then he did a slashing motion across his neck.

Dobrynya shook his head.

Everyone seemed disappointed even as they ducked down to hide.  Xandor pulled up the cowl of his mottled cloak, concealing his face, and crept to the other side of the stairwell so he would be at the orc's back if it entered the basement.

The orc passed Xandor's position, and everyone breathed a sigh of relief when the ranger signaled 'all clear.'

Two more orc soldiers followed the first.  It was obvious as they passed that something had them agitated.  Xandor didn't understand their harsh language, but by the tone of their voices, it was clear they weren't happy.  Shouts erupted down the hall, and the three orc soldiers ran off, brandishing their weapons.

Climbing down the stairs, Xandor stepped close to Dobrynya and whispered, "This place is an armed camp.  Have you found the entrance to the smuggler's run?"

Staring at the map in his hand, Dobrynya's brow furrowed in concentration.  "Not yet."

Xandor slapped the youth on the back for encouragement and turned toward the tunnel.  "Chert, can you join us?"

The dwarf said a quick prayer and emerged from the adit with his helmet in one hand, and his shield strapped to his back.  He gave the two men a questioning look as he approached.  Showing Chert the map, Xandor and Dobrynya described what they were looking for.  The dwarf turned a full circle, studying each of the walls.  "It's not here."

"What do you mean it's not here?" Dobrynya hissed.

"I mean, there is no secret tunnel entrance in this basement."

"You didn't even look," the youth argued.  His storm-grey eyes narrowed, and he scowled at the dwarf.

"Yes, I did."

Xandor leaned close to Chert and said, "You could have at least made a show of it."

"I'm sorry," the dwarf said patiently, "but it's not here."

"How can you be so sure?"

With a look of disbelief, Chert explained, "I know rocks and dirt and how they go together.  No offense, but human hands made these walls.  The stones are weak, and most of the mortar joints have crumbled away.  We're lucky they haven't collapsed under their own weight."

"What about magic?"

"What about it?"

"Could they use magic to hide the entrance to the smuggler's run?"

"Sure, I guess they could, but these were smugglers, right?  They probably had ties to the owners here at the inn.  Do you think they would have used magic to hide it when they could use this whole building?"

"It's not likely, but..."

"Get Jasper to look if you want, but I don't think he'll find it.  I bet it's either in the wine cellar or under the kitchen floor."

"Why not here?"

"Because it's not here," Chert said confidently.

Xandor shrugged and said, "We'll have Jasper take a quick look, just in case."

"Fine.  But you're wasting your time," the dwarf said.

After a moment, the tip of Jasper's staff clacked against the floor.  The mage crawled out of the adit and brushed himself off.  "You have some antsy soldiers down there.  You need to get them out."

Dobrynya said, "We will, but first I need you to see if the entrance to the smuggler's run is hidden in this room somewhere."

"Have you asked Chert?  He's the expert."

"Thank you," Chert said, his arms crossed.

"We have.  He didn't find anything."

"You suspect magic?" Jasper asked, somewhat surprised.

"Maybe."

Jasper nodded and said, "I'll check."  Raising his staff, he closed his eyes and whispered a few unintelligible words.  When he reopened them, he scanned the room.  "Sorry," he said when he was done.

Disappointed, Dobrynya put his hands on his hips and asked, "Now what?"

"We search the rest of the inn," Xandor said, unperturbed.

# CHAPTER 27
# THE WIND RIDER

## October 28, 4235 K.E.

**1:39pm**

Using the layers of smoke for cover, Yana searched the city below. She breathed deeply, letting the magic of her helmet filter the corrupt air.

Yana had already swept past the Keep on the eastern shore of the White River and over what remained of the Chernigov port. At the former, she identified the siege engines, memorized their placement, and got a rough count of orc forces. At the latter, she carefully studied the watercraft, trying to find at least one that would serve their purposes. She was delighted to identify three.

Looking down now at the teeming horde of humanoids inside the city walls, what she saw disheartened her. The sheer numbers were hard to believe, and the fact that King Kraagor had managed to put together an alliance of orcs, dreyri, and who knows what else was simply amazing. More than that, though, he had succeeded in holding the alliance and the city together for over a decade.

She shook her head sharply and took herself to task. They were not here to take the city, and she did not have time for woolgathering. Her mission was first to identify what engines were placed where, then neutralize as many of them as possible.

The city's defensive wall roughly followed the outlines of the original town before the bridge was built. It was irregularly shaped — not square and not quite round. At each of the cardinal directions, wide gatehouses supported ballistae and smaller, swivel-mounted scorpions. The battlements angled back and away from the gates to four towers she decided were the corners, each defended by a tall leaf-spring catapult flanked by a pair of smaller onagers. Interior buttresses supported platforms and braced each wall. The platforms bore additional catapults, ballistae, and scorpions. Yana counted two buttressed platforms plus the eastern gatehouse and the two towers on the eastern wall corners that could range the bridge.

Defenses and artillery placements firmly in mind, she turned her attention to the troops on the walls and the city below. The amount of movement was overwhelming. From her vantage point, Chernigov resembled a kicked-over ant hill. Turning, she followed the northern wall as it ambled westward.

Ten minutes later, she completed her circuit of the city and lined up for her first attack run at a tower. She had thus far kept to the lower edge of the smoke to make herself harder to both see and hit. For reconnaissance, that altitude was preferred, but she had to go lower to get good hits on the engines.

Tucking her chin, she dove at the northeast corner tower, gaining speed as she fell. The silk airfoil rippled under the pressure, and the small ants walking the walls became humanoid-shaped.

Seconds before release, a guard looked up at her.

Reaching out, Yana tugged on the cord to the pouch on her right wing, spilling a few black orbs onto the catapult and onager emplacements. The guard opened his mouth to shout a warning — and his world dissolved into noise, fire, and pain. Waves of heat caught the wings of her flyer, and Yana used the updraft to shoot into the safety of the smoke.

Waiting only a few seconds, she dove for the northern gatehouse. The guards there were caught gaping at the destruction of the first tower and had no hint that they were the next target. She tugged on another cord, and another pouch opened. A handful of orbs spilled out, bouncing off the gatehouse and striking its war engines.

Nothing happened. She glanced down and saw them roll across the gatehouse roof.

Suddenly, one exploded, setting off a chain reaction of its peers. The heat and concussion threw her haphazardly back into the sky where she fought to regain control as she climbed for height and safety. She swore as she recalled the Leftenant's comment regarding the age of the bombs. Glancing at the remaining pouches, she could only hope.

In the seconds it took her to line up on the northwest tower, the orcs were waiting for her. Archers launched their black arrows as soon as she came within range.  She evaded to the left, but several tore through her wing.  Some bounced off struts, cracking one.  Two hit her: one, her armor took; the second grazed her right arm, preventing her from releasing the bombs.

She had to get out of there.  Shifting her weight, she banked right and spiraled upward into the smoke.

Below, orcs frantically prepared for her next attack.  The stairs filled with the foul beasts as they climbed, looking for their chance to kill the Trakyan flyer.

Shouts drifted over the city.  The orcs were loading their war machines.  '*Great,*' she thought.

Yana's glider nose-dived out of the smoke, and she aimed directly for the western gatehouse.  Orcs hurried to aim their scorpions.  Rushed, the first crew loosed the spear-like missile early, and it flew harmlessly to her right.  The second crew fumbled their loading and would not be ready before she passed.  The ballistae were too slow to reorient and fire at her, so at least she did not have to worry about them.

The archers, however, were quite good.  Five black arrows put holes in her airfoil, and three hit her.  Her armor turned two, but one pierced her left thigh.  The agony from the barbed head as it penetrated brought a shriek.  Still, she pulled the cord and dumped a measured load of bombs onto the gatehouse.  Some were duds and simply bounced and rolled.  Others exploded in a fiery wave, sending orcs and machinery over the wall.

Using the heat, Yana pulled up.  The forces her body felt, normally exhilarating, caused her to scream again as the barbed head of the arrow tore at her flesh.  She ground her teeth as she reached the safety of the low-hanging smoke and then turned west away from the city.  She had bombs for two more targets, and there was no way she was going back with dragon pellets left.

The pain became excruciating as she banked for a return to the wall.  This time, however, she was going to cross the wall rather than follow it.  The gambit paid off.

The orcs were looking north as she swooped in from the west to hit the southern platform on the west wall.  They never saw her coming.

Yana pulled the cord, dumping pellets from her starboard pouch, and obliterated both engine and crew in a cloud of greasy smoke. The attending archers were swept away by the shrapnel.

She caught the updraft and climbed for the sky. Below her lay the city proper, with its teeming masses. Frowning, she realized that if she went down here, there would be no chance of escape. Not while wounded.

A few delinquent arrows hissed through the sky, chasing after her. The wind rider breathed a sigh of relief as she gained enough altitude to clear the smoke and escape their range.

Before turning, Yana took a few deep breaths and prepared herself for more pain. Her expectations proved right. The agony was enough to tear another scream from her lips and bring tears to her eyes. Banking sharply, she felt hot blood running down her leg and knew she couldn't stay up much longer. However, she had only a single load of bombs left to drop. She headed back toward the northwest tower.

Two minutes later, she made a slow, lazy turn east and stooped for the wall. Changing her pattern again saved her.

The Trakyan flyer streaked out of the smoke. Yana saw the orcs scanning for her in the sky, but they were looking down the parapet line. One of them spotted her and began to shout. The orcs raced to turn the catapult. She flew low, and the gunner cut loose with a shower of five- and ten-pound stones: scatter shot. Joining the stones, arrows arced toward her like a swarm of bees.

Frantically shifting her weight and tapping into the magic stored in the small craft, the glider banked while simultaneously gaining altitude. The heavier stones fell short. Had one hit, she would have followed it to the ground. However, the lighter arrows kept climbing as she strove to get above them.

With a grimace, Yana counted at least six arrows she couldn't avoid. Four put holes in her airfoil. She wasn't as lucky with the other two: her barbute turned one, but the second slipped past her armor and sliced her left side. It wasn't a fatal hit, being close to the surface, but the pain was incredible.

Screaming, she swept through the cloud of arrows toward the tower and loosed the last of her dragon pellets.

Over half were duds.  They hit the tower with only the sporadic accompaniment of explosions.

When the last bomb dropped, she banked hard and climbed desperately for the safety of the pall of smoke, trailing a hissing tail of barbed arrows hunting for revenge. She threw a quick glance behind her just before entering the clouds and frowned.  Those last few bombs had spewed more smoke than flame, making it impossible for her to assess the damage she had done.

**1:50pm**

Xandor climbed back up the stairs while Jasper and Dobrynya stood at the bottom, waiting for the signal.  Behind them, a dozen grimy Rhodinans stood ready, with more emerging from the tunnel every minute.  Chert stood next to the adit, helping the soldiers crawl out and keeping the wall open.

Shouts from outside breached the thin walls of the inn, and an occasional distant explosion caused the men to wonder if the city was under attack.

Pulling the basement door open slightly, the ranger looked up and down the hallway.  It bisected the inn with doors on either side and a door at each end.  Not seeing anyone, he took a cautious step.

Motioning for the others, Dobrynya and Jasper led the soldiers to the top of the stairs to take his place.

As Xandor traveled down the hallway, it quickly became apparent that very little of the original inn depicted on Dobrynya's map remained.  In some rooms, the interior finishes on the wall had been stripped, leaving the timber studs exposed, some with the bark still on them.  Lapped, wooden siding was fastened to the exterior side of the studs, but many of the planks were rotten and let in daylight.  The wooden floors sloped this way and that, and Xandor wondered what the orcs had been doing here earlier.

Outside, there was a lot of running, shouting, and cursing.  A whip cracked sharply, and someone screamed.

Steeling his nerves, he continued down the hallway, toward where the map indicated the old kitchen lay.  He stopped at a section of solid wall flanking the doorless entry to the old dining room. Xandor peered around the jamb.  The room was barren of furniture, and broken windows lined the exterior wall.  Glass, stained yellow, hung like jagged teeth.  His mind reeled at the thought that this was where Trakya's Kral and the Korol' of Michurinsk had signed their treaty.  It should have been treated with respect, not left to the whims of humanoids.

In the center of the far wall, a pair of undamaged shutters covered what could only be a pass-through window.  The door at the end of the hallway had to be the kitchen.  He darted past the gaping dining room doorway and waited on the other side with his back to the wall.

Dobrynya and Jasper crept toward him, staying low.  Like his brother, August, Dobrynya couldn't sneak past a sleeping deaf elephant.  His armor clanked with every move, and his heavy, heel-toe gait thunked loudly on the wooden deck, yet the warrior remained blissfully unaware of the noise he made.  Xandor shook his head and wondered what Yana would have said.  Probably something pithy and unpleasant.

The ranger motioned for the others to stay put near the dining room while he continued to the kitchen.  At the end of the hallway, the thick door planks were grey with age, gouged in some places and scorched in others, making him wonder if they were the originals.  The door was closed, but someone had torn a huge chunk out of the edge near the handle.  Peering through the hole, he saw that most of the kitchen was still intact.  Some of the utensils looked recently used in fact.  As quiet as a mouse, he stepped inside.

Grime, grease, and soot covered every surface.  The ranger had no idea what orcs ate, let alone cooked, and he didn't want to know.  From the hall, he heard Dobrynya's clanking approach.  Shaking his head, he searched for a trapdoor and hoped Chert's instincts were right.

"Here it is," the vityaz said a few minutes later, kneeling beside a small table.  He traced a seam in the floor with his fingers, drawing a thirty-inch-square outline in the grime.

"Where's the latch?"  Xandor said as he knelt beside Dobrynya.  Moving the table aside, the two pried at the edges with their daggers, but all they accomplished was chewing up the wood.

"Maybe we need Chert to open this," Dobrynya whispered reluctantly.

"Don't do that. You and I would never hear the end of it," Xandor replied quickly. "Jasper, what do you see? I'm not even sure which way this thing opens. There's no hinges or anything."

The mage stepped from the hallway, where he had been keeping watch, and knelt on the far side of the square. "Let me try a little magic." The two gave the mage some distance. Jasper assumed a hurt look but had a hard time keeping a straight face. The smile faded quickly, replaced by a look of concentration. Muttering, the mage waved his hand, and the trapdoor buckled as if under a tremendous strain. The edge of the wood floor split and the trapdoor popped loose. Everyone held their breath, anticipating someone outside had heard, but nothing happened.

"You weren't supposed to break it," Xandor whispered.

"I didn't mean to," Jasper whispered back. "It was stuck."

Reaching down, Dobrynya said, "There's nothing for it now. We'll just have to deal with hiding it when the time comes." He gripped the edge of the wood and lifted the trapdoor. The rank stench of dead fish quickly overwhelmed them. Covering his mouth, the vityaz turned his head and gagged.

Jasper glanced down the dark hole with interest. The top of a rusted spiral staircase disappeared into the gloom. "I think we found it."

**2:00pm**

The stone was still hot when Bregu Kraagor and his entourage surveyed the damage on the northeast tower. He kicked at the debris on the battlements. The destruction of the engines on this tower was complete. There was a surprising lack of blood. Perhaps it had burned off in the fire that still smoldered, he noted with dispassion.

Kraagor turned his gaze westward, where four of his towers and one engine platform still smoked. His anger swelled, and the red in his eyes glowed. He would have killed the fools who let this happen. Fortunately for them, they were already dead. Turning, he glared at the gathered tohan.

"What are the humans doing?" he demanded.

His advisors looked nervously at one another, not wanting to attract attention from their irate liege. Finally,

Toha Darolsh stepped forward. "That was one of the Kral's flyers. The Rhodinans," he spat the word, "must have allied with the Trakyans and are intent on taking the city. They move to attack us. Dobrynya Sabe's incursion must have been either a feint or a reconnaissance, or both!"

Another advisor nodded emphatically and added, "This attack is preparing the way for an assault on our city. We should send out more patrols and torture some east bank farmers to learn of their troop locations. Then we can lay in ambush and destroy them to the last man!" The other advisors growled agreement and beat their fists on their chests.

Bregu Kraagor studied the orcs, trying to discern if they were speaking true or working to maneuver him into an unwise move. They met his scrutiny with an open desire for blood and revenge, but not treachery.

He nodded. "Toha Darolsh, your words are wise. The humans," he spat on the floor as he uttered the contemptible word, "have pushed too far. It is time for them to learn the error of threatening Chernigov!"

The voices of agreement from his advisors overwhelmed all else for a moment, then Kraagor continued, "Bring me a farmer, a merchant, anyone from the east bank! We shall learn the truth of their plans. We shall rout their forces in the field, run them to ground as they flee, and feast on their flesh!"

Roars of approval from his advisors echoed, and the heartbeats of those orcs nearby raced with excitement and bloodlust.

After the noise subsided, Kraagor turned to one of his orc advisors and said, "Toha Borrag, see to having these engines repaired or replaced; Folcgesíþ Karnor and Folcgesíþ No'Kal, put extra patrols on all three exposed sides of the city." In acknowledgment of the orders, the indicated advisors struck fists to chests.

# CHAPTER 28
# SACHA'S PLAN

### October 28, 4235 K.E.


**2:00pm**

Grendel and Sacha were the last to crawl free of the adit. They stretched and worked out the kinks, happy to be out of that hole.

Chert waited until the two were clear before he ducked back inside.

Soldiers pooled in the basement and lined the stairs. At the top, Ilya checked the corridor. The excitement around him was contagious. They were going home. Pointing to five men, each with an injured man hoisted over their shoulder, Ilya gestured for them to move out. They quickly disappeared through the broken doorway and down the hall. Their boots tromped on the floorboards loudly at first but faded quickly as they made their way toward the kitchen.

Taking the necklace from around his neck, Grendel turned to Sacha and said, "Thank you."

She took it and dropped it in one of her pockets, watching Grendel resume his normal size and appearance.

From within the adit, they heard grumbling. Chert thrust his helmet from the opening, and Grendel took it. The dwarf's hand disappeared, and they heard muted cursing. Then everything went quiet. A small cloud of dust escaped the tunnel, followed by an ominous sliding noise. Alarmed, everyone turned toward the opening in the wall. Grendel and Sacha knelt and peered through the blackness but couldn't see anything.

They backed away when Chert stepped out of the adit covered in dark black soil, spitting dirt. The dwarf brushed himself off and turned to face the opening.

"What happened?" Grendel asked quietly.

"Organics."

Sacha and Grendel shrugged as they stared at each other questioningly.

The dwarf worked the edges of the adit and slowly closed it until there was no trace left of the tunnel. Finally removing himself completely from the opening, he allowed the stone walls to close with a click.  Taking back his helmet with a muttered thanks, he glanced around.  The line of soldiers had shortened as the crowd in the basement thinned.

When the last of the soldiers took their places in the line on the stairs, Grendel, Chert, and Sacha followed suit.  Those near the top of the steps heard shouting from outside along with the occasional movement of heavy equipment, but the inn seemed to be ignored.

Ilya signaled for five more soldiers to proceed down the hallway.


In the kitchen, Dobrynya stood anxiously at the doorway, motioning for his men to hurry.  Each had looks of concentration on their faces as they tried to walk quietly, but the old floorboards squeaked and thumped with every step.  Behind him, the trapdoor lay open, filling the room with the noxious smell of dead fish.  Despite the stench, his men didn't hesitate to descend into the murky depths of the smuggler's run.

The next group of men had made it half-way down the hall when a soot-covered orc wearing a black apron appeared in the doorway of the old dining room.

At first, he didn't see or hear the humans on either side of him.  He had one clawed hand on his forehead, muttering to himself.  The soldiers froze.  Dobrynya had the brief impression the orc had forgotten something, then the creature looked up.  The orc gave one slow blink before his eyes flew wide and he did what any sensible person would do when outnumbered by a well-armed enemy — he ran.

The soldiers made to chase after him, but Dobrynya stopped them with a signal and gestured for them to continue into the kitchen.

Ilya, seeing the incident, rushed everyone out of the basement.

Outside, the lone orc shouted loud enough to raise the dead.

The last to enter the kitchen, Ilya closed the door behind him and followed the other soldiers down the hole.  As his second-in-command disappeared below, Dobrynya turned to face Xandor and said, "Come with us.  There's no chance for secrecy now.  Once we reach safety, we can team up with your men on the other side the river and sneak back across later tonight or tomorrow.  Those crates aren't going anywhere."

The ranger listened to the growing noise outside and knew Dobrynya was right.  He was about to agree, but a light hand on his shoulder stopped him.

"Once word of our presence reaches Kraagor, he'll hide those crates deep down, maybe even hide each one in a different part of the city.  If we leave and come back, we'll never know if we destroyed them all.  Our only chance is to act now," Sacha said.

Xandor looked her in the eyes, searching for a reason to believe her.

Dobrynya saw the doubt and whispered, "She's a Madasgorski first.  Remember that."

A decision had to be made quickly.  He asked, "What's your plan?"

She told them.  They listened as she laid it out, and, as she finished, Dobrynya's eyebrows rose in surprise.  "You can't be serious.  That's suicide."

"It's our only chance.  We do this now, or we forget about stopping the soap," Sacha said.  Grendel and Chert remained silent, leaving the decision to Xandor.

Jasper stood, leaning heavily on his staff, and said, "We might catch the crates on the river later or in a wagon, but she's right.  We'll never know if we got them all, and even a single bar of soap is dangerous.  It only took a handful to take down the White Circle.  Imagine what happens if a whole crate were to slip through our fingers.  With the Iron Tower at their door, they're bottled up right now — just like us."

Muttering of orc voices and heavy footsteps in the dining room made everyone glance toward the hallway.  Time was up.

"Dobrynya, get your men out of here.  Don't wait for us," Xandor said.

The vityaz clapped the ranger on the arm and shook his hand.  "Until we meet again on the other side."

Xandor nodded, smiling sadly, and repeated, "On the other side."

Dobrynya ducked below the trapdoor.  Xandor shut it behind him and motioned for Grendel to give it a shove.  With a groan, the warped frame fit snugly into the opening, stuck for good this time. The ranger swiped his boot over the edges, smearing the grime.

Sacha pulled out her gold chain and handed it to Chert. "Strip down and when you're done, put this on. Now."

With a grimace, the dwarf looked at Xandor, clearly questioning the sanity of her request.

"Do it. We have to lead the orcs away from here."

With help, Chert quickly took off his armor, clothes, and boots and handed them to Jasper, who dumped them into the magical bag he had brought with him from Pazard'zhik. The dwarf placed the necklace around his neck and Sacha gripped it with both hands, whispering words of magic. The short dwarf grew taller, and his skin took on an odd, greenish-brown hue. His beard disappeared, and wispy strands of black replaced the mop of curly brown hair on his head. When she was done, an average-looking orc stood naked in the kitchen in the place of Chert Joalheiro.

"I don't know why I have to be an orc" Chert said awkwardly, unfamiliar with the elongated canines and sharp, pointed teeth.

"Because if they see a dwarf in here, they will attack first and ask questions later."

"And we don't want that why?"

Giving the former dwarf a look, Sacha turned to Grendel and asked, "Can you find your friend here some clothes and weapons?"

The half-orc nodded with a grin and peeked out the kitchen door. Two orc soldiers slowly headed their way, led by the small orc wearing a black apron. Holding up three fingers, he mouthed, "They are coming."

Chert stood naked in the middle of the room while the others moved into position. Xandor and Sacha each found a dark corner. Grendel stood behind the door. Jasper closed his eyes in concentration and vanished.

Footsteps stopped outside the kitchen. The door jarred slightly when the orc in the apron checked to see if it was barred. With a loud creak, he pushed it open and cautiously stepped inside. A wide grin broke out on his face when he saw Chert standing in the middle of the kitchen. Motioning to his companions, all three approached the naked orc and started laughing.

Chert scowled at them, but didn't speak, which made the newcomers laugh harder.

Grendel eased the door closed behind them.  He launched a fist at the closest, striking the orc solidly in the throat.  There was a loud crunch followed by a soft whimper that caused the other two to whip around.

Attacking from behind, Xandor and Sacha took down their orcs, the ranger with a simple thrust of his longsword and Sacha with a slice of her dagger.  The surprised orcs fell dead before they realized what had happened.

"This language barrier may pose a problem," Chert whispered as he piled the bodies against the wall.  "I didn't understand a word they said."

"Don't worry.  Just act deaf and mute," Sacha said.

"Actually, that's a problem for all of us," Xandor said, stripping off the shorter orc's clothing and handing them to Chert.  Next, he nudged aside the body and picked up a rusty scimitar.

The former dwarf held up the clothes and made a face.

"Put them on," Xandor ordered.

Grumbling, Chert donned the clothes and stepped into the orc's iron-shod boots.  The transformation amazed the ranger, and he had to look twice to reassure himself it was Chert.

"Jasper, you still with us?" Xandor whispered.

"Yep," came the disembodied reply.  He flickered and became visible again.

"Ready for the next part?"

"No," came the unanimous reply.

Everyone stared at each other before they quickly busied themselves with part two of Sacha's plan.  Grendel stood beside the door, listening for another orc patrol, but none came.

Jasper helped everyone prepare in the kitchen.  Even though he was putting on a strong front, he could feel his strength waning.  The magic he had poured out at the monastery was taking its toll, and it was an effort to do the smallest of tasks, like when he put away Chert's clothes and equipment.

Reaching into his sporran, he pulled out a bit of acacia gum wrapped around an eyelash.  As he did, he felt something cool brush against his hand.  It was the barest of touches, but he had no doubt as to what it was: the *Veritas autem Sutekh.*  He jerked his hand back as if stung, but the feeling didn't go away.  It whispered to him.  All he had to do was use the book and his strength would return — more powerful than before.  He could take down the entire city.  Grimacing, Jasper cinched the sporran tightly and concentrated on his next task.

Xandor put on his cloak, and Sacha held her hand out to him.  The ranger paused, doubt gnawing at him.  Reluctantly, he undid his belt and handed it to her.  She gave it to Grendel and turned to face Xandor again.  She eyed him suspiciously, and her foot tapped impatiently.

"That's everything," he whispered.

"Your daggers and knives?  Where are they?"

"I don't have any."

Sacha's eyes widened in surprise, but he didn't offer an explanation, and she didn't ask for one.  She grabbed both his hands and crossed the wrists.  Reaching into her pouch, she produced a black silk cord.

"Stand still," she said when she placed it over his wrists.  The silk cord quickly bound Xandor's hands, and he flinched when it finished tying itself into a knot.

"That's an interesting little toy," he said.  "Who else have you used this on?"

Ignoring his comment, Sacha said, "Just stick to the plan.  And don't forget the word I told you earlier.  It will release you."

Sacha pulled the hood of the ranger's cloak up far enough to conceal his face.

"Are you sure it will work with me?"

"Do you want to give it a try?"

Xandor brought his bound hands up and whispered.  The silk cord immediately loosened and untied itself.  Sacha picked up the cord and placed it over his wrists again, binding them.

"Will it do that every time?"

"Yes.  Now quit playing with it and let's go.  Chert, you take him.  Grendel, you stand with me."

Chert stepped up, holding the scimitar.  Xandor pointed toward the hilt, and the former dwarf gave him a wry look.

"I know how to hold a sword, human," the dwarf said.

"Sorry, couldn't tell from where I was standing."

"You ready?"

"Let's get this over with."


**2:17pm**

Sacha stepped boldly into the street where a crowd of orcs had already gathered.  Grendel, Xandor, and Chert waited behind her.  The foul-smelling creatures surrounded them, brandishing their wicked blades.  Sacha didn't stop.  She took up an air of disdain and walked into their midst like she belonged there.

"Orcnéas, hwyrfaþ!" she commanded.  *Orcs, move aside!*

The orcs hesitated, and their swords wavered.  They stared at one another, unsure what they should do.

Getting directly in the face of the nearest one, Sacha said, "Móton grétan Toha þínum.  We have a prisoner that must be taken to Bregu Kraagor immediately!"

The orc eyed the woman greedily, not disguising his lust.  With a blur of motion, Sacha pulled her dagger and slit the orc's throat.  She stepped in front of the next orc before the first body fell.  Shocked, no one moved.

"Ic eom on ofeste!"  *I am in haste!*

The second orc glanced at the fallen body of the first and licked his cracked lips with a blue-black tongue.  His beady eyes traveled to the dripping dagger.  "Hwæt syndon gé?" *Who are you?*

"Ic eom Aleksandra Madasgorski.  Ic gáän séon Bregu Kraagor." *I am Aleksandra Madasgorski.  I seek an audience with King Kraagor.*

"Show me this prisoner," he replied in orcnéan.

Sacha stepped aside and motioned for Xandor to be brought forward.  Grendel moved with Sacha, and Chert shoved Xandor ahead of him.

"We heard that many Rhodinan dogs were hiding in here," the orc said, staring at the cloaked figure.

"That was obviously overstated," Sacha replied.

"How did he get in here?"

"He's one of the Kral's rangers."

An angry murmur spread through the group of orcs.

Bowing obsequiously, the orc said, "My apologies, Milady. I was unaware of your presence in our city. Gewítaþ forð beran waépen ond gewaédu. Ic éow wísige." *Go forth bearing your weapons and armor. I will guide you.*

A crowd had gathered in a plaza surrounding the foundations of an old stone fountain. Curious, many of the orcs stood atop piles of rock to see the newcomers. They pointed to the pair of humans. Vicious snarls and taunts greeted the ranger from all sides. Chert made sure he kept Xandor between himself and Grendel, and away from the rowdier orcs.

Xandor stared at the fresh plumes of dark smoke billowing from several of the towers posted along the city walls. The smoke fanned out briefly, revealing the wrecked remains of war machines. Between the towers, orcs ran frantically along the tops of the walls, trying to put out the fires and repair the damage.

The group kept moving, and a cluster of ramshackle wooden buildings blocked his view. Like the inn, the former houses and shops looked to be rotting from the ground up and were on the verge of collapse. At first, he thought they were vacant, but he occasionally caught a glimpse of someone or something staring back at him from a window or doorway.

Conforming to the shape of the old wall, present-day Chernigov was but a shadow of its original self. At its widest, Xandor guessed the city spanned a bit under a mile in each direction. Dilapidated one- and two-story buildings, black from soot, flanked filthy streets. Interspersed between them were tall earthen mounds that looked to be entrances into tunnels beneath the city. From somewhere near the center of town, black smoke continuously billowed and fed the ever-present gloom.

It was no wonder the Korol' of Michurinsk had opted to let the city be.

Several muscular orcs forced their way through the crowd, and the noise subsided. Behind them, a fat orc with a long face and droopy jowls that rested on his multiple chins casually stepped forward.  He wore grimy reddish-brown robes and held a spiked mace aloft like a symbol of authority.

"What have we here, Wēigen?" the newcomer rumbled.

With a clumsy flourish, the orc answered, "Garedon Styrr, let me introduce Lady Madasgorski.  She has captured one of the Kral's rangers."

"Indeed," the fat orc said, openly suspicious.

He glanced past Wēigen and saw Sacha standing beside Grendel.  "Your brother said you were dead."

"Garedon Styrr, as you can see, I am not dead."

"Obviously.  How did you get into Chernigov?"

"I followed this ranger into the city.  He was able to sneak past your orcs, and so was I.  Of course, Bregu Kraagor will be informed.  I doubt such laxness will go unpunished."

Orcs stared at each other nervously.

"One of the Kral's rangers, Lady Madasgorski?"

"Yes.  See for yourself."

Walking around Sacha, Garedon Styrr threw a furtive glance at Grendel and continued past.  He stopped in front of Chert and Xandor and gestured toward the cloak.  The former dwarf pulled back Xandor's hood.  The ranger was hating this more and more, but he kept still, his mouth shut.

In crude Trakyan, the orc said appraisingly, "Lord Madasgorski mentioned a ranger.  We've never caught one alive before.  This will be a rare treat."

The orc chieftain turned to Chert and said bluntly, "I don't recognize you.  Who are you?"

Interrupting, Sacha stepped forward and said, "Garedon Styrr, I found him near the mudpots, fighting the ranger.  During the fight, his throat was damaged and rendered him unable to speak.  If it hadn't been for my arrival, he would be dead.  He owes me a life debt."

Facing Chert, he said, "You fought the ranger by yourself? Impressive."

The former dwarf stared blankly.  He kept his eyes averted and held Xandor tightly.

Rounding on Sacha, Garedon Styrr said, "Lady Madasgorski, this prisoner is mine.  I will be the one to present him to Bregu Kraagor.  You may accompany me if you like."

Everyone took a step backward as the tension suddenly ratcheted upward.  Sacha's eyes narrowed dangerously, and she said, "This is my prisoner, Garedon Styrr.  I alone will be the one to take him to your king."

The Garedon beckoned, and the edge of the crowd formed a circle around them.  A giant of an orc broke through the line with a growl and stood next to Garedon Styrr.  Similar in appearance to Grendel, his large-boned frame, dark-colored skin, and bestial face suggested he was an óhreint — the unholy union of eotenas and orcnéas.  He wore thick plate armor and held a massive two-handed sword.  Several nicks scored the edge, and flakes of black blood decorated the flat of the blade.

"You are traveling through my domain, Lady Madasgorski.  Therefore, you and your prisoner are now mine," Garedon Styrr said with an evil smile.  "Count yourself fortunate that I do not feed you to my dogs."

Sacha looked at Grendel.  The half-orc was slightly smaller than the Garedon's champion, and she watched, fascinated, as he hefted his battle-axe and stretched and flexed his muscles.

"I am no prisoner, you fat slob.  I say you are a coward, Garedon Styrr, and Bregu Kraagor will hear of your laziness."  She pointed to the crowd of orcs and continued, "Everyone here knows I am a princess of Zhitomir.  You have no right to revoke my claim to passage or take what is my spoil of battle."

Screaming, the obese orc shook his mace violently.  Spittle trickled down the folds of his greasy skin.  He grabbed the monstrous orc by the arm and pushed him into the circle.  "Skyld, kill them!"

Grendel and Skyld walked to opposite sides of the circle.  Sacha grabbed Chert's arm and directed him to a spot that the crowd of orcs cleared for them.  Xandor followed her lead but inside, he seethed — this was not part of the plan.  They were surrounded, with no chance of escape.

Grendel studied his opponent.  Skyld was taller, possibly stronger than him, but moved slower.  The more Grendel considered the óhreint, the more he believed the other's armor was more of a detriment than a boon.  The thick steel was black from dirt and ash.  Underneath, it was solid, but it was also heavy.

Skyld, like Grendel, fought for a living. Approaching cautiously, he studied Grendel in turn. Knees slightly bent, he kept his center low and held his two-handed sword with the hilt up near his left shoulder, the tip of the blade pointing toward the smoky sky.

Lifting his axe in front of his heart onehanded, Grendel dipped his head. "Alea iacta est." Stretching such that several vertebrae popped, he gripped his weapon loosely in front of him, his hands apart. The two circled, waiting and watching.

With a loud, phlegm-dripping growl, Skyld attacked. Leading with his wrist, he snapped the heavy blade of his two-handed sword forward. The long blade blurred with motion as it cut toward Grendel's head.

Taking a step back, Grendel brought up his axe to block. Sparks flew as metal struck metal. Skyld quickly drew his sword back to his right shoulder before Grendel could catch it between the upper curved hooks of his axe blades.

Snapping his blade forward, Skyld cut at Grendel again, this time from the other side, and again, Grendel took a step back and stopped it with his axe. Step by step, Skyld forced Grendel backward into the waiting crowd.

With the power of the eotenas backing each of his opponent's strikes, Grendel backpedaled and stayed on the defensive as cut after cut came at him. The crowd of orcs loomed behind him, their hoots and howls accompanying each blow.

Changing his grip, Skyld performed a complete outside moulinet. Continuing the motion, he rolled his wrists, and the two-handed blade circled on his opposite side. Building momentum, the blade began an upward and forward motion. It arced down from overhead and slammed into the waiting haft of Grendel's weapon. The diagonal cut clanged loudly, and the vibration nearly shook the axe from Grendel's hands.

Surprised the half-orc was still standing, Skyld found himself overextended.

Grendel kicked the side of the poleyn protecting the knee that supported most of Skyld's weight. The knee buckled, and the óhreint stumbled sideways with a groan. The awkward position caused the joints in the plate armor to bind. Focusing his attention on not falling, he left his head open to attack — a fatal mistake, had he faced any other opponent.

Using the axe haft, Grendel pushed aside Skyld's blade and disengaged. Skyld stepped back, bewildered that he was still alive. He looked at Grendel with a questioning expression.

Enjoying the fight immensely, Garedon Styrr taunted, "Skyld, he's a coward. He is no match for you!" It was obvious he wasn't going to let it go without shedding blood.

"You'll have to kill him," Sacha yelled in Trakyan.

"I do not kill unless I have to."

"Don't tell me. Tell that fat orc over there."

Grendel glanced over at Garedon Styrr and instantly recognized the type of person he was. It didn't matter if he was orc, human, or minotaur. During his bouts in the ring, he had seen many of them standing in the audience, and he hated each and every one of them. They were the ones who drew a perverse pleasure from watching the fights. The bloodier, the better. They fed off it.

Favoring his knee, Skyld advanced, his two-handed sword held out in front with the hilt low and the tip at eye level — the en garde position.

Lunging forward, Skyld attacked with an overhead cut aimed at Grendel's exposed shoulder. The half-orc stepped diagonally while closing his grip. With a loud ring, the blade fell on the haft just below the axe blade. Grendel rode the sword's momentum and, twisting his haft, pinned the weapon inside the curved lower hook of his own steel.

Sparks flew when Skyld wrenched his blade free.

Grendel swung his mighty battle-axe and pivoted while stepping forward with his left foot. Skyld leaned back to avoid the attack, narrowly missing the sharp tips of the axe blades. Pressing, Grendel stepped forward with his right foot and swept his axe back across, letting its long reach keep his opponent off balance.

Timing his parry, Skyld stopped the half-orc's swing cold.

Using his right foot for leverage, Grendel push-kicked with his left and hit Skyld squarely in the stomach.

The weight of Skyld's armor shifted, and he toppled backward. Gripping his sword with one hand, he reached back frantically with the other to catch himself.

With a quick swipe, Grendel hit the flat of his opponent's sword, knocking it away.  He stepped forward and pressed the tip of his axe blade against Skyld's throat just above the gorget.  "Yield!"

Skyld's eyes darted toward Garedon Styrr.

Livid, the fat orc commander yelled, "Hildlata! Ábréatan!" *Battle-shirker!  Break him!*

In a move that surprised everyone including Grendel, Skyld rolled and struck the battle-axe with his steel vambrace, shoving it aside.  The axe sliced Skyld's neck, but the óhreint didn't seem to notice.  Black blood welled from the wound, making it difficult to determine the severity.

Using his gauntlet for protection, Skyld grasped the long blade of his sword with one hand.  With a herculean effort, he whipped the quillions and pommel of the oversized weapon around and aimed it directly at Grendel's head.

Grendel hunched and blocked the attack with his shoulder.  Red blood spattered the hilt and ran down the blade.  A shocked murmur resonated through the crowd. Holding his shoulder, Grendel staggered back under the crushing blow.

Skyld was on his feet in an instant.  Flipping his sword, he gripped the hilt with both hands and brought the sword back to his right hip with the tip angled toward the sky.

Letting go of his shoulder, Grendel gripped his battle-axe with both hands and brought it up in a makeshift salute.

"Hwæt bist ðu anbidung?  Ácwylman sé dóc!" the orc commander shouted.  *What are you waiting for?  Slay that bastard!*

The orcs surrounding him yelled taunts.  One of them, overcome with blood lust, brandished his scimitar and madly flung himself at Grendel.  Catching the orc by the scruff of the neck, Skyld tossed him back into the crowd.  Jeers erupted, while others seemed on the verge of trying their luck.

Taking advantage of the distraction, Skyld charged Grendel, bringing his sword up for an overhead cut.  Grendel turned and caught the falling blade between the tips of his axe.  Using Skyld's forward motion to his own advantage, Grendel twisted left and brought his axe down and back, maintaining contact between the two weapons and allowing the two-handed sword to continue sliding past.

Twisting suddenly back to front, Grendel broke contact and cut at Skyld's stomach with a short, vicious swipe. The blade struck the bands of steel below the cuirass even as Skyld dodged back, trying to avoid it. The armor held, but a large rent opened between the bands, exposing the padding beneath.

Two screaming orcs rushed out of the crowd toward Grendel, their scimitars held high. Noticing them out of the corner of his eye, Grendel quickly turned and caught both blades on his axe. Before they could recover, he made a two-handed swipe at their chests. The first evaded the cut, but the second was sliced open cleanly and collapsed, a black smear running across the front of his leather armor.

Opposite each other, Skyld and the orc eyed Grendel cautiously. Skyld resumed his en garde position while the orc assumed a less professional stance with the tip of his blade pointed directly toward Grendel.

With both hands on the haft of his battle-axe, Grendel lunged at the orc with a diagonal swipe from high to low, striking the proffered blade near the quillions and knocking it out of the orc's hands with a metallic clang. Stepping forward with his left foot as the orc backed away, he reversed his grip and direction of the battle-axe and caught the orc unawares. The axe buried itself in the newcomer's chest, and black blood gushed from the wound.

Advancing as the orc fell, Skyld thrust his blade toward Grendel's back.

Feeling death looming over his shoulder, Grendel yanked and tugged at his axe, but it was embedded in hard bone and wouldn't come loose.

With nothing else available, Grendel choked up on the haft, turned, and dodged to one side. He tried to use his axe to parry the strike, but the dead orc weighed it down. The steel handle struck the two-handed blade a glancing parry and searing pain coursed through Grendel's body as the tip sliced across his ribs, under his arm.

Skyld drew his blade back for the fatal blow. The two opponents stared one another directly in the eyes, waiting for the telltale sign.

With a flick of Skyld's wrist, the two-handed sword snapped forward. Grendel released his axe, spun to the side of the flashing blade, and lashed out with a roundhouse kick to Skyld's chin.  The heavy boot landed with a solid thud that sent Skyld crashing to the ground and the sword flying.

The display stunned the crowd.

None too gently, Grendel stepped on the dead orc and yanked his axe free with a sickening crunch while Skyld sat up groggily, still dazed by the fierce attack.

Smiling evilly, the fat orc commanded in Trakyan, "Kill him.  He is worthless to me now."

"No," Grendel said, resting his bloodied axe on his shoulder.  "He is defeated.  Let it go."

Garedon Styrr's smile faded.  He looked at Sacha and then at Grendel.  "I have given you a command, half-breed.  Do you dare defy me?"

Moving faster than anyone expected, Grendel suddenly stood in front of the orc magistrate and growled, "I dare."

Xandor and Chert made to assist, but Sacha held them back with a hand on Chert's arm.

The fat orc's eyes grew wide, especially when Grendel raised his axe.  Shaking in fear, Garedon Styrr raised his mace in defense, but Grendel batted it away contemptuously.  The sour smell of urine wafted up, and the orcs surrounding the garedon backed away, disgusted.

Using the knob of his axe, Grendel pushed Garedon Styrr into the crowd of orcs.  The waiting masses tore into the disgraced leader with an animalistic frenzy.  Given the way the mob moved, Garedon Styrr didn't die immediately.  Rivulets of black blood escaped around the orcs' stomping feet, and horrible, ripping sounds made Grendel turn his back on the ravenous crowd.

Skyld regained his senses, walked past Grendel, and disappeared into the mob.  A solitary scream erupted shortly thereafter, followed by wicked laughter.  Skyld pushed out of the crowd bearing the garedon's bloodied mace.

"Brúc ðisses sigorléan, lindgestealla," Skyld said as he held it out for Grendel to accept.  *Take this trophy of your victory, shield-brother.*

Sacha licked her lips expectantly as Grendel took the mace.  His brow furrowed with confusion, he stared at it briefly before tucking it away in his belt.

Sacha's eyes practically sparkled with triumph.

Watching her, Xandor couldn't help but notice that none of what had happened surprised her. A sinking feeling hit the pit of his stomach when he realized that they had been played all along.

# CHAPTER 29
# THE GAREDON

### October 28, 4235 K.E.

**2:40pm**

"Næfre ic máran geseah ordfruma ofer þæt eldland!" Skyld announced. *Never have I seen a greater warrior in the land!*

Raising their fists, the orcs shouted and struck their chests in response.

After the shouting subsided, Skyld struck his chest with his fist and said, "Skyld." Understanding the gesture, the half-orc pointed to himself and replied, "Grendel."

"Making new friends?" Sacha asked when she had pushed her way through the gathered orcs. For some reason, she seemed completely comfortable surrounded by the vicious creatures, which put Grendel even more on his guard.

"I do not know. I think so," Grendel answered.

Chert and Xandor walked close behind her, the former dwarf still holding Xandor's arm tightly.

"What now?" Xandor whispered in Sacha's ear.

The crowd of orcs had not dispersed. In fact, it seemed to only grow larger. The circle had closed, and Grendel felt claustrophobic from the press of bodies all around him. He had found instant fame. It was a lot different than being in a human city, and a part of him liked it.

Skyld shoved the orcs aside roughly, knocking some of them to the ground. "Hwæt! Fæste hwyrfaþ!" he yelled. *Hear me! Make way quickly!*

The orcs scampered out of the way, giving Grendel and Skyld room. When the line of orcs retreated, a small knot of female orcs, wearing hide skirts and leather bodices, stood openly appraising the half-orc. Except for being a bit shorter, they were similar in stature to their male counterparts; however, their coarse, black hair was much thicker, and the fronts of their bodices were loosely strung together, revealing ample amounts of green bosom.

Unaware of their gaze, Grendel listened as Sacha and Skyld conversed. They repeated the word Kraagor often, and Skyld pointed toward the center of town.

The knot of orc women drew closer, making Xandor and Chert nervous.

Noticing the women for the first time, Skyld grimaced and said, "Garedon Grendel, séo brýd sigores tó léane." *The brides are a victory gift.*

Glancing at the women, Grendel almost choked when he caught the word *bride.* Not being able to help herself, Sacha hid a smile behind her hand and laughed quietly.

With a loud clap of his hands, Skyld yelled, "Earm ides hondgemóta!" *Wretched women battle hand-to-hand!*

His eyes wide, Grendel was shocked by what happened next.

Cheering erupted as the seven orc women split up and immediately went after each other tooth and nail. Hair was pulled, clothing ripped, ears bitten, and faces clawed. Hoots and hollers from the crowd accompanied the screams from the women competing for Grendel.

Horrified by their savagery, Grendel stepped into their midst, pulled two apart, and flung them into the nearby audience. As a reward for his efforts, he received several deep scratches on his arms. With another step, he grabbed two more by their hair. Misinterpreting his intentions, the seven women gave him toothy grins.

A scrawny orc brought forward a large iron goblet filled with a vile-smelling liquid. Taking the goblet, Skyld handed it to Grendel and said, "Onfóh þissum fulle, fréodrihten mín." *Take this cup, my lord.*

"Sacha?" the half-orc queried, holding the goblet.

"Yes," she replied, still smiling.

"What is going on here?"

"I suppose you might call it a marriage ceremony, although I doubt these orcs would describe it that way. They have considerably fewer restrictions when it comes to copulation. I believe the phrase you would use is *might makes right.*"

"Who are these women?"

"They were the former garedon's property; they are now yours."

"Former garedon.  Who is the garedon now?  Skyld?"

Sacha shook her head, her hand covering her mouth, but he could see the mirth glinting mischievously in her eyes.

The answer dawned on him, and the sudden realization hit him like a brick.  "Oh no."

The crowd of orcs noticed the reaction, and their shouts of jubilation quieted down.  Silence reigned in the street, letting the sounds of the orcs fighting the flames on top of the wall reach them.

Every eye was on Grendel.

Sacha took the goblet from the stunned half-orc and turned it upside down, pouring its contents onto the street.  She had their undivided attention.

"Nú sy ne ándaga gebréman!" Sacha said loudly, addressing the crowd.  "Þínum wráþum standan ætforanweall!  Ne bídan oþþæt burgweg heoru-dréore ond blóde bestýmed!"  *Now is not the time to celebrate!  Your enemy stands at the walls!  Do not wait until your streets are filled with gore and smeared with blood!*

She paused as the orcs turned toward the north, letting her words sink in.  Their ferocious smiles became fierce grimaces as they listened to the shouts and screams of their people on the wall.  Sacha could see it in their faces — they knew she was right.  The enemy was outside their gates and would be attacking their people again at any moment.  Now was not a time for celebration.

"Atole ecgþræce ábidan!  Ábregdan sweord ond helm ond feoht!" Sacha concluded.  *The terrible storm of your weapons awaits!  Rise up with sword and helmet and fight!*  Her eyes practically shone as she watched the orcs.  New shouts erupted, but this time all merriment was gone, replaced by the lust for blood.

Feeling the emotion of the crowd turn, Xandor understood what had just happened.  He grabbed Sacha by the arm and said, "What the hell are you doing?"

Jerking her arm away, she rounded on him and replied, "You know damn well what I'm doing.  I'm saving our skins."

"You're sending those orcs into battle.  What's wrong with you?"

"Do you want to get to those crates or not?"

"Of course, but..."

"We can't reach them standing here watching Grendel choose his next bride.  Before long, these orcs will start drinking.  Trust me, we don't want to be here for that."

She made to step away but stopped herself.  She glanced back at the ranger with an odd look, leaned close to his ear and whispered, "Steel yourself for what is yet to come.  This is not a pleasant place.  You will face things that most people find abhorrent.  Just remember, you can't rescue everyone."

Sacha walked away, letting her words do their work.  She found Grendel standing beside Skyld, who scanned the angry mob for any signs of a threat directed toward their new leader.  Her bodyguard now had a bodyguard.

Sacha placed a hand on Grendel's shoulder.  He leaned down so she could whisper in his ear, "Tell Skyld exactly what I say."

After she finished, he straightened and stepped in front of Skyld.  Working his way around the strange words, he said, "Skyld, feorran cumene þæt wé fundiaþ Bregu Kraagor sécan." *Skyld, having come from afar, we are anxious to find King Kraagor.*

Skyld lowered his head, said, "Ic gefremman sceal," *It shall be done* and motioned down one of the streets.

Behind him, Grendel heard the women, now under a temporary truce, in deep discussion.  It wasn't difficult to figure out their subject matter given the looks they kept giving him.  Throughout their conversation, he kept hearing the phrase "loc túsc" repeated.  He looked at Sacha, but her face was purposely devoid of emotion; however, the sparkle in her eyes hinted at the meaning.

Following a gesture from Skyld, several orcs separated from the crowd and formed a small escort for Grendel and his entourage.  One of them held a container of paste.  He approached Grendel and motioned to the half-orc's wounds. Sacha nodded, and Grendel let the orc apply the paste to his various cuts.  When the ointment touched the wounds, Grendel felt like a hot iron had hit him.  His hands involuntarily clenched, and his nails bit into his palms. Steam hissed as the paste cauterized the wounds, closing them.  As soon as he got over the shock, Grendel made to punch the orc, but Sacha stopped him.

"That stuff hurt," Grendel growled.

"Don't get hit next time," Sacha said.

With the excitement dwindling, the orcs left the plaza and went back to their duties and chores. As they filed out, Xandor thought that the orcs must have been blocking the wind or something because when they left, a foul stench wrapped itself around them and clung like a second skin. The miasma made him want to retch.

Xandor found himself surrounded by a half dozen stout orcs carrying rust-stained scimitars. They grinned at him viciously, looking for an excuse to test a ranger of the Kral. Chert stepped closer, making sure everyone knew that the prisoner was his.

With a shout, the band moved down one of the main streets.

Having lost Grendel in the crowd, Xandor kept an eye toward the dark windows of the ruined buildings to either side, expecting at any moment for their ruse to be called. Fetid odors accosted them from all sides, and random lumps of excrement lined the old street gutters. He didn't want to know what caused the streets to have that slimy sheen.

Watching the arrival of the new garedon, orcs stood along the side of the streets, many of them old, toothless women. As Xandor walked past, they shouted curses at the ranger and threw rotten fruits, vegetables, and feces. The orcs guarding Xandor miraculously avoided the juicy projectiles, letting them fly unhindered. Most landed harmlessly in the street, but some managed to strike either Chert or Xandor and burst open in a shower of pulp and goo. Both Chert and Xandor took the abuse stoically.

Yelling from behind the old women distracted Grendel. Out of the corner of his eye, he saw a rail-thin, naked human boy dart behind a building. Chasing him were two orc children. They wore crude, brown furs and waved long pieces of wood in front of them like swords.

He wanted to intervene, but Sacha's fingertips brushed his hand. Her face was a mask, and she kept her eyes straight ahead, but he noticed that something worried her. Maybe she had seen the boy, too.

As they moved deeper into town, they spotted vegetable gardens neatly tucked in the alleys. Two or three humans, hunched over and wearing dirty rags, worked the land. In most cases, they were tilling the previous year's efforts under, while others were harvesting cabbage and other winter crops. In the latter case, small baskets lined the road, ready to be picked up. Orcs carrying heavy whips and scourges patrolled the grounds.

When Grendel and his escort walked past them, whips cracked, and pain-filled screams followed in their wake. Grendel's eyes narrowed, and he looked as though he was about to stop.

Sacha murmured, "What's your plan? Do you really think you can get to all of them? There are hundreds of them in this city."

"Why are they doing that? Those humans haven't done anything wrong."

"The orcs are showing you their respect."

"By hurting the humans?"

"Yes."

"I cannot turn my back on them."

"You're not. You are going to hurt these orcs where it counts."

"But that boy..."

"What about him?"

"What will happen to him?"

"If he's not fast enough, those orc children will catch him."

"Then what?"

"Grendel, these orcs view humans as a source of food. Remember that. Those crops we saw — they're not for the orcs. They only eat meat."

Alarmed, Grendel turned to face her.

"Keep walking," she hissed.


Chert and Xandor, having made their way back to the front, overheard Sacha's conversation with Grendel and found themselves struggling. Their hearts lurched at the thought of what was happening. They passed more humans, and the look in their eyes confirmed what Sacha said.

Hatred built up inside Xandor, and he couldn't tell who he hated more: the orcs for the life they led, Sacha for being so cold about it, or himself for not stopping them.

They passed through a plaza where orc soldiers stood in formation, their leader marking their faces with red blood. The ranger couldn't understand what was being said, but it was obvious they were preparing for the fight across the river. Some of them followed the ranger with their eyes as he was marched down the street. Some stared openly at the strange half-orc being led by Skyld.

There were so many of them. How could they have possibly thought that there was even a remote chance they could steal the chuck wagon? It seemed impossible. He recalled Sacha's plan, and with it came the dread feeling they were in way over their heads.

The walk through town ended at one of the earthen mounds. Beyond it, they saw a deep pit spewing smoke and ash. The smell of burnt flesh was overwhelming and competed with the smell of raw effluent.

Skyld directed them to one side, near the entrance to a tunnel. Orcs dressed in chain armor and wielding spears guarded the opening. At the group's approach, they crossed their spears, barring the way.

Human bones lay discarded beside the entrance, and a stone marker engraved with crude symbols stood at the top of the mound. Skyld stepped forward with Grendel and announced, "I bring you the new garedon of the south district. He has come to speak to Bregu Kraagor and present his gift." Skyld snapped his fingers, and the orc escort parted, letting the guards see Xandor and Chert. The guards growled and bared their fangs, but otherwise didn't move. The whole affair had the feel of a ceremony.

Sacha lightly touched Grendel's arm and discretely pointed. The half-orc stepped forward as she indicated and waited. One of the guards in the middle handed his spear to the orc on his left and broke ranks to greet Grendel. At his side, Sacha asked, "May I act as your interpreter?"

"Of course," Grendel responded, unsure exactly what was happening.

The orc guard turned to her and said, "There is no need. I understand the human speak."

For the first time, Sacha appeared apprehensive.

"Half-breed, state your name and your purpose," the orc said contemptuously.

Grendel didn't know how to respond.  He quickly glanced at Sacha, but her face was neutral.  He wished she had given him some kind of warning.  At least if she had told him that he would be tested on orc etiquette, he would have paid attention.

Looking around, it was obvious his delayed reaction had not gone unnoticed.  He tried to think about his recent crash course in their customs.

Inspiration struck him.  Handing his battle-axe to Skyld, Grendel pulled out the bloodied mace and hit the insolent guard across the bridge of his nose.  A loud crack echoed off the nearby buildings.  It wasn't a fatal blow, but it could have been, and everyone there knew it.  The guard doubled over and grabbed his nose.  Black blood gushed between his fingers and dripped to the ground.

"Tell them to stand down so that a garedon may present himself to Bregu Kraagor."

Sacha recovered quickly and did as Grendel ordered.

One of the orc guards responded and his tone, while respectful, held a negative tone.

"He says that Bregu Kraagor is not available.  He is currently occupied."

Grendel strode forward and said, "Tell him to send a messenger to Bregu Kraagor, and tell him that we will wait for him in his throne room."

Sacha relayed what Grendel said and then added something afterward.  The guard's eyes went wide.  He seemed like he was about to argue, but his eyes drifted to Grendel's mace.  Thinking better of it, he barked orders.  A guard at the end of their line grunted and disappeared around the back of the mound, heading east.  The other guards stepped aside.  Behind them was a reeking hole dug into the ground.  Foul mist wafted up, followed by the occasional scream.

Grendel stared into the dark maw of the orc's underground city with a heavy sense of foreboding.  He could feel the danger emanating from the pit like a cold wind on his skin and wondered if there was anything he could have done differently.  It was too late to change course.  To turn back now would not only let Marko win, but would, in all likelihood, sentence him and his friends to a horrible death.

Swallowing his dread, Grendel entered the underground city.

End of Book II

Don't miss the exciting conclusion:  <u>Blood of Cayn</u>!

## THANK YOU FOR READING!

We hope you've enjoyed <u>City of Cayn</u> as much as we enjoyed bringing it to you!  No author would be where they are without readers, so please accept a HUGE thank you for taking a chance on our endeavor.  Whether you loved it, hated it, or landed somewhere in between, it would be of immense help to us, as well as other readers, if you would take a moment to leave a review on Amazon and/or Goodreads.  Even a single sentence will mean a lot.

We love to hear from readers!  Feel free to drop us a line at mcdonald.isom@gmail.com  Let us know what you loved (or what you hated).  If you have questions about the story, we'll do our best to answer them.  For more information about cultures, countries, creatures, and races of Gaia, visit the glossary on our website, www.mcdonald-isom.com.  You can also find us on Facebook, @McDonald.Isom.author.

There are more adventures yet to come!

Turn the page for a sneak peek at <u>Blood of Cayn</u>!

# CHAPTER 1
# YANA RETURNS

### October 28, 4235 K.E.

**2:05pm**

Squire Patrick Anders burst into Lord Fergusson's command tent. Around the central map table, half-a-dozen knights reached for weapons. Tall, blonde, and blue eyed, Dame Astrid Wolfelschneider, the only female Detchian knight with whom Fergusson had ever served during his years with the Iron Tower, had her blade half-drawn before she recognized the squire.

"Laytenant Marchenkova's back, Sir!" Anders shouted.

Lord Geoffrey Fergusson, sixth baronet of Yorkshire, closed his eyes and counted to five.

"Squire!"

Anders snapped to attention. "Sir!"

"Step back outside and try that again."

"Yes, Sir!" With a nod, the young squire exited. Thirty seconds passed in silence.

"Permission to enter, Milord?" the squire called.

"Granted."

"Laytenant Marchenkova has returned from Chernigov, Sir. They've taken her to the healer's tent."

"Discipline, Squire, discipline. It makes the difference between a live soldier and a dead one," Lord Fergusson admonished.

"Yes, Sir," Anders said with a bowed head. "I'll take you to her when you're ready."

Lord Fergusson signaled for Leftenant Brian Gallagher to carry on with the planning before he followed his squire to the healer's tent.

On the way, they passed the edge of the training field where a small crowd of the curious had gathered to inspect Yana's abandoned glider. The soldiers parted to allow their leader a closer look at the holes riddling the dark silk sail.

After removing three black arrows still caught in the material, Lord Fergusson grabbed a random soldier by the elbow and instructed, "Get those holes patched immediately. Move!"

The man snapped a hasty salute and took off at a run.

Outside the field hospital, a group of camp runners, the young sons of sutlers and camp followers, huddled around one of their number. "...and when the chirurgeon shoved the needle and thread all the way through, blood just *gushed* out..." At sight of Lord Fergusson, the boys scattered, leaving the storyteller behind.

"Zack, I take it Lady Sehraine is inside with Laytenant Marchenkova?"

"Yes, Sir," the boy said.

Inside the tent, a woman screamed in agony. Fergusson saw his squire grow pale. "Anders, wait here with Zack. I'll call you if I need anything."

The wind rider lay face down, her right arm and left side swathed in thick bandages. A streak of bright red blood soaked the white sheets beneath her. Yana maintained a death grip on the edge of the operating table with her eyes shut tight. Sehraine gripped Yana's forearms, tears welling in her eyes.

Yana bit down on a wooden stick and screamed through the block when the healer shoved the barbed arrowhead through her thigh and out the other side. The wind rider dropped her head to the table in exhaustion. A moment later, her torment by the chirurgeon resumed as he stitched and bound the wounds.

Lord Fergusson watched in silence until the bandage was tied, and then said, "I thought I told you to be careful."

"I was," she replied in a raspy voice. "The orcs didn't start shooting and throwing things at me until I blew up the first tower. I have the information you need about their fortifications."

Yana slowly pushed herself up to a sitting position, but it was too much, too fast. Her face drained of color, and she slumped over. Sehraine caught her, holding her tight.

"I'm thirsty," Yana whispered, gesturing toward a cup.

"You need to lie back down," Sehraine said.

"I'm fine."

"Lie down anyway," Sehraine demanded. She eased Yana back onto the table and placed a kiss on her forehead. "Stay still," she commanded before turning to Lord Fergusson with a narrow-eyed look that reminded the older man of the looks he'd seen some of the sutlers aim at their children.  "She needs to rest."

"I can come back later," Lord Fergusson said.

"No, Sir.  I'm fine," Yana croaked.  "Sehraine, please get me some water."

The elf nodded and crossed the tent to retrieve a pitcher and cup from a trestle table near the washbasins.  Beside her, the field chirurgeon scrubbed Yana's blood from his hands.  Fergusson saw her lean close to the healer.  The two of them whispered back and forth, casting glances at Yana. The man nodded and hurried from the tent, still drying his hands.

The commander waited patiently while Sehraine helped the wind rider sit up.  Seeing the two of them sitting side by side, the elf with a slender arm around her friend, it struck him how much the average person could learn about kindness and friendship from these two women.

Yana drank greedily from the cup, draining it twice before she spoke again.  "Just so you know, Sir, those dragon pellets are not worth the money you paid for them.  They're unpredictable."

He drew in a deep breath and let it out in a short sigh of acceptance.  "Some worked, though, correct?"  She gave him a single nod in reply.  "Considering their age, I suppose we should be glad any worked at all.  So what do you have for me?"

"Let's go back to your tent so I can reference your maps." She slid from the table and swayed on her feet for a moment before sitting again.

"Yana..." Sehraine protested.

"Stop mothering me," the wind rider said.  "I have a job to finish."

"You need to wait."

"There's no one else who can use that glider, Sehraine, and I'm sure as hell not staying in this tent while Xandor and Jasper are in that cesspool of a city."

"I know," she replied, laying a hand on her arm, "but you need to rest a few more minutes until Bris returns.

"Anders!" Fergusson shouted.  The squire stepped inside, eyes carefully trained on the ground.  "Take word back to the senior officers:   Tell them I'll be there with Laytenant

Marchenkova in ten minutes.  Send Zack to ask Knyaz Dorinkov and his senior officers to join us."

Anders bobbed his head and took off at a run.  At the tent flap, he barely avoided a collision with the returning healer.

"Normally I recommend bedrest for wounds like yours," the chirurgeon said, "but your friend was very clear that's not going to happen, so drink this."  He offered Yana a small glass vial containing a milky, pale blue liquid.  When she hesitated, he gave her an exasperated sigh.  "It's a healing draught."

"I'm accustomed to blue, but why is it so thick?" Yana asked, tilting the vial side to side.  She pulled the cork and took a whiff of the contents.  "Ugh!  That smells vile!"

"Makes it work better," he replied.  "Drink up."

"I think I'll pass."

"You'll drink it if you want to walk out of this tent," Sehraine said.  "I'm not above tying you to a cot."

Fergusson bit the inside of his cheek to keep himself from laughing at the wind rider.  She'd already lost the argument; it was just taking time for her to realize it.

"Fine," Yana groused and drained the vial in one swallow.  Her face twisted in disgust.  "That stuff needs to come with a shot of rakiya to get the taste out of your mouth!"  Despite her words, her color instantly improved.

"The worse it tastes, the better it works," Bris said, handing her a cup of water.

Sehraine laughed.  "In that case, her homemade rakiya should cure everything."

Yana gave her friend a reproachful look.  "I'll remember that the next time you beg me to go to the apothecary for a winter ague remedy."  The drawn and haggard look she'd worn when Fergusson first entered the tent vanished.  Sliding off the table, she tested her leg again and smiled widely.

"Thank you, Bris," she said and patted the healer's shoulder.  It was a few minutes' work to get Yana dressed and into her armor.

"I need some silk scraps to patch a few holes on the glider," Yana said.

"Already handled," Fergusson replied.  "Let's focus on what you learned."  He reached for the door flap, but almost immediately dropped it.  He eyed Sehraine.  "Milady, you might want to straighten your hat.  There is a definite chill in the air these days, and we wouldn't want your ears to get cold."

The elf's eyes grew wide, and she tugged on the hat. "Lord Fergusson, I know it's too much to hope there are any players in the area, but are there any... um... *painted ladies* among the sutlers?  I need a better disguise than this hat."

Fergusson shook his head.  "If there are, they're among the Rhodinan camp, and not likely to be willing to help.  Keep the hat on and stay among friends."


**2:30pm**

Inside the command tent, a group of men and women milled around, discussing strategies and pointing to the various flags and clay figures on the Knight Commander's map table.  A second, older map of Chernigov, the bridge, and the Keep was pinned to another table and propped up where everyone could reference it.  Someone had marked the locations of several harpax and small ballistae along the bridge and far shore.

Yana studied the group while Leftenant Gallagher called them to attention, and they shuffled into a semblance of order.  Including Brian, there were six Iron Tower knights. An equal sized group of Rhodinans gathered around a middle-aged man with a thick mustache and long, black beard.

"Knyaz Dorinkov, ladies, and gentlemen," Fergusson said, "allow me to introduce Laytenant Yana Marchenkova, in service to the Kral of Trakya, and Lady Sehraine Marchenkova of Pazard'zhik.  Laytenant Marchenkova has just completed her reconnaissance of the enemy fortifications."  He gestured for Yana to stand beside the map of Chernigov.  "Laytenant, you have our attention."

"Yes, Sir," Yana replied.  She gave a slight bow to the Rhodinan leader.  "Your Highness, thank you for the use of your treasure."

Turning to the others she continued, "Ladies and gentlemen, as the Knight Commander said, I am Laytenant Yana Marchenkova, Black Dragon Squadron, of the Trakyan Wind Riders.  We utilize gliders, mostly for reconnaissance and message delivery, but aerial attack is also in our purview.

"Two hours ago, Lord Fergusson asked me to conduct a three-stage reconnaissance. Stage one was the Keep at the eastern foot of the Rainbow Bridge. Stage two was to sweep across Chernigov's port to identify possible transport for Vityaz Dobrynya Sabe's evacuation. Finally, stage three was to overfly the walls of Chernigov and identify the siege engines emplaced there. Afterwards, my mission was to destroy as many of the orcs' war engines along the northern approach as possible."

"Excuse me, Laytenant," interrupted a gangly knight with a purple scar along his cheek.

"Yes, Sir?"

"Stephen Daughtry, Spearhead Patrol." He raised an eyebrow. "Did you say 'fly'?"

"Yes, Sir, I did."

She scanned the small crowd. More than half openly grinned at her. To her chagrin, she realized most, if not all, of them had witnessed her initial antics and minor crashes with the antique flyer. She gave the group a rueful grin and said, "Yes, despite my earlier difficulties, I flew as requested by the Knight Commander, taking advantage of the orcs' perpetual smoke screen."

"Don't let her fool you, folks," Lord Fergusson commented as he passed the three barbed arrows he collected from the glider to Brian for the group to inspect. "The Laytenant and her flyer came back wearing those."

A low whistle cut through the group. "These are nasty business, Sir," a short, broad-shouldered man said. "They're a lot better quality than orcs usually have, too." He gave Yana a sympathetic look. "Franklin Engval, ma'am. Wildcats."

Yana nodded back and resumed her reconnaissance brief. "I'll start with the Keep, since that is our primary target. Your map is accurate, as far as the outer walls and towers are concerned, but they have block and tackle rigs at the towers for hauling up ammunition. They've also widened the battlement walkways on either side of the gatehouse with wooden platforms, giving them enough room for two ranks of archers, possibly three. In addition, there is an onager and two springalds on the gatehouse roof."

Theodore Tolliston, Leftenant Gallagher's squire, marked the platforms and siege engines on the map with a charcoal pencil as Yana described them.

"The eastern face looks pretty solid.  Major weak points are the obvious ones: the main gate and the sally port.  The eastern towers hold onagers.  Based on the debris littering the clearing around the Keep, I'd say their range is the full two-hundred yards to the tree line.  These two," she said, indicating the westernmost corner towers, "hold small ballistae on swivels.  They also have a handful of scorpions on the western walls."

Gesturing toward the map, she continued, "I counted three buildings inside the Keep, each large enough to house a troop of orcs.  I saw no evidence of tunneling, but there's a heavy presence of orcs patrolling the walls."

"I made a final 'just-in-case' pass along the western side.  The walls run right up to the bridge abutment and tie into the bridge defenses.  The walls themselves looked relatively well maintained, but the steep riverbank is another story.  Have your people look at this section along the northwest corner — from the air, it looked like the foundations had partially eroded."

"Mattias and I can check that," one of Knyaz Dorinkov's aides said.  "Perhaps an explosion, like the one Lord Fergusson discussed using on the front gate earlier, could drop that corner of the fortification and let us storm the Keep from the waterside."

Knyaz Dorinkov nodded to his senior aid.  "Go, Mikhail.  Let us know what you find."

Mikhail and Mattias saluted and left the tent without another word.

Yana waited for them to leave and then continued, "The bridge is lined with stone battlements and has small war engines along its length to attack the traffic along the river, but the humanoids could easily rotate them to defend the city from an attack originating on the eastern shore.

"Next, I passed over the docks and identified three possibilities for you.  All are single-mast, cog-like boats, but with a little crowding, could hold twenty to thirty men for a river crossing.  They are here, here, and about here."  She pointed to different piers marked on the map north of the bridge as she spoke, and Tolliston drew a small symbol beside them.

Yana paused and looked at Lord Fergusson.

He raised an eyebrow. "You have a recommendation on which boat?" he asked.

"Yes Sir. At first glance, they are all equal. But this one," she pointed to the southern-most boat, "is crewed by orcs, while dreyri crew the cogs here and here."

"That works well. The tunnel Dobrynya is using will drop them out about here," Fergusson said as he pointed to a blue dot on the map slightly closer to the centermost ship. "This boat is the best option, especially since Dobrynya's men will be on the run. Let's plan on the shortest route. Plus, it's practically within the shadow of the bridge — too close for the engines on the parapet to be of any use."

He pointed at the boat again. "This will be your second mission objective in the morning, Laytenant Marchenkova. We'll need a strike team. Can you handle the planning?"

"Yes, Sir, but I'll have to cancel my next flight to do it," she replied.

"Vassily, don't we have men who know these waters?" Knyaz Dorinkov asked.

"Yes Highness," the Rhodinan knight replied. "I believe the Ivanov twins would be perfect. They were river pirates before they joined our camp."

"Fergusson, Laytenant Marchenkova has a lot on her plate. Let our men take care of Dobrynya's rescue. Besides, pirates are better suited for this type of mission than a wind rider."

The Knight Commander's brow clouded. "You may be right, Highness. Brian, pull a pair of volunteers to assist Knyaz Dorinkov's men."

"You are knights — not thieves," the prince said.

"I may be able to help," Sehraine said. Everyone in the tent turned to her, including Yana, who opened her mouth to protest, but closed it in the face of Sehraine's glare.

Fergusson stared at the elf, hardly believing what he was hearing. "Lady Sehraine, I cannot ask you to put yourself in harm's way. I don't know the circumstances that brought you here, but you yourself admitted to a lack of fighting skills."

"Knyaz Dorinkov is right.  You don't need knights," she said.  "You need stealth, which means disguises.  As a Trakyan Royal Player, I'm an expert."

"Surely you jest!  You have no place in this battle," the prince said.

"Your Highness," Yana said, "with all due respect, you're wrong.  I personally vouch for her and the value she could add to this mission.  We've both been on the Chernigov side of the river and are familiar with the patrols.  In fact, she was instrumental in getting our horses and us across the river.  However, if she goes, so do I."

"Fergusson, what say you?" Knyaz Dorinkov asked after a moment of contemplation.

The Knight Commander remained quiet as he studied the young-looking elf.  Reaching a decision, he said, "Lady Sehraine, it goes against my better judgement but, if you are *absolutely certain*, I accept your help.  I believe it will work out better this way, since we need the laytenant to focus on reconnaissance and her part in taking the Keep tomorrow morning.  She can join you on the river once we breach the gate."

"Vassily, contact the Ivanovs, and let them know that we have a task for them," Dorinkov ordered.

"Yes, Your Highness," the knight replied with a bow.

"As for you, young lady, this is my second-in-command, Poruchik Vassily Tirinko.  Meet him at our camp after this debrief.  We'll see just how much you know."

Lady Sehraine bowed.

"Laytenant, please continue with your account of the city," Lord Fergusson directed.

Yana nodded, looked from Knyaz Dorinkov to Sehraine, and then continued, "I overflew the waterfront from north to south, then looped back to check out the eastern wall of the city..."  She went on to delineate engines by type and location, beginning with the northeast tower.  Tolliston dutifully marked positions on a map as she spoke. That part went quickly.  When she got to the southeast tower, she slowed, placing particular emphasis on the eastern wall defenses.

"King Kraagor has emplaced several large siege engines on the walls.  He has a mix of catapult-type weapons: scorpions, onagers, and mangonels.  Some of the mangonels are unusual.  Instead of the torsion system we are used to seeing, they have spring-driven mechanisms; I have no idea how this may affect their range or ammunition capacity."

Lord Fergusson nodded.  "I saw them in action earlier this morning.  They easily ranged four to five hundred yards with reasonable accuracy."  Several of the younger officers exchanged worried glances.  "We'll need you to pay special attention to those contraptions on your next flight."

"Additionally, they have trebuchets," Yana continued, pointing to various positions along the walls of the city, with Leftenant Gallagher's squire dutifully marking what engines were placed where.

"The eastern wall is the only portion that I made a second pass.  When I got back to the northeastern tower, I climbed for altitude, circled out over the water, and started my attack run.   I hit several of their towers and received heavy resistance."

Yana looked at Brian and said pointedly, "The dragon pellets are not dependable.  Most exploded like they were supposed to, but there were a fair number that simply spewed smoke or did nothing at all."

Unconsciously rubbing the fresh wound on her leg, she continued, "We surprised them this time.  I don't know if we'll be as lucky the next time.

"I'm confident that I destroyed four or five of their engines.  I am certain that I damaged at least one or two more, but not confident on their destruction."  She shrugged. "Pending any questions, that concludes my report, Milord."

The Knight Commander responded promptly, "What can you tell us about the numbers of enemy personnel, Laytenant?"

"The Keep looked to be about a hundred.  However, after seeing the city, I would double, maybe even triple that count, at the very least.  It's hard to tell exactly since they like to stay underground.  When I overflew the city, I saw them entering and exiting burrows; however, as I mentioned earlier, there were no visible burrows in the Keep.

"As for actual numbers, there's no way to get even a rough count.  I would hazard to guess that fifteen thousand is a gross underestimate."

Lord Fergusson nodded grimly and looked around the tent.  "Ladies, Gentlemen, do any of you have additional questions about Laytenant Marchenkova's reconnaissance or attack?"

When no one responded, he turned to the wind rider. "Laytenant Marchenkova, I suggest you make ready for your next run.  The fewer engines they can aim at us in the morning, the better."

With that dismissal, the room came to attention.  The officers and squires saluted their commanders, then filed out to prepare their troops.

Knyaz Dorinkov stayed behind, eyeing the map.

"You better be right about this, Fergusson.  I'm risking a lot of men on this attack."

"I understand, Your Highness.  Our mission is to open the bridge, hold the river, and give our ranger and his team time to cross.  Everything else, including extra casualties, is secondary to the information they hope to bring us.  I'm not saying that I don't care about casualties, because I do, but if we do not find a cure for the rising plague, many of your countrymen and mine are going to die.  In the face of that, we are all expendable."

Knyaz Dorinkov's face soured, "I want that cure as soon as they cross the bridge.  I received a message this afternoon from the Korol' — the plague has reached the capital.  It started in a fishing village several miles south of here with reports of a ghost ship and spread both north and east.  Luckily, we haven't seen any signs of it here in camp.  At least not yet."

"Your Highness, we discussed this.  I can't guarantee they'll even *have* the cure.  My agent has gone dark." Fergusson's eyes flicked to the journal sitting on top of a folding table.

"How do we even know he's alive?" the Rhodinan prince asked.

"We don't, but what choice do we have?" Fergusson replied.  "The signal's been given.  We attack at dawn."

# ABOUT THE AUTHORS

## Jason McDonald

An engineer by day and a world builder by night, Jason is an advocate for using both sides of the brain. Unfortunately, it seems his best (and worst) ideas come to him while driving — much to the chagrin of his family and coworkers.

With his stepfather as a guide, Jason traveled the worlds of Edgar Rice Burroughs, Robert E Howard, and JRR Tolkien at an early age. As he grew older, he discovered Dungeons and Dragons and the joys of creating his own campaigns. Combined with the creative genius of his co-writers, whom he met in college, these adventures grew more complex, and an entire world sprang to life.

During all this, Jason graduated from Clemson University, embarked on a career in engineering, and became a partner in a successful engineering firm. Still a practicing engineer, he continues to design a wide range of projects. His attention to detail and vivid imagination helps shape the various scenes and adventures that challenge his characters.

## Alan Isom

Alan began his adventure with science fiction and fantasy literature as it should begin: with JRR Tolkien's The Hobbit, read to him as a child by his father. Since that auspicious beginning, he has fostered a love of reading a variety of fantasy and science fiction types and that led him to RPGs, most notably Dungeons & Dragons, where world building became a fascination.

Growing up in northeast Alabama, Alan moved north to South Carolina for college. He fell in love with the Upstate of South Carolina and forgot to go home afterwards. While initially majoring in Physics at Furman University (Go Paladins!) and then moving on to Clemson University for additional studies in Civil Engineering (after deciding that his options for a Physics career were decidedly thin), he became a licensed engineer and now works for an international Engineering-Procurement-Construction company.  During all of this he served a number of years as a soldier with the Army National Guard.  Each of these careers, as well as a multitude of hobbies, helps bring depth and creativity to the characters and worlds he brings to life.


## Stormy McDonald

Born in the midst of a thunderstorm in the darkest hours of a solstice morning, Stormy has been told she has a personality to match:  full of sound and fury, and highly unpredictable.  She comes from a family of traditional, oral storytellers, so it's little wonder that she's driven to weave words as well.  She can't remember a time when she didn't love books — from the feel and smell of the pages, to the information they hold, to the tales that they tell.  However, storytelling is a labor of love, which doesn't always pay the bills.  Over the years, she's worked a ridiculous variety of side jobs to support her writing habit, including waitress, security guard, library minion, engineering drafter, and small business owner.